# THE DOCTOR'S SECRET

AN UNPUTDOWNABLE GRIPPING PSYCHOLOGICAL THRILLER WITH A KILLER TWIST

**COLE BAXTER**

ILLUSTRATED BY
**NATASHA SNOW**

EDITED BY
**ELIZABETH A LANCE**

Copyright © 2024 by Cole Baxter

All rights reserved.

**Cover design** by Natasha Snow

**Edited** by Valorie Clifton
**Edited** by Elizabeth A Lance
**Proofread** by Dawn Klemish

No part of this book may be reproduced in any form or by any electronic or mechanical means, including information storage and retrieval systems, without written permission from the author, except for the use of brief quotations in a book review.

This book is a work of fiction. Any resemblance to persons, living or dead, or places, events or locations is purely coincidental. The characters are all productions of the authors' imagination.

# CONTENTS

| | |
|---|---|
| Mailing List | v |
| Chapter 1 | 1 |
| Chapter 2 | 9 |
| Chapter 3 | 21 |
| Chapter 4 | 31 |
| Chapter 5 | 45 |
| Chapter 6 | 57 |
| Chapter 7 | 67 |
| Chapter 8 | 77 |
| Chapter 9 | 87 |
| Chapter 10 | 99 |
| Chapter 11 | 105 |
| Chapter 12 | 113 |
| Chapter 13 | 123 |
| Chapter 14 | 131 |
| Chapter 15 | 139 |
| Chapter 16 | 149 |
| Chapter 17 | 159 |
| Chapter 18 | 169 |
| Chapter 19 | 177 |
| Chapter 20 | 187 |
| Chapter 21 | 195 |
| Chapter 22 | 207 |
| Chapter 23 | 217 |
| Chapter 24 | 223 |
| Chapter 25 | 233 |
| Chapter 26 | 243 |
| Chapter 27 | 251 |
| Chapter 28 | 261 |
| Chapter 29 | 271 |
| Chapter 30 | 281 |
| Chapter 31 | 291 |
| Chapter 32 | 301 |
| Chapter 33 | 309 |

| Epilogue | 317 |

## DON'T OPEN THE DOOR

| Chapter 1 | 331 |
| Chapter 2 | 343 |
| About Cole Baxter | 355 |
| Also by Cole Baxter | 357 |

To get updates about new releases, please follow me on Amazon! You can also follow me on Bookbub! Or join my reader Facebook group! Sign up for my VIP Reader Club and find out about his latest releases, giveaways, and more.

# CHAPTER ONE
STACY

T*he victim has now been identified as Gabrielle Unwin, 25. Her role as a sex worker in the city's seedy underbelly has police investigating whether or not her death was in connection to a recently busted sex trafficking ring that saw girls being 'imported' through Seattle's port.*

"Gosh, that's terrible, I had no idea." Stacy Lewis was watching the news through her fingers, like it was some gory horror movie.

Her fiancé, Henry, was sitting on the other end of the couch watching the same report with a detached boredom. He sighed and asked the question he knew Stacy was expecting. "Was she one of yours?" he asked, not turning away from the television.

Stacy nodded; her face still buried in her hands. "I examined her today. Came in as a Jane Doe. They managed to find identification just as I was about to cut into her. Her mother identified her through the window. She hadn't seen her daughter in over a year; thought she was already dead." Stacey trailed off as the reporter continued to describe the grisly scene.

Gabrielle Unwin had been found in an alleyway, completely naked, her legs and arms spread out wide. A restaurant dishwasher found her as he came in for his morning shift, tripping over one of her legs. She was lying beside the dumpster, her body badly bruised and her neck red from strangulation. It was the sort of thing Stacy thought she should be used to by now. She had worked at the city morgue for a year, as an official coroner. Before that she worked in the city's biggest hospital as a medical examiner and pathologist. She had seen patients in much worse conditions come through her door, there was no reason this young woman should have affected her as much as she did.

"Why are you so upset about it?" Henry asked, reflecting her morbid train of thought. "She can't have been the first prostitute to be beaten up in this city, nor will she be the last."

"It's not about that. I don't know maybe..." Stacy trailed off again. She didn't want to admit it but the real reason she was so shaken up was that Stacy thought Gabrielle looked like her. She could have been the sister Stacy never had. It was a silly thought, but there was no getting it out of her mind.

"What is it? Stacy, you keep doing this," Henry sputtered, exasperated.

"Doing what?" she demanded. "Caring about the people who come across my table? I would have thought you'd have a little bit of compassion," Stacy said, whipping around to face Henry on the couch.

She could see him recoil in disgust — Henry hated it when Stacy was anything other than passive and gentle. He complained that it wasn't 'ladylike' and would sulk for hours afterward.

"I didn't say you shouldn't care. Only that you keep starting sentences and not finishing them. You seem to be off in your own little world today." Henry pursed his lips at her. "Why don't you tell me what's going on in your pretty head, rather than letting it fester and make you even more anxious than you already are."

He had a point. Turning the image of Gabrielle Unwin's lifeless, beaten body around in her head was doing nothing but making Stacy more anxious. Would Henry understand? He was a celebrated ER doctor, practically famous in Seattle. There were rumors that a big Hollywood executive who had been treated by Henry was going to make a show based on his life. There was no denying he was absolutely brilliant, but like many brilliant men, he could be a little insensitive. It was a result of having to work on so many traumatized bodies — the less you thought of them as people, the easier you could make difficult, life-altering decisions about them.

Stacy felt some of that, it went hand in hand with her job. As a medical pathologist she faced death every day. There were plenty of people who refused to come down to the morgue because they thought it was creepy, while Stacy felt the space was peaceful. Far from the rush of the ER or surgery room, down there you could actually hear your thoughts and solve little mysteries of death in your own time. Today had been different. Today, Stacy had to face one of her biggest fears — seeing a woman beaten to death. It made her think—

"Stace? Stae? Hello? Earth to Stacy Lewis, come in please?" Henry waved his hand in front of Stacy's face. The news had moved on to their second story — a heartwarming human interest piece about a little girl raising money for the city's homeless population.

*Winter is coming, but Suzy Atherton isn't afraid of any evil, fantasy creatures. She's facing the very real problem of the city's houseless population — the freezing cold temperatures and high winds.*

"Huh? Sorry I—" Stacy started.

"Were you thinking about the homeless guy at the end of the street? He has somewhere to go, you already went through all this with him. You can't save everyone; you know that, and I do too."

"I know. I guess it just freaked me out."

"What? The winter? In that case you're living in the wrong city—"

"No! Obviously not, I meant that girl!" Stacy said, recoiling into her corner of the couch. She wanted to get away from Henry's touch, far from anything that might remind her of the bruises on Unwin's delicate frame.

"Still? Stacy, come on. That girl wasn't the first prostitute to come across your table, nor will she be the last."

"I know that, but... she looked like me," Stacy fretted, worrying at her lip with her teeth.

"So she had dark hair, what's the matter with that? You're perfectly safe, and you will be for a long time," Henry said, patting Stacy's foot. "Now can we move on? You know I hate discussing your work. It's disgusting."

"Why'd you ask a coroner to marry you, if the thought of death is so disgusting to you?" Stacy retorted.

Henry didn't answer, he just got up and went into the kitchen. Stacy and Henry shared a recently converted townhouse — one of those fancy new builds, which was probably supposed to look like an upscale loft. Everything was open concept and it felt as if there was nowhere for you to hide. Stacy watched as Henry went into the pantry that served as a wine cellar and pulled out a new bottle of her favorite red wine.

"I was thinking we should order a case of this for the wedding. We could have them put custom labels on it, like 'Lewis & Goldberg' and the date — or maybe do something a little more cutesy like have them call it the 'Lewisberg' blend. What do you think?"

"Sure," Stacy said; — classic Henry, changes the subject to the farthest thing from her job. They hadn't even sent out Save the Date cards for their wedding yet, and Henry was already thinking about the booze.

They should have already done it. The wedding was supposed to happen at Christmas time. It would have been a small, classy affair. A courthouse ceremony followed by a reception at their favorite restaurant. Stacy didn't have much family to invite — apart from her estranged half-sister and her best friend, there weren't many people to fill her side of the aisle — and Henry had agreed to only invite his immediate family to keep the numbers down.

Henry's mother wasn't a fan of the idea.

In fact, Henry's mother wasn't a fan of most ideas surrounding Stacy. She hated the fact that Stacy had stolen her precious boy, hated how much attention he gave her and how easily their lives entwined without her.

The wedding had been postponed indefinitely since Amanda Goldberg's suicide. She left no note, she was found in her bed clutching a photo of her and her son. The last portrait they had taken together before Stacy came into the picture. Amanda had experienced depression and was possibly bipolar, though Stacy never knew for sure. Henry refused to send his mother to a therapist, refused to ever acknowledge that their relationship was a strange one. He'd only gone against her wishes once in his life, when he announced that he planned to marry Stacy Lewis, at Christmas time, and Amanda Goldberg could be there, or she could miss it. Henry's mother had threatened to kill herself many times in his life, usually when a girlfriend was getting too close for her comfort, but no one could believe she'd ever go through with it.

*"We were close,"* Henry had explained, *"when I was growing up all we had was each other. You could never understand."*

Beyond that, he never explained to Stacy anything else about his mother. When people would ask how he was doing, he'd say he was grieving and change the subject. Stacy suggested therapy — a normal thing when you're going through the grieving process — but Henry vehemently rejected the idea.

*"I've gone to shrinks before,"* he'd explained, *"all they want to do is bash my mother for doing her best with what she had."*

"Stacy, are you even listening to me? What is the point of talking if I'm talking to the wall?" Henry said, his voice tensing up.

"Sorry, I'm just really distracted tonight. I thought you didn't want to think about wedding stuff yet?"

"It was just an idea. I know we're probably going to be doing something smaller, but I still want to have a little special element to it. Maybe each guest can take home a bottle of wine? We could even spend a day creating our own blend at a winery. I know Dr. Spellman did that with his wife, it seemed cute. Very up your alley." Henry smiled his disarming smile.

Stacy couldn't help but giggle. The thought of Henry with his pinkie up, tasting blends of wine made her laugh. He was such a scientific man; it would be funny to see him try to parse out the science of a wine tasting. She'd have to tell Lillian that; it was bound to crack her up.

"You? At a winery? You know they don't have labs and test tubes, right? It's just a guy pouring fermented grape juice out of barrels."

Henry froze, the color draining from his face.

"Wait— what? That's how they do it? They just pour different wines together and swirl them around? They don't even measure it first?"

Stacy smiled — there was a reason she had been so taken with Henry. Sure, their relationship sometimes felt more like roommates than lovers, but he had a sort of childlike innocence combined with immense ego that somehow turned out extremely charming.

"No, usually the winemaker just guesses. It's all trial and error and then they serve it to you once they get a blend that they think you'll like. I went to a wine tasting for a bachelorette once, they did it right in front of us. It's pretty impressive when they do it."

"Not scientific at all," Henry muttered, staring at the wine bottle as if it had betrayed him.

Stacy got up from the couch, turning off the TV as she did. That was enough for one night, they could catch up on the news some other time. Besides, with their careers, they probably knew more than the tv stations did.

"I'm sorry I've been so distracted today. That girl was beaten so badly, it shocked me. I can usually put up a wall between myself and my work, but I thought about my past, about my father, and I realized I could just as easily be that girl, lying on a slab with bruises up and down her body." Stacy fought back tears.

Henry put down the bottle and wrapped her in a long warm embrace. "You don't have to explain, I should have known. I'm so stupid, I—"

"It's not your fault."

"Well, of course not," Henry winked, "I'm the perfect man. And for the record, it's not your fault either."

"Because I'm the perfect woman?" Stacy smiled up at her tall, handsome doctor.

"Exactly." He kissed the top of her head and turned away.

Satisfied that they'd avoided a real fight, the two went back to their places on the couch. Henry brought over a glass of wine, and each of them picked up the book they had been reading from their respective side tables. They each read for precisely one hour, before going to bed early so they could get started on their day — they were both morning people who needed to wake up early. Death and accidents didn't sleep in, after all.

---

STACY STARED up at the ceiling, still thinking about Gabrielle Unwin. Each time she closed her eyes she saw the young sex worker staring back at her from the slab, her dark hair radiating around her. It made her stomach turn, the way the darkened bruises stood out against Unwin's pale skin tone. Stacy shivered, even though she was safely ensconced in a warm duvet. Beside her, Henry lay sleeping, still as a board, off in a deep dreamless sleep. She wished he would hold her tightly against his chest as she slept, stroking her hair, her waist, maybe even explore between her legs. She wanted to wrap herself around him, lose herself in the scent of her fiancé and forget about the dead bodies and crime reports that waited for her in the morning.

That wasn't really their style. They had a comfortable, solid relationship — the kind of thing Stacy never had in the past. She knew Henry would be by her side all night long, no matter when she fell asleep, and she knew he would be up to make her breakfast the next morning — a healthy smoothie and bowl of his homemade muesli. He was charming and romantic in his own, slightly nerdy way, the perfect partner for the rest of Stacy's life.

She lay back in her bed and stared up at the ceiling, listening to Henry's slow and steady snore, allowing his breath to carry her off to a dreamless sleep.

# CHAPTER
# TWO
STACY

Just as she predicted, the next morning Henry woke up first, showered, and prepared breakfast for the two of them. Stacy woke up as he was leaving the bathroom and started her morning routine. They ate together, Henry kissed her on the forehead, and they left for work. He drove her to work, she kissed him on the cheek, and exited the car.

Same as it had been every morning for the past six months.

Their relationship hadn't always been so prescriptive. In the beginning, Henry had wooed her like the best of them. He sent flowers to her work, took her on elaborate dates, and they made passionate love just about any time they were together. Even before they got together, back when Stacy still worked at the hospital, Henry would discreetly flirt with her and look for reasons to visit her down in the morgue. There was a time when Henry was competing for her affection, when he was the shoulder for her to cry on after her ex-boyfriend proved he was more violent than she ever believed.

There was a time when their relationship was spicy. Nowadays, it was lacking salt.

The peak of their relationship happened when Henry asked

her to marry him. Stacy hadn't expected it at all. Of course, they knew each other well, having worked together for some time before starting to date. He planned a weekend on the San Juan Islands at a secluded hotel. It was apparently to celebrate her new job, and Henry's latest promotion — to Head of the Emergency Department at St. Vincent's Medical Center, the undisputed best hospital in the city. It rained, yet somehow that made the night even more romantic. Henry had booked the private dining room in the restaurant and filled the space with Stacy's favorite flowers — Calla and Cobra lilies adorned every table, spilling onto the floor and even hanging from the ceiling. It was pure magic. Stacy had never been surprised like that before. Henry was standing in the middle of the room, holding a small ring. It was a vintage baguette cut diamond on a simple gold band; just what Stacy had always wanted. Nothing flashy, nothing that might get in the way of her work — if she ever chose to wear it, just a small but beautiful distillation of their love.

Stacy and Henry spent the night making passionate love all over their hotel room. The second they walked in the door, Henry had ripped off her dress sending the dainty buttons to the floor. He'd wrapped his tie around her wrists and teased her on the way to the bed, nipping at her neck and kissing her ear. It drove Stacy insane, and she thought about it constantly. All those nights she lay in bed next to a stiff board, Stacy would replay the night of their engagement in her head and wonder if she'd ever get that version of Henry back. Their relationship started to go downhill the next morning, when Henry's mother, Amanda stormed into their hotel room. Apparently, Henry hadn't told her where he'd be that weekend, nor that he was finally asking Stacy to marry him.

"I can't believe you'd do this to me!" she shrieked, standing over their bed.

Stacy woke with a start, pulling the covers up to her chin. She knew Henry's mother was a little… off. She'd raised him on his own after his father left, and Stacy often thought their relationship was a little *too* close.

"You're going to kill me, you know that, Henry!" she cried. "I'm going to kill myself if you're just going to abandon your mother like this. What? You think you're going to turn your back on me because some Amazon of a woman wormed her way into your mind! Don't you see what she's doing to you — to us!"

Amanda kept screaming as Henry, wearing only his boxers, fireman-carried her out of their hotel room. Stacy could hear her cries all the way down the hall, she would not be silenced. Amanda had given Stacy no illusions about how she felt. Henry's girlfriend was persona non grata, and more than once she tried to manipulate Henry into believing Stacy was cheating on him, just so they would break up. He was away most of the day. Stacy passed the time walking around the grounds of the hotel. She joined a historical ghost tour, and watched the other patrons jump out of their skins every time Amanda shrieked at her son. Henry returned to their room looking like he had been to hell and back. He didn't say a word to Stacy, he just collapsed in their bed and went to sleep.

Things went downhill from there. For a while it suited Stacy just fine. She grew up in an unstable home and to her the ultimate love came in the form of steadiness — a steady man, a constant presence, no fiery arguments, or crazy drunken behavior — that's what love really was. Stacy was happy to trade passion for consistency, at least she was at first. Half a year down the line, she was starting to rethink things — what if it never improved? What if they remained distant for the rest of their lives? Would Stacy be content living with an imitation of the Henry Goldberg she fell in love with? The question plagued her thoughts, and every couple of days Stacy considered coming home and telling Henry that she was calling off their engagement. The poor corpses got the brunt of Stacy's indecisiveness.

She didn't have a large circle of friends, but she was very good at talking to the lifeless bodies on her autopsy table and imagining what they would think of her problems.

"He's nice, he really is. He truly does take care of me, just as he did his mother until she…" Stacy said to the latest heart attack victim on her table.

"Until she what?" She imagined Mr. Matthew Perreira saying back to her. "What did his mother do?"

"She killed herself. Because he got engaged. She always threatened to do it, but finally—"

"The former Mrs. G pulled the trigger when she realized she wasn't the only woman in her son's life. It's pretty common, I see it a lot in my line of work. A mother feels she's being replaced by the pretty young thing her son brought home."

"You were a used car salesman, Mr. Perreira."

"Exactly! Bring in the old car, trade up for a new model. You see it all the time."

The corpses weren't always the most helpful.

He was right, Amanda Goldberg didn't let Stacy forget that she felt abandoned and replaced, which was odd because Henry still saw his mother multiple times a week, often staying over at her house rather than coming back to the apartment, leaving Stacy alone in his house. Whenever he did, he'd make it out to be some kind of grand misunderstanding, saying that Stacy couldn't possibly know what it was like since she was mostly raised by her abusive father. Henry's favorite line when it came to issues with his suffocating mother was to tell Stacy she was out of line, and couldn't possibly know what real familial love was.

He had inherited his mother's manipulative streak — it was always worse after a visit with Amanda — and he took it out on Stacy. He always apologized after, saying that it was his complex trauma talking, not him, and Stacy always took him back into her arms and consoled him. It was probably true, she was reading into his relationship too much, and couldn't possibly understand what it was like to have a parent who loved you so much that you actually *wanted* to see them every other day.

Stacy was turning this over in her head when her best friend, Lillian Kelly, came through the door.

"Another day, another body, am I right, girl?" she said, gesturing around the room with her camera lens. "I'm here to photograph Gabrielle Unwin, the beating victim. Apparently, the police are looking further into her case."

Stacy beamed at her friend — finally another living person to talk about her problems with.

"I heard about it on the news last night, the city is trying to make a case that it's part of some sex trafficking ring, right?"

"Sure is. Don't know what they're gonna find on some poor girl's beat up body, but here I am, ready to take detailed photographic evidence as if she had never lived a day in her life."

Lillian allowed her emotions about the job to show through more than Stacy did. It was probably because Lillian was an artist, she had to stay close to her emotions for her artwork to be powerful. She was the only person in the coroner's office who actually *tried* to make friends with Stacy when she started working there. Everyone else had been so emotionally deafened by their job that they were more content to keep their heads down and live in their own morbid worlds than get involved in someone else's life.

Lillian always said it was a wall of protection, so that if their friends ever came across the slab they wouldn't break down and cry. Stacy thought the only thing standing between her sanity and psychopathy was getting personal with her coworkers. Just like that, Lillian became her best friend, the one person who could see the beauty in caring about your work — even if your work was as close to death as you could get without dying.

Stacy went over to open the shelf of the young sex worker so that Lillian could get to work.

"I'm glad you're here, actually," she said, "I've been having The Great Debate again."

Lillian rolled her eyes. "You're the only woman I know who is having this much difficulty deciding whether or not to call off the engagement. Most women I know would call it off the first time they thought, 'gee, maybe this guy ain't the right guy for me.' Meanwhile every time I come into this office you've flipped to the other side of the coin."

"I know, I know it must seem silly, but I just can't tell if I'm panicking about settling down or if I'm really worried for my and Henry's future. It all seems so long."

"Dump him," Lillian deadpanned, snapping photos of the red ring around Gabrielle Unwin's neck.

"Well, that was fast," Stacy muttered; she knew Lillian wasn't the biggest fan of Henry, but she could at least listen to Stacy's reasoning.

"I'm sorry, Stae, I know you think I should be a little more kind. But I think you should dump him and get back together with Hot Matt."

Hot Matt was what Lillian called Stacy's ex-boyfriend, Matt Ensor. Sexy, tumultuous, dangerous Matt who beat Stacy's father to a pulp one night. Lillian saw Matt more often than Stacy nowadays, she'd see him whenever she had to deliver corpse photos to the precinct.

"He still asks about you," Lillian continued, "always very politely asks how you have been 'holdin' up', asks if you're still with Henry and if Henry's mother is treating you well. Asks if you've been eating and I always tell him that yes, the brains of our city's corpses provide you all your necessary vitamins and minerals." Lillian smirked as she zoomed in on the bruises on Unwin's chest.

"He doesn't ask how my father is, does he?" Stacy said through gritted teeth. It was the straw that broke the camel's back. Matt was passionate but he was also unpredictable and could be aggressive. The night she broke up with Matt, he left her father a bloodied mess on the floor after beating the old man to a pulp. Oliver Lewis had definitely deserved it, he was a mentally-ill abuser of his wife, child, and any drug he could get his hands on. Still the incident shook Stacy, and she knew she'd never be able to look at Matt the same way after that.

"No," Lillian said quietly. "He doesn't ask about your meth-addicted father who was stalking you, and was ready to attack you with a knife the last time he saw you. Besides, your father is criminally institutionalized. Matt doesn't need to *ask* about him."

"How nice to know Matt can barge into my father's room and beat him to a pulp whenever he wants to."

"Hey! He may have gone too far, but he did it to protect you. Your father was going to kill you. If I had been in Matt's situation, I would have done the same thing. I've seen what meth addicts can do, and frankly, I'm glad Matt was there because I don't ever want to be photographing your body in this morgue."

The conversation fell flat after that. Stacy drifted back to her office and pretended to check over her notes until Lillian was finished with Gabrielle Unwin's body.

"Knock-knock," she said, hovering in the door of Stacy's office, "I'm all finished."

"Great." Stacy pretended to be deeply engrossed in a document about post-mortem bruising. "You know where to sign out."

Lillian sighed — "I knew I should have just changed the subject rather than engage with your debate about whether or not you should go through with your engagement."

"Maybe," Stacy replied, keeping her eyes averted from her friend.

"Look, you know that I think Henry's nice demeanor cloaks a manipulative perfectionist. I should let you come to your own conclusions about him. You're the one who's marrying him, not me. As far as Matt goes, I'm not going to pretend that had Matt not protected you, you would have died that night. And if you had, I'd never have gotten to know you and that's just sad."

Stacy frowned and looked at her friend.

"I was thinking of grabbing some lunch. There's a new souvlaki truck in the square where all the food trucks park."

"Sounds like a recipe for food poisoning." Stacy said, turning back to the same page she'd been staring at on her document.

"Probably," Lillian shrugged, "if only I had a loyal friend who would help me to the hospital in case I did get sick."

She waited in the doorway until Stacy looked up again. Lillian looked at her with puppy dog eyes, trying to convey an apology without having to actually voice one. Stacy stared back at her for a moment, before she sighed and picked up her bag.

"We'll have to stop by the drugstore and get some antacids first," she said, brushing past Lillian.

---

ALL THEY REALLY NEEDED WAS SOME questionable food from a truck to knit their friendship back together. Stacy had to admit, she was wrong about the new souvlaki truck — it was one of those new hipster trucks that were twice as expensive, and not as tasty as the old trucks that had questionable hygiene. Lillian and Stacy laughed as they taste-tested their way through lunch. Stacy came back to the office in a much better mood than she left it in, thinking that maybe Lillian had a point about her relationship with Matt Ensor.

It was true, Matt had protected her from her father. Oliver Lewis had never gotten over his drug problem and likely never would, no matter how much time he spent in a padded cell. He had been obsessed with Stacy's mother, Heather, never being able to let her go. When Stacy was a child, her mother tried to escape him multiple times, but he always managed to track them down. Restraining orders couldn't stop him, and even when Heather

Lewis changed her name and appearance, he had still managed to find them.

Stacy and her mother had always suspected someone was helping him — a family member or someone else close to the them, who was easily manipulated into aiding the abusive man — but they could never prove it. Once he'd realized he'd never be able to control Stacy or turn her against her mother, he'd backed off, descending further into his addictions. Stacy had thought she was rid of him for good, but he'd reared his ugly head after her mother passed away.

Somehow, in all those years trying to escape Oliver Lewis and cobble together a life for her and her daughter, Heather Lewis had managed to save some money and put it into an investment account. By the time she died, she'd amassed a small fortune passing it all to her only daughter, Stacy. Of course, Oliver found out about it and started to harass Stacy for his 'share'. For years she had been embroiled in one battle after another, with her father trying every trick in the book to get Stacy's money. Luckily, her mother contacted an old family friend who tied it up in so much legal paperwork that no matter what Oliver tried, he couldn't so much as sniff the money.

Maybe if she had caved, he wouldn't have stalked her. Maybe, if Stacy had let him manipulate her, maybe lied about how much money her mother left, he wouldn't have attacked her. If Stacy and her mother had been able to find out who was the family leak all those years ago, maybe Oliver would never have found out. These maybes swirled around Stacy's head on the daily. None of these maybes pulled her out of the reality she faced — her father had attacked her while high on meth. He'd tried to mug her while she was on a date with Matt. Matt shoved Oliver out of the way, but Oliver attacked him. The two men got into a fistfight with Matt quickly overpowering the older and weaker Oliver, but he didn't stop there. Matt unleashed a side of him that Stacy had never seen, a rageful and angry side that reminded her of her father. Stacy could do nothing but stay frozen to the spot and watch as Matt unleashed his anger in the name of protecting Stacy.

She ended things a day later, in total fear of what Matt could become.

Despite all this, she had to admit that she missed Matt Ensor. He was charming and sexy, and always pushed Stacy to do better than she thought she could. In all aspects of her life, she received so much encouragement from Matt that it was almost annoying. It had been almost a year since they broke up. It had been nice to hear that he still asked about her — and was courteous enough to ask about Henry.

*Should I call him?* Stacy wondered, retreating further into her memories. The night with her father was easily replaced with the many other nights that she and Matt twisted her sheets into knots as they made love into the morning. Oh, and the many sweet gestures he'd done for her, outside of the bedroom. He had been the one to suggest she apply for the job at the city coroner's office. He knew she was more interested in criminal autopsies than medical post-mortems, and had even recommended Stacy by name to someone he knew in the office.

*Maybe I should call. Just to tell him the job is going well.* Would that be wildly inappropriate? She knew Henry would think so. If Henry saw a call to Detective Ensor on her phone, he would turn sullen for days, forcing Stacy to feel guiltier and guiltier as the hours went by.

*I could tell him it's related to the assault case. Matt was involved, it's only logical he'd call to update me.* Stacy pulled her phone out of her purse and scrolled through the contacts, her thumb hovering over Matt Ensor's name. She could delete the record of the call, and Henry would never know.

Just as she was about to tap his name, Stacy's phone rang, and Henry's dimpled face filled her screen.

"H-Hello?" she stammered, shocked back into reality.

"Hi — Stacy?" Henry asked.

"Yes, hi, it's me. Sorry, you surprised me I, um, I was just thinking about you." She closed her eyes trying to push Matt Ensor from her mind.

"Oh, well, what perfect timing. Listen, I just called to say there was a pile up on the I-90, just south of the city."

Stacy knew what was coming next. A highway accident could only mean one thing coming from an ER doctor.

"Do you want me to make you a plate?" she asked, knowing that Henry was about to make excuses for being home late.

"No, it's still early. Sounds like there wasn't a truck involved, so with any luck it'll be a couple of bruised bodies and a bad case of whiplash. I just heard about it, so I wanted to give you a head's up, and tell you to avoid the 90 on your way home, traffic is bound to be painfully slow."

"Of course, thanks for the tip, babe."

"I'm just trying to look out for you," Henry said, quieting his voice. For a moment he didn't say anything, and all Stacy could hear was the beeping and bustling of the hospital. "I love you, Stacy, you know that right?"

He was suddenly so earnest that Stacy was caught off guard. It was as if he knew what she had been thinking about just moments earlier.

"I know that. I love you too, Henry, I love you sideways," she said, smiling into the phone as she heard Henry's quiet laugh. It was true, she did love him. Their relationship was dull, but it was serious and steady. It was the stable force she needed in life, the complete opposite of the impulsive passion that Matt Ensor embodied.

"I have to go," Henry said. "Be careful out there."

The phone darkened for a moment, before going back to Stacy's contact list. There was Matt Ensor, his phone number, all his details still up on her screen. She had to keep him there for now, in case something came up with her dad. Always helpful to have a friend on the police force when your family was stalking you, she learned that when she was just a kid. For now, that's all Matt was — a connection. He didn't have to be anything more than that.

Stacy closed her phone and got in her car, turning onto a side street so she could avoid the throughway that cut through Seattle, following her fiancé's advice.

## CHAPTER
# THREE
STACY

"The accident was way worse than I realized, at least four cars and a couple of idiots who slowed down to take a look. I'm going to be late, but I'll bring home some sushi to make up for it. I have to run, see you at home! I love you, Stacy."

Stacy got Henry's voicemail just as she was pulling into their little driveway. It took her almost twice as much time to get home. Whatever the accident was, it had tied up the city with commuters avoiding the highway and clogging up the other thoroughfares and bridges around the city. Henry's voicemail was a welcome relief from having to think about what to make for dinner. Whether she realized it in the moment or not, Stacy's day had been draining. From arguing with Lillian, to re-evaluating her relationship, her mind felt like it had run an obstacle course. All Stacy wanted to do was veg out in front of the TV until dinner was ready. If only she could get Henry to hand feed her the sushi rolls.

Stacy decided to take a long relaxing bath to wash the day off of her. Seeing Gabrielle Unwin's body again hadn't felt good, it brought up the same foreboding feeling she had last night — that it could have been her on the slab rather than the young sex worker. She went all out, adding the expensive essential oil Henry had bought for her to make up for the ruined engagement weekend. Stacy lit a candle that was way too expensive and popped open a bottle of wine she had been saving for a special occasion.

*I think deciding to stay with my kind and loving fiancé rather than leave him for an aggressive and overly passionate ex is cause for celebration, no?* she thought as she popped the cork. Ever the steady head, she also filled a water bottle and kept it beside the bath, so she didn't get too dehydrated.

The bath was exactly what Stacy needed. She lay back listening to her favorite true crime podcast — a cheesy-sounding tale of art-world fraud that Lillian recommended to her — and settled in to the bubbles. Nothing could disturb her peace in here. She could forget the argument, forget her second thoughts, even forget about her dull fiancé from her place in the bath. It was incredible how a little scalding hot water and scented oils could relax Stacy's mind and carry her off onto another plane. Maybe this was all she needed after all. She had a part to play in her lagging sex life, after all. The past year had brought back stressors that Stacy had believed were in the past — her father's attack led to months of court appearances and legal hoops to jump through that re-triggered feelings of paranoia and abandonment that Stacy had thought she had left behind.

Until her phone rang.

Stacy reached a wet hand out of the bath to her phone to see who interrupted her peace. It couldn't be Henry, from how it sounded, he was going to be at the hospital for another couple of hours at least. Stacy blinked at the caller display before dropping the phone. She let it ring out, waiting for the caller to give up and for her voicemail to answer. A minute later the ringing stopped, and her phone dinged to notify her of an unheard voicemail.

Stacy's podcast came back on, and her scene settled back into relaxing familiarity.

Except that Stacy was no longer relaxed. The caller couldn't have had good news, she recognized the name and they never had anything good to say. Not only that, but it had been weeks since they called — what could they possibly need? Stacy could feel her heart rate rising and she closed her eyes trying to calm down. She used a technique her former therapist taught her — deep breath in through one nostril, hold your nose closed, slowly exhale through the other nostril, repeat until your head cools down and your heart stops racing, and your breath doesn't catch in your throat. Once Stacy caught her breath again, she sank back into the bath, cradling her glass of wine. It was all going to be just fine, and she shouldn't be panicking this much over a single unanswered phone call. Stacy closed her eyes and lost herself in the sound of her podcast and the lavender-scented bath.

*Relax, Stacy, just relax.* She willed every cell in her body to relax.

The phone rang again. It was the same caller. Stacy didn't need to look at the caller ID to know. Maeve never let the first unanswered call stop her.

*Just breathe, relax, she'll give up and you can go back to your bath like Maeve didn't call you.*

Stacy wondered what her half-sister could possibly want. There was a time when the pair were close, but in the past year, Stacy hadn't heard much from her younger sister. Both during and after the trial, Maeve made it clear whose side she was on, and Stacy quickly got sick of hearing how Maeve thought their father was framed, and that there was no way he would have done any of the things he was accused of.

Maeve was lucky. Her mother was never really in a relationship with Oliver Lewis — he was too obsessed with Stacy and Heather for that. Any time Stacy and her mother managed to escape, Oliver got back together with Maeve's mother who was always ready to welcome him back and try to 'fix' him. According to Maeve, their father was mentally ill, and Stacy's mom refused to acknowledge it or get him any help, and now he was institutionalized thanks to Stacy's crazy cop boyfriend. In the aftermath of their father's attack, Maeve was the one to show Stacy how erratic and dangerous Matt could be and for that Stacy was thankful.

After a while, it got to be too much. Her sister's unconditional love for their father felt suffocating, and the two grew apart, but Maeve still called at least once a month to nag her sister about visiting their father. As time passed, she became more obsessive about it, reflecting one of their father's worst qualities.

The call finally went to voicemail again. Stacy's podcast came back on, but she was no longer paying attention. Her body was tense, bracing for the next time her phone would ring. Maeve always tried three times, and then would give up for the day. Stacy was accustomed to the routine. She just had to wait for that third call, resist the urge to pick it up, and then she could go back to her bath. She waited, and waited, but that third call never came.

"Maybe she finally understands that if you call someone and they don't answer they either can't or don't want to talk to you," Stacy muttered, taking a sip of her wine before letting her head fall back onto her inflatable bath pillow. At the back of her mind, she knew this wasn't the end of it. The last time Maeve called the two of them ended up in a screaming match and Stacy cried herself to sleep — talking about their father's abuse and addiction issues always brought out Maeve's mean streak. That had been at least three weeks ago, which meant Stacy was due for another nagging phone call from her sister.

"Just as long as she doesn't call again while I'm in the bath." Stacy sighed, and turned her phone's ringer to silent mode.

## THE DOCTOR'S SECRET   25

JUST AS STACY PREDICTED, by the time she exited the bath there were three voicemails from Maeve waiting for her.

*"Hi! It's me, Maeve, I'm guessing you're stuck in all this traffic. Must have been quite the accident — give me a call when you get the chance, I need to talk to you about some stuff. It's urgent."*

Stacy deleted the message.

*"Hi! Me again! I mean if you're stuck in traffic, you might as well answer. I was just checking to see if you're out of it. Or if you're screening my calls again — just kidding. I know you'd never screen calls from your beloved baby sister! Okay, well call me back when you get home. Okay? Okay. Bye."*

Maeve was nothing if not persistent and completely illogical.

*"Okay, third time is not the charm, I guess. Call me when you get home, it's important. It's family stuff, and I know you have pretty much set yourself up with a brand-new family, but we do still exist, unfortunately for you, and we need your attention as well. I really need you to call me back, it's important. And urgent. Call me back, please, or at least text to say you saw that I called.*

There were no voicemails after that, however her sister had sent text messages with just her name in all caps:

*Stacy.*

*Stacy!*

*STACY!*

This was all accompanied by countless 'missed call' alerts, all from Maeve. Stacy was starting to doubt herself. Maybe she was wrong, and this really was an emergency. She wasn't a completely heartless person, while she didn't want to have a relationship with her father anymore, she also didn't wish the worst on the man. She had accepted that he would never 'get his act together', the way her mother believed he would for so many years, and Stacy learned to deal with the disappointment that she would never have a normal family, especially since her mother died. She wished she could talk to her. Stacy had always been close to her mom, but when Heather finally cut Oliver out of her life, the two of them had grown even closer, more like sisters than mother and daughter. Stacy used to go to her mom for advice on everything, and she missed her mom the most in times like these when she could use a kind but stern word.

Stacy knew she had to call Maeve. Her baby sister would not stop calling until Stacy answered; that she could guarantee.

"Please don't make me regret this," she said to her phone screen.

Maeve answered almost immediately. "Oh my god, Stacy, I thought you had died!" Maeve screamed into the phone, causing Stacy's muscles to contract.

"Why would you think that, silly? I had to work late and then got stuck in all this traffic. You know I don't check my phone when I drive — and you shouldn't either, by the way."

"Ya, sure, whatever," Maeve said, dismissing her sister's concerns being as she was the typical twenty-three-year-old who thought she was invincible. "I was about to call your boyfriend at the hospital, you should at least check your phone when you're at a red light. What if there's an emergency and someone is trying to call you? Like me, hello? I have been freaking out like, all day long waiting for your call."

"You called me less than an hour ago, Maeve. Why have you been worried all day?" Stacy took deep breaths, willing herself to calm down. There was a time when she and Maeve were close. Their father drove a wedge between them and drove Maeve's anxiety to new heights.

"Because you said you'd go visit Dad, and I checked in today and he said he hadn't had any visitors, so I double-checked with the nurse and the receptionist, and they both said he was right, and no one had come by all day. I told you a week ago I would be working a double *today* and you said you'd go and visit *Dad,* so that he wouldn't be alone all day so obviously I got worried thinking that something had happened to you, and then I heard about this accident on the highway—"

THE DOCTOR'S SECRET 27

"Maeve, I never said I'd visit today. Besides, it's a Wednesday — I have work, remember? I can't just take off in the middle of the day," Stacy replied, mentally repeating to herself that Maeve wasn't *trying* to drive her crazy.

"Why? The dead bodies are still going to be dead on Thursday."

"Yes, but my supervisor and the many people waiting on their autopsy reports will be asking where I disappeared to all day. Besides, I never said I'd go visit him today. Also, he wasn't alone all day. He's surrounded by nurses and other patients all day long, *and* he has court-mandated therapy. He's just fine."

Stacy could feel her jaw getting tight and her heart starting to race. Arguing with Maeve brought back memories of that night. Her father's crazed look as he attacked her, Matt leaping in front to block him, the sound of a fist hitting a bloody target over and over and over...

"Stacy," Maeve said, cutting through the noise of Stacy's memory, "he is surrounded by people who don't care about him. He needs us to show him care and attention so that he doesn't go crazy in there. If your *boyfriend* hadn't locked him up and thrown away the key, then maybe he wouldn't be as lonely and depressed, but since Matt gaslighted you into thinking our father was dangerous—"

"Our father *is* dangerous, Maeve! He came at me with a knife after stalking me for over a month! He tricked you into telling him where I was and almost killed me. He also tried to frame you in court, claiming that you blackmailed him into attacking me— don't you remember any of that?" Stacy cried, her attempts to calm herself down failed.

Maeve struck a nerve that she couldn't control. On the other end of the line, Maeve was scarily quiet.

"Stacy, our father wouldn't do that. He was desperate, he had his back up against the wall thanks to your crooked ex-boyfriend. We both know he planted that weapon on our dad.

Why would a father try to stab his own daughter?" Maeve argued.

"Because he wanted my money! The money my mother left me, the money she painstakingly saved up while also putting me through school and paying for lawyers to keep my abusive father away from me!"

"*Our* father was never abusive! Your mother—"

"Maeve, do not bring my mother into this. Don't you dare, or I swear I will block your number. I'm always here to listen to you, but not if you're going to turn this into some self-righteous lecture about my mother. She went through enough without having you slander her memory."

"I won't. Oliver told me about your mom, how she was depressed and stuff. I wouldn't do that; I was just going to say that she had her own mental health issues, and you always supported her. Now that your father is going through the same — because addiction is a disease, you know, just as cancer and heart disease is — you have turned your back on him. I know Dad was never going to hurt you, and I was always willing to stand by him on that. Matt *planted* that knife; his fingerprints were all over it and the police conveniently forgot to investigate his role in the attack. It's just like cops to stand by their own and throw an innocent person under the bus — I just never thought you'd be one of them."

Stacy could hear Maeve's ragged breathing through the phone. She was probably crying. She could never handle the real truth about their father. *Her mom did a great job sheltering her,* Stacy thought.

"Maeve, I'm sorry. I didn't want to turn this phone call into an argument, it's just that I never promised to visit our dad today and I am concerned for your anxiety. You freaked out over nothing, and I'm worried about *you*, that's all. Listen, I'm going to say this calmly because I want you to understand that I am not blaming you." Stacy paused, and heard Maeve sniffle. "We were raised by different fathers. The Oliver Lewis I grew up with was addicted to drugs and alcohol, and was an obsessive and controlling man. Your mom managed to shield you from his worst qualities, and for that I think you're lucky. I'm glad you're able to have some kind of relationship with him, and maybe even help him in his recovery, but I can't do that. He was worse with me and my mom, he was never as controlling with you. When he attacked me — and yes, he did attack me — it made me realize that he'll never change. He will always put his needs above everyone else, and he will always react with violence when he thinks you aren't under his control. So no, I'm not going to visit him, and I don't care if you think he's lonely. I have to go. Henry just came through the door with dinner—"

"Don't lie to me, Stacy," Maeve said, her voice steely now. The tears didn't work, so she dried them up and moved on to her next tactic. "I know your mom and your boyfriend brainwashed you into thinking he's the worst thing imaginable, but he's sick and he needs our help. If you aren't going to step it up as a daughter, then—"

Stacy didn't wait to hear Maeve's threat. She hung up the phone and blocked Maeve's number. Not forever, she hoped, but definitely for the rest of the night. A long time ago she and Maeve made a pact that they would never blame the other's mother for how she dealt with Oliver. Over the past year, as they drifted apart, Maeve seemed to forget about that pact, and in a weird way was starting to sound more and more like their father. There was no good way of dealing with it, and the topic made Stacy angry. It was yet another way Oliver Lewis exerted his power over her life — dangling her sister's sanity over her, just out of Stacy's reach. She wished there was a way she could bring Maeve back down to earth, pull her away from the delusional life Oliver had drawn her into.

*If only there was some way I could have just a little control over someone else's emotions,* Stacy thought, *maybe then I could relax.*

# CHAPTER
# FOUR
STACY

Henry got home even later than Stacy expected. She was still waiting, her stomach growling, at 8, 9, 10 at night, with no sign of Henry or the promised sushi. Stacy checked the news on her phone for news of the accident or some clue as to why Henry was still out, but she found nothing. The accident barely made the evening news, it was just a short report explaining the bad traffic, buried halfway into the 7 o'clock news. Stacy cobbled together a dinner made up of questionable leftovers and various snacks, knowing that Henry would get moody if he found out she ordered takeout for herself when he was coming home with dinner.

He couldn't be hurt. It was more likely that he got caught up in some other accident at work and forgot to tell her. Still, it was unlike Henry to come home this late without any warning. Sometimes he even got one of the nurses to call, if he had to go into an emergency surgery.

*I could call the hospital,* Stacy thought, *they could at least tell me if he's still there.* She did her best to calm down and keep from panicking. She often panicked when things didn't go as planned, that sense of unpredictability triggered feelings of fear Stacy thought she had either buried or worked on with a therapist. That's the whole point of being with Henry — that he didn't come home late unexpectedly or disappear without warning. He was her rock, and in moments like this Stacy felt like the ground was shifting underneath her feet.

"Stay calm, Stacy Lewis, there's no need to go off the rails. Henry has come home late before, today is a little later than expected. You feel vulnerable because of that phone call with Maeve, and you need to be comforted, that is why you feel a little more on edge than usual. Wrap yourself in a weighted blanket, take a deep breath, and call the hospital to check on Henry. He likely forgot to call when he got pulled away for an emergency — which is the nature of his job."

Stacy continued to monologue as she took a few slow, deep breaths. It was a tactic an old therapist had taught her — literally talking herself down off a ledge. Speaking aloud helped reinforce the reality of the situation and drown out the panic at the back of Stacy's brain. Her spiral soon slowed to a stop and when Stacy was ready, she called the emergency department.

"St. Vincent's Emergency Department, how may I help you?" a frazzled nurse answered almost immediately. Stacy recognized most of the voices, but this one was new to her.

"Hi, I'm looking for Dr. Henry Goldberg? I'm his fiancée," Stacy replied. "He isn't home yet, and I was just wondering if he was pulled in to a surgery or something?"

The night shift nurse sighed, and Stacy could practically hear her eyes rolling. The night shift nurses were all hard as bricks, and didn't like answering calls they thought were a waste of time. "He's not on the board, and it doesn't look like anyone was scheduled to have an emergency, so it looks like he isn't here."

"Can you page him?" Stacy asked, bracing herself for the answer.

"I'm sorry, ma'am, this isn't the information center at Disneyland. I can't just page a doctor at the request of someone who *claims* to be his fiancée over the phone. If I see Dr. Goldberg, I'll tell him to give you a call, I assume he has your number? Now if you'll excuse me—" the line clicked, and the nurse disappeared.

"So much for compassionate care," Stacy muttered.

The nurse must be new, even the overworked night staff were usually pretty accommodating for her — a former colleague and soon-to-be-bride of the hardest working doctor at St. Vincent's. She sent Henry a text, waited for a moment and then sent another. It was past their bedtime, even if he had brought sushi they weren't going to eat it now. She could call the police station — or better yet, she could call Matt. He was still in her phone, and would probably do more than the missing person's line. Her finger hovered over Matt Ensor's name, once gain Stacy was deciding whether or not it was worth opening that can of worms.

Just then, she heard a thud coming from downstairs. Stacy crept out of bed, clutching her phone. She slowly walked to the staircase, and heard the same thud. It was coming from the front door, a loud heavy thud against the wood. Stacy tiptoed down the stairs, listening to the strange shuffling and jingle of keys — it reminded her of her father coming home drunk late at night — but it couldn't be? Henry never got that —

"Fuck!" She heard a cry outside the door followed by another thud. It was Henry all right, and he definitely sounded drunk. She hadn't heard his car come up the drive, Stacy hoped it wasn't wrapped around a pole somewhere as she scurried to the front door. She whipped the door open, and Henry practically fell through, stumbling into the hallway and reeking of whiskey.

"Henry? What's going on?"

"The stupid key won't work. It doesn't fit, did you do something to the door?" he slurred, slumping down to the floor. "I think you did something to the door. It rejected my key."

Stacy looked outside and saw Henry's keys — his car keys — lying on the welcome mat.

"That's because this is your house, not your car," Stacy said, her voice deadpan and her jaw clenched.

Henry was wasted, she could hear his groaning as he picked himself off the floor. Stacy threw the keys into a bowl, harder than she needed to, and Henry winced.

"What, are you angry? Are you *mad*? I figured you'd be used to this, someone coming home drunk. It's nothing you've never seen before anyway," Henry said as he stumbled into their living room and collapsed onto the couch with a sigh. "I'm drunk, Stacy. I need some water."

"I'll get you a coffee," she said through clenched teeth.

She couldn't believe a moment ago she was actually worried about Henry. Meanwhile he was out at some bar drinking with his work buddies, not even thinking about Stacy and the fact that she was sitting at home going hungry. When she came back into the living room, Henry had kicked off his shoes and thrown his coat to the floor, and was sitting with his head between his hands.

"Henry? Are you okay?" Stacy asked, this behavior wasn't something she was used to. Henry rarely drank, and when he did, he could hold his liquor better than any drunk she'd ever known. Something must have happened on the operating table, or—

"How can you even ask me that? Today, you seriously asked me if I'm 'okay' TODAY?" Henry roared at Stacy before dropping his head back in his hands and violently sobbing.

Suddenly it dawned on Stacy that today was the three-month anniversary of his mother's suicide. Amanda was found in her apartment next to an empty bottle of sleeping pills and a half-finished glass of whiskey. All day Stacy had been questioning whether Henry was the right person for her, meanwhile he was mourning the death of his mother — a death that had been caused by his engagement to Stacy. Neither truly believed that Amanda would do it — she was hysterical and often made empty threats when her beloved son wasn't doing as she said. Neither thought she'd take her own life in protest of their marriage. Both were wrong, Amanda Goldberg would stop at nothing to get her way.

"Henry, I'm so sorry." Stacy collapsed into the couch next to Henry and wrapped her arms around him. "I didn't even—"

"Yeah, you didn't even say anything. I thought you might say something when we were on the phone, but there was nothing at all. You just ignored me."

"I'm so sorry, Henry, I really I—I must have got the days confused. I've been a little turned around lately — I didn't — I wish—"

"You wish, you apologize, blah, blah, blah," Henry said as he pushed Stacy off of him and got up, grabbing his coffee as he did. "I'm gonna go to sleep. I'll stay in the guest room, so I don't *disturb* you."

Henry stumbled off and Stacy sat there, listening to him bang into the wall as he plodded into their guest bedroom and slammed the door.

*I probably deserve that,* Stacy thought. She couldn't believe she had forgotten. The day was burned on Henry's memory, his mother — the person he was closest to — had died very suddenly. He had probably been thinking about her all day, meanwhile Stacy was debating whether or not she should break off her engagement, and she'd almost contacted her ex-boyfriend twice in one day. Stacy felt like a complete idiot, she wanted to crawl out of her own skin in shame. How could she have forgotten today? Years later she never forgot the day her own mother died. The date was etched into her soul, she remembered even when she tried to forget, of course, Henry would be feeling the same way.

Stacy quietly picked up after her fiancé and went upstairs. Behind the door to the guest room, she could hear Henry snoring. It was too late for her to apologize again; she would have to wait until the morning. She slipped a piece of paper under the door, her final apology for the night, before padding down the hall to their bedroom and putting herself to bed.

THE NEXT MORNING, Stacy woke up early and prepared breakfast for both of them. Henry barely spoke to her; he ate in silence and grunted his thanks before leaving for work. She felt relieved she hadn't brought up her hesitations about their wedding, it would have only made matters worse. Stacy went to work stressed out about how things had been left with Henry. How could she make it up to him? This wasn't exactly a situation in which you could buy a 'sorry I forgot your mom died' cake. She couldn't send flowers to his work because they'd likely get lost in the chaos of the ER. Besides, Stacy didn't want to catch any more angry comments from the nurses. She had all day to think and stew in her guilt. Henry didn't answer any of her text messages — except one, to tell her to stop messaging him, and they'd talk at home that night.

"This is probably how Maeve feels when I'm avoiding her," she said to the corpse on her autopsy table.

The corpse stared blankly into the atmosphere in return. Stacy resolved to stop turning Henry's feelings around in her head. He was allowed to be upset, after all. She would have been just as upset if Henry callously asked her, "What's for dinner," on the anniversary of her own mother's death. He was probably hungover this morning, not exactly in the mood to talk. Stacy was just glad he didn't drive home last night; she couldn't handle any more guilt over his feelings.

"Maybe I'll get him flowers on my way home. Dahlias, he loves them and will never admit it because he thinks it makes him less manly or something. I'll bring home a bottle of wine too, and we can sit and talk about our feelings like grown-ups. That seems like it could be a good idea, right?" Stacy asked the body on her table. She gently nudged the dead woman's head, so it looked like she was nodding. "That settles it then. I'll bring home I'm-sorry flowers and a bottle of his favorite red. I'll cut out of here early and make his favorite dinner, then when he's home we can talk in a way we couldn't have done yesterday."

Stacy sighed, settling the matter. She finished her work quickly and efficiently, eager to get out of the morgue that day.

---

"HONEY? I'M HOME!" Stacy called out to the empty townhouse when she arrived carrying a large bouquet of dahlias and the 'Special Menu B' from their favorite sushi place.

Henry didn't answer, but Stacy knew he was home, his car was parked in the drive.

"Henry? You home?" She listened for the sounds of life as she tiptoed through the house, still hoping to surprise Henry with the flowers. He was nowhere to be found, not in the kitchen nor his office upstairs.

*"Hey, hon, where are you? Stuck at work again?"* Stacy texted Henry, hoping this was all some misunderstanding and that she hadn't forgotten another important date.

*"Obviously,"* he replied, *"I'll be home soon just finishing up."*

Stacy's heart sank. He was still angry, which meant tonight was going to be a quiet one. She put the dahlias in a vase and left the sushi on the kitchen counter. Stacy decided she'd give him an hour before she dug into dinner herself. She knew what this night was going to be like — passive-aggressive silence from Henry, confrontational avoidance from her. If their loving relationship had become boring, their arguing had become tense and quiet. They didn't passionately argue and make up anymore, the tension just stretched below the surface, pulling them farther away from each other, until finally one of them gave up and eased the tension.

Once again, Stacy started to feel as though she had made the wrong choice in accepting Henry's marriage proposal. But what could she do? She couldn't break up with him now — not while he was grieving his mother, the woman who would rather commit suicide than see her son get married. Stacy thought about having another bath, or maybe doing some yoga while she waited for Henry. All she could think to do was try to find some balance in herself, so that maybe she'd be able to get Henry to actually *talk* about his feelings for once.

He arrived an hour later, seemingly in a good mood. Henry smiled at Stacy, thanked her for the flowers and kissed her on the cheek.

"Did you already make dinner, is that why you texted?" he asked, fingering the sharp petals on the dahlia.

"No, I figured we could have that sushi dinner, since we couldn't have it last night." Stacy smiled and pulled out the takeout containers from behind a bread box. She saw Henry smirk, but couldn't figure out what emotion was behind it. He could be pleased — but he could also be annoyed that she dared mention anything that happened last night.

"That's cute, making up for a lost sushi dinner. To be honest I didn't much care about it, I wasn't craving sushi yesterday, it just seemed like an easy meal to pick up after work."

"Isn't any meal an easy meal to pick up?"

"Well sushi is served cold, so it doesn't exactly *matter* when you pick it up, right? For all I know you picked this up at lunch and it's been sitting around all day."

"Why would I pick up our dinner at lunch time?"

"Because it was more convenient for you, I don't know. It was just a hypothetical answer, I know you prefer to do what's convenient for you."

*Well, I guess we're having another passive aggressive night.* No matter how relaxed or calm Stacy was, Henry's anger was penetrable. He was still upset and no matter what she said or did, he'd continue to live in his funk until he decided enough time had passed. Stacy could just back away, wait until this round of passive-aggressive anger was over. She didn't have to talk to Henry about his mother and what feelings might have been dredged to the surface on the anniversary of her death. What was the point? After all, in their day-to-day life Henry was doing pretty well. Anyone would react poorly and get the blues while remembering their parent's death, even if the relationship they had with that parent was strained.

But for some reason, that night Stacy just couldn't let it go. She couldn't let Henry retreat into himself and push her away. Stacy needed something more, if only to remind her why she fell in love with Henry in the first place. Why it was even worth being with a man whose mother was so overbearing that she could control his emotions from beyond the grave.

"Henry, I want to say something."

"I'm all ears, Stae," Henry said, pressing his lips together until they stretched into a smile.

"I'm really sorry about last night. I should have remembered that it was the three-month point since Amanda died and I'm sorry if you felt I was being insensitive. I know her death was traumatic for you, and I wanted to know if you wanted to talk about it with me." Stacy smiled and gently placed her hand over Henry's. She could feel his fingers tapping the table beneath her own.

"Nope, I'm fine." He smiled again and reached for the sushi.

"It's okay to not be okay, you know. Obviously, your mother was never very...impressed with me. I know she was very manipulative, and you didn't believe that she'd actually...*do* anything like that. You know it's not your fault, right?" Stacy asked, her voice calm and gentle.

"I know," Henry said, stirring wasabi paste into his soy sauce.

Stacy was quiet for a while. Henry scrolled on his phone as he chewed on his California roll.

"Aren't you gonna have any?" he asked, gesturing to the small sushi platter.

Stacy nodded and snapped apart her chopsticks. Why was Henry so content to avoid real emotion? He tapped the edge of his plate with his chopsticks, clearly agitated, all Stacy wanted was for him to let go a little bit and let her in.

"Henry, have you thought about seeing a therapist at all?"

Henry's head whipped up when Stacy said it. The unspoken rule between them was broken — Stacy was determined to force a conversation about feelings, emotion, and trauma. Henry finished chewing as he watched Stacy carefully select a piece of Spicy Salmon Maki and bring it to her lips. Shee didn't know if he was angry or aroused, but every cell in her body was on edge at his look. He looked as if he wanted to get away, or that he wanted to strangle her, or maybe he wanted to throw up, and cry all at the same time. She couldn't determine which of those thoughts were true though.

"What?" he said, in a monotone voice that hid his clear inner turmoil which swam in his eyes.

"When my mother died — and I know it was under different circumstances — I went to a therapist, and it helped me a lot. Especially on those days that were particularly painful, like her birthday and the anniversary of her death. Even on Mother's Day, it was really helpful to have someone to talk to," Stacy said, avoiding eye contact with Henry.

"Isn't that what you're here for? For me to have someone to talk to?" Henry asked, his voice practically at a growl.

"Of course, but—"

"But? What do you mean 'but'? If I can't talk to you — and if I can't communicate to you that I don't want to talk and have that boundary respected — then what are we even doing this for?" His voice was starting to get louder. Henry seemed to be straining against his anger trying as hard as he could to stay calm.

"*But* last night you came home wasted, I practically had to carry you up the stairs to bed. You've barely said a single word to me all day, and I've been trying to talk to you, but clearly you can't for some reason—"

"I just don't want to talk about it right now, why is that so hard for you to understand? I want a little space and I want you to just leave it alone, it's a sore subject, you should know better than to push my boundaries like this!"

"I wouldn't push your boundaries if I wasn't concerned! I just want to know that you're okay, but you keep coming at me with sarcasm and—"

"When was I sarcastic? I think I've been pretty clear that I just don't want to talk about my mother today — or any other day for that matter! The reason she is dead is that I decided to be with you, isn't that enough? I feel guilty about it constantly, but I don't want you to feel that because I know it isn't your fault and I don't want you to think that. My mother was controlling and manipulative and I work against that every single day. Sometimes I don't want to open that can of worms, sometimes I just don't think there's much of a point. The moment has passed, it's a new day, I've had a long work day, and I want to eat this sushi in peace, is that too much to ask?"

Stacy took a deep breath to fight down the lump in her throat. She could hear Henry taking his own long deep breaths to control his own temper. The two of them went back to their sushi, and didn't say another word during the meal. The cloud of their argument hung low over the tempura and California rolls. When they were finished, Henry cleaned up and Stacy went into the living room and turned on the TV. She expected Henry to go straight upstairs, but he sat down next to her and handed her a glass of wine.

After an episode of some dumb sitcom, Stacy cleared her

throat and said, "I'm sorry for pushing you. If you don't want to talk to me, I still think it's best you see a therapist."

"I'm fine, Stacy. If anything, it's a relief to be out from my mother's suffocating shadow," Henry replied.

"I know— I believe you. Last night scared me, that's all. I think you'd feel better if, every once in a while, you could talk to someone without worrying about judgement or anything."

"Stacy, I am fine. I'm sorry about yesterday, I went for drinks after a stressful day, and I went a little overboard. You don't have to worry about me turning into a drunk." Henry got up and took their empty glasses back into the kitchen. Without another word, he went upstairs. Stacy soon heard the shower running.

*I'm fine, I'm fine, I'm fine, that's all he'll ever say,* she thought. She didn't know if it was because of his manipulative mother or just because he was a man, but Henry dismissed just about every emotion that passed through him. It frustrated Stacy to no end, seeing him bottle everything up. Stacy was slowly starting to realize it wasn't actually that much better than the opposite. Her father and her ex-boyfriend had both allowed their emotions to take over and govern their actions. To Stacy, the sign of stability was someone who could keep all that under control — but Henry took it one step further. It made Stacy feel a strange combination of anxiety and fury, keeping her restless until their long drawn-out low-key argument was over. Since their sex life had stalled, she didn't even have an outlet for her restless anxiety.

"Maybe I'll book a spin class or something," Stacy muttered as she went upstairs and got ready for bed.

Henry smiled as she came into the room, giving her a hug and a perfunctory kiss on the forehead. They took turns brushing their teeth and changing into pajamas before crawling into bed with their books. Not even twenty minutes later, Stacy turned off the light and closed her eyes, hoping she could trick her body into feeling tired and falling asleep. Henry did the same a minute later. Stacy could hear that he was wide awake, but felt too nervous to say anything to him.

*What's the point,* she thought, *we'll just keep going round and round in passive aggressive circles.* She stared at the ceiling and waited to sleep.

Stacy managed to fall asleep, but not for very long. She woke up to the sound of Henry getting out of bed and padding down the stairs. She turned to the clock by her bedside to look at the time — barely even 10 p.m. Henry was going for a drive, an old habit of his. Whenever Henry couldn't sleep, he'd drive around the city until he felt tired enough to come to bed. There was a time when this little habit added to Henry's mysterious allure. Nowadays, Stacy saw it for what it was — yet another way for Henry to avoid having any emotions.

*Let him drive. Maybe he'll drive into a therapist's office and finally get some help.* Stacy fitfully turned over, but she couldn't get back to sleep. She was awake for hours, staring at the ceiling, waiting for Henry to come back. Lying with her thoughts, she couldn't help but wonder if she had trapped herself in a gilded cage. It was her fault Henry's mother died, so she couldn't very well break up with him — yet Stacy was growing increasingly unsure that this was the right relationship for her.

*It's fine, Stacy. You had a fight, so what? Sometimes relationships are just fine. Everyone goes through growing pains; everyone goes through rough patches and boring spells. Just because it isn't all fireworks and euphoria doesn't mean it's not a good relationship. You are fine. Just let it be fine.*

She repeated that mantra over and over again, until she finally drifted off to sleep.

# CHAPTER
# FIVE
STACY

"Did you go out last night?"
"I just needed to clear my head."
Stacy nodded. Their morning was quiet, but Henry seemed to be in a much better mood than the night before. He woke her up with freshly squeezed orange juice and a homemade breakfast sandwich.

"You put up with me," he said with a smile. "That's why."

Just like that it was all over. Their fight, the anger from the night before, even Stacy's doubts. She knew Henry would always be there in the morning, even when they argued, and that was what she needed. Passion was all well and good, but what did passion matter when you were left wondering if your partner would come back to you? Henry always came back, and maybe over time Stacy could work on his emotional connection.

---

STACY'S GLOW didn't last the whole day. She had planned to work from home that day, hoping to catch up on reports, when her reverie was interrupted by the phone.

"They found another one, same as before. They need you in here to examine the body."

"Another what? Same as who? And why does it have to be me, I'm not the city's only medical examiner you know." Stacy was talking with Trevor, the morgue's semi-useless intern.

Somewhere in the coroner's lunch room was a secret calendar that counted down the days until his placement was over — until then, Stacy had to field phone calls where she received only half the information she needed.

"I dunno, that's what they said. To call Stacy Lewis and tell her she needs to get down here to examine another body, pronto." The phone clicked as Trevor hung up, failing to explain anything.

Stacy sighed and poured her fresh coffee into a thermos.

---

"JANE DOE, late twenties, found in an alleyway near the Fremont bridge." Stacy read out the file that Trevor handed her. "Why is this assigned to me?"

The boy just shrugged and went back to his game of solitaire.

Stacy, irritated at the interruption to her day, stalked off in the direction of her boss, determined to figure out why she needed to be called in for a Jane Doe. She didn't even notice a person coming out of her office, and almost collided with him in the hall.

"Watch where you're going!" she screeched, scrambling to pick up her files, "I could have been holding something sharp." She looked up to see her ex-boyfriend, Matt Ensor.

"Sorry! I was looking for you, you weren't in the autopsy room, so I figured you'd be in your office."

"I was working from home today until I got called in for some emergency autopsy, but no one will explain to me *why* I had to be the one to do it—" Stacy was about to go in for a rant about

Trevor when Matt silenced her with a finger to her mouth. It sent shivers down her spine, followed by a wave of guilt.

"You're about to go off like a bottle of Coke loaded down with Mentos, I can tell," he said, softly dropping his hand to his side. "Before you get that poor kid fired, *I'm* the one who insisted you get assigned to this case. It's another Jane Doe in an alleyway, the second in as many weeks. Her body was found in an alleyway, completely naked, covered in bruises, with her hands bound behind her back — just like Gabrielle Unwin. I want a little consistency, and I want it done quick, just in case we have a serial killer on our hands."

"It's two bodies, that's hardly a series," Stacy said, dismissing Matt and reopening the Jane Doe file.

There it was, the initial crime scene Polaroids — an antiquated way of doing things, but it came in handy. The girl's body was covered in bruises, and she was completely naked, her legs and arms spread wide, just like Gabrielle Unwin. Matt was right to think it might be a serial killer, it wasn't every day you got two nearly identical crime scenes.

"Maybe, but I'd rather be safe than sorry. Besides, I always want the best on my case, and I know you're the best." Matt smiled.

She whipped her head back to the file. He could not have chosen a worse moment to rear his ugly head. The last thing Stacy needed was a constant reminder of the man she had broken up with for Henry. Matt wasn't exactly a 'traditional' charmer. He was a large, burly, hairy man with a raspy voice that made it sound like he had been born with a cigarette in his hand. He had a slightly bent nose and a scar on his lip, both souvenirs from his days as a boxer, each serving to remind everyone that he could break them in two if he wanted to. He didn't make silly jokes or wink his way through life, but he often had an unmistakable twinkle in his eye that could put anyone at ease. True to Stacy's type, Matt had a hard shell around his emotions, but unlike Henry he was more willing to let someone take a crack at it.

## MATT

Whether Stacy knew it or not, Matt still felt the need to protect her, and once he noticed that the two murder victims bore a striking resemblance to his ex-girlfriend, he became determined to keep Stacy close at hand.

"Her body is waiting for you in the autopsy room," he said, breathing down Stacy's long neck.

Matt missed her, but he understood why she had broken up with him. He probably would have done the same. He wanted to ask how she was doing, if Maeve was giving her any trouble, and if Henry was treating her well, but he doubted Stacy would be willing to give up anything about her life. After the night of the attack, Stacy barely said two words to Matt, calling on her friend Lindsay to pick up her stuff from his apartment.

"We should go," Stacy said, clearing her throat and taking a step away from Matt. "I obviously have some catching up to do."

Matt watched Stacy, perched on the same stool he'd sat on back when they'd been together. He glanced at the victim who was practically identical to her — same build, same dark hair, and auburn eyes — and once again he had a sick feeling in the pit of his stomach. It could have been her lying on the slab rather than some anonymous woman, and that scared the piss out of him.

"Any idea who she is?"

"So far, no, but I have a team working on it," Matt replied, twirling a small metal brush in his hands trying to distract himself from what he was thinking.

"Maybe you should call them," Stacy said, grabbing the brush and placing it back on her tool tray. "There could be updates."

Her voice was tight, and if Matt hadn't known her so well, he would have thought she was just annoyed. He could tell there was something else to the tension in Stacy's voice, knew that she was bothered by her resemblance to the young woman lying dead in front of her. He was glad she was seeing the resemblance and appeared to be concerned about it.

"How's Henry doing?" Matt asked, pretending to scroll through the messages on his phone.

"He's fine," Stacy replied. "Why do you ask?"

"Just wondering how your life is. You don't exactly send me updates." He kept his eyes on his phone.

"Sorry, I didn't think you'd be interested in the newsletter."

They sat in an uncomfortable silence for a while, the only sound was Stacy's pen scratching at her notepad.

"You know I still care, Stace."

Stacy nodded, but didn't say anything.

"I heard St. Vincent's got a new board head or something. Must be stressful, having a promotion and then a new boss all of a sudden."

"I think he can handle that."

"What makes you say that?"

"The man routinely sees people who had to be cut out of their cars and could be on the brink of death. Something tells me a change of the guard at work wouldn't be too hard for him to handle." He could hear the annoyance in her voice.

"It's a different kind of stress, answering to a new authority. Dead bodies don't scare me anymore, not after working as many homicides as I have, but I still faint at the doctor every time they try to draw blood," Matt answered, watching Stacy's body language closely. He had never trusted Henry Goldberg — and not just because the man had inadvertently stolen his girlfriend from him. Henry had a manipulative streak that people around him didn't seem to notice. He was like a pickpocket, charming his victim before robbing them blind. Even Matt's partner was sick of hearing him talk about the doctor — there was zero evidence that he was a bad guy or that he'd treat Stacy poorly. He even stood up to his emotionally abusive mother in order to be with her. However, Matt still didn't believe Henry was truly the right person for Stacy. He knew that their relationship was irreparably broken after the night of the attack, but he still cared about Stacy, and he still wanted the best for her. The woman deserved it after what her life had been, and Matt couldn't shake the feeling that even though Henry seemed like the perfect man, that perfection was nothing but a façade.

"Matt, what is this really about? Or do you honestly think that Henry Goldberg — a grown man and celebrated surgeon — is going to lose his mind over a new boss?" Stacy asked, putting her hand on one hip.

Matt almost blushed — Stacy was unbelievably sexy when she put her foot down. "No, but I do know he's been through a lot lately. His mother's death couldn't have been easy, the two of them were…extremely close. Who knows what could trigger someone in that situation. I'm just being a detective, following my leads."

Stacy opened her mouth, probably to defend her fiancé, when Matt's cellphone started ringing.

"Ensor—" He put a finger up to Stacy and hurried out of the room.

---

## STACY

Stacy rolled her eyes and resisted screaming at him. Matt hadn't changed, and she was swiftly reminded why he was the most *irritating* partner she'd ever had. It was practically impossible to win an argument against him because he had the memory of an elephant, and forget trying to keep a secret — the man's job was to read clues and discover what people were hiding. The most irritating thing was that he always managed to get a phone call *just* as you were going to eviscerate him with an argument of your own. Stacy shook her head and went back to the body.

*"Bruising on the neck and arms consistent with strangulation. Bruising pattern indicates large hands, I'm guessing a large man at least six feet tall with some muscle on him. Bruises up and down her arms and torso...even some on the legs. Upon initial examination there is no sign of sexual assault, but I'll send a rape kit to the lab just in case. There is some material under the victim's fingernails indicating that she tried to fight off her attacker, but was unsuccessful. The back of her head has a...a lump? But that could be her hair...dried blood in the hair, the attacker hit her up against something like a wall or the ground...I'll have to examine that wound further to see if there is debris pointing to the location of the attack..."*

Stacy was still muttering into her voice recorder when Matt came back in. He tiptoed over to the desk and doodled as Stacy finished, gently prodding and lifting the body to get a clear picture of what happened before she did her initial surgery. He waited patiently until she was done.

When she removed her gloved, Matt finally said, "Audrey Wells, thirty-one years old, owner of Bechdel Wonder, a comic book shop in Ballard."

Stacy stared down at the woman lying on her table. She was only three years younger, the two of them could be sisters. She had a long nose, Stacy could imagine the thick rimmed glasses that perched upon them. There wasn't a superhero to save her that night, no Batman, or Wonder Woman to swoop in from the dark and fight off her attacker.

"What can you tell me?"

Stacy shrugged. "I don't know if the sex trafficking theory is going to pan out."

"But you think they're related?" Matt asked, taking a step closer to Stacy.

She could smell his cologne cutting through the formaldehyde, Matt was forever using a bottle when just a spritz would do.

"I'd have to check my notes, but the bruising pattern seems consistent with what I saw on Gabrielle Unwin. Big guy, big hands."

"Perfect, that's great, Stacy, thank you."

"Is it great?" Stacy burst, Matt could be incredibly insensitive when it came to dead bodies. Stacy worked with murdered people all the time too, but she didn't forget the fact that they lived complex and sprawling lives before they ended up on her table. "Is it perfect that this young woman is lying here after being attacked rather than at home with her family or like…at her comic book store? Her employees are probably standing outside the shop waiting for her to come open or…maybe there's a regular who asked…maybe she has a fiancé or a girlfriend…she could even have cats, whose feeding her cats right now?"

Matt led Stacy over to the desk and sat her down, handing her a bottle of water.

"Stacy," Matt said in the calming voice he used for panicked witnesses, "is there anything you want to tell me? Anything at all, it doesn't even have to be about the case, I can tell you have something you want to get off your chest."

*Sure, Matt, well it all started a couple of days ago when I was questioning whether or not I should go through with my marriage and that spiraled into whether or not I should ever have broken up with you. That, of course, led to a fight with my fiancé, who you hate, even though he doesn't know that I am secretly feeling guilty about thinking that I should break up with him and go back to my ex-boyfriend, you, on the three-month anniversary of his mother's suicide. Which, coincidentally, is my fault! On top of that, women who look a lot like me keep turning up murdered around the city.*

"No," Stacy mumbled, "just…always a little freaky when the vic looks like you."

"I don't think so. I think that's just a coincidence."

"Matt, you're a man, you're huge, you're an ex-boxer, and you're a cop. Our perspectives about getting murdered in an alleyway are a little different."

That shut him up. Matt stroked Stacy's arm in silence. Stacy let him, it felt nice.

After a few minutes Matt cleared his throat and Stacy stood up. "If she was a comic book store owner you can probably dismiss the sexual angle. I'll do a rape kit and send it to the lab anyway, just in case."

"Stace—"

"There wasn't a sexual attack on Gabrielle Unwin, so if you're thinking this is serial and it's the same guy it seems sexual violence isn't really his thing."

"Stacy, are you okay? Really, please just tell me. I care about you, you know," Matt pleaded with her, but Stacy was determined not to go off track.

"I can have a full report done for you in two days. Tomorrow if you think it's that urgent."

"Is something going on with Henry?"

"Today I have a lot of paperwork to catch up on, and we're backed up as it is. Apparently, some family is insisting on a post-burial autopsy to settle some kind of a will dispute, can you believe that?"

"Stacy." Matt lowered his voice and grabbed her by the elbow. He was gentle, but his touch was strong enough to stop Stacy from moving away and make her stomach flip over itself. "If something is going on, please tell me. I know you. I know what you're like when your head is somewhere else. I miss you, okay? I miss you and I just want to know that Henry is treating you right." Matt's words were mere whispers, as if he almost didn't want her to hear them..

"I'm fine, Matt. I'm fine, Henry's fine, we're fine individually and as a couple. His mom's death was three months ago, he's still working on it. He's doing well."

"I don't trust him," Matt muttered. "I don't trust any guy with a mom like that."

"Well, unfortunately for some of us, we can't pick and choose who our parents are." That comment sent Stacy over the edge. How dare he accuse Henry of being an untrustworthy partner because of his abusive mother? Is that what Matt thought of her, that she was some manipulative psychopath because her dad was an obsessive addict?

*Of course not, I'm a woman. Matt thinks of me as a victim.*

"I didn't mean it like that, of course he didn't *choose* his mom—"

"But he deserves to be thought of as weak and devious because of her, right? You know what, Matt, just go. Please leave my office, I have a ton of work to catch up on — your murder isn't the only death in the city, in case you didn't know." Stacy pushed Matt out of the room. He let her — she couldn't get him out the door if he hadn't, the man was built like a stone wall.

"I'll go, you don't have to shove me out. Just promise me you'll say if something is wrong."

"I promise I'll let you know if something goes wrong with the victim in this murder case. As for my personal life, you'll have to ask Lillian, who I'm sure keeps you very well informed."

Stacy shut the door and beelined back to her stool, dropping her head into her hands. Matt was impossible — telling her he missed her while they were working on a *case?* That was absurd. Stacy was practically married! She was engaged, she shared a house with her partner, and Matt thought he could come in here, stroke her arm a couple of times, tell her he *misses* her, and what? She'll dump Henry, go back to Matt, and they can ride off into the sunset solving crimes?

*I mean, you thought the same thing a day or two ago.* Lillian's logical voice echoed in her mind. The whole situation was a double-edged sword, she'd have to get better at balance if she was going to work with Matt.

The rest of the day was a complete wash. Stacy tried to work, but all she could do was dream up scenarios that usually ended with Matt and Henry getting into a very sweaty fistfight, or with her and Matt in bed together. Matt whispering, "I miss you," was a recurring theme, she could practically feel his breath on her ear, and it made her shiver every time.

This was going to be a long and complicated case.

# CHAPTER SIX
STACY

Stacy was glad for the paperwork-heavy day. Anything else and she'd actually have to pay attention to what she was doing. Her wandering thoughts wouldn't help her on a normal work day. Thinking about Matt getting close to her, stroking her arm, and claiming that he missed her, and still cared about her, would have compromised her examinations.

It was fine that she kept writing, "I miss you," under 'observations'.

The day crawled along until it was finally over. Stacy made her way home practically in a daze, hoping she could shower and wash off the day before joining her loving fiancé for dinner. She kept thinking she could smell Matt's cologne on her — but that was impossible. They didn't get *that* close. Still, Stacy hoped she could shower before Henry made it home.

---

"HONEY, YOU'RE HO-OME!" Henry sang from the kitchen.

Stacy hung her head, *shit.* She wanted a moment to clear her head, to forget her day and not have to confront her fiancé while her ex-boyfriend was swirling around in her head. Henry bounded out of the kitchen wearing his favorite funny apron, wrapping Stacy in a salty-scented hug. She hoped he couldn't smell the cologne; she closed her eyes and prayed it was all in her head.

"Busy day? You seem tense," he muttered into her neck.

"Mm-hmm...got called in unexpectedly, then a lot of computer work. My eyes are practically glazed over." Stacy forced a laugh and gently untangled herself from her fiancé.

"I told you that you need a better chair. Those creaky rolling chairs from the seventies are horrible for your posture, and you spend almost every day bent over." He kissed her forehead and backed away, back into the kitchen. "Have a shower, I'll warm up a hot water bottle for you to put across your neck. By the time you come down dinner will be ready!"

Stacy sighed, relieved that Henry didn't notice Matt's scent, and that she could shower and collect her thoughts before dinner. Henry was finally in a good mood again, and she didn't want to ruin it by bringing up her ex-boyfriend. Stacy took extra time shampooing her hair, doing a deep conditioner, a body scrub, and a body oil. She wanted to feel reborn by the end of it. She wanted the scalding water to burn away her doubt so she could go downstairs as in love with Henry as she was months ago.

"I was half expecting a brand-new fiancée to come down the stairs, you were in there for ages," Henry joked when Stacy reappeared for dinner. He had changed out of his apron into a dapper pair of slacks and shirt.

Stacy almost felt underdressed in her at-home uniform of a cashmere-silk lounge set.

"How come you didn't wear what I laid out for you?" Henry asked, doing a poor job of hiding his disappointment.

Stacy saw the slinky lounge dress laying out for her, but she wasn't really in the mood to seduce Henry. She half expected him to still be sulking when she got home.

"I'm feeling a little cold," she said, "and the dress is pretty skimpy. I can change if you want, I didn't realize you were making a formal dinner. What, are you planning on proposing all over again?" She smirked, trying to make a joke out of it, but Henry didn't budge.

"I'd like it if you changed," he said, his face growing serious. "I'll turn up the thermostat for you."

*I guess I don't have much of a choice.* Stacy trudged back upstairs and soon heard the low hum of their thermostat coming to life. When she came back downstairs, Henry had dimmed the lights and lit a few tapered candles. He greeted her at the bottom the steps with a bouquet of roses and a little teddy bear holding an "I'm Sorry" heart.

"The heart is made from chocolate." Henry grinned and Stacy awkwardly took her gifts.

She didn't know where to put them, wasn't sure if Henry would be offended if she just left them on the side table. She smiled and clutched them in her arms, deeply breathing in the scent of the bouquet to show her appreciation. Thankfully, Henry took both of them back, arranging the flowers in a vase, already full of water and flower food, on the table, tucking the teddy bear in beside it.

"For tonight, I've gone with a classic French dish of coq-au-vin, some warmed up French baguette and butter on the side, as well as a fresh arugula salad with a Dijon dressing." Henry opened the steaming dutch oven with a flourish, serving a small portion of the French stew for Stacy before pouring her a glass of red wine.

He was so proud that it was easy for Stacy to be taken in. This was why she had chosen Henry, his stability and mature romance. He could apologize without having to investigate an argument, he knew just how to perform a romantic gesture, even if he did go a little overboard sometimes. Stacy let herself relax and melt into the smell of red wine and herbs de Provence. Henry didn't have to know about Matt, she didn't have to stress over Matt's behavior or his regret. She could bathe in the warmth of a loving fiancé who knew how to make a delicious coq-au-vin, and planned out a surprise dinner date, right down to her outfit.

"Do you like it?" Henry asked, watching Stacy take her first few bites.

"It's delicious, where'd you get the recipe?"

"My mom used to watch Julia Child when I was little. I talked to one of the psychologists at work, they suggested focusing on the positive memories of my mother, what she did to enhance my life rather than focus on um—"

"That's really nice," Stacy interrupted, putting her hand on top of Henry's. "To keep your mother's memory alive rather than try to suppress it. I'm glad you found something you can remember her by."

Henry stroked her hand with her thumb and went back to his dinner. "So I was thinking maybe this weekend we can pull out the binder."

"*The* Binder? Are you sure?"

Henry nodded. "It's about time we started planning our wedding. All the nurses keep telling me if I don't do it soon, you'll go find yourself a man who can finish what he started."

"I mean, they're not wrong. Lucky for you most of the men I see aren't exactly stiff competition."

"Or are they?"

The couple laughed. It felt normal, nice, comfortable, *stable.* It was as if their fight the previous night never happened. Yet at the back of Stacy's mind and in the pit of her stomach, something felt off. It was probably that girl on her table, the woman who Stacy would have to examine the next day, the woman who looked as though she could be her sister.

"I figure we can pull out the binder and go over what we already decided, to refresh our memories and also maybe examine if that's what we *really* want, and then build from there? I think venue touring might be a little bit of a stretch, but I may be able to pull some strings and get us in. There's a couple of wineries in Redmond that get absolutely fantastic light around sunset, perfect for photos. One of them has llamas or something which I'm sure you'd love…Stacy?"

"Yes?" Stacy realized she hadn't been listening to a word Henry was saying. Something about a llama winery? She ought to focus, she knew they were talking about the most important day of her life, but her mind kept wandering back to the woman on her table. Was Audrey Wells married? Was she engaged to someone? Did they do wedding venue tours in preparation for the big day? Or was she still single, but the type of woman who fantasized about what it would be like walking down the aisle?

"Earth to Stacy, come in please, we're talking about your wedding. Or do you not care? Would you prefer a quick little courthouse affair?" Henry smirked and stroked Stacy's hand, pulling her back into the moment. Dinner, romance, a little wine, and a little business rolled into one.

"To be honest, I think I would. That way I wouldn't have to invite Maeve." Stacy stabbed at her plate a little more aggressively than she wanted, causing Henry to flinch.

"Oh, well that's not what I expected but sure, I guess we could have a party or something afterward."

"It could still be in Redmond. I think that might be kind of fun, takes the pressure off our guests too." *And that way no one will be asking why my father isn't the one walking me down the aisle.*

"I guess neither of us has much family who will be offended if we don't have a big thing," Henry muttered.

Dinner was quiet after that. It wasn't much fun to think about a wedding when you were reminded of the fact that your parents were either dead, abusive, or both. They still had a lovely evening. Stacy was still enamored with Henry, Henry was still on his best, most charming behavior, as they settled into their routine — each with a glass of whiskey, on their own side of the couch, as they watched the evening news and compared notes.

"That accident wasn't nearly as bad as they say. The truck driver came in to St. Vincent's — he was the worst off. He had one leg up on the dashboard to 'stretch a lil' bit' and his femur broke in three places. That was the worst of it — pretty gruesome as well," Henry commented.

Stacy was waiting, bracing herself for what she knew was coming.

*"...And now for our top story of the night. The body of a woman was found bound and beaten in an alley, bearing striking similarities to the recent homicide of a sex worker. Reports say the previous homicide may have been connected to an ongoing investigation into sex trafficking in the city's port, however police may have changed their theory. The most recent victim's identity has yet to be confirmed, but her body was found in Seattle's Ballard district — known for its trendy restaurants and avant-garde shops. Police have not confirmed, however, locals fear the city is in the clutches of another serial killer. Joining us is Dr. Richard Conwyn, an expert in the psychology of serial killers..."*

Stacy blinked back tears. "Their bodies were the same all right. Same height, same build, same hair color, same cause of death—"

"How do you know all that?"

"She was on my table today." Stacy took a deep breath as Henry shifted in his seat.

"I thought you were going to work from home today," he asked, "finishing up old reports and the like, that's what you told me."

"I told you that got called in," Stacy mumbled, hoping to dodge the next, obvious, question of, 'by who?'. "They could see the cause of death was similar to Unwin, and knew I worked on her. The police want to keep this contained, in case it's a serial killer."

"That's ridiculous, it isn't a serial killer. They wouldn't be so obvious."

"You never know, maybe he wants to get caught. Maybe he's doing all of this for some sick grab at attention." Stacy could feel the tears tumbling down her cheeks again. She couldn't help but feel overwhelmed. Not only was she hiding the fact that her ex-boyfriend Matt, of whom Henry wasn't a fan, was the lead detective on the case, but she also felt on the verge of a breakdown, fearing that she could be the next woman found beaten and strangled in an alleyway.

"Stacy, it isn't a serial killer. Besides, no one would be so stupid as to kill the city coroner."

"How would they know? I'm not famous, I don't exactly walk around with a vest that says, 'city medical examiner, please don't kill me.'"

"Well then why don't you get yourself reassigned, there's plenty of people who can examine dead bodies."

"I can't."

"Why not?" Henry leaned in, his looming presence was calming and intimidating at the same time.

Stacy felt as though he could see right through her.

"It's Matt. Matt is the lead detective. He requested me specifically. I just know that he will badger everyone in the coroner's office to make sure I'm the one working on this case. He's really annoying when he doesn't get his way."

Henry didn't say anything, he just backed away to his corner of the couch. He set his jaw and turned up the volume on the interview with the serial killer expert.

*"So, what I'm hearing you say, Dr. Conwyn, is that the prevalence of serial killers in Washington State can be attributed to Seasonal Affective Disorder?"*

*"Yes. Hilary, what you may not understand is that S.A.D is a*

*complex mental illness, and contrary to popular belief it can affect people all year round. In most of us that just means we need to take a little vitamin D, or get some extra exercise, but for those with underlying psychological problems, it can trigger uncontrollable feelings of anxiety and rage. When someone has a sociopathic illness, for example, S.A.D can be the straw that breaks the camel's back, so to speak."*

*"Interesting. Well, I will certainly be picking up some vitamin D, and maybe a bottle of pepper spray as well. Thank you for joining us, Dr. Corbyn. Up next, a new koala has been born at the Seattle zoo! More on this cute little critter after these messages."*

"You know statistically speaking, many serial criminals are police officers," Henry said.

Stacy barely heard him. She didn't need Henry's opinions of Matt right now, she just wanted to be comforted.

"Sure, but a police officer would know better than to strangle a woman with his bare hands. That gives us so much information about the killer — how large he was, the angle at which he attacked his victim, he could have left DNA under her fingernails or have her DNA under his. Audrey Wells — that was her name —"

"I don't want to know her name, Stacy!" Henry roared so suddenly that it made Stacy jump, "I hate how morbid all this is, I don't want to be talking about your crazy ex-boyfriend and the dead bodies you're cutting up all day. It gives me the creeps, and you know it."

"Henry, nothing is going on with me and Matt, it's just business. I thought you should know that he's the lead detective. I know I would want to know if you were working closely with an ex."

Henry scoffed. "I'm not worried about Matt. I am creeped out by how obsessed with work you have been lately. It's concerning. I think you should bring it up in therapy or something. You never talk this much about work."

"I suppose you're right. It's just a little frightening lately, I guess. Seeing these women who look just like me."

"You're seeing what you want to see, Stacy. You don't look anything like that hooker or that other woman — who was probably also a hooker, why else would she be creeping around alleyways late at night. You aren't some lowlife like they are, you are an intelligent, beautiful, and brilliant woman and no one in their right mind would chase after you as a victim. You're powerful, and you know how to fight back." Henry was gripping her arm, staring right into her eyes as he said it.

He filled Stacy with confidence, made her really believe that she had nothing to worry about. Henry was right, she knew how to fight back against a man attacking her — thanks to Oliver, Stacy had a lot of experience in that department. The best thing she could do, was help solve this case before any more women were murdered.

Stacy changed the channel; it was a rerun of a sitcom she and Henry both liked. They retreated back to their comfortable silence.

"I really would like to be able to talk to you about my day," Stacy said, practically at a whisper.

"I really don't want to have a morbid discussion at the end of mine," Henry intoned.

That was the end of that conversation. Stacy knew better than to press the issue when Henry got into his monotone mood. *His mother's death is still fresh. That's probably why he doesn't want to talk about it.* Besides, it's probably best to leave it alone while she was working with Matt.

Later that night, Stacy and Henry made love. When he turned the charm back on Stacy thought maybe tonight was the night that they'd finally rekindle the passion they had months ago.

That was not the case.

They made very nice, comfortable, stable love. Henry kissed her where she wanted to be kissed, she stroked him where he wanted to be stroked. They each climaxed, in turn. At the end of it all, Henry held Stacy for a few minutes, before kissing the top of her head and going to sleep.

Stacy turned to her side of the bed, and found herself wishing it was Matt lying beside her, rubbing her back as they fell asleep, each of them exhausted by passion.

# CHAPTER
# SEVEN
STACY

"The rape kit found no sign of sexual assault, and her toxicity screen came back as normal." Stacy presented Matt with the findings from her report. She'd come in early that morning, knowing Matt would be back at the office breathing over her shoulder as soon as he could. She only paused her work to allow Audrey Wells' mother to come identify her daughter's body. Afterward, Ms. Wells could be heard crying all the way down the hall — she'd raised Audrey as a single mother, and often helped out in her daughter's comic book shop, whenever Audrey needed an extra hand. In fact, on the night of the murder, Ms. Wells was supposed to be the one to close up shop — Audrey stepped in at the last minute, so her mom could go on a date.

"It could have been me. It should have been me!" Ms. Wells wailed.

Stacy heard her from behind the one-way glass, blaming herself for her daughter's death. Stacy's stomach flipped on itself as she realized the woman would probably drown herself in guilt for years to come. She put in earplugs to drown out the sounds of a mother's cries.

What were the chances that Stacy and Audrey both came from broken homes? Had Gabrielle Unwin been the same? Was the killer motivated to stalk women with daddy issues? Stacy's blood started to boil as she thought of some pathetic man chasing down women who had been saved by their mothers, who left their fathers behind.

"Disgusting," she muttered to herself.

Stacy was in a pessimistic sort of mood. She had spent the night fitfully dreaming of Matt's arms around her. They wrapped her in a warm embrace, but just as she sunk in and let him hold her, Matt's arms tightened, and he started choking her. She dreamt that she crumbled to her knees in an alleyway as Matt stalked off into the night. She could almost feel the raindrops falling on her naked body as her soul waited for someone to find her, but no one ever did.

---

"STACY? YOU'RE FAR AWAY AGAIN." Matt said, waving his hand in front of her face.

"I-I'm sorry. Didn't get much sleep — where was I?"

"The toxicity report, you said no alcohol was found in her system, but I asked about any drugs — rohypnol or any other Benzedrines that could be used to knock her out?"

"Oh...no, there was none of that either." Stacy cleared her throat and moved over to the x-rays. "You can see that her windpipe was crushed. So that's consistent with our earlier hypothesis — that the killer asphyxiated her with his bare hands. He was definitely larger than her, by at least a half a foot. Muscular, but I mean I guess you don't need muscles if you've managed to disarm someone another way. Her arm has a hairline fracture — I'm guessing he grabbed her by the arm, and she tried to twist herself away."

"If she was hurt, she probably wouldn't have fought back, am I right?"

"Bingo. She was hurt, she went down, he killed her. No rape, just murder."

A black cloud descended over Stacy and Matt. It was a relief to know the killer wasn't interested in rape, but it made the killer that much more dangerous. A man whose only desire to control a woman was to kill her — was he just killing these women for sport? Or was he trying to work something else out.

"What I don't understand," Matt said, breaking the silence, "is why he left them like that? Completely naked, tied up with her legs spread out."

"Maybe he wanted to humiliate them. He didn't tie them up to disable them — there's no rope burn or anything that indicated he bound these women before he killed them. His motive was to kill them, humiliation came after."

"So, he's weak. That explains it, he's a sniveling, pathetic man who can't hold his own against a woman." Matt kicked the edge of a table and sat down, his temper already starting to boil over.

"'*Can't hold his own against a woman?*' Why do I feel like that's code for '*Women are weak*'?"

Matt flinched. "That's not what I meant. I just mean he didn't even give these women a chance to fight back, he kicked them when they were down, literally."

"He's a smart killer. He knows that the more chances there are for someone to fight back, the more likely it is they'll end up with your DNA under their fingernails."

"Was there any DNA under her nails?"

Stacy shook her head. "Nothing, not even her own. The material I found was just dirt. The killer snuck up on her, like he was waiting for her. I will say — I don't think she was killed in that alleyway. There are some scratches on her knees that indicate she must have been dragged. She wasn't dragged very far, but it means the surrounding area might have some evidence lying around."

"I have officers canvassing local businesses, checking over their surveillance tapes. They swept that alley up and down, and didn't find a thing."

"Have them look again, maybe a piece of her clothing—"

"Fine!" Matt snapped, and Stacy froze. He knew she didn't react well when he had an outburst, and took a deep breath to calm himself down. "I'm sorry, this case is stressing me out. I really do think we have a serial killer on our hands. I have people down at the precinct looking into recent homicides to see if anything takes shape — there must be some kind of a pattern here, serial killers don't just spontaneously jump out of the woodwork."

"Do you really think so? I thought maybe there's some connection between the women—"

Matt was shaking his head and rubbing his forehead. "Think about it, Stacy. Two women, similar age, build, height, features. Both with long brunette hair, both with brown eyes, both killed before they were bound and beaten. Both were strangled by someone who was larger than they were, and that person wasn't interested in attacking them sexually, he wanted a punching bag. He wanted to take his anger out on these women."

"I guess you have to start asking why," Stacy replied. "Why would a man want to do that? Some incel misogynist who's bragging to his friends online, maybe?"

"Maybe. Some weak, pathetic man who hasn't worked out his mommy issues or something."

Stacy winced when Matt said that. She knew it was how he felt about Henry. She didn't want to bring her fiancé into this again, didn't want to have to balance on a tightrope between them any more than absolutely necessary.

# MATT

"I didn't mean Henry," Matt said, knowing her thoughts went immediately to him when she flinched. "I mean, I do think he hasn't worked out his mommy issues, but I'm just not sure he's a serial killer."

"Thanks, I guess?"

"C'mon, Stace, you can't blame me for resenting the guy at least a little bit." Matt's voice was low, barely above a whisper as he spoke.

He'd been holding back, determined to make sure he hid his true feelings while he was working this case with Stacy. She didn't need to know what he was really thinking — that he hated the fact that Henry had won Stacy over. Matt kicked himself for what happened with Stacy's father, hated that what he did made her afraid of him.

"What do you mean you resent him, what did he ever do to you?" she asked, the anger starting to rise in her voice.

"He won you," Matt said, so quietly that he was sure Stacy hadn't heard him. "He won you over and I'll never get you back. I'll never be able to get over what happened with your father, and Henry knew it. He took that opportunity and snatched you up before I could ever explain what I knew. Now you two are engaged, and I lost the best thing that ever happened to me."

Matt looked at Stacy, who was trying her best to look at anything except him.

"Detective Ensor, this is inappropriate." Stacy said.

Matt flinched when she used the formal, 'Detective Ensor'. It was as if they didn't even know each other.

"Stacy, you'll never understand how much I miss you. These women look like you, they could *be* you... don't you understand? I need to keep you close."

"You *need* to keep your distance. I'm engaged. We're going to spend the weekend touring wedding venues. I can't keep having these conversations and then going home and acting like they never happened."

"I can't help it that I miss you, Stacy. I will obviously try to keep things professional…from now on. But I had to say it. I had to bring it out into the open, y'know, or else it would just eat me up inside. I know you're engaged; I know you've moved on. I can't get rid of this feeling and…I don't know what else to say."

"I think you've said enough, Matt."

He nodded, and Stacy made some excuse to leave the room. With a sigh, he grabbed the pad of post-it notes and wrote his email address down for her then left.

## STACY

Stacy felt herself fight back tears and had to get out of there before Matt saw her. When she came back, Matt was gone, but attached to her computer screen was a post-it note from him. She crumbled it up and threw it away. She already had his work email, so she didn't need a handwritten copy of it. However, maybe emailing him would keep him at the distance she needed.

She decided to call Lillian and ask her to lunch. Maybe she'd have some insight into Matt's behavior.

"HE SAID WHAT?"

Stacy had to hold the phone away from her ear, one more outburst and Lillian might have deafened her.

"He said he missed me," Stacy replied. She had wasted no time asking Lillian to meet her for lunch and telling her about Matt's visit. Lucky for her, Lillian was already downtown, meeting with a gallery curator about an upcoming photography show. Stacy had hoped their phone call would be brief, and she could talk to Lillian in person, but Lillian didn't want to wait for the juicy details. She made Stacy give her a play by play of the morning, sparing no details.

"I CANNOT BELIEVE THIS! YOU HAVE GOT TO BE KIDDING ME."

"Lil! You have to stop screaming, someone might hear you!"

"SO? I'M DOWNTOWN, NO ONE'S GOING TO KNOW WHICH SPECIFIC—"

"I meant someone on *my end of the call.*" Stacy looked around and ducked into a supply closet so no one could hear her.

"Oh, right, I forgot you were still at work. So, wait, he didn't say goodbye or anything? Just left a post-it with his department email? Don't you already have his department email?"

"I think it was a gesture. Y'know a sign he's going to be a bit more professional moving forward."

"Riiiiight, he's completely embarrassed himself so now he's going to act like this never happened."

"I hope so."

"What does this mean? Are you going to go back to him, are you going to break it off with Henry?"

"Three months after his mother committed suicide? I don't think so. Besides, I love Henry, he's a million times more stable than Matt and this proves it. What kind of person does that, confesses their love while we're talking about a *serial killer.*"

"Detectives are all desensitized to that stuff."

"Fine — what kind of a person confesses their love to their ex-girlfriend while she's engaged to another man, after he beat up her father?"

Lillian paused. "You have a point there."

"I just don't know what's happening. I feel like my life was finally stable, for months I didn't think about Matt, I moved on with my life, things were falling into place. Now all of a sudden it feels like that's all been turned upside-down again. You know, last night Henry made me dinner and brought up wedding planning again? It's like Matt knew. It's as if he's bugged my house and has been waiting for Henry to come out of this funk just so he could mess everything up all over again."

Stacy sank to the floor, almost falling into a mop bucket in the process. She couldn't decide if she wanted to scream or cry, or both.

"Stacy? Are you still there?" Lillian asked.

Stacy replied with a sniffle.

"Good. Listen, you understand that this isn't your fault, right? Unfortunately, we can't control how other people are feeling, we can only control our own thoughts and emotions. Matt confessing his love to you over a dead woman isn't professional, and honestly, he shouldn't have put you in that place. It's totally fair for you to be feeling confused because Matt put you in a confusing situation. *Your* life is still stable, your worries about Henry are perfectly normal for any engaged person. How Matt feels about you isn't a reflection of you — you didn't tempt him or lead him on, that's all on him. You aren't to blame here, got it?"

Stacy nodded and sniffled again.

"Sorry I said that stuff about going back to Matt. That was unfair of me."

"It's okay, you got excited. Caught up in the drama of it all."

"It's easy to do when you're not in the middle of it. Listen, I have to hang up, I can see the curator. Can we meet up for a quick lunch when I'm done? I'll come to you. You can rant about your feelings, and I'll actually listen and not treat your life like a soap opera."

"That would be nice." Stacy could feel a lump rising in her throat. The men in her life were chaotic, but at least she could rely on Lillian.

"Okay, I'll talk to you in a bit. Try to bury yourself in work or something."

The line clicked and Stacy took a deep breath. She could drown herself in work for an hour or so, and then maybe fake sick, and go home, take a mental health day or something.

Unfortunately for Stacy, everything in her office reminded her of Matt. The post-it note was still in the trash, the victim in his case was still lying on her autopsy table, and she had a reminder pinging her to update her reports. How was she going to plan a wedding with this cloud over her?

*Who knows,* she thought, *maybe the serial killer will get me, and I won't have to.*

# CHAPTER EIGHT
## STACY

"Azaleas or lilies?"

"For the centerpieces? We should do lilies, they're more wedding-y I think."

"I was hoping for azaleas. My mom had azaleas at her wedding so I thought we could do something to honor her, but if you prefer lilies—"

"Why don't we do azaleas for the head table and lilies for everyone else, or a combination of both?"

"That seems fair."

*That seems fair.* Stacy had lost count of how many times she'd heard that phrase all weekend. She and Henry were trying to decide basic details of their wedding — flowers, food, venue. They hadn't even got down to the nitty gritty yet and already they were arguing.

No, they weren't arguing. They were *disagreeing,* which according to Henry, was worse.

"It just seems as if you don't have an opinion on anything. I feel like I'm making all of the decisions myself," he kept saying.

Stacy held back telling him that it was because he *was* making all of the decisions himself, but not because Stacy wasn't offering her opinion. It seemed every time she made a suggestion, Henry had a perfectly good reason why *his* choice was better for the whole wedding. It was starting to get exhausting. What happened to men disappearing for eight to ten months and showing up on the day of the wedding, ready to go in a freshly cleaned tux? But of course, Henry was raised by a woman and not only that; he was raised by a very *opinionated* woman who rarely took no for an answer and passed that quality along to her son. Sometimes Stacy thought he was making decisions just because if his mother were there, Henry would have to defer to her choices. He was so ecstatic that he could *make* a decision that he lost the ability to compromise.

It was still annoying, even if Stacy did understand why he did it.

In the days leading up to their weekend, Stacy brought out the wedding binder each night after dinner, and she and Henry started going over what they had previously decided. She noticed that a lot of the pictures she cut out — of her wedding dress, decor inspiration, even menu ideas — had been replaced.

"I took the liberty of making some edits," Henry said, offering no other explanation. "My mom shared some ideas with me and frankly I think they were really good ones. I figured you wouldn't mind, since we were going for a fresh start."

"Sure," was all Stacy could think to say.

She was speechless that Henry had gone over every page and replaced it all with *his* ideas. It made Stacy's blood boil, though when confronted, she realized she hardly remembered what was on the pages in the first place.

"You see," Henry said when they argued about it, "you barely remember. That obviously means you weren't married to those choices in the first place, so it's still a fresh start! I just added my two cents, which I hadn't done before because I was busy trying to get my mother on board. I'm sorry I didn't tell you; you've been so busy with work it seemed like a bad time to bring it up."

Now here they were, sitting in traffic on a bridge over Washington Lake, *not* arguing over flower arrangements.

"I would definitely prefer azaleas for the head table. Then maybe we can see how lilies will look," Henry added after a moment's silence. This was not how she imagined wedding planning was going to go.

"This wedding is getting complicated. Couldn't we just do a courthouse thing and then rent out a restaurant for our friends to party at?"

"It's still simple. A simple dinner and wine tasting while we say our vows isn't complicated. Besides, we're just going to take a look around and maybe sample some wine, we don't have to put down a deposit today."

Henry was way more excited for this venue tour than Stacy could ever be. She supposed he wasn't distracted by thoughts of a serial killer hunting women like her throughout Seattle; that would make life a lot less complicated.

"I'm not saying it isn't simple. I guess I just didn't think all these little details would start adding up the way they are. The flowers, the theme, the colors, even my dress are all starting to get a little more…detailed than I expected."

"It's a wedding, Stacy. It's the beginning of our lives together, this day is never simple. There's a lot to think about as we join our two lives—"

"Our lives are already joined! We own a house together, don't we? We have two cars, we have a joint account that's connected to all our bills, what more could we 'join'?"

"Well, I don't have access to all your accounts. There's investments you've made, and I have no idea what's in there. For all I know you're in mountains of debt and I have no idea."

Stacy looked at Henry as though he had grown an extra head. There was no way that sentence came out of his mouth, unless his mother had possessed him and was controlling him from beyond the grave. Henry never cared about that sort of thing; he had defended her to his mother countless times as Amanda accused Stacy of being nothing but a gold digger.

"Why do you need to know what's in my investment accounts? And for the record, the only *debt* I owe is the house we purchased *together* and that mortgage is in both our names."

"You could be lying to me. I would never know it until after we got married. You lock me in without a prenup or anything and then…Stacy, I didn't want to have this discussion in the car, I knew you'd take it the wrong way."

"Which way was I supposed to take it?" Stacy screeched. "Months and months into our engagement and suddenly you *care* about my investments and my debt? You've been quiet about it as you've turned my whole wedding on its head, and now you mention it, as casually as if you asked me what we're having for dinner tonight."

"Like I said, I didn't want to bring it up this way. I wanted to sit down and really go over everything. This isn't all for me, you know, you can make requests for the prenup as well."

"Wait — are you actually serious? You really want a prenup?" Stacy suddenly felt hot and like her seatbelt was choking her. The subject of prenups had come up before, with his mother. Amanda had insisted on one and spent a solid week calling at every hour of the day and night with new 'suggestions' of what Henry should put in them. They ranged from adding an infidelity clause to requiring Stacy to have weekly drug tests for the first ten years of their marriage. Whenever Stacy asked for an explanation, Henry would just sigh and say his mother was protective. Then he'd bend down and kiss Stacy on the forehead and whisper some sweet nothings about how their love would rise above a prenup.

So much for that.

"It's perfectly normal for a man in my position to want a prenuptial agreement, Stacy. It's not a reflection of our relationship or of how I see you, it's a really normal thing. Many couples get them, and it has no effect on your relationship."

"A man in your position?" Stacy asked incredulously. "What position is that?"

"I'm a well-respected doctor who is pretty well known throughout the city. Not to mention my hefty salary, it's natural to want to protect that."

"Henry, we make the same amount of money. If you don't believe me, I have the mortgage documents to prove it."

"How would I know? We only have the joint account to prove what you've been contributing; I can't see anything else. For all I know you've been using the joint account as your only account."

Stacy couldn't believe what she was hearing. It was as if, when Amanda died, she began to inhabit her son's body. Henry had been subtly manipulative in the past, Stacy had come to expect that sort of behavior from all men, but this was a new side of him. She could see the gears turning in his head, spinning with the lies about women that had been fed to him by his mother. This was monstrous, this was ridiculous.

"You're fucking crazy, Henry," Stacy said in a low growl. "If you think, especially after the life I've had, that I'll ever let you touch one of my bank accounts."

Henry flexed his hands on the steering wheel.

"I'm not crazy, Stacy."

They fell silent after that. Stacy was stewing with anger, she wanted nothing more than to get out of the car and run as far away from Henry as she could.

---

"AND THIS IS where your guests can dance the night away. The bar is usually set up in the corner by the window there, but some guests like to keep it outside so they can have a little more dancing space.

You can also set up a photo booth in the corner, or even a gifts table, it's a pretty multi-functional space." The poor tour guide stuck to her script despite the fact that the couple were clearly in the middle of a major fight. No matter, it wasn't the first time, and it certainly wouldn't be the last that she had to give a tour to people who were on the verge of breaking up over their wedding decisions.

"Do you have any questions?" She smiled at Stacy, probably hoping she'd be a little more sympathetic than her glowering fiancé.

"Well, I wondered—"

"I have a question. Do you split the bill for the venue? Y'know just in case a couple wants to keep their financial lives separate for no apparent reason?" Henry interjected.

Somehow, even through his sarcasm and anger, he was still charming, asking the question with a flash of his dimples.

"Of course! We can break it all down however you like, it's pretty common that couples have multiple financial sources for their nuptials. When we negotiate the venue contract, we can specify who will be paying for the venue and how you expect to pay for it —"

"He didn't really mean that," Stacy commented, her arms crossed, and her gaze bore through Henry. She hoped he could feel it. She hoped he would spontaneously combust on the spot and come back as the charming doctor she agreed to marry.

"It's not a problem, really. Most couples have some kind of an arrangement depending on whose paying for the wedding. Parents or grandparents sometimes..." The venue guide trailed off.

Somehow, Stacy knew that the guide knew the breakdown of cost wasn't the problem here.

The woman cleared her throat. "I'll leave you two alone to discuss. When you're ready, just meet me downstairs and we can do a little wine tasting." She smiled her brightest, and probably her fakest smile, and hurried out of the room as politely as she could.

Stacy could imagine her thinking, *Bridezilla strikes again, third one this week,* as the woman ran away from them.

"Well, that was unnecessary," Henry scoffed wandering over to the window. "It's a nice place. A little small, but I guess that's what we're going for."

"You guess? You agreed to having a small affair."

"I know I agreed to it, but I figured you'd change your mind. What little girl doesn't dream of this day—"

"This little girl," Stacy interrupted. "I don't care about the wedding, I care about our marriage. Remember that part? It lasts a little longer than a day."

"Stacy there's no need to be bratty about it, I agreed to have a small wedding, we can have a small wedding, it's no big deal. There's no need for you to start yelling."

Stacy took a deep breath to keep from exploding. Ever since they got out of the car, Henry had been finding subtle ways to undermine her. It started with the questions, the way he sighed at everything Stacy asked as if she was being completely ridiculous. It continued with his pace. He was rushing through the place like there was a prize for 'Fastest Walkthrough of a Wedding Venue.' Then he started criticizing the venue, but making it sound like it was Stacy's opinion.

*"You don't have to lie, Stacy, I know how much you hate weeping willows."*

*"Stacy always says you can really tell a venue is good by its ceiling height. I personally never understood what that meant."*

The comments he made were ridiculous, but Stacy could see they had an effect on their guide. By the end of the tour, she felt like Henry had painted BRIDEZILLA across her forehead, and the guide didn't want to even look in Stacy's direction. She directed all the answers to questions and her tour spiel directly at Henry, and avoided Stacy's gaze as much as she could.

"I just thought," Stacy started again, slowly, trying to keep her temper under control, "that we wanted the same thing. But if you want something different, we can discuss it."

"Apparently we can't. Every time I make a *suggestion* you get upset."

"It's only because I feel like your suggestions are demands. Somehow all the decisions we were supposed to make *together* come out on your side."

"Well, there's no need for you to be sour about it."

"I'm not sour, Henry! I'm just trying to figure out what the hell is going on. One minute you're happy with the selections *we* made for the wedding, and the next you're picking each and every thing apart!" Stacy exploded, her voice echoing through the empty dance hall.

"Oh?" Henry asked, his voice rising. "Like what? Like the lilies you decided on when my mom was threatening to kill herself over our wedding, or the fact that you decided we should have a courthouse wedding when I was burying my mother?" Henry's face turned bright red, and he clenched and unclenched his fists.

Stacy wanted to back off but she knew that wasn't true. "Don't try to gaslight me, Henry. You're making it sound like I manipulated you into these decisions, but we sat down and talked about them *months* ago, and you were just as excited as I was about them. All this vineyard, venue bullshit is brand-new, likely because some rich patient stroked your ego and you wanted to bask in the glory of it, brag to me about all the free shit you get. The courthouse thing was *your* idea, and I agreed because I didn't want to have to deal with family breathing down my neck. I made the suggestion of flowers because I fucking love lilies, you never mentioned azaleas until today in the car. All the comments you made to the guide, those were your own thoughts, your own opinions, but you're making me out to be a bridezilla in front of her!"

"I think you're forgetting that this is my day too, Stacy. I also get to be a part of this, which means I also want some input —"

"And you can have it! But you don't get to make every decision and manipulate me into going along with it."

"I'm not manipulating you! I'm stating my opinion, and if my argument sways you that isn't my problem. God, everything just *has* to go your way, doesn't it? Not a single soul can have their own desires or needs, it's just always about you—"

"Is this about the stupid prenup again? Henry, you're right, a prenup is a pretty normal request, but having access to all my bank accounts because you don't trust me? That's on another level."

Henry's face turned dark. Stacy didn't know what to do, she was fighting back tears and fighting the desire to run away and never see Henry again. She was right — wasn't she? Asking for access to everything she had, that was taking pre-marital precaution a little too far, wasn't it? Stacy wasn't so sure anymore. She was so caught up in flowers and vineyards and a stupid argument about wedding planning to really know anymore.

"Stacy, it's not that I don't trust you. It's not that I'm manipulating you, in fact, the desire for a prenup has nothing to do with you, and maybe if you were a little less of a hypersensitive, controlling, obsessive, *bitch* you might be able to see that."

Henry spoke in a deafening whisper. He stomped past Stacy, out of the room and down the stairs of the venue. Stacy wavered in place as she heard the muffled voice of Henry charming the guide at the bottom of the stairs. She quietly started to cry when she heard the sound of a car driving off.

Luckily for Stacy, the venue guide was used to couples arguing.

"It comes with the territory," was all the guide said, before calling Stacy a trusted car service.

Stacy got home in record time, where she was greeted by a completely empty house. She had no idea where Henry had driven off to, and didn't want to wait around to find out. Stacy grabbed her keys and went for a walk by herself. She walked for a few hours, stopping at a bar to rest her feet and have a glass of wine. She needed to clear her head, sort through the mess of manipulation Henry had made.

She drank more than she expected. Stacy remembered ordering one last gin and tonic, before calling herself a cab. She woke up on the couch around midnight, her keys still in her hand and one muddy shoe on her foot. She stumbled upstairs and into the shower, letting the hot water wash her clean of the day. Downstairs she heard the front door open, and slam shut — it made the hair on her arms stand to attention. Wasn't Henry home already?

"Hello?" she slurred. "Who is it?"

"It's me," Henry slurred back. "I brought you something."

Henry stumbled into the bathroom, still wearing his muddy shoes and raincoat. His face and hands were scratched, and Stacy gasped when she saw him.

"What happened to you?" she asked, suddenly feeling a lot more sober.

"I hurt myself, but I got you this." Henry smiled and head out a single crumpled rose, clearly torn from someone's garden. "it's a comp-*rose*-mise."

Stacy could have cried right then and there. She took the rose and fell into Henry's arms.

"We could have roses. It's the most romantic," he said, stroking Stacy's hair. "Right? It's the sign of love or whatever."

Stacy answered him with a kiss.

# CHAPTER
# NINE
MATT

Matt sat in his car, staring at the half-formed message on his phone.
*Hey! Hopefully you haven't blocked this number yet lol. I just wanted to say that I am sorry, and I really am happy for y-*

That's about as far as he got. He wanted Stacy to trust him again, but he couldn't lie to her. He wasn't happy for her, he wanted her to find another man, any other man would do. Preferably him, but he knew he'd ruined his chances months ago. What Matt really wanted to say was that he was pretty sure Henry Goldberg was a psychopath and he was going to end up killing her, but that was proving difficult to say over text.

His partner knocked at his window and Matt jumped.

"They're ready for us. You okay?" Detective Cardoso could apparently see right through Matt's hard exterior to the heart-broken bum underneath.

Matt cleared his throat and locked his phone before nodding and getting out of the car.

"Shaddup, Andy," Matt said, answering his partner's smirk.

"I didn't say nothin', man, but if she's already engaged then like it or not, she wants to forget you," Andy replied.

Matt had spoken to him at length about Stacy and how he'd lost the love of his life, but Andy's answer that it had been long enough and that Matt needed to move on was something that Matt couldn't do.

"It's not about that...not entirely," Matt mumbled as he passed under the yellow police tape. Another alleyway in another part of town, still upscale just like the last victim.

"Currently a Jane Doe, but we're working on an ID," Cardoso reviewed. "Found about an hour ago by the dishwasher, who thought she was some strung-out junkie dumpster diving for leftovers. She was completely naked, just like the other girls, her legs draped over the dumpster. The dish washer flagged down an officer who, luckily, heard about the other couple murders on the news the other night and knew to call you. Must be nice having a fan, huh?" Cardoso nudged Matt, probably trying to get him to focus.

Matt was listening, but his mind was elsewhere, thinking about Stacy and how all these dead women looked so much like her.

"Anything we can pin on the perp?" Matt said, running a hand over his face trying to get his head back in the game.

"Nothing yet, no signs of sexual assault, no torn clothes or anything. But it looks like this time he didn't get away easy — she's got a couple of scratches on her arm, and CSI says there's something under her fingernails. Could be some useful DNA under there."

*That means a trip to the morgue,* Matt thought and his heart fluttered a little bit. It was a perfectly good excuse, he had to collect the coroner's report anyway. He could apologize for professing his continued love to Stacy and—

"I'll go ahead with the body. The CSI is almost done with the photography, the evidence techs are finishing up. I'll ride alongside. Why don't you do some witness statements and uh, damage control." Detective Cardoso nodded to the crowd that was already forming, and the tv crews preparing their intros for the night's news. "You're always better at that stuff — with your gruffly handsome appearance, it's always a hit with the worried housewives of the greater Seattle area." Andy smirked.

"Sure," Matt said, hiding his disappointment. "We'll touch base later today."

Cardoso slapped Matt on the back. "It'll be good for you." He winked, and turned to where the CSI team was finishing their evidence gathering.

Matt's apology to Stacy would have to wait.

---

## STACY

Stacy stared down at the body in front of her. Still unclaimed, the woman lay on a slab, her eyes closed facing the ceiling.

"She was found in an alley, just like the others," Cardoso said from someplace far away.

He kept talking, describing the latest details, what CSI reported and the potential for DNA, since this victim seemed to fight back.

Stacy nodded along but she wasn't listening, she was staring at the girl in front of her.

Same height, same age, same dark auburn hair. If her eyes were open Stacy was sure they'd be the same amber-colored irises she had. She'd never felt less unique in her life. The two women were identical, down to the manicured hands. Stacy wondered if they went to the same manicurist. It felt as though Stacy was looking into a funhouse mirror, or a crystal ball.

*Am I dreaming? The air feels heavy and it's hard to breathe. I must be dreaming. Any minute now I'm going to wake up and I'll be in my bed nursing a hangover with Henry. I need to pinch myself or something.*

"Stacy, are you all right?" Detective Cardoso touched her elbow, gently leading Stacy to a chair. "You look a little...like you're gonna be sick."

Stacy didn't know what to say. She thought she knew Andy pretty well; he and Matt had been partners for years. The two of them used to go on double dates with Andy and his wife. He didn't see what she saw, what Matt had agreed to seeing too, but then maybe they both were going crazy. That's the only explanation for how casual he could be as he brought in a woman who looked *exactly* like Stacy.

"I am gonna be sick, Andy. Do you see her?"

"Yeah, of course I do."

"She looks exactly like me, Andy. Like...exactly."

Andy Cardoso looked behind him and appeared to be studying the victim. Stacy could see him debating. She imagined what he was saying in his head. *True, there are similarities, but you and victim are far from identical. Stacy, you're taller, for starters, and the victim's hair is lighter than yours.* He probably figured she must be panicking — and why wouldn't she, if she fit the profile of a serial killer's victims?

Instead of voicing his actual thoughts, he said, "No way, you're much prettier." He smiled, probably hoping to disarm Stacy a little and get her out of the panicked spiral she was going down. He grabbed her bottle of water off the desk and held it out to her. "Here, drink this, and take some gum. I've got wintergreen, it's the best for when you feel a bit of a panic attack coming on."

He offered Stacy a stick of gum, she accepted it in a daze. He was right, the cool mint taste made the water sharply cold, bringing Stacy back to the present.

"Stacy, I know you and Matt have some history and you

might feel…compelled to be on this case, but you really don't have to be."

"Andy, I'm the chief medical examiner. It's my job to be on high profile cases like this one, it'll look weird if I reassign myself. It's just a little…jarring to see them."

Andy nodded. "I admit having a serial killer roaming the city stresses me out worrying about my wife coming into contact with this guy, but I guess you have it worse. I can't imagine what it must feel like to perform autopsies on women who look like yourself, wondering if—" he stopped abruptly and looked away.

Stacy swallowed hard. "Thanks for the gum, but I have to get to work." Stacy stood up.

Andy nodded. "I'll be in contact when we hear more about the identity of the vic." He gave Stacy a sympathetic looking smile before walking out the door.

---

"Whoa, you think it's the same dude?" Trevor droned somewhere next to Stacy.

She felt like he was too close and a million miles away at the same time. Trevor reached out and poked Lacey Daniels in the side of the arm.

"Stop that!" Stacy screeched, causing Trevor to jump. "She may be dead now, but she was alive once. She isn't some weird toy or a prop in a movie, Trevor, she's a human being."

Trevor looked terrified. He nodded and mumbled some excuse while backing away from Stacy and out of the room.

The victim had a name now. Lacey Daniels, twenty-eight, a computer programmer at an up-and-coming tech startup. Graduate of some college for women in tech, she was last seen coming home from a fundraiser for the same college that was being held at the Washington Park Arboretum. Her fiancé worried when he came back from a business trip to an empty apartment. Two days later, he got the dreaded call from the police department — someone was found, but that someone was dead.

Stacy was still exhausted. She felt hungover, and was delirious from lack of sleep. Since their fight, she and Henry had avoided talking about the wedding, but that didn't stop Stacy from waking up every half hour from another nightmare. It always started the same, she was walking down a path toward her wedding at a vineyard in Redmond. Then the path turns into a small copse of trees, and suddenly it gets dark. Stacy keeps walking, but the makeshift aisle keeps going and going, deeper into the dark of the forest, until she starts running — but was she running toward the altar or running away from a pair of heavy footsteps that suddenly started chasing her? Stacy never found out. She always woke up in a cold sweat.

"Knock, knock." Lillian appeared at the door, jarring Stacy back to life. "They called me in early, is this a bad time?"

Stacy stared at her best friend with tears in her eyes. "No," she said through sobs, "it's fine."

"Hey, are you okay?"

Lillian closed the door behind her and led Stacy to a chair. The same chair Andy had sat her down in when she started freaking out just a few hours earlier. Lillian wrapped her in a hug as Stacy cried it out.

"I'm fine—" she said, wiping tears from her eyes. "I'm fine I'm just tired. The wedding stuff...and now this, and they all...I didn't sleep last night...or any night really. I feel like I'm going to be next like I'm being—"

"Don't even say it," Lillian said, dabbing at Stacy's eyes with a tissue. "You can't know that."

"Lillian, have you seen these girls? They all look like me — they look *exactly* like me. We're all around the same age, same build. It's like the killer is wandering around looking for me, but he keeps getting it wrong."

Lillian bit her lip. "You have a point — I wouldn't go so far to say the victims looked *exactly* like you, but they share certain characteristics, and that's always a serial killer's MO; they have a profile, and they follow it."

Stacy pressed her lips together to keep from panicking further.

"Stacy...I don't mean to—" Lilian cut herself off.

Stacy pulled away from her friend and searched for the rest of the question in her eyes.

"What, Lil? Just say it, honestly you can't make me more afraid for my life than I already am."

"When's the last time you talked to your father? Or your sister? You don't think he could be..." Lillian trailed off again.

Stacy's breath got caught in her throat. Could it be? Was it possible that Oliver had somehow escaped the facility he was in, and that now he was trying to find her? He knew she was the city coroner, and a trail of dead bodies would surely get her attention. Maeve could have helped him escape, she'd do anything for their father, and even if the man dangled a dead body in front of her face, Maeve would probably never believe he was a killer.

But then it hit her, and she shook her head. "It's not possible. I talked to Maeve a couple of weeks ago, she was back trying to get me to visit him. From what she says that place is basically one step down from a prison, there's no way he could leave. Besides, even if he did, I know Matt keeps tabs on him. If my father had escaped, he'd have a uniform on his tail and another at my door faster than you could blink." Stacy sniffled, she was starting to calm down, but she was still having a hard time looking at the body of Lacey Daniels.

They were quiet for a moment. Lillian got up and started setting up her equipment, carefully selecting which lens to use. Stacy could tell Lillian had more to say, but was obviously keeping her mouth shut. Stacy had to wonder if she'd been speaking to Matt. She knew that Lillian and Matt were friends still and it bothered her that Lil took his side, but she tried not to let it get to her. Lil had never been a fan of Henry's.

Now Stacy wondered what it was that Lillian wasn't saying. Did Matt have a theory and he told Lillian about it? Was that what she wasn't saying? And why keep that from her? If she was keeping it from her. She shook her head, trying to dismiss those thoughts. They weren't helpful. With as little sleep as Stacy was getting, she was probably reading too much into Lillian's quietness right now.

"This is the third victim, right?"

The question pulled Stacy from her thoughts. "Sure is."

"I guess that makes it official. We have a serial killer on our hands."

"I know. I was hoping it wouldn't come to this." Stacy sighed, gazing at the woman lying in her examination room. "Matt seemed to be expecting it," she admitted.

"Oh?" Lillian clicked away, obviously trying not to pry, since she kept her eyes on her camera. "How much do you guys talk about the case?"

"Lil—"

"I only mean you've made it sound as if Matt has other things on his mind."

Stacy frowned. Lillian probably already knew Matt's theory, but she wasn't going to admit it, so she decided to voice her own opinion along with Matt's theory. "He mentioned...well, he implied, that the killer was a woman-hater with mommy issues. Obviously, the subject of my *fiancé* came up, but I don't know if I can really trust Matt's opinion on this. He's clearly jealous of Henry, and he's said he's still in love with me. I mean what if he's manipulating things behind the scenes?"

"You don't really think Matt would do that, do you? Frame Henry just to get back together with you? I think he knows better than to meddle too aggressively in your private life, especially since the whole incident with your dad is the reason you two broke up."

Stacy shrugged. Lillian changed the lens on her camera to get up close to the bruising on the victim's neck.

"He always strangles them, huh, and with his bare hands."

"He's probably a manual laborer. How else can you explain it?" Stacy suggested.

After a brief pause, Lillian said, "How's Henry been?"

"Ugh." Stacy rolled her eyes and blew her nose. "We haven't talked about the wedding at all since the venue tour. He won't budge on the prenup, and I still think it's weird and invasive that he wants access to all of my accounts. I think it's his mother talking, he never cared about that before."

"Didn't you say he was kinda beat up the other night? After your fight, I mean."

"Yeah, he said he walked through some rose bushes trying to pick me one. We were both drunk, it made no sense to me at all."

"That's weird, don't you think? He just disappears for hours at a time and then comes back with scratches on his arms and blames it on a rose?" Lillian replied.

"Well, we were both drunk. I don't know how long he was gone. And I'm sure he wouldn't have been hurt so badly if he had been sober."

Lillian nodded. Stacy was sure that Lillian had more to say, but was wisely keeping her mouth shut on that topic. Instead, she went back to the fight that Stacy and Henry'd had. "How do you feel about the prenup? I mean, I personally think it's insane and wildly controlling for Henry to have access to all of your money, especially since you won't be getting the same thing *and* you already have a joint bank account. But then again, I'm not in love with him, you are."

Stacy could feel herself getting defensive. It wasn't normal, that part was true, and she still didn't know what to do about it, but she had hoped Lillian could give her some unbiased advice on the subject.

"Do you ever miss Matt?" Lillian asked after a moment of silence between them.

Stacy nodded. "Sometimes I do. Life with Matt was…sexier. He was just a little more passionate than Henry, who is much more stable and methodical. I thought that's what was missing in my life, but now that I have it, I want the sort of back and forth I had with Matt. I'm sure if I were to leave Henry, I'd find out Matt was controlling in other ways. You know he keeps tabs on my father? He put him into the institution and yet still feels the need to 'make sure' he's there. And I just know I'd end up with a police detail following my every move just in case something happened to me."

Lillian went quiet again. Stacy felt like she was in an interrogation, but she wasn't sure who was being interrogated or why. Lillian kept trailing off or asking random questions with zero follow up. It was driving her crazy and she wished she'd just tell her what she was really thinking.

"Do you have something to say about it all? Because if you have any answers, I'd welcome them. Our fight the other day was…scary. Henry left me in Redmond without a car, and didn't even bother to ask how I got home. He's manipulated our wedding into being a party he has complete control over, and now I'm seeing that he's going to want control over the rest of my life as well. Seriously, Lillian, if you have anything to say, now's the time, I'm actually ready to hear it."

"I think you should dump him," Lillian blurted out. The look on her face said she immediately regretted it, and she clamped her hand over her mouth and almost dropped her camera to the floor.

"What?" Stacy stared at her in shock.

"I-I think he's controlling and manipulative, and I think you'll regret it if you do go through with this marriage. I know you want stability, Stacy, but I don't think Henry is the kind of stable you need. The longer you're with him the more you'll see this scary version of him. You remember what his mother was like, all I'm saying is I think the apple doesn't fall far from the tree."

Stacy was stunned, she wondered how long Lillian had been keeping this from her. The thing was, Stacy kind of agreed with Lillian. She had been so afraid of Matt's temper and how much it reminded her of her father, that she forgot about the other, subtler hints that Henry was destined to go down that path as well.

"He's just stressed about his mother," she countered, ignoring the little voice inside her head. "You would be too, if your mom unexpectedly committed suicide. She meant for him to see it as a punishment, and he does. He's so guilty over it, I think you'd see it too if you were around him more. He's grieving right now, honestly, I think we should call off the wedding just because of that. No one should be planning a wedding while grieving a parent, even if that parent was abusive."

"You're probably right." Lillian sighed, taking Stacy's hand in hers. "I don't spend a lot of time with Henry, and I do see Matt pretty often because of work. I'm probably just as biased, listening to your ex's version of things. I do worry about you though. And I do think your boring boyfriend might be a little more like his mom than you think, and I don't want you to find out when it's too late."

"He's just boring, Lil. He isn't dangerous. He's like me — a broken weirdo with fucked up parents."

"Yeah, and I get that he's grieving his mother, but she would have found some other way to destroy your relationship and punish her son for loving you. What's the excuse going to be next time?"

Lillian's phone alarm went off, indicating she had to leave. She gave Stacy a hug and packed up her equipment.

"Stacy," she said before leaving the room, "I just don't want you to throw away what could be a wonderful, dynamic life for a guy who is so unbelievably controlling that he comes off as stable. It's just not worth it."

Stacy nodded and watched Lillian go out the door. She turned back to the body to begin her investigation. She couldn't think about it now, the men in her life were a source of trouble from every angle. Sometimes she felt as if there was barely a life to throw away.

# CHAPTER TEN
STACY

With Lillian's voice ringing in her ears, Stacy continued with her examination. She documented every bruise on Lacey Daniels' body, the scratches on her arm, and the debris under her fingernails. The process took longer than usual. Stacy was determined to find the person who killed Lacey, before he could find her. The bruising around her neck was consistent with the other victims. Large hands, putting pressure on their trachea — someone holding these women down and slowly draining the life out of their bodies. The bruising happened post-mortem. The person — the man — who killed them was angry either at himself or at all women, and he beat and kicked the women while they were down. They were probably already naked when it happened, because on all three of the victims the skin was broken in the places where the perp landed a few nasty kicks.

It made Stacy sick, but she documented all the ways Lacey Daniels' body was the same as Gabrielle Unwin and Audrey Wells. Lillian's suspicions haunted her, she couldn't believe that Henry was involved, but she could see how Matt might think so. He'd never trusted Henry, and was forever making comments about Henry's relationship with his mother. What did Matt know? He came from a stable home. He didn't understand how you could love your parent, even when they were abusive. That strange, impossible back and forth that goes between your head and your heart — wanting so badly to forgive, but knowing that it wasn't healthy. He had so much power, and so many people who trusted him, Stacy feared the ways Matt could abuse it.

---

"Zero matches."

"Not a single one? Not even relative DNA?"

It was the next day, and Stacy was presenting her findings to Matt. She wished she could be more relieved, but it would have made things much easier if the DNA she'd found under Lacey Daniels' fingernails had a match in Washington's criminal DNA database. She could feel how angry Matt was, his frustration was sucking all of the oxygen out of the room.

"Do you have any leads?" Stacy asked.

Matt flinched "I can't share that kind of information with you…not yet at least."

The room went quiet. Stacy stared at Matt, trying to find out if what Lillian had said was true. The fact that there was no matching DNA in the database could lead to Matt continuing down the road he was on, one in which Henry was the prime suspect, but Stacy couldn't see how that would stick. Nothing had been found that would point to her fiancé, the only common aspect was the fact that each of the victims resembled her, but that was hardly enough evidence to go on. All serial killers had a 'type', it just so happened that this guy was after someone who looked like her. If that was all Matt had to go on, Stacy's sister Maeve was just as likely a suspect as Henry.

Maeve had the motive — she was perpetually resentful of Stacy because their father seemed to love her the most, despite the fact that Stacy wanted nothing to do with the man. Her sister was a nurse, she had enough strength to bring any woman to her knees and strangle her if she wanted to. The sexual nature of the victims' humiliating poses was a bit of a wild card, but then again, Stacy had no idea what went on in Maeve's head.

"Stacy, I need to tell you something." Matt's voice cut through Stacy's internal monologue.

She turned and saw he was holding out a chair, inviting Stacy to sit down.

"I was really hoping you'd tell me something…a little more definitive. As it stands I—" Matt cut himself off and stared down at his hands.

"What, Matt? What do you have to tell me?" Stacy asked.

Matt turned away from her. He twiddled his thumbs, he played with a pen on her desk, he looked everywhere but in Stacy's direction.

"Matt? Stop avoiding me, just spit it out."

"There was some physical evidence at the scene." Matt snapped to attention, glaring at Stacy. "CSI couldn't identify it at first, there was a clump that looked like it could be vomit, a dead rat, or just street trash, but they processed it anyway. It was hair, blond curly hair mixed in with some dirt. We think the victim must have been trying to pull the killer's hair, but he managed to subdue her before she could get a good fistful."

"There was some bruising on her wrist, could be consistent with him grabbing her and holding her down," Stacy replied, she could already see where this was going. The room suddenly felt way too small, like she had eaten a mysterious cookie from Wonderland.

Matt nodded and continued, "They were blond curls, Stacy."

Stacy took a deep breath, shrinking the room even further.

"Do you know the building where Lacey Daniels was found?" Matt asked, abruptly changing the subject.

Stacy wondered for a moment if *she* was under investigation.

She knew this was one of his tactics, to distract the interrogation subject and throw them off their guard. "No, I wasn't on the scene. I didn't really pay much attention to the building, was busy investigating the dead body in the alleyway," she spat.

"It's a loft building, an old factory that was converted into community spaces. It was in the news a few years back; some developer wanted to buy it and turn the building into luxury condo lofts. The community came together and petitioned high-profile people in the city to purchase the building and turn it into something else, something that hopefully wouldn't drive up rent prices in that area of the city."

"I remember that. The hospital hosted a couple of fundraisers for it, to help convert the building and bring it up to code."

"That's right, it was around the time you were working at St. Vincent's. The building got turned into a community arts center. It's got a clay studio, some painter's lofts...still attracts all the yuppies and doesn't do much in terms of gentrification but there's a couple of community outreach classes that—"

"Matt, what are you getting at? This woman was found near the botanical gardens, in an alleyway, what does that have to do with the hairs you found?"

"The building is owned by Henry Goldberg. We found out during the initial investigation after we had some calls from an insurance company. He bought it about five years ago, with help from his mother and a co-investor, who he bought out about a year ago. The hairs found at the scene are pretty similar to his cherubic curls, and he had more than enough motive to be there. We're bringing him in for questioning. I just...I wanted you to know."

Stacy was speechless. Lillian was right, Matt had his eyes on Henry.

"That's a bit of a stretch, don't you think?" Stacy scoffed, dropping down into a chair.

"Why? Because he's your fiancé? I'll have you know that we

questioned the owners of all three buildings where the murder victims were found."

"But did you bring them down to the precinct? Did you strap them in a chair and turn the lights on them?" Stacy started to raise her voice, causing Matt to flinch again, which made her glad.

"No, I didn't, but I also didn't find evidence that matched their descriptions, and none of them resisted passing along security camera footage of the area. Not to mention the victim profile—"

"Don't you dare bring that into it—"

"Fine! I won't. I know you think this is all some scorned ex-boyfriend stuff, but it's not. I don't have to explain my investigative process to you, Stacy, but I would hope you know me well enough to know I'm not some crooked cop chasing a grudge."

"Please, Matt," Stacy said, tears stinging the corners of her eyes, "don't do this."

"Stacy, if Henry has nothing to hide, he'll be perfectly fine. We're not about to bounce him off the walls, but we do need answers to some of our questions." Matt stood up and strode toward the door. He stopped, pausing at the door without looking at her. "For the record, I'm hoping it's not him."

STACY LOCKED herself in her office for the rest of the day. Twice Trevor knocked on her door attempting to deliver a message from her supervisor, and twice she yelled at him to go away. She busied herself by staring at the phone and trying to decide whether or not she should call Henry and warn him.

On one hand, it shouldn't make a difference. If Henry was innocent, he'd go with the police willingly, answer a few questions, and be on his way.

Then again, there was a chance. A small chance, sure, but a chance that Matt was right. He was a talented detective, but there's no doubt in her mind that he was biased in this case. She hoped his partner, Andy, would talk some sense into him. Andy was a level-headed guy, the 'good cop' to Matt's 'unpredictable rebel cop'. He would never allow Matt to follow a hunch that didn't have something behind it.

If she did warn Henry, what would he do? He was a proud man, and he hated Matt. There was a chance he'd run, drive out of the city to avoid the police's questions — but that would make him seem even more suspicious. If she warned Henry, Stacy might be able to talk some sense into him, maybe even persuade him to go down to the police station himself and volunteer to be questioned. She'd never be able to persuade him over the phone, she had to do it in person, maybe even drive him down to the station. That would relieve some of the suspicion around him, wouldn't it? No serial killer in their right mind would volunteer to be questioned by the police.

Stacy grabbed her keys and jerked open the door, almost knocking Trevor to the ground as she attempted to leave.

"Sorry, I have to go," she muttered as she pushed by him.

It was too late. Stacy got home just in time to see Andy leading Henry out the door in handcuffs. Some people were on the street filming the incident on their phones. Henry's face was dark, and he flinched away from the detective when he opened the door for him.

"Wait! Wait, I need to know where you're taking him. Is he— he isn't supposed to be under arrest he's—"

"He punched me in the face, Stacy — I mean, Ms. Lewis. He's being brought down for questioning, and then we'll decide if he's being charged for assaulting a police officer." Detective Cardoso guided Henry into the backseat and closed the door.

Stacy could only stare into Henry's eyes and watch as the cruiser drove away.

# CHAPTER
# ELEVEN
STACY

Stacy walked back into her house like a zombie. The people recording the arrest turned their camera phones toward Stacy, screaming at her as she trudged past them into her house. She didn't care. Their footage would either appear on TV or on social media soon. Besides, she didn't really want to relive her day.

She collapsed on the couch and started to cry. She sobbed loudly for the better part of an hour, letting the stress of the past week wash over her. Henry was odd, he was boring, but he was far from dangerous. Stacy had been around dangerous men all her life, Henry was probably used to being manipulated by his mother and he definitely had some unresolved issues that required the expertise of a therapist, but there was no way he was a *serial killer*.

This was all Matt's doing.

Matt was the one who pushed himself onto this case, Matt was the one who insisted he and Stacy meet for briefings of the victims, Matt was the one who targeted Henry. Because of his involvement in the case, Stacy had been flipping back and forth between wanting to get the wedding over with and finally settle down with Henry, and possibly leaving her kind fiancé for the passion she yearned for. If she hadn't done that, then maybe she and Henry wouldn't have argued that day at the winery, and maybe...

*Stop it, Stacy. You're just like Matt, jumping to conclusions that have a perfectly reasonable explanation.*

She waited by the phone for Henry to call. He got one phone call, right? She figured he'd call his loving fiancée, but Stacy fell asleep on the couch waiting for the phone call that didn't come. Henry must be angry, or he called his lawyer, or Matt has been grilling him for hours about a crime Henry knew nothing about. He didn't even want to listen when Stacy talked about it, that's how removed from the case he wanted to be. Stacy's head was spinning when she woke up, the imprint of her couch cushion on her cheek. She hadn't felt this anxious in a year, and there was only one person who could help.

"I'll be right over," Lillian said before Stacy even opened her mouth to say anything into the phone.

Lillian appeared less than twenty minutes later carrying two bottles of Stacy's favorite wine, and a pizza.

"I was going to bring tequila, but I figured you'd have a big day ahead. Besides, I have to be at the gallery, and I *cannot* have a tequila hangover." She winked as she glided past Stacy on the way to the kitchen. "Should we do a movie, or would you rather just vent?"

Thank goodness for Lillian. The best friend with a sixth sense, who never complained about how formaldehyde-y Stacy smelled.

"Movie, I want a bad movie that we can talk over."

"Perfect, I'll cue it up. Why don't you go take a quick shower."

"I'm sorry to call you so late I just, I—"

Lillian popped back out of the kitchen and looked Stacy dead in the eyes.

"Stacy, it is 9 p.m. I don't know what kind of elderly sleep schedule your fiancé keeps you on, but it is far from late at night. You need to go upstairs and wash your face before we comfort you, and then when you come down, we can talk, and you'll feel like a normal person," Lillian said. "Besides, even if it was 1 a.m., I'd still be over here." She disappeared into the kitchen again and Stacy heard the sounds of the wine opening on her way up the stairs.

She turned the shower to its hottest setting, allowing the water to wash and burn away her day. She had to stop overanalyzing everything, she knew she had to leave the investigating up to the detectives, that they would come to a dead end and be forced to let Henry go. Stacy spent longer in the shower than she expected, but she didn't cry. It seemed fruitless to cry, what would it do? She wondered if she had somehow contributed to the suspicion against Henry. It didn't seem possible. All she could identify about the killer was the fact that he — or she — had large hands — Henry wasn't the only man in the city with large hands — he wasn't even the only one in the neighborhood with large hands. The only logical reason to have pointed the finger at Henry was the fact that Matt was the lead detective, and Matt lost her to Henry.

Stacy came out of the shower angrier than when she went into it. It was clear that Matt should have taken himself off the case, or at least not insisted she be the medical examiner. Someone else could have done the work, there was no reason for Matt to be 'protecting' her through his investigation. The fact that he told her what was going to happen also enraged her — how dare he! He was about to haul her fiancé under a bright interrogation light, and he comes to her, as if she can stop it? All that did was make Stacy feel guilty that she didn't do more. Henry was stressed about his mother and the wedding, it's no wonder he attacked Andy when he came by. The man worked a high-stress job and came home to a police officer? After having to deal with the guilt surrounding his mother's suicide, wedding planning, fights about wedding planning, and a dead body found in the alleyway of a building he owned, he was met with a policeman at his door — it was no wonder he snapped—

"Stace? Is everything okay up there?" Lillian called from the bottom of the stairs.

"It's fine! Just having a mental argument with myself, you know how it is!" Stacy tried to sound as normal as possible, but she couldn't hide the wavering in her voice.

Lillian stomped up the stairs and opened the bathroom door. "You can't hide from me, you know. I can hear you blaming yourself from the kitchen."

"I could have warned him, Lil. Matt warned me, you hinted at it. I should have said something so that—"

"What? So that Henry could get angry and manipulate you into thinking this was your fault?"

"He wouldn't do that. He at least would have known what was coming, it wouldn't have been a surprise."

Lillian sighed and hugged her friend. "You care too much. Henry is fine, he's a level headed guy. If you had told him, you'd be feeling guilty that you somehow roped him into the world of this serial killer or something. He's not the type to take blame. Maybe you could have prevented him from trying to punch Cardoso, but that's about it."

"I feel bad. I feel like I'm the reason there's a tornado of stress around him. I feel like if I could just—"

"Stop, Stacy, you don't have to do anything. *You* aren't the reason, you're the solution. He knows you aren't to blame for any of this."

"You have to admit, if it hadn't been for me, Matt probably wouldn't be looking at him for the murders. He's clearly biased against Henry, and took the first most convenient chance to pin it all on him. I mean c'mon, curly blond hair found at the scene, and he hauls *my fiancé* in for questioning?" Stacy was starting to get worked up all over again.

It didn't help that Lillian's response was to stare down at the floor. She was right then, Matt might not have been a crooked cop, but his bias was clear in this situation.

"Let's go downstairs. Let's have some wine and pizza and gossip over a movie. All you can do now is to wait. Henry is a methodical man; he's going to answer their questions and come home. It might be later tonight, it might be tomorrow, either way he'll be fine and when he's home you can find a way to help him, okay?" Lillian gently led her to the bedroom to change.

Stacy put on sweat pants and a t-shirt in a daze, stumbled down the stairs and plopped down on the couch beside her best friend.

She barely paid attention to the movie, didn't listen as Lillian complained about the creepy curator at the gallery, just drank and listened for some clue that Henry was arriving. Hours passed, but Henry didn't show.

"He'll be here in the morning," Lillian reassured her. "Do you want me to stay?"

"No, it's fine. I'm just gonna go to sleep, maybe stare at the ceiling for a couple of hours as I overanalyze every sound I hear."

Lillian held her and gave her a sympathetic smile. "Well, call me if you think any of those sounds are a killer on the loose." She winked as she walked out the door.

Stacy left the debris of their dinner on the coffee table and dragged herself upstairs to bed. She'd deal with it in the morning, just like everything else.

The next morning Stacy woke up to an empty bed, the wine glasses and pizza box still sitting on the living room table. She felt panic rising in her chest. Henry still wasn't home. His car keys were on the hook and his car was in the driveway. Henry was still at the station, probably still in an interrogation room somewhere. She toyed with the idea of going down there. She was familiar with most of the staff and knew how to get them to let her in. She could say she had business with Matt. That used to work when they were dating, and Stacy came down for a mid-afternoon tryst.

*I can't do that,* Stacy thought, *I'll just be angry and irrational.* There was a perfectly good explanation for why Henry wasn't home. Maybe the cops had dropped him off and he'd gone for a walk, trying to clear his head. He might be getting coffee for the two of them. He wasn't answering his phone, but it was probably dead anyway, the police weren't going to give him a charger if they forced him to stay in a cell all night.

There had to be some way for Stacy to find out where her fiancé was, but she didn't have time to figure it out. The wine last night had gone straight to her head, and if she didn't leave soon, she'd be late for work. Stacy put aside her anxiety to clean up, make sure the house looked spotless for Henry's arrival, before jumping into her car and racing to work.

When she arrived, she found an envelope waiting for her on her desk. It wasn't hers, it looked like an internal memo from the Seattle PD crime lab. Stacy's hands shook as she opened it.

*Thought you might want to see this before it goes public.*

It was a detailed report examining DNA evidence of the few curly blond hairs, as well as tissue samples found under the victim's fingernails. The DNA was a match to that of Henry Goldberg.

Stacy's knees buckled, she only just caught herself on her chair. She read the words on the report over and over again, willing them to change. She had no idea who sent this to her, it was probably Matt, but there was no signature on the note. It could have been one of the technicians from the crime lab, the city coroner's office did a lot of work with them, and Stacy had got to know some of the technicians pretty well.

She didn't have a lot of time; the information was likely being drafted into a press release at that very moment. What could she do? She could very easily hide at her work, her exam room was in the basement, making it very easy to hide from the world down there. She could go home, but she knew there would probably be camera crews and photographers eager to get an exclusive for their story about the Alleyway Strangler. She could go to Lillian's, but if Stacy was being honest with herself, she really wanted to be alone. She buried her head in her arms and tried to ignore her churning stomach. Stacy couldn't believe these results were real, she just couldn't, she knew deep down that Henry couldn't be the killer, despite the findings sitting in front of her.

Of course, there was one possibility. She knew of Matt's bias against Henry, knew that he was a talented, but also ruthless, cop who would stop at nothing to chase down a lead. There was plenty of time at the scene for him to plant just enough evidence to turn the investigation Henry's way. There was a possibility that Matt — or someone — had framed Henry. They could have planted the body at the loft building he owned, left hair fibers near the body, all in a careful ploy to indicate blame. Either it was some psychopath who was trying to shift the heat off himself, or it was someone in the police department who knew of the case and knew they were closing in on Henry.

Stacy was convinced that there was no way her boring, steady fiancé could have done this. True his mother had scrambled his brain, but not in a way that turned him into a serial killer. Someone had set him up, someone was trying to ruin Stacy's life, trying to send a message to Stacy that she may not be as safe as she thought she was.

# CHAPTER
# TWELVE
## STACY

"Mr. Goldberg was brought in for questioning yesterday, in connection with the so-called Alleyway Strangler. The latest victim, Lacey Daniels, was found near a building owned by the well-respected doctor, and police became suspicious after he blocked the release of footage from a security camera that faced the alleyway. After connecting a DNA sample taken from the scene, police have now arrested Mr. Henry Goldberg on suspicion of the murders of Lacey Daniels, Audrey Wells, and Gabrielle Unwin."

Stacy stared at the screen, only half listening to what they were saying. Her boss sent her home early that day, after he found her sobbing into her hands at her desk. She got home and turned on the tv, only to find wall-to-wall news coverage of her disgraced fiancé and his connection to the serial murders in Seattle. The story was even being covered on the national news channel, so it was either listen to reporters break down Henry's life all day, or watch the soap operas that she hated.

"Mr. Goldberg's mother, Amanda Goldberg, was a local socialite who was reported to have a very close relationship with her son. She was found dead in her apartment from undisclosed circumstances three *months ago. Up next, we'll be talking with Dr. Bill Wakely, who will be breaking down the history of parental trauma in serial killers."*

It took them absolutely no time to find the skeletons in Henry's closet and pull them out for their personal gain. It was a ratings circus, and Stacy could hear it happening in real time just outside her house. Her cellphone was ringing off the hook, but she didn't answer anyone's call. *Let it go to voicemail, they only care about what they can sell to the tv stations anyway.*

There was one call she answered, and it came on their landline.

"Stacy?" Henry's shaky voice came down the line. "Tell me that's you."

"It's me!" Stacy squealed. "Of course it's me, who else could it be?"

"I'm sorry I-I didn't know...I thought maybe someone broke in or...I don't know, Stacy. I'm exhausted."

They were quiet for a moment. This was the phone call Stacy had been waiting for.

"I tried calling your cell but—"

"I haven't been answering," Stacy interrupted, wanting to keep Henry on the line as long as she could. She missed him; more than she wanted to admit. She missed his large body sleeping next to her in bed, and she missed hearing the mundane noises of Henry living alongside her in their house. All the anger and confusion that she felt, it melted away listening to his voice. He sounded vulnerable and unsure.

"I get it." He cleared his throat, clearing away all the shakiness and vulnerability from his voice, "I need you to take care of some things, can you handle that?"

"Of course, what do you need?"

"I already called a lawyer. He's pretty confident we can get all this cleared away pretty quickly, this is obviously some kind of revenge from Ensor." Henry's voice sounded cold. He was a man with a plan, and nothing else. Stacy realized his vulnerability might have been because he couldn't secure his *own* situation, not because he was concerned about her. "You need to call Kitagawa, my family's lawyer, and he'll handle everything. Any press or weirdos coming out of the woodwork and trying to bother you, just send them his way. You can just forward all the calls to his number."

"I can't do that, Henry, I also get calls to my phone."

"That's obviously not what I mean, Stacy. I mean the calls you get from numbers you don't recognize, people who are clearly reporters or other hack jobs, just send them along to him. Their office knows what they're doing, my family has used them before."

"Okay, I just—"

"I understand. You don't like sharing your private information with me." Henry's voice grew colder. He sounded angry, but whether upset at his situation or at Stacy, she couldn't tell.

"We're going to get past this, Henry. What they're saying is bogus, just—"

"I know that, Stacy. I didn't call for a tearful reunion, I called to make a plan. Is that something you think you can handle? Because if not, I will have called Kitagawa himself, I thought you might like to hear from me, but I guess you're already updated about my situation."

"I'm not, Henry, please don't go there. I had no idea this was going to happen, I only found out they arrested you when I came home and saw it on the news."

"You went to work today?" Henry asked.

Stacy let the question hang on the line. She had no idea what to say, this morning when she left, she had no idea Henry could be arrested. She regretted not saying anything when she could, maybe Henry could have got away and he wouldn't be rotting in a jail cell right now.

"I didn't know— I didn't know what to do. I didn't think you'd be arrested. Someone sent me the DNA report and I went straight home but—"

"It's fine, Stacy. I understand. You couldn't have known what was going on in here," Henry replied, and went silent again.

Stacy had nothing to say, she didn't know how to reassure Henry or make him understand what had been going through her head.

"I'm running out of time; I have to go."

"Okay," Stacy gulped, "I love you."

But Henry had already hung up.

Stacy felt her stomach sink. She felt guilty, and exhausted, and worried all at the same time. She wished her mother was still here, she'd know what to do. Henry was so cold and disconnected on the phone, he wasn't even angry, he sounded disappointed, which was so much worse. She wished she could be a fly on the wall of his interrogation, so she could know what Matt had said to him. Did he tell Henry that he'd given Stacy fair warning that they were going to bring him in?

*It's fine. Henry knows they can't pin anything on him, DNA is only one part of the puzzle.*

Stacy sat down listening to the commotion going on outside her house. She dialed the number for Kitagawa's legal office, put a plan in place for all the press inquiries that were already coming through to her email, and probably Henry's as well. She mentioned the crowds outside her door, and less than an hour later they were gone. Cleared thanks to the impromptu press conference she could hear happen on her front stoop. She hid inside, avoiding the reality of what was happening in her life. She could hear the questions about whether or not her engagement was still on, and if she, as city coroner, had been hiding evidence on Unwin and Wells' bodies. She ignored it all, sipping on the wine that Lillian had left behind. Stacy thought back to those examinations, looking up the reports on her computer. There was no DNA found anywhere, no hairs on the bodies, nothing beneath the fingernails, not so much as an errant fingerprint. It was only on that last body, which seemed strange to Stacy. The one body with DNA, and its immediately traced back to her fiancé?

Could it be a crime of opportunity? The body was found in an alleyway outside his building, Matt knew exactly who owned it, the curly blond hair wasn't discovered until a day later. Could he have planted the evidence? Even if it wasn't Matt, someone might have been able to do it. After murdering the woman, leaving her in a humiliating state, they planted just enough evidence to have Henry arrested on suspicion. Matt was already biased, already suspicious of Henry, this finally tipped the scales in his direction — it was too convenient.

*That's not possible,* Stacy thought, *it's more likely that I'm the one who planted evidence.*

Stacy froze. That's why Henry was acting so strangely over the phone. He obviously knew *he* wasn't the killer. Matt might have been grilling him about the DNA evidence found on the woman. Henry knew how much access and influence Stacy could have over an investigation. He was afraid and exhausted, he wasn't thinking straight, and all that could point to Stacy. It didn't help that this arrest came on the heels of their fight at the wedding venue.

Stacy got up. She felt restless, like she needed to *do* something, but she wasn't sure what. She didn't feel comfortable going outside for a walk — it sounded like the camera crews were gone, but for all she knew they were lying in wait at the end of her street or something. She didn't feel like going for a drive; that was too much time alone with her thoughts without enough distraction.

She looked around the living room, and slowly realized she

hadn't cleaned in days. There was dust on the mantle and glass rings on the coffee table. That would keep her mind off things, give back a tiny bit of control over her life. She'd clean until she forgot about everything that was and could be happening to her fiancé.

---

STACY WAS in the midst of power scrubbing the bathroom when her phone rang. Thinking it could be Henry she answered without checking the caller ID.

"Stacy, is this true? The news said they hauled Henry in for those insane murders that have been happening all over town!"

It was Maeve. *Shit.*

Stacy sighed. "Yes, Maeve, they brought Henry in for questioning and then...I don't know I guess they found more evidence that kept him in there."

"Does he have bail? Do you need money? I can loan you some money if you want, obviously, I would need it to be paid back because not all of us have a fancy job like you, but if you need help with his bail—"

"It's fine, Maeve. He's being held without bail. I couldn't bail him out even if you wanted to donate to his bail fund." Stacy rubbed her temples. The last person she wanted to be talking with was Maeve. She also knew anything she told her sister would be passed along to their father, and Stacy didn't want him knowing anything about her life.

"How is he being held without bail? What kind of proof do they have on him, they can't just throw him in there and get rid of the key, Stacy, you have to start asking questions. I know you have a load of *faith* in the justice system, but sometimes they get things wrong, and it can really traumatize a person. Just think of Dad, he probably wouldn't be in a mental institution right now if it wasn't for the *judicial system* getting its way, you know?"

"I get that, Maeve, but they haven't told me much. Matt just said they found enough evidence to hold him and bring him in for questioning."

"Matt? Matt Ensor, what does that lowlife have to do with anything?"

"He's—he's the lead detective on the murder investigation."

Stacy immediately regretted telling Maeve even an iota of the truth, but she was tired of walking on eggshells around her sister. Stacy wanted to get her mind off of the arrest, she wanted to get off the phone and back to scrubbing the mysterious ring around her bathtub.

"Maeve?" she asked, after hearing nothing but her sister's heavy breathing. "Are you okay?"

"I'm angry, Stacy. I know you were clouded by love in the past, but I'd have thought you'd be over it by now."

"What do you mean?"

Maeve sighed. "Stacy don't you see what's going on? This is all a revenge ploy by your ex-boyfriend who is completely unable to regulate his emotions and is in a position of power in this city. He obviously planted the evidence that he needed to hold Henry, and greased the wheels of the justice system to make sure he was denied bail! Don't you see that?"

"Maeve, Matt wouldn't do such a thing."

"How would you know? You've never worked with him directly. Even as a medical examiner you're one step away from the investigation. Sure, your exam might not have been biased, but think about all the other cogs in that machine."

She had a point. The evidence found at the crime scene, the hair that Matt immediately assumed came from Henry's blond, curly head — all that was completely out of her jurisdiction. She only had access to the debris under Lacey Daniels' fingernails, but even in that case it was easy for someone on the investigative team to tamper with the body. She had to be processed and transported to the morgue, a lot could have happened between the time her body was found and the time she was put in front of Stacy for her autopsy.

"I think it would be a pretty elaborate set up, Maeve." Stacy's voice lowered; she was less sure of herself now.

"Well, I doubt that any successful set up would be basic, Stacy," Maeve deadpanned.

Her sister was against Matt and would be for the rest of time. He was punished for having attacked their father, but of course the older man got the worst of the deal. Matt had to see a therapist for a few weeks, Oliver had his freedom stripped away and was now monitored and medicated 24/7. Seeing Henry's situation from that perspective was sure to create some doubt about how legal the investigation was.

"Think about it, Stacy. He could plant evidence and his department would be none the wiser. I bet he could do it without his partner even knowing. Then he gets his way — your fiancé, his competition for your heart, is finally out of the picture. This isn't going to be the end of it, you know."

Stacy didn't know what to say. Her sister managed to convince and confuse her about the whole situation. Would Matt really do such a thing? If he was ever found out, it would jeopardize his whole career, and it didn't guarantee that Stacy would get back together with him. While she missed the passion of their relationship, she also didn't think she could commit to a man who was so volatile, especially after the dull security of her relationship with Henry.

"Maeve, I—I have to go. I have food in the oven and — I mean, on the stove, and I need to—"

"I get it. You should process what I said, you probably hadn't even thought about it because your mind is complete mush when it comes to these things. You just follow what you're told, like a little sheep, and you never give anything a second thought. I for one am glad I could get you to start thinking about what is sure to be called a 'conspiracy' when I go to the media about it."

"Maeve, please, don't do that. I don't want to deal with any more media coverage, I can hardly leave my house right now because there are camera crews waiting by my door. Please, Maeve, please will you just—"

"Will you come visit Dad, like you keep promising and putting off?"

*Dammit, I should have known it was an empty threat.*

"No, Maeve, I won't. You know what, I take that back. Go ahead and tell anyone you want, it's not as if you can make things any worse than they are. My fiancé is in *jail,* and I can't go get him, I have you in my ear telling me he's being framed by my ex even though you have *zero* evidence to back it up, meanwhile every time I close my eyes, I see these victims who look exactly like me, bruised, and strangled staring up at me. So, you know, do whatever you want, for once you're the least of my worries." Stacy hung up.

Her sister could go to the media with her conspiracy concerns if she wanted to, any journalist who did two minutes of research would see that she clearly had a vendetta against Matt. Stacy took a deep breath and leaned against the bathtub. That nagging feeling, that Henry was being framed, came back. This time her sister's voice was in her ear telling her there was plenty of opportunity to plant the evidence against Henry.

*Matt wouldn't do such a thing. He wouldn't go to those lengths. Sure, he's biased, but its unconscious.*

For the millionth time that day, Stacy ran over the events of the past few days in her mind. Matt warning her that they were bringing Henry in for questioning, Henry being led out of their house by Andy, and then finding the envelope with the DNA results on her desk. If Matt was planting evidence, he wouldn't have given her so much warning, it would be too dangerous for him. Besides, he'd never been to their house or been anywhere near Henry — how could he have found enough hair or skin to plant on Lacey Daniels? No, Matt was definitely biased, and probably more eager to follow the Henry lead than anything else, but he didn't have the opportunity to collect enough DNA evidence against Henry. Someone else was doing this, someone who had more access to Henry — but who?

# CHAPTER
# THIRTEEN
STACY

Stacy finished cleaning her house. It took hours, but when she was done it felt like no time had passed. She was still worried, guilty, all the emotions she had been feeling were exactly the same — except now her house was cleaner than it had ever been. There was nothing left to do but wait. She opened her computer to do some work, but found an email from her boss saying she could go on leave for a few days.

*"I know you're committed to your job, but I think it's best if you rest for a couple of days. This investigation has already been quite stressful, I can only imagine the events of yesterday and today have made it even more stressful. Take a long weekend, and come back on Monday."*

Part of her felt grateful that she worked at a place where they took your mental health seriously. Another part of her felt like they were just trying to keep the heat off the morgue. Not that they had anything to hide, after all, they did examinations on dead people, how many secrets could they have? But Stacy was sure someone higher up decided that the city coroner's office didn't need a crowd of journalists and camera crews camped outside the building all day. That meant that Stacy had nothing to do, nowhere to go, and no one to talk to until Monday when her life could start again. Rather than be alone with her paranoid thoughts, Stacy called Lillian.

"I'm on my way, shall I bring pizza and wine or sushi and wine?"

"Sushi, I think, I just cleaned. I'd rather not get my cushions all greasy."

---

LILLIAN ARRIVED WITHIN TWENTY MINUTES.

"Were you already on your way here or something?" Stacy asked as her friend came through the door.

"I've been ready to come over for the past two days, I knew you'd call when you were ready." Lillian turned and wrapped her in a tight squeeze.

For the first time in days Stacy felt her muscles relax into the comfort of another person.

"It smells clean in here."

"I cleaned. I cleaned everything. This house hasn't been this clean since we moved in, I even pulled the fridge out and dusted behind it. I kept cleaning so I could think about anything except my fiancé getting arrested by my ex-boyfriend, under suspicion of being a serial killer. Now I'm done and that's all I can think about."

Lillian squeezed Stacy's hand and led her to the couch. "Lie down, Stae, I'll get plates."

"I just don't know what to think anymore," Stacy called out. "Maeve called and she got in my head and now I'm even more confused."

"Maeve? Your sister? That can't be good, what did that nut job say?"

"That Matt framed Henry because he's jealous of my fiancé."

Lillian didn't say a word. She sauntered back into the living room with an 'you-have-to-be-kidding' look on her face.

Stacy just nodded. "She was pretty convincing."

"Yeah, most delusional conspiracists are. Did she somehow find a way to guilt trip you into going to see your dad in all of this? Or tell you about how the medication *Matt* prescribed is causing your father's brain to leak out of his ears? Or that the facility he's in has bugged his room?"

"She didn't go that far, but she did almost agree to get me to go see him. She's tricky like that. I dunno, she had a point. The only evidence they have against Henry is the debris under Lacey Daniels' fingernails, and a couple of hairs found at the scene. Anyone could have planted it, even Matt."

"Yeah, but he's also the owner of the building and the only person who refused to turn over security camera footage when asked."

"His lawyer says the release of the footage has to get approved before the police can see it, because it's a community building run by a board or something? I didn't really understand, I heard the press conference through the door." Stacy groaned, dropping her head back onto a pillow.

Lillian crept away and got their dinner prepared, presenting it delicately like they were at an omakase restaurant.

"That makes sense, why didn't the police take that into account?" Lillian asked, shoving a spicy salmon roll into her mouth.

"I don't know. I think it was Matt, he's never liked Henry. The second this case pointed to him, he probably barreled through protocol for the chance to arrest him," Stacy said between bites. "He's the only building owner that they brought down to the station for questioning, everyone else they met outside the station. Matt said there were other factors to consider, but I can't help but feel…"

"Like the outside factor was that Matt hates Henry and will

do anything he can to break you guys up?" Lillian finished Stacy's thought.

All Stacy could do was nod along. They were quiet for a while, each absorbed in her own thoughts, savoring the dynamite rolls in front of them.

"Henry never struck me as a murderer. He's not my favorite guy in the world, but he's too…well, he's a bit too much of a wuss to be a murderer. I feel like without his mom he's just this kind of manipulative, sad, traumatized child who doesn't even understand what it is to make a decision with another person, y'know? Like he never learned how to compromise so he doesn't comprehend what that means, all he learned was how to manipulate and be manipulated. He's not angry or psychotic, just kind of sad," Lillian finally said.

"His mom really was a piece of work, huh?"

"Mm-hmm, and you can't deny that it probably broke him, long before she died. You're right that bringing him down to the station for questioning seems sketchy, like they were just trying to stall for time before they could arrest him. Then again…I think framing him would be a little too far, Stace. Matt might be biased, sure, but he's not a dirty cop. He wouldn't do something like that, especially if he knew it would hurt you. I mean, do you even know where Henry was that night?"

"Well…no, that was the night we had that fight."

"Where he abandoned you in Redmond, I remember. You drunk-texted me a lot that night."

"He showed up later that night. He brought me a flower."

"Didn't you say he was all scratched up? Be honest with yourself, could those scratches have been made by another person?"

Stacy tried to think back to that night, but her memory was hazy. He brought her a rose, claimed to have climbed through a bush to get it for her, but later when she tried helping him treat his scratches, he flinched away from her.

"The scratches seemed pretty deep, but I mean Henry was

drunk. He probably fell or cut himself on thorns and leaned into the bush, not realizing it was hurting him, everyone's more careless when they're drunk."

"True," Lillian said, stirring some wasabi into her soy sauce, "but you've seen plenty of scratches, and so have I. They look different, they're wider and deeper than any thorn from a rose bush could be—"

"I was drunk, Lil, I hardly remember what *I* did that night, and I wasn't paying attention to his scratches. I wasn't standing over him measuring and taking notes on the quality, I was drunkenly stumbling back to bed with my fiancé and caressing a rose he got me."

Lillian bit her lip. "I know you don't want to think of this, but there is a chance he did it. Sometimes the simplest explanation is the right one, and in this case that means Henry murdered someone. She looked like you too, doesn't that freak you out?"

"Of course, it does! Of course, it freaks me out, I keep thinking I'm the next one, I'm gonna be the next serial killer victim in Seattle. I've had dreams of my photo coming up on the evening news as the latest 'Alleyway Strangler' victim, and that's the only way I'll be described for the rest of eternity. I just don't see how Henry could kill someone who looks like me, it doesn't make any sense."

"Maybe that's why. The night Lacey Daniels was killed he was angry with you, right? Maybe he found a very bizarre way of taking it out on someone else."

"He wouldn't do that, Lillian, he doesn't have rage blackouts like that. Henry is a mild-mannered man, he's more of a silent-treatment guy than the type to scream and shout. I would know if he was a psychopathic killer, okay? We spend just about all of our time together; I think I would have seen the signs."

"You mean a crazy controlling mother wasn't enough of a sign?" Lillian scoffed.

"I can't believe you would bring that up right now. His mom

is a sensitive subject, she literally killed herself because she finally couldn't control her son's life anymore. He still feels guilty about her death, he's still in mourning. It was only three months ago, and I just—his mind must be reeling. It took me ages to get over my mom, sometimes I think I'm still not over her death. If there was some kind of guilt or I felt like her death was my fault, it would drive me crazy."

"Well, it seems like maybe it did drive Henry crazy," Lillian said, ushering in another extended silence.

Stacy sat with what her friend said, unable to resolve it with what she knew of Henry. He wasn't crazy, he wasn't a killer. He was a sympathetic man, who was still untangling the years of abuse inflicted on him by his mother, who had to do it all from a jail cell because her ex-boyfriend seemed to have a bias against him.

"Matt said, early on in the investigation, that the only person who would do this kind of thing was some 'weak, evil man who hates women and probably has mommy issues.' It's obvious he was already thinking of Henry, long before there was any connection to him in the case. I hear what you're saying, but it just seems impossible to me, I still think—"

"I know," Lillian said, gently stroking her arm. "I get it. You can't just turn off your feelings for Henry. Just please think about it before you join Maeve on her conspiracy crusade against the Seattle P.D, okay?" Lillian wrapped Stacy in a long, tight hug.

---

LILLIAN LEFT LATER THAT NIGHT. The camera crews had returned to Stacy's doorstep, eager for a nighttime news exclusive. Stacy decided to hide in the kitchen and pretend she wasn't home. Today felt long, and she knew that the upcoming days would feel longer. She sat in her kitchen drinking wine, angry and sad at her conversation with Lillian. She knew her best friend was trying to be supportive, but her questions felt like they weighed hundreds of pounds.

Stacy didn't want to consider that Henry might actually be the Alleyway Strangler, and that Matt was following a good lead in his investigation. Stacy just wanted to forget about everything she knew, she wanted to stop trying to remember what kind of scratches were on Henry's face that day, she wanted to get rid of the temptation to ask the crime lab for their DNA reports on the other women.

Because Lillian made some good points.

There were a few questions that Stacy couldn't answer. Like why was Henry so reactive when news about the serial killer came on at night. Why he was so adamant that he didn't want to talk about this investigation — beyond the fact that her ex was leading it.

There were so many questions, and no one was around to answer them. Stacy shivered; the house felt colder without Henry's presence. He managed to bring a dorky positivity to their daily activities, when he was feeling happy. Stacy could have used an over-the-top, restaurant quality dinner tonight, rather than picking at cold sushi. She missed Henry, missed his comforting touch, missed the feeling of not being alone or afraid of who might come through the door. Sure, they'd had their fights, especially lately, but overall, Henry was a good man, a stable man.

Wasn't he?

# CHAPTER
# FOURTEEN
STACY

That night Stacy dreamed she was running down an endless alleyway. There were cameras pointed at her recording every step, and no matter how fast she ran the person chasing her was keeping up with every step. Stacy's breath got slower, her ribs hurt, and her legs were cramping but she knew that if she stopped moving, she was going to die. She just needed to find a door, a corner, some way to get away from the man who was chasing her. He smelled like Henry and her father, but his footsteps sounded more like Matt's. Then she tripped, she hit her foot on a loose brick and tumbled down to the ground, falling face first, and as her body hit the ground her clothes disappeared. She backed away into a wall trying to cover herself as best as she could, and saw the cameras turning away from her. Then a pair of hands came out of the dark, a face appeared, but it kept changing between Oliver, Henry, and Matt. They all laughed as she died. They laughed as they slowly walked away from her, leaving her in the alleyway.

STACY WOKE UP WITH A START, falling off the couch and to the ground. She never made it upstairs the night before, and her head was pounding. The last thing she remembered was sitting down with some of Henry's whiskey, listening to the low din of reporters packing up their camera equipment just under her window.

"She must be hiding out at a hotel, there hasn't been anyone in there since the friend left."

"Did anyone see a car leave?"

"No, we had someone at the end of the street after the lawyer came, they said no one came outside, just the friend."

"She must have gone out the back. Hey, get the intern to check the hotels in the area, see if anyone checked in that matches her description."

The people outside didn't seem to care if she heard. *I guess they all think I ran off. Kind of them to think I have a back entrance to escape from.* Soon after that Stacy drifted off into a fitful sleep, thanks to the whiskey. She woke up with breath worse than her father's when he was on a bender. Stacy dragged herself upstairs to shower away the night. She'd been taking a lot of these cleansing showers lately, with no sign of stopping. Every time she stepped in, she turned the water to the hottest it could be, feeling as though she could burn her skin right off and grow a newer, thicker skin in its place. The dream kept coming back to her in flashes; the feeling of helplessness as she ran through an endless alleyway and the faces of the three most important men in her life all trying to kill her.

Henry, who may or may not be a serial killer; Matt, who struggled with a violent beast inside him; and Oliver, who had no desire to hide the worst part of himself, and then there was Stacy, stuck running from all three. The water wasn't hot enough to wash the dream away. Stacy stumbled out of the shower unsure of what to do. She wasn't going to work, she had already cleaned the whole house, there was no way she was taking another bath lest she turn into a prune. Maybe now was the time she should tackle the never-ending pile of books to be read, or tv show recommendations to watch. She could finally veg out on the couch and take that staycation she had been promising herself for years.

Or should she be researching past cases of police corruption, killers who had been framed, any way she could possibly get Henry out of jail and back into their house where she knew he'd feel safe.

All of her options felt pointless. What she really wanted was to have Lillian back, she was the only person who could take Stacy's mind off of everything that was going on, but she couldn't keep dragging her friend over. Lillian had a life, she had a photography exhibit to plan, Stacy couldn't expect her best friend to drop everything just because Stacy's life was falling apart.

*I guess I could start with breakfast,* Stacy thought, and she slowly dragged herself downstairs to the kitchen, standing in the doorway when she got down there. *Now what? Breakfast for one person just feels...sad.*

Just then Stacy's landline rang. She jumped, as if she'd never heard the sound before. Stacy had turned her phone off last night to avoid the 'concerned' calls and text messages, the house was so silent without that constant ping that the sound of her landline ringing felt foreign to her.

"Henry?" Stacy asked, answering the phone. He was the only person she could conceive of who would call her this way.

"No, it's Matt."

His voice echoed down the line and Stacy felt her blood start to boil. How dare he call her after he put her *fiancé* behind bars!

"You've got to be kidding me—" Stacy said, and moved to hang up the phone.

"Wait! Stacy, don't hang up, please, I just want to talk."

"Talk?" Stacy growled. "Now you want to talk? You want to explain why you targeted my fiancé? You want to apologize for putting me in the shittiest position by basically implying that you were about to arrest him, and then have to make the decision about whether or not I should say anything? You want to apologize for the fact that I can't leave my house because there are camera crews camped outside my door? C'mon Matt, go ahead, talk about whatever you want to talk about."

Stacy was fuming. The absolute audacity of Matt calling her house to talk blew her mind. How unbelievably cocky could he be, thinking that she would *want* to talk to him after all that he put her through.

"Y'know, Matt, I should have known. Every time you appear in my life, it seems fine, you seem like a perfect gentleman, and then you absolutely go nuclear on someone right when I least expect it. I don't know why I didn't see this coming from the moment you stepped into my office."

"Hey! Cut me some slack," Matt said, interrupting Stacy's rant, "I know how you must be feeling, and I just called to see that you were okay. Believe it or not, I don't *want* the men in your life to ruin you, Stacy. I know you probably don't believe it, but there's other evidence that points to Henry, and I didn't want to pursue the lead because I knew it would hurt you. I chased down every other lead I had until I got to a dead end, it was Andy who had to convince me to go back to Henry and bring him in for questioning."

"You really expect me to believe that? You've never liked Henry, even before we were official, and Henry and I were just coworkers you aways had a chip on your shoulder about him."

"That was different. He obviously liked you, as did I, and I was jealous. I admitted it to you, I even remember you saying it was cute."

"Well, it's obvious that your bias against him colored your investigation. Maybe back then it was just petty jealousy, but I know you were angry to find out we got engaged, that Henry got the prize, and you were alone again. You should never have been on this case in the first place. The second you had an inkling of suspicion against my fiancé, you should have passed it along to someone else. You're the one who was always going on about how bias can infect an investigation, and here was your chance to put your money where your mouth was and properly recuse yourself, but of course you couldn't help it. You couldn't help but go through with your little revenge fantasy, could you?"

Stacy's voice was getting louder. She was very aware of how close the phone was to the front door, that anyone outside was probably listening in on her phone call, but she didn't care. It was better that the media learned about who was 'protecting' this city.

"A serial killer is a serial killer, Stacy. This isn't about you and me, and frankly you don't need to believe that. I talked with my superiors, they were fine with me on the case, Cardoso is there to keep me in check. Like I said, he was the one who said we had to take our foot off the break when it came to Henry, remember? Probably not, you're probably so wrapped up in your anger, in your expectation that the men in your life are only there to disappoint you that you're not even listening to a word I'm saying." Matt's calm facade was beginning to break down. "I knew it would hurt you if Henry was locked up, so I tried to treat you with as much consideration as I could. Not a single other cop would have done the same, and you know that."

"Maybe I should let someone know, that you are letting your feelings get in the way of an investigation. Revealing potential suspects, giving me little clues, those are all grounds for suspension, aren't they?"

"If you want me suspended, then go ahead. The case can and will go on without me, and Henry is still going to be a prime suspect. All that will change is that you'll have no one holding your hand through it. You think you're going to keep getting DNA reports from the crime lab? You think you won't need to take a *suggested* leave of absence from your job? If Henry really is a serial killer, they're going to start to look at you as well, you know."

"How is that going to affect my job?"

"You really think the city is going to let you perform medical examinations if they think you're involved in the murder? All your cases will get reassigned, all your previous reports will be reviewed. Believe me, it's better for both of you that Henry cooperates and that we are miraculously wrong. This was a courtesy call, Stacy. I called to check on you, make sure you were holding up okay. Obviously, you're panicking and becoming paranoid. I don't want you to go down that road, okay? Just please, trust that I am doing my job."

"How can I when you're investigating my fiancé?"

Matt took a deep breath in. "That's fair. I guess if the roles were reversed…yeah, I'd also be upset. But I'm not that kind of officer. I do everything I can to find out the truth, but that's it. I don't just make up suspects based on who cut me off that morning. You know that."

Stacy didn't know what to say. When she picked up the phone, she was convinced she was right — that Matt had allowed his bias against Henry to cloud his judgement in the investigation, but maybe she didn't have all the facts. It was true, Matt had his partner and his superiors who would check him if they thought he was going down the wrong path in an investigation. If they hadn't stopped him from arresting Henry, then it must mean Matt wasn't the only investigator who suspected he was involved with the murders.

"Stacy? Are you still there?" Matt asked after she was quiet for a while.

"Mm-hmm."

"Do you…are you feeling safe at home? Do you need someone to come and—"

"I'm fine, Matt. I think you've done enough for me, thanks." Stacy cut him off, unwilling to accept any more of Matt's 'help'.

She hated this feeling, of being a damsel in the dark, not knowing who to trust. This morning she was so sure, but now…

"Okay. Well, you have my number if you need anything."

"I need my fiancé out of jail, Matt."

"Yeah, but I need your fiancé in jail. You…you mean a lot to me, but I have a duty to the public, and that means more to me than you can understand." The line clicked as Matt hung up the phone.

Stacy slumped down onto the couch, staring up at the ceiling trying to organize the thoughts in her head.

Last night and this morning she had been sure that Matt had allowed his bias to skew the investigation. After talking to her sister, she was convinced that Matt was a ruthless detective who would stop at nothing to prove his own hunch, unable to accept any other theories of a case. After talking to Lillian, she wasn't entirely sure that Henry *wasn't* the Alleyway Strangler, after all he was AWOL the night Lacey Daniels was murdered, and she didn't get a good enough look at the scratches on his face to see if they really were caused by thorny roses. Now, after talking with Matt, she wasn't sure it was all bias, that maybe there was more to the investigation than she realized, and maybe Matt was trying to look out for her when he notified her about bringing Henry in for questioning.

She didn't feel like she could tip off his superiors about anything. She had no evidence that anyone planted Henry's DNA at the crime scene, and if Matt was taken off the case, she probably wouldn't have the inside look at it anymore. She would be reassigned, maybe her superiors would start to look at her examinations. If she and Matt had a past, and Matt was biased, they could start to think that she was biased too, and they were working together somehow. Stacy groaned out loud, releasing the anxiety from inside her chest. She truly didn't know who to believe anymore.

*Maybe I need to stop listening to other people, and start listening to myself.*

She couldn't trust anyone else's investigation, but she could still trust herself. It would give her something to do, something other than staring at the ceiling worrying about Henry and what was going on in that downtown jail. *There must be something in my notes,* she thought, *something I or Matt missed that clears all of this up.*

Stacy got up off the couch, ignoring the part of her that wanted to do nothing, and went up to her office. She was going to find some alternative, or at least figure out her *own* opinion on this case.

## CHAPTER
# FIFTEEN
STACY

Stacy made herself a coffee and went up to her office. Her work files were backed up to a cloud, but it would take a minute for them to download, since the city's data system was ancient. While she waited, she took out a notebook and made some notes.

1. Find an alternate theory of the case.

That meant she had to find some other reason these girls were being murdered, something that hinted the killer wasn't a *"weak evil man who hates women and probably has mommy issues."* She remembered that Gabrielle Unwin was a sex worker and made a note to see if she could follow up somehow. Maybe the other victims got in the way of a transaction and some pimp killed them.

1. Find a connection between the women.

So far, there wasn't any connection. Except the fact that they all had similar physical attributes, the women had different lives and lived in totally different parts of the city. They weren't even really the same age; it ranged from twenties to mid-thirties. There had to be some other connection that the detectives had missed, maybe even the same doctor or visit to a hospital at some point.

Finally, the files downloaded, and Stacy started going through her notes with a more keen eye. She needed to find something that would turn the case away from Henry. She felt horrible that he was sitting in a jail cell, stewing in his own thoughts, with no idea what was going on in the investigation. Matt stuck his neck out by providing hints to Stacy, but Henry wasn't getting that benefit. All he knew was his DNA was a match to something, and his reluctance to turn over security footage quickly was somehow a suggestion of his guilt. He was sitting there grappling with grief over his mother, probably getting angrier at Stacy, and he was probably bored out of his mind.

At the back of her mind, a little voice told Stacy that it was actually a relief not to have to talk about the wedding details or Henry's desire for a prenup. When she went to bed at night, she didn't feel the need to pretend to be asleep to avoid boring sex with her fiancé, and while she was cleaning the house yesterday, she felt like she could pour herself into the task without feeling Henry's eyes on her making sure she was cleaning the house to *his* preferences, which were the same as her own — spotless — but Henry always needed to see it with his own eyes. She could sit in her office blasting whatever kind of music she wanted, could keep the lights dim if she wanted, and at no point did she have to explain herself to anyone. It felt good. Stacy had forgotten what it was like to live alone. Before Henry she lived with Matt, before that she had a steadily rotating door of roommates, and before that she was with her mother. It had been a long time since Stacy felt this kind of peace.

Of course, as soon as she acknowledged it — how peaceful her home life was without Henry — Stacy felt a bubble of guilt rise in her throat. This wasn't a vacation from her fiancé, this was a murder investigation. This was a mission to exonerate him, not fantasize about what it would be like to have her own space and time uninterrupted by Henry's neediness.

She clicked on the report for Gabrielle Unwin, deciding to go chronologically first before comparing the three side by side. Gabrielle Unwin was found near the Seattle port, just north of Pike Place Market. She wasn't really known to the area, her 'corner' was on the other side of town. Apparently, she wasn't working that night, but no one knew where she was going or why she was down by the port. A close friend said Unwin liked to take long walks through the city, especially when she couldn't sleep. Stacy reviewed the photographs of her body; it looked like Gabrielle was waiting for someone to fall into her arms. According to her report, Stacy hypothesized that Gabrielle had been moved into that position after she was killed.

*Henry wouldn't like that.* She thought, *He was a strictly 'hold each other in missionary' kind of lover.*

The marks on Gabrielle's neck suggested strong hands, that the killer used bare or gloved hands to strangle her. The bruising was most concentrated on her larynx, which means the killer knew what he was doing. The bruising on the rest of her body was primarily on her legs and face. Her nose was broken, also post-mortem, like the killer wanted to disguise her identity. That was why the initial investigation veered toward the sex trafficking industry — it would be even harder to identify her if her face was disfigured. The killer took his anger out on how she looked, and maybe the fact that she had tried to run away.

Stacy closed the file, finishing up the notes she needed before combing through Audrey Wells and Lacey Daniels. In all three cases, the women were strangled, and the killer crushed their larynx to interrupt the flow of oxygen to their lungs. That meant he was in front of them, and he knew what he was doing. He wanted to go quickly; this wasn't about their sexuality it was about killing them *before* inflicting violence.

*He wanted a punching bag.* Stacy thought, *He wanted someone who wouldn't fight back.*

All three victims were found completely naked, in their most vulnerable state, but there were no signs of sexual violence on any of them. The killer had a single iota of decency, or that just wasn't what he was after. He wanted to attack these women for some other reason, take his anger out on them because of their looks or the power they felt walking alone at night. Since the first body was found, Stacy noticed that almost every women that she saw on the street was accompanied by a friend. Recently, someone started a social media campaign where you could call a number and they'd find a walking buddy if you needed one. Stacy wasn't sure that would deter this killer, he could be like a Ted Bundy kind of guy — someone who persuaded you to help them and attacked when you least expected it.

She couldn't imagine any of these women would follow a stranger into an alleyway. Maybe Gabrielle Unwin, but if her friends' statements were true, she wasn't looking for that kind of action that night. Audrey Wells lived and worked in Ballard, it was possible she was going through a familiar alleyway as a shortcut to get home, before being jumped by the killer. Did he wait in these places until he saw someone, or did he follow these women and attack when he knew they were alone? What Stacy found interesting was that, according to the news, there were no reports of screaming or loud noises from any of the crime scenes, but there were no traces of chloroform or other sedatives in the women's systems. She checked again in her notes for each of the women — they all came back with clear toxicity screens. None of these women had even a shot of tequila in them.

Three dead women, all with auburn hair and brown eyes. All of them between twenty and forty years old, and slightly above average height. Their physical description matched Stacy's, which was another reason she couldn't believe it was Henry. They had their problems, but he never indicated that he wanted to hurt her. He was rarely ever violently angry, more the type to sit and stew in his anger or give her the silent treatment for a few days. This was the work of someone who was truly violent, more on the level of Matt's inability to control himself after he blew up. A small part of Stacy thought it could also be her father. A man desperate to get to his daughter, someone who wasn't paying attention to who his victim was, just looking for her most prominent features, attacked her and then to cover his tracks made it look like the work of a psychopath who was afraid of sex. Her father also wouldn't sexually attack a woman who looked like her — he was cruel, but never that cruel.

*Stacy, maybe this isn't about you. Maybe you have to look beyond the scope of your world for a bit.*

This killer might not be related to her at all. Some random weak little man with a vendetta against auburn-haired women. Wasn't there another serial killer in the 70s who always attacked women with their hair in a ponytail? He had no connection to them, just waited for a victim to cross his path, always attacking at night.

*A killer all over the city, he doesn't even need a car. But he must be from Seattle because all of these locations are hidden from public view.*

At every scene, the person who found the body was a worker, someone who would only come out in the morning. Two of the women were found by restaurant dishwashers taking out the trash or going for a smoke break. That indicated that the killer knew the areas well enough to know where to dump the bodies so that it would take a long time for them to be found.

*Familiar with the city, a thing for redheads, and a guy who needs a woman to be a punching bag. All this work and I'm nowhere.*

Nowhere in her notes could Stacy find a piece of evidence that would point to another man. The only victim who had any *specific* evidence on her body was Lacey Daniels. She was the only woman who fought back, the only one to get a good scratch on him. Either that or the killer was rushing that night, he didn't clean off the woman's body as well as he had his previous victims. Did this man go out with the intention of killing a woman? Did he leave home with tools in a bag; an undetectable drug to sedate them, gloves that had no seams, a cloth to wipe their bodies with. And where were their clothes? For all the women, no one had found their clothing. What did he do with it? Did he burn them, or dump them into Lake Union?

Stacy combed through her notes and news reports for hours. She tried going over every piece of evidence at her disposal and there was nothing specific she could find to turn suspicion against Henry. The only connections between the three women were their looks, and the more Stacy turned over the case, the more she found she agreed with Matt. This could only have been done by a weak, evil man who hated women. Whether or not he had mommy issues seemed too specific to tell.

Stacy felt defeated. She spent an entire afternoon looking over the available facts of the case only to decide there was a very good reason she wasn't a detective. She could gather all the evidence from a dead body, analyze the cause and surrounding circumstances of their death, but she still didn't have any access to the interviews or security camera footage that the police had. Based on the evidence available to her, and the anecdotal stuff she researched online, the only way Stacy would be able to clear Henry's name would be to bait the killer. She was the perfect victim — the killer didn't seem to care about wealth or social status, he only cared about their physical features, and she matched his profile perfectly. She could go out for a walk, late at night, and taunt the real killer out of hiding. If he was smart that's what he'd be doing right now — hiding away until the media scrutiny died down and he could go back to taking his anger out on dead women. She could wander the city alone for the next few nights, switching up which neighborhoods she was in, dangling herself as bait for the killer. That would conclusively prove that the killer was still out there, and the police would have no choice but to release Henry.

*What's the point of that, if you don't live to see him free?*

Henry would be free, but Stacy would be dead. She wouldn't even know if her plan had worked, clearly this killer was strong enough to detain any woman, smart enough to wrestle her to her death if she attacked him. Stacy could wander around the city with a knife, but that would probably make her seem suspicious. If what Matt said was true — that the police would start looking at her as a potential accomplice, that would make the case worse for Henry and for herself. This plan was too risky, there were too many factors at play, and no guarantee that it would even work. She opened up the photos again to see if there was a footprint she'd missed — the police hadn't yet searched her home, she still had all of Henry's clothes. She could try to match the prints to some of his shoes.

Stacy printed out all the photos and ran to Henry's closet to grab his favorite boots. The ones he wore on hikes, but also wore to death on weekends, horrendously ugly and boring looking shoes that Stacy was always trying to get rid of. She brought them to the photos with a magnifying glass to see if maybe, *maybe,* there was the faint outline of a shoe print on the women. If the shape of a bruise matched the shape of the toe — but it was fruitless. She contorted the boot and the photos as much as she could, but couldn't make a match. That should be enough to exonerate Henry, right? His clean, mud-free boots didn't match up. It was a relief to her, but there was no one she could share that with. She emailed Matt the details, and received an automated response that just said he was too busy to check his emails right now. Figured, he was probably drowning in media requests at the moment.

She felt like a chicken running around with its head cut off. Every moment getting up from the computer to follow a new lead, but all this evidence collecting wasn't sticking. It was all pieces of a puzzle but there was no picture in what she was trying to create. What was the point of showing that there was no connection between Henry's shoes and the bruising on the bodies if she also couldn't come up with a new suspect? Why profile herself and give herself up as bait when there was no guarantee she'd be able to defend herself. The phone rang downstairs, shocking her out of this downward spiral.

"Hello?" Stacy said, her voice hoarse and shaky.

"Hey, it's me, I just wanted to see how you were doing?"

Lillian's voice was comforting, and reminded Stacy that there was at least one sane person in her life who would really hate it if she went out and tried to get murdered by a serial killer.

"Your call came at the perfect time. I was just about to start another downward spiral about how all of this is somehow my fault."

"What? How? Do you need me to come over? This time I'm bringing salad because at this rate—"

"No, no, your phone call is enough. And believe me, I don't need another junk food dinner. I've just been going over the reports I made for each of the victims, and I feel like there's something I'm missing, but I can't figure out what."

"Something you're missing?"

"Yes, some connection between these women beyond just their looks. Something that can point to someone, anyone else other than Henry. There's plenty of angry men in the world, right? Henry isn't even *angry*, really. He's just a boring doctor, it's not as if he's been muttering in his sleep about killing women all this time."

"Well, he hasn't been stressed about his mother and a wedding for all the time you've been dating. Some things can really... change a person," Lillian muttered.

"That's true... that's very true. I don't know, I feel like I'm all over the place, just trying to solve this case—"

"Stacy, stop it, that's not your job. Going over the autopsy reports was enough; you have got to let it go. Listen, if Henry is innocent, they're going to realize they don't have the burden of proof or whatever and can't take him to court. If there really was something you missed in the autopsy then yeah, pass it along to Matt, but you have to realize that he's the one in charge here. He's the one with the resources to follow up on leads and check on Henry's whereabouts and all that."

"That's another thing — why haven't they asked me anything? I've been sitting at home for the past three days going insane, but not a single cop has been by to search my house for evidence or ask me where my fiancé was on the nights of the murders. Don't you think that—"

"That Matt pulled some strings and is trying to give you some space?" Lillian interrupted, "Any other person would be up to their ears in cops and their stupid protocol right now, but thanks to the fact that the detective *genuinely* cares for you, you have a little breathing room. Obviously, you've decided to use this breathing room to suffocate yourself with guilt."

Stacy groaned and slumped down farther in her couch. She knew Lillian was right. She knew she was going to get nowhere with her 'investigation'. She knew all of this, but didn't feel like she could stop herself.

"You know, I almost want to go out there and—"

"Do not finish that sentence. If you do, I will call Matt right now and he'll have an armed guard outside your door before we even hang up. Don't do anything stupid, please?"

"I won't! I promise. I decided it wasn't worth it, I'll either get killed and martyr myself for a man or I won't find anything at all. I feel crazy, Lillian, if only you could see my office right now, it's a mess of notes that don't make sense and printouts of reports with highlighter circles all over them."

"You're driving yourself crazy. Take a bath?"

"I can't take another bath, I'll permanently prune. I can't clean, I've already cleaned."

"Do you have a book of crosswords? Or just a regular book? Drink yourself to sleep? Scroll through social media until your eyes bleed? I don't know, Stacy. I can come over and distract you if you want, I'll even do cartwheels in your living room if it means you'll stop this dummy investigation of yours."

"You don't have to." Stacy sighed. "I'll find something to do. I'll bake a cake or… I don't know. Something."

"Okay, well I called to see how you are and you're definitely going stir crazy and doing a lot worse than I expected, but I hope my sensible words and threats to destroy your living room with my cartwheels get you somewhere a little more stable." Stacy heard Lillian chuckle on the phone, trying to lighten the mood. "I hope you can get a little sleep tonight."

"Goodnight, Lil, I hope you never have to deal with my manic mind ever again."

They hung up and Stacy was back where she was that morning. Lying on her couch, staring at the ceiling, worrying about her fiancé and powerless to do anything about it.

# CHAPTER
# SIXTEEN
STACY

T he next few days were spent in a daze. Stacy moved from room to room, spending time in each like they were little vacations. She read every murder mystery in the house, until the stories became too familiar, and she had to stop. She made elaborate meals for herself, like homemade pasta from scratch filled with truffle ricotta and honey. She had enough time to try the recipe multiple times in a day and have a perfect version by dinnertime, donating all the less-perfect trials to Lillian. The time spent alone was starting to feel refreshing. She rearranged some of the furniture in a way she preferred, ate foods she never ate around Henry because he found them disgusting and managed to read up on some scholarly articles about the field of autopsy work.

Henry hated it when she did, he found those publications to be depressing, *"And besides,"* he'd always say, *"they're dead, how much more research into the study of dead people could there possibly be?"*

*A lot, actually,* Stacy thought, responding to the Henry in her mind, *new imaging techniques, new research into the formation of clot-*

*ting, it's not as if medical examiners stop trying to find the truth just because their subjects are dead.*

A few days without Henry had started to clear up Stacy's thoughts. She was reminded of all her hobbies and interests that she'd given up in order to give Henry the attention he needed. She wasn't upset about that; the past few months had been a struggle and she wanted to be there for him. He would have done the same thing for her, because that's what you did in a partnership sometimes. Made sacrifices for the other person.

Henry had to sacrifice his mother for Stacy, the fact that she kept most of her academic publications at work seemed pretty minimal in comparison. Henry's mother never liked Stacy, Amanda felt that Stacy was too independent and wouldn't be able to truly devote herself to Henry — at least, that's what she said out loud. Privately, Stacy knew that Amanda didn't want anyone to come between her and her son, and so any girlfriend of Henry's had to be weak enough to be manipulated by Amanda. Stacy remembered all the hospital gossip. It started with the head of pediatrics at St. Vincent's — she was this tall, leggy, modelesque doctor with long, reddish hair and classical angular features. Dr. Katrina Foy could have stepped out of an operating room into an issue of Vogue and looked perfectly comfortable in both. She was extremely intelligent, highly accomplished, and when rumors circled that she and Henry had started seeing each other the whole hospital buzzed with the kind of excitement felt when watching the red carpet special before an awards show. They were set to be a Seattle power couple, until one day St. Vincent's Medical Centre Administration received a short resignation letter, signed by Katrina Foy, with no explanation given as to why she wanted to resign. The hospital staff went into a whirlwind panic mode, trying to contact her or find out what happened. They didn't know if she received an offer from another hospital, or if she had just decided to move halfway across the world without telling anyone — her patients were left scrambling for appointments, and her staff didn't know who to report to anymore.

A week later, Katrina burst into the hospital. She demanded an immediate meeting with the, very shocked, board of directors, in order to figure out what had been going on.

Apparently, on the same day the hospital received her notice of resignation, Katrina had received a notice of termination from the hospital. She'd been away on holiday, so she didn't get the email until she came back, and as soon as she saw it in her inbox she stormed into the hospital for an explanation. The hospital said they didn't send the letter, she said she never sent one either, and the IT department couldn't trace where the emails had been sent from.

Gossip started to spread, and while some of it was *wild*, there was a little truth in there. Apparently, Amanda was angry that Katrina had refused to give up her work and become a stay-at-home girlfriend for Henry. When Katrina went away for a family holiday — one that *didn't* include Henry or Amanda, much to the matriarch's chagrin — Amanda decided to take matters into her own hands. Katrina and Henry were never seen together after that incident, and she ended up leaving Seattle and taking a job in California, in part because Amanda kept bothering her about breaking Henry's heart.

Stacy asked Henry about it when they started getting to know each other. She remembered teasing him about 'the one that got away,' one night while she was crying over Matt.

*"She wasn't the one. If she was the one, then…"* he'd trailed off.

Stacy never got a real answer from him. Henry always did a swift job of changing the subject when his mother's meddling was involved. Before they got together, he brushed it off as a single mother's care for her son.

*"She doesn't have anyone else to rely on,"* Henry had said, *"and I think she struggles with that a bit. She feels guilty that she couldn't be*

*the mom and the dad, and that causes her to be a bit of a helicopter parent."*

*"I get it,"* Stacy had responded, *"my mom was the same way. She was always so worried about my dad and giving me the best life in spite of him. Sometimes I think it really messed with the wiring in both our brains."*

Their shared mommy-trauma bonded them, even when Stacy was dating Matt — Matt didn't understand what it was like to have a mother like that. It had taken ages for Stacy to understand that Heather Lewis and Amanda Goldberg were very, *very*, different people.

Amanda was a very demanding woman. She came from old money — just enough that she grew up getting everything she wanted, and a little inherited psychological trauma to boot. Stacy never found out what happened to Henry's father, he left when Henry was a kid and Amanda raised him herself.

That part was relatable, Stacy's mom was the same, she raised Stacy mostly on her own while running from Oliver — but Amanda wasn't running away from anyone. She was obsessed with her son, and convinced she was the only person who could know what was best for him. She was determined to eliminate any woman who got in her way — that's why she wanted Katrina out of her job, so that Katrina didn't have the power to say no to her anymore.

She and Stacy never got along; Stacy was too stubborn for Amanda's meddling. Unfortunately, Stacy was very used to dealing with meddling family members thanks to Oliver and Maeve, so she knew how to deflect their demands very well. Amanda never liked that, she needed control over every person in her and her son's life, so she just openly hated Stacy instead. Amanda criticized Stacy at every opportunity and from every angle. She attacked Stacy's father and his addiction problems, her 'weak' mother who could never shake him for good, and Stacy's 'morbid' job. Amanda always managed to find some new article or podcast episode talking about the rate of necrophilia in coroner's offices around the country, causing Stacy's blood to boil over at many weekly dinners.

Henry was useless in terms of defending her. Rather than say anything to his mother, he just stopped bringing Stacy around, stopped mentioning either woman to the other. Often when he came back from visiting his mother he'd be in an angry, resentful mood; sometimes he'd even ghost Stacy for days on end, but at no point would he ever admit that his mother was overbearing or wrong. That was when Stacy started to feel distant from Henry. She still loved him, still felt he was the steady force she needed in her life, but some of the intimacy was gone from their relationship. Stacy didn't feel like Henry would defend her against anyone. After all, if he couldn't stand up to his mother, then how could he stand up to someone else? If Oliver appeared on their doorstep, would Henry retreat and avoid dealing with him too?

For months it had felt like Stacy was in a relationship with only half a man. Her Henry came home and made beautiful dinners, listened to her talk about work, encouraged her to apply for a promotion, and cared for her as she dealt with the aftermath of Oliver's attack. The other Henry left every Sunday morning to have brunch with his mother, and came back sullen and resentful. If Stacy texted asking when he'd be home, she'd receive a call full of vitriol, with the other Henry demanding she calm down and allow him some time to be with his mother. Stacy thought she might be doing something wrong, that maybe she needed to try more with Amanda, after all, she loved Henry and it hurt her to know she was causing him pain. Both Henrys wanted his Amanda and Stacy to get along, her Henry knew it was impossible because of Amanda's demanding nature; other Henry claimed it was impossible because Stacy was getting in her own way. It was the beginning of the downward spiral of their relationship. Stacy never felt she could get close to Henry, and Henry kept her an arm's length away. She supposed this was Henry's way of protecting her, knowing that his mother was capable of anything as long as she got her way at the end of it.

---

*Being alone is going to drive me crazy.* Stacy thought. She was back to sitting on her couch, mindlessly flipping through a magazine Lillian had dropped off, letting her mind wander. It wandered back to Amanda, the theme of her most recent thoughts. She was never able to confirm if the rumors about Dr. Foy had been true, and Henry always brushed them off as petty hospital gossip. He asked his mom, she said it was nothing, and Henry accepted that answer, but always bristled at the subject. Stacy wondered if there was more to it.

"Were you ever rebellious?" Stacy once asked.

It was an early date, the two were flirting furiously and playing footsies under the table of the restaurant, both politely eager to take each other home.

"Rebellious?" Henry asked. "What, you mean like hot-wiring cars and cutting class?"

"No, I mean… did you ever try to run away, get out from under your mother's watchful eye, that sort of thing."

Henry's face clouded over as he stared into his drink. "No, no I'm not like that, I like my mom. We only have each other, I wouldn't do something to hurt her."

Stacy laughed it off. "You can be rebellious and still like your mom. I loved my mother, and I still got a tattoo as soon as I turned eighteen, even though she found them disgusting."

"Why would you do that?" Henry replied. "Hurt her like that, just flippantly go against what she wanted for you?"

Stacy's smile faded from her face. "It didn't hurt her; it was just a tattoo. My mom got over it, she—"

"But you hurt her, you realize that, right? You hurt her feelings, you were careless and callous with her desires. She wanted what was best for you, probably realized that a million tattoos would prevent you from getting a good job and you just sort of... threw that in her face."

Henry was making himself angry talking about it. Stacy didn't see why; it was just a flirty question. The kind you ask on a first date and joke about for years later, but it struck a nerve. This was long before Stacy ever met Amanda, and she hadn't experienced the kind of guilt she passed on to her son.

"I'm sorry, I—I never saw it that way. My mom and I talked about it; she was okay. She got a matching one a few weeks later actually, I found it so embarrassing."

Their dinner was quiet and awkward after that. It was a pattern Stacy came to get used to, and find some comfort in eventually. Henry went to his mother's house, he got sullen and quiet, and then he came around with a romantic gesture after a few days. In those few days, Stacy could be alone with her thoughts.

---

EVERY DAY, Stacy woke up and hoped to get an email or phone call from someone regarding Henry's jail time. She waited for word from the lawyers, or even from Matt himself about how the case was progressing. Any time she asked, she received the same answer — "We can't disclose anything further at this time, but the case is progressing well. Stay positive!"

What was she staying positive for? Days without Henry in the recesses of her mind had Stacy rethinking her entire relationship. Why was his mother able to come between them so easily? Why was it that Stacy felt it was her fault that—

*Well, it kind of is your fault, Stacy.*

The threat that Amanda made on the night Henry proposed marriage. Stacy hadn't believed it at the time; she'd thought his mother was exaggerating. She'd thought Amanda would be content having ruined the actual proposal and then she'd retreat into the background of Stacy's life again. She could deal with that — a mean mother-in-law was practically a cliché. Thinking about it now, Stacy was reminded of her idea to offer up herself as bait to the real serial killer — what was the point, if you didn't live to see the result? Amanda threatened to kill herself if Henry went through with the engagement, but why go through with it if you couldn't reunite with your son?

Apparently, that didn't matter, what mattered was the guilt and shame Henry would feel for the rest of his life, and how that would affect their relationship. It was true that Amanda's presence had been felt more in death than in life. Anything Stacy said, any time she disagreed with Henry, the spirit of his mother hovered nearby as if to point out how wrong Stacy was for Henry. Stacy sometimes wondered how long it would take before the specter of Amanda would dissipate from their lives. Would she still be there as Stacy was giving birth, or sending her daughter off to college? Or would Henry get sick of her by then?

Henry's mind worked in a mysterious way. Stacy thought about it, and she truly never knew what he was thinking. That's why their argument about the prenup was such a surprise — at no time had Henry ever mentioned that he was concerned about their shared finances. He never mentioned anything about Stacy's contribution to their shared household, and never cared that she was adamant about keeping her personal finances separate. He knew why, she'd told him when they moved in together, that after the way her father treated her mother, and how he stalked Stacy over her inheritance, she didn't trust having her finances split with someone else. It was too easy to be taken advantage of, when someone else could control your access to money. Henry knew, he agreed, but did he harbor and idea that he could change Stacy's mind?

*He changed your mind about Matt, I bet that made him think he could change your mind about anything.*

Henry was Stacy's at-work confidante when she was dating

Matt. At the time, Henry was this platonic entity — a good listener who didn't want to sleep with Stacy. In fact, she thought he might be gay when they first met. Whenever she and Matt got into a fight she would go to Henry. They'd sit and have a coffee and Henry would listen as Stacy talked about all the ways Matt reminded her of her father, or how she wasn't sure it was ethical to date a police officer if she wanted to work at the city coroner's office someday.

Henry was gently encouraging, and he seemed to give good advice. He was the one who encouraged her to stick up for herself, to follow her instincts when she saw Matt's violent side rear its ugly head. It didn't feel strange at the time, to have your work-husband give you advice. A friend who also had a fucked-up parent and could understand what it was like to navigate that kind of relationship.

But what if Henry just said all that to build a bridge between them, and destroy Stacy's relationship with Matt?

It was a nugget of an idea. A seed planted months ago, when she and Matt were breaking up. Stacy was getting her things from Matt's apartment, and she brought Henry with her to protect her. Matt was very respectful, he'd put all her things into a box, and left a small note for Stacy.

"I don't know if I want to read it," she said, handing the note to Henry.

Henry took one glance, before guffawing and tearing up the note.

"What did it say?" Stacy asked.

"Ridiculous, he was practically blaming you for your father's imprisonment, basically, it's not worth reading it'll only make you feel guilty."

His voice was dripping with disdain for Matt, Henry immediately turned on his heel and walked out the door. "I'm gonna keep an eye out on the hallway, make sure he doesn't show up unannounced. Let me know when you're through."

Stacy nodded. Henry left and she went over to the trash, staring at the pieces of paper in the trash. All she saw was a heart, and 'sorr—" written in Matt's signature chicken scratch. If Matt had been truly apologetic back then, Stacy probably wouldn't have broken up with him. If that note had an apology or an explanation, then maybe Stacy wouldn't have left the apartment with Henry. Maybe they wouldn't have gone for a drink, and maybe Henry wouldn't have been able to charm Stacy into staying with him that night.

All those maybes swirled around in Stacy's head. Maybe if she hadn't entertained Henry's attention during her and Matt's relationship, she'd have been able to repair it. Maybe if she had tried a little harder with Amanda, she wouldn't have committed suicide when her son got engaged. Maybe if she had talked to Dr. Foy, Stacy would never have gotten together with Henry. Maybe if Stacy had just agreed to the prenup, Henry would be here arguing with her about wedding flowers. There were too many factors to consider, too many roads untraveled, too many ways for her anxious mind to spend its time. Stacy felt like she was drowning in her guilt and had no power to save herself. All she could do was wait, but the longer she waited, the less sure she was about anything in her life.

# CHAPTER
# SEVENTEEN
STACY

"Go away! No one's home!" Stacy yelled from the couch. She had officially spent too much time alone with her thoughts. Between trying to solve the serial killer case from her office and re-evaluating her entire relationship with Henry, Stacy had given herself a massive headache. She was lying on the couch with an ice pack over her forehead and a tea on the counter, trying to count sheep and force herself to sleep.

"Stacy, it's me," a familiar voice called through the door.

Stacy had to pinch herself to make sure she wasn't hallucinating. "M-Matt?" she stammered. "What are you — what time is it?"

"Um, it's about 8 o'clock. There's no one else out here, if that's what you're worried about. They're all down by the station, they've given up trying to get a glimpse of you."

Stacy stared at the ceiling for a minute weighing her options. If Matt came in, then maybe she could persuade him to drop the charges against Henry. Maybe she could ask what was really on that note he left her.

"How do I know you don't have a camera crew hiding behind you?" she asked, still lying on the couch.

A moment later she felt her phone vibrate from somewhere in

the couch cushions. It was a selfie from Matt, showing that he was alone on her street. There was no one behind him on the stoop or in her driveway.

"I'm happy to prove that I'm not wearing a wire either," he said, "this is just a courtesy call. You haven't been to work in a few days, and this is a stressful time. Lillian called to tell me you were going insane, so I figured I should check on you. It's the least I could do... given the circumstances."

Stacy stared at the photo on her phone. Matt's intense brown eyes and his square, dimpled jaw stared back at her. He looked like he was hoping that she would find it in her heart to just open the door. He still had his looks, he still had that tortured puppy dog look in his eye, he still looked like he could protect her from the world beyond her little stoop. She knew he'd go away eventually. In the past few days, Matt had texted her to make sure she was doing okay, but Stacy ignored him, this was obviously his last resort. She wanted to know what he had to say for himself, and she wanted some company. Her self-imposed house arrest really was driving her off the deep end, and it would be nice to feel grounded in reality for a moment.

"Fine," she said, "you can come in for a few minutes. But just because I need to talk to another human being before I go insane."

"Uh...okay," Matt said. "A win's a win I guess." He chuckled as he swept past Stacy into her room.

Matt was holding a pint of ice cream and a cheap grocery store bouquet. He awkwardly held both out to Stacy, who took them with her into the kitchen. She hated to admit it, but these were her favorite kind of flowers. Because they had to appeal to as many people as possible, they were usually the brightest available, and Stacy loved that they would always be a surprise. You couldn't go in and curate what was going to be in the bouquet. Sure, there were the grocery store staples — roses, daisies, and carnations — but it wasn't like a carefully selected, overly thought-out florist bouquet. These were spontaneous, they said, "I was just thinking of you, at the most unexpected time." It was a concept she could not explain to Henry, who didn't grow up with an appreciation for spontaneity.

"You loved these, I picked the one that had a lily in it, but the lily hasn't bloomed yet so you can't see it," Matt stammered; he was obviously uncomfortable.

It made sense, the only time they had spent alone had been in Stacy's office or examination room. Stacy also felt a little weird. What would Henry think, knowing that Matt was standing in his house, sitting on his couch, while Henry was rotting in a jail cell.

*It's your house too, remember? And this is your couch, you're the one who paid for it!* Stacy had to remind herself. She was finding that the guilt over Henry's arrest had made her start to forget herself.

"How are you holding up?" Matt asked, perching himself on the kitchen counter. It was a familiar stance, and it made Stacy want to fall into his arms and be wrapped up by him, smelling his cologne and—

"Stacy?" Matt asked. "Earth to Stacy?"

Stacy shook her head. She stopped paying attention and the vase was overflowing with water. She was off in another land, one where she could be intoxicated by Matt and give in to her desires.

"Sorry, I'm okay. I feel a little out of it, to be honest."

"How come?"

"I just feel like I don't know what's going on. I was angry at first, then I was convinced you had made a mistake, *then* I was convinced that you were just after Henry because of some petty revenge, but Lillian put me off that idea. Then I tried to see if there was something you were missing in the evidence, but I realized I'd never have as much context as you do *and* I couldn't find anything to contradict Henry as a suspect, and then I spent most of yesterday re-evaluating my relationship."

"Sounds like you've spent too much time alone," he said, helping himself to a scoop of ice cream.

Stacy sighed and stood next to Matt.

"You know I'd never do that, right? Arrest Henry as revenge. I don't like the guy, but I wouldn't do anything to hurt you."

"Arresting him doesn't hurt me," Stacy muttered.

Matt just laughed. "You just described the week-long spiral downwards you had into your own psyche, and now you're going to tell me arresting your fiancé doesn't hurt you? Try again, Stace. I know you; I know you want a stable life with a guy who can be there for you and doesn't have to hide half his life from you. Arresting Henry sets your world off balance, and that hurts you very deeply. Trust me, I know. I've done it before, remember?"

Stacy opened her mouth to say something, but Matt quieted her by putting his finger over her lips.

"Stacy, it happened with your dad, and it broke us up. You don't have to be strong right now, I'm admitting guilt, okay?"

Stacy nodded and Matt dropped his hand, wiping it on his jeans as if to wipe away the moment. There was something between them, a casual intimacy that was missing in Stacy's relationship with Henry. Even though she felt weird about Matt being in her house, it still felt comfortable to sit and share a pint of ice cream with him.

"So, did you find anything new when you reviewed your notes?" Matt asked.

Stacy shook her head. "Nope, everything was just as I left it. Came up with a couple of good conspiracy theories though, if you want to listen to them." She laughed. "Seriously though, the only evidence that conclusively points to Henry is the DNA found on Lacey Daniels, and I just can't believe there wasn't a moment between the initial sweep of the crime scene and my exam where the body could have—"

"Why do you think this?" Matt asked, his defensiveness

starting to creep up in his voice. "Who would have it out for Henry, and why would they go to all this trouble?"

"I don't know. I don't think they're framing him for any reason other than convenience — didn't you always say that most crimes happen because of opportunity, not planning? I think maybe the killer had the opportunity to plant some evidence, so they did."

Matt furrowed his brow. "Do you think Henry is going to blame you for letting him get arrested? Because it's not your fault, you know. You had nothing to do with it, you couldn't do anything except your job, and your job is to observe and analyze a major piece of evidence — the body of a woman who was brutally murdered, by a man who did not care about her."

"I don't think he's going to blame me," Stacy said, ignoring the rolling ball of guilt in the pit of her stomach, "he wouldn't do that, but I just can't believe he's a killer. He's a mild mannered, boring guy; that's what makes him such a good emergency surgeon — he's able to keep a level head under pressure. He's not some angry killer guy."

"You never know what might set someone off. But, whatever, maybe you can tell me something I haven't heard yet. Maybe there is a hole in this case that I'm skipping over, why don't you tell me what you found," Matt said, putting his notebook on the table and leaning in to Stacy.

She felt dizzy being this close to Matt. It dredged up long-dormant desires to feel his body on hers, his lips on hers, her fingers running through his hair.

"Well," she said, clearing her throat, "for starters, Henry isn't familiar enough with some of these neighborhoods to know where to dump the bodies. Each was found by a worker who had to check something in the morning, right? A dishwasher, for example, or someone taking out the trash. That means, in every case, the killer found an alleyway that was trafficked enough that the bodies weren't lying there forever, but not so frequently that it would be found right away. Henry isn't familiar enough with Ballard or the Port, he hates going there. If he killed these women, he'd be dragging them around trying to find someplace suitable to dump them."

Matt scribbled down — *unfamiliar with locales.* "Okay, anything else?"

"The bruising was done by someone who was very violent, someone without control. Henry has the opposite problem, he has too much control. Even when his mom died and he went a little off the rails... he doesn't even go to the gym, Matt, he isn't about to take up boxing on a naked dead girl."

Matt nodded, gesturing for Stacy to continue.

"And finally, there's no reason these three killers are connected, except for their looks. That's weak... that's pretty weak, isn't it? Their profiles, like, so what if their profiles match that's true about so many people in this city, and—" Stacy suddenly broke down in sobs.

Now that she was saying all this out loud it seemed even weaker than when she was creating her conspiracy notes in her office. *Unfamiliar with the area, what kind of explanation is that?*

"Stacy, can I ask you one question, if you can... if you're willing to answer," Matt asked, handing her a napkin so Stacy could dab her eyes.

She nodded.

Matt continued, "Can you tell me if you were with Henry on any of these nights?"

"Huh?"

"Were you with Henry, or did you know where he was, on any of the nights where Gabrielle Unwin, Audrey Wells, or Lacey Daniels died?"

Stacy thought about it. A chill ran down her spine and her stomach twisted in on itself. She didn't want to say the truth, which was that she didn't know. She could hardly remember the night Lacey Daniels was killed, but she didn't want to think about what those scratches could have been…

"Stacy?" Matt asked, gently stroking her arm. "I know it can be hard, but if you can tell me."

"He was home, I think. One of the nights… when Lacey Daniels… I don't know; we had a huge fight that day, I was out all night and I hardly remember getting home so I'm probably not the most reliable um… witness." Stacy stumbled through her statement.

Matt only nodded and put away his notebook.

"I have nothing," Stacy said, tears rolling down her face. "I can't help him right now, and I feel so guilty."

"Why do you feel guilty?"

"I'm the reason his mom killed herself, for starters. I'm the reason he's in jail right now — "

"Okay, I'm going to stop you right there. You're not the reason he's in jail, if anything you're the one thing that kept him out of jail longer. Second of all, you're not the reason his mother committed suicide. She was an unhealthy, unstable woman. Just the same way that it's not your fault Oliver tried to attack you, or that he's an addict. If Henry can't see that… well he's in for a rude awakening. It's impossible to control the world around you, Stace, you can't control his mom, your dad, his actions, or the serial killer stalking the city. All you can do is be careful, and work through your own grief."

*Why is this the healthiest piece of advice I've heard in days, and why is it coming from the mouth of my ex-boyfriend?*

"When did you get so wise?" Stacy sniffled.

"When it was *strongly suggested* I take some time to examine my extreme reaction to your father's attack. I went to therapy because it was required, and now I just go because it's good to talk to someone about all the fucked-up stuff that goes on at work, and how often it's gotten in the way of my personal life."

Stacy suddenly realized that she was snuggling into Matt's

arms, her head in the crook of his neck, and his arm gently stroking hers. It felt so natural that she didn't even know when she'd done it. He was saying all the right things, everything Stacy wished he said when they were together. She had begged him to go to therapy and Matt refused, seeing it as a sign of weakness. Nowadays she found herself saying the same thing to Henry, who dismissed the suggestion because he didn't like strangers knowing his 'secrets'.

"Matt, can I ask you something?" The memory of clearing out her things from Matt's apartment came back to her. She even dreamed about it the night before, turning the memory over in her mind. "When we broke up, and I came over to pick up my stuff, you left me a note."

"You didn't read it. I saw the scraps in the trash."

"What did it say?" Stacy asked, looking up at him.

Matt looked back deep into Stacy's eyes. Her worries suddenly melted away; she couldn't remember why Henry was the 'better' choice.

"It doesn't really matter, does it? You did what you thought was best for you at the time."

Their heads came together, Stacy felt as though there was a thread tied to their hearts pulling them closer together. She could smell the coffee on his breath as she closed her eyes —

"I have to go," Matt blurted out, standing up and catching Stacy as she fell into his chair, "It's getting late, and I have to go back to the station to follow up on some things. Plus, you need to make dinner and I'm sure there's other stuff you need to do. Henry might call, and you'll want to talk to him, since you're engaged to be married and all."

Matt hurried to the front room, apparently desperate to leave now.

Stacy watched Matt go from her front window. As he drove into the night, she thought about what almost happened. She wanted to talk to Lillian, but her calls went straight to voicemail.

Stacy needed to get out of her own head, because for a second there she really thought that maybe...

It couldn't be. Matt missed her because his ego was bruised. Henry was right for her because he was a stable man. Stacy needed to stop flipping between these men in her life and start getting herself back on track. She sniffed an armpit and recoiled — did she really think she was going to seduce Matt smelling like that? Stacy needed a hot shower and a good, healthy meal. Tomorrow she was determined to go for a walk, no matter how paranoid she felt about the news media outside her door. She was starting to go insane in here, and she couldn't bear another day of trying to figure out how to clear Henry's name.

*"Were you with Henry, or do you know where he was, on any of the nights where Gabrielle Unwin, Audrey Wells, or Lacey Daniels died?"*

Matt's voice echoed in her ear. Stacy didn't want to admit the truth — she didn't know where Henry had gone. In fact, throughout their relationship when they argued Henry often disappeared for a few hours. He drove around to clear his head, or went for walks late into the night. He was a man, they could do that sort of thing and not worry about serial killers or psychopaths.

*Nonsense, it's all nonsense.*

# CHAPTER
# EIGHTEEN
STACY

Stacy had a fitful night of sleep after Matt left. It could have been the fact that she finished that pint of ice cream by herself and washed it down with whiskey, or it could be that Matt left her with less confidence that Henry was innocent. She wracked her brain trying to remember where he was, tracking his every movement. She even went into his device history, to see if his phone would give away his location, for better or for worse. If she could at least find Henry an alibi, maybe it would help alleviate the guilt she was feeling after last night. Having Matt in their home felt strange, leaning on him for comfort felt like a betrayal.

Then again, there was something powerful about having Matt over. He would truly do nothing to hurt her, and that added to his sexiness. Maybe she was just starved for affection or something, after all it had been a few days since Henry got arrested, and they didn't have a very active sex life before that. Matt remembered her strange love of cheap bouquets, he was sheepish the whole time he was here, nervous. When Stacy went over the visit in her mind, she felt a current of excitement run through her body. What if Matt had stayed, and they'd moved their discussion onto the couch? What if he didn't pull away when she leaned into his body? What if she could feel Matt's touch on the back of her neck, traveling down her back to land on her ass once again. He'd always loved her ass, always playfully complimented, or smacked it as Stacy walked past him. What if he had stayed, would he wake up in her bed, appreciating her body once again?

It was enough to make Stacy blush. Time away from Henry allowed her time to re-evaluate her relationship. Henry's mother was a suffocating presence when she was alive, and she was just as suffocating now that she was dead. Living in this house alone felt like breathing fresh air for the first time, and it made Stacy nervous. What was going on in her mind when Henry was around, that living without him felt like a vacation? She didn't have to load the dishwasher his way, she could have dinner whenever she wanted, wander around the house completely naked if she pleased — all the things that would piss Henry off.

*I doubt I'm the only one. Most people go a little crazy when their partners aren't around.*

Her thoughts drifted back to the beginning of her courtship with Henry. How he never wasted an opportunity to throw Matt under the bus, even making him seem more violent than he actually was. For months Stacy felt like Henry was the safer option, and in a week that idea completely crumbled. She wanted to talk to someone, but lately it felt as though her mind changed every time she did. Everyone in her life was divided — they were either Team Henry or Team Matt, and there was absolutely zero crossover. Lillian would always defend Matt and cast doubt on Henry; Henry would obviously never admit Matt had a single decent quality; that left Stacy confused and alone.

Someone kept calling Stacy, enough times to get through her phone's 'mute' setting. That could only be one person.

"Maeve, I think I've heard from you more often this past week than this past year."

"How did you know it was me? Well, I guess you have caller ID. Of course, I'd call you more often, you're going through a crisis. It's all I wanted when Daddy was going through his arrest, and even though you never called me then, I figured I'd extend the olive branch and call you now. Do you have any updates?"

Typical of Maeve to somehow turn Stacy's pain into a jab.

"Thanks, Maeve. And no, I don't have any updates. I talked to Matt yesterday and he—"

"You *talked* to Matt *Ensor?* Jesus, Stacy, why? Why would you do such a thing?"

"He asked how I was holding up, and actually listened to my answer, might I add. He was over here just making sure I didn't go completely stir crazy and I talked to him about the case a little bit."

"Stacy, why? Don't you see, he's going to use whatever you say *against* Henry! If you tell Matt anything, he'll be able to turn it into evidence, you have to be completely mum if you see him, you know? Anything you say can *and will* be used against you, didn't you know that?"

"Of course, I know, Maeve, he was asking how *I* was holding up and I told him, again, that I don't think Henry is the killer."

"Did he ask you any questions?"

"Only asked if I could remember where Henry was those nights—"

"You see!" Maeve screeched. "That's how it starts, he's going to make sure Henry doesn't have an alibi by poking holes in whatever you tell him. Lemme guess, he kept asking if you were 'sure' about where Henry was, right? That's just a trick they use to make you second-guess your own memory. That way their lawyers can gaslight you into thinking you were lying about everything."

Maeve was exhausting. She kept droning on about some tv crime drama and the tactics police and lawyers use to entrap innocent victims. Stacy wasn't paying attention; she was distracted by the flowers that Matt brought over. The lily was starting to open up, soon it would smell like lilies in the living room.

"Stacy? Are you even listening to me? What, did Matt cast a spell on you last night that you don't listen to reason? Was he at your house, by the way? Because he's not allowed to do that, just come, and go as he pleases. For starters, that's the house you share with Henry, Matt should feel afraid to go there, he should feel embarrassed to even set foot on that block."

"He did seem uncomfortable when he was in here last night."

"Last night! Did he think this was a date?"

"I highly doubt that, Maeve," Stacy muttered, staring at the flowers.

It would have been a nice date, something cozy just as Stacy liked it. A small romantic gesture, the opportunity to get close...

"It's obvious he's trying to entrap you, Stacy. He's probably digging for some way to plant more evidence on Henry. You didn't tell him anything, did you?"

"We talked through some of my notes. I've been going over my old reports to see if there's anything I missed."

"And?"

"He wrote some stuff in his notebook, but for the most part it looks like it was all stuff the police have gone over already. Either that or it just didn't hold enough water."

"Did Matt say that, or did you come to that conclusion on your own? Honestly, Stacy, you are so gullible sometimes, you'd be the first fish to catch plastic bait, you know that? He's dangling his charming personality in front of you in order to plant *just enough* doubt in Henry that you won't be able to testify in his defense! Everything you say to him, he'll take that as an opportunity to solidify his case, you're practically sending Henry to jail yourself. Is that what you want?"

"No, of course not, I—"

"Well, then why do you keep talking to that gorilla? This is exactly what happened with Daddy, you know? You let Matt get in your ear and he slowly changed your mind and made you see the absolute worst in our family before anyone was able to talk to you. He manipulates the narrative and before you know it, you're parroting everything he says. Soon you're going to be siding with him, looking for evidence to help prove his case."

"Maeve, I really don't have it in me to talk about our dad right now. I see what you're saying and... I guess you're right. I probably shouldn't have talked to Matt, and I didn't really answer any of his questions. It seemed like everything I said he already knew."

"Of course, he isn't lazy. He doctored the whole case, he's probably just excited that he managed to trick you."

"Can you not say stuff like that? It isn't even because of Matt, but you're really making me sound like I'm bad at my job. I examined those bodies thoroughly, I never found anything that pointed to Henry except for with the final body. That wasn't because Matt managed to scrub the bodies clean — I can tell when someone does that too."

"Fine, I'm sorry." Maeve took a deep breath. "I get a little worked up when it comes to Ensor, you know that. He turned you against our family, and now it seems he's going to turn you against Henry. You should really examine why you were so ready to turn against your poor innocent fiancé. He's only been gone for a few days and already you're entertaining your ex-boyfriend, if I didn't know any better, I'd say you were close to believing the slanderous lies against Henry. Henry is a good guy, and his mother was an eccentric. We know all this best, we also grew up with crazy mothers in our lives, we're just lucky to have had a good father to guide us through. Henry needs you to be his guide, not his executioner. He's going through a horrible time in his life — his mother is dead, and now his fiancée thinks he's a serial killer. Have you even tried talking to him? If I were in your position, I would be down at the station every day demanding to see my fiancé. There must be some kind of privilege you have, isn't there? Well, I bet Ensor has pulled some string to make sure you can't see Henry. If you went down there, they'd lead you to his desk and leave you two alone and let him seduce you, what does the state care anyway? They have their scapegoat; they have the perp they're going to trot out in front of the media…"

"Maeve, I have to cut you off, you're going off the deep end," Stacy muttered an interruption. She knew where Maeve was going and didn't have the patience for it. "I want to help Henry, you know. I did all I could but there's only so much I can do from my side. The police have evidence and notes that I don't have access to. All I have is three dead bodies and the weak theories—"

"Weak? Why are you downplaying your abilities like that, Stacy? You are such a smart woman, I'm sure you can find a way to help Henry out, if that's really what you want to do."

"It is."

"Then you need to gather evidence or something. You need to find an alibi for Henry, even if it's not exactly *truthful* you could at least say something that will give him time, or get him released. Stacy, you're a medical examiner or a coroner or whatever, don't you have access to criminal files through work? You can look into his file and delete a couple of things—"

"Maeve, I'm not going to do anything illegal—"

"Well, you have to do something, Stacy!" Maeve screamed. "You have to think of something because I'm a little busy with our father who you abandoned, so I can't solve all your problems as well as my own. Figure it out!"

Stacy jumped as Maeve hung up the phone with a flourish. She must have been at work, that's the only way she could have made so much noise. She pictured her sister, huffing and puffing at the nurse's station, her eyes darting around as the other nurses turned to stare at her. Maeve was dramatic, they were probably used to scenes like that. It made Stacy exhausted. She wanted to call Lillian, but knew that her friend was setting up an exhibit of her photographs today, and Stacy didn't want to bring down the mood.

She wished she could get an update, but her calls to Henry's lawyers went unanswered. *This must be a tactic of his* she thought, *a new level of silent treatment.* If he'd known what she'd been going through... he'd probably still be upset. Stacy had been flip flopping between being convinced of Henry's guilt and then of Henry's innocence. She'd re-evaluated their relationship and almost cheated on him with her ex-boyfriend if only in her head. Every day brought a new level of rock bottom she didn't know was there. Maeve was right about one thing, she couldn't solve Stacy's problems, Stacy had to figure it out. She had to decide if Henry was guilty or innocent, and find a way to help him if he wasn't.

# CHAPTER
# NINETEEN
STACY

It was a clear night, rare for Seattle this time of year. Stacy looked up and she could see the moon and stars peeking through the rose bush above her. Her heart was racing, but she didn't know why. She wasn't being chased and the night was bright enough that she could see all around her. Still, something ominous was hanging in the air, causing the hairs on Stacy's arm to stand on their ends. The city was quieter than usual, she could hear the occasional car, but other than that it was just animal sounds and the smell of a cool night air.

Suddenly, Stacy heard someone behind her. Their footsteps were getting faster as they headed toward her. She didn't know who they belonged to, but she knew she had to run. She picked up the pace, tried to find a path, but when she looked down there was only grass. No matter, she just had to start running. Her breath quickened along with her heartbeat as Stacy tried to run through the rosebush maze, but she kept getting tangled in the brambles. The thorns were scratching at her face, she could taste blood where a thorn tore her lips.

"Stacy! We just want to talk to you!" the voice called out to her. It felt familiar but Stacy couldn't place it. "Stop running, it'll only be worse if you run!"

She couldn't stop. The voice wasn't friendly, she didn't know what kind of trap the voice had in store for her. A phone rang in the bushes. She reached out and grabbed it while running, the caller ID said it was Henry, so she answered.

"Henry" Stacy said, "I'm running!"

"You better run; they won't care what you say if they catch you. You'll be locked up beside me, we'll both be in trouble."

"Henry, I think I'm already in trouble. I can't catch my breath I—"

"This is why I tell you to work out, Stacy. You're on your own, there's nothing I can do for you now. They found the girl; they won't stop until they get you."

"Which girl? Who are you talking about? Henry! Henry!"

He was gone, the phone in Stacy's hand melted away, like it didn't exist. Was it evidence? She didn't know, she shook the residue off her hands and kept running. Henry was right, she really ought to work out more, Stacy's legs were starting to seize up. Behind her she could hear a team of search dogs barking in the night, sniffing out her trail. She could try to outsmart them, but there were no trees. She was running through a labyrinth of thorned vines, vines that seemed to climb up onto brick walls before disappearing in the dark. Where was she? Was Stacy still in Seattle?

"Stacy, we will not make this offer again. Turn yourself in now and we can work out a deal! There's no deal if you keep running away from us. We only want to talk to you; we want to ask you a few questions," the voice boomed again.

"If all you want to do is ask me a few questions, why do we have to work out a deal?" Stacy yelled back to the voice.

"We only want to talk to you, Stacy," it said, ignoring her question. "We only want to ask you a few questions."

Stacy couldn't. She knew she'd never get a fair trial. She kept running until finally she could see the end of the tunnel. The grass and thorns changed to brick and concrete, and something else she couldn't quite put her finger on. She sped up, using the last little bit of energy she had, and spat out of the grassy maze. She landed on the pavement with a thud, splashing into a sticky puddle. Slowly, Stacy realized she was lying in a puddle of blood. It was still warm; the body must be close by. She looked up to see herself lying in an alleyway, covered in bruises. There were no open wounds, Stacy couldn't see where the blood was coming from, but it was slowly leaking from her body. She wanted to scream and cradle her dead doppelgänger, but there wasn't any time. Her body felt like lead, but she knew she had to pick herself up and keep going. There was blood all over her now, they'd never believe it wasn't her.

"Stacy, c'mon, don't do anything stupid," the voice called out again.

She started to recognize it as a blend of all the men in her life. Her father, Henry, Matt, even his partner, Andy. Sometimes they harmonized, sometimes one voice came to the fore, it was always intimidating to hear. Stacy looked down and realized she was covered in her own blood — but how could she get in trouble for being covered in her own blood? Obviously, she hadn't killed herself, she was still running down the alley. This must have been a different body, this must be —

Stacy looked back but the body was gone, an empty metal gurney sat in its place illuminated by a bright LED bulb. She crawled back on her hands and knees desperate to get away. The alley was lined with cameras, they were all slowly turning to focus on her now. Soon it wouldn't matter if she could run from the voice chasing her, soon they'd have everything they needed. She wasn't a killer, but she was covered in blood and there was a body missing, anyone could put two and two together.

"Where is she?" It was Audrey Wells' mother, she was leaning out of the window, crying out for her daughter. "You know where she is, you know what they did, why won't you admit it, you weak woman, why won't you admit what you've done!" Her voice sounded hoarse, like she had been screaming for days.

"Audrey's dead! You held a funeral for her! This isn't Audrey, this is me! This is my blood!"

Stacy's cries were drowned out by Mrs. Wells' wailing. The woman *didn't care, she was out for Stacy's blood, just like the voices of the men in her life. Ahead of her, in a dumpster, another phone was ringing.*

*"Hello?"*

*"It's me again, why are you waiting around, they're going to catch you."*

*"Henry, I don't know what I did, there's all this blood—"*

*"Whose blood?"*

*"I don't know, I thought it was mine but maybe it's—it's—"*

*"Is it mine? Stacy, you know it's not real right, it can't be mine, I'm not even around!"*

*"I know you're not— Henry where are you? I need you; I need to find you—"*

*Stacy opened her mouth to speak, but the phone dissolved in her hand again. In its place she held a pair of black gloves. Just then, a group of police dogs burst from the end of the alleyway followed by Matt, Andy, and the rest of their precinct.*

*"Put your hands up!" they all screamed in unison. "No one else has to get hurt. Put your hands up and back away from the bodies."*

*Stacy looked down and saw that she was surrounded by women's bodies. They all looked similar to her, but some were taller, some were bigger, there was one woman who had an amputated leg. They were all on the tall side, with auburn hair, and brown eyes that stared at Stacy, accusing her of killing them. They were completely naked and unmoving, except for their eyes. The eyes of the women followed her as the police arrested Stacy and led her through the never-ending alleyway.*

*"It wasn't me! It can't be me, I just showed up here; I—"*

*"That'll be for a jury to decide," Matt cut her off, pushing aside one of the bodies so that Stacy didn't step on her.*

*The eyes stayed on her, angry and betrayed that another woman would let them down. Stacy let all these women down because she didn't find the real killer, she didn't believe the real killer even existed.*

*"I told you; I don't know who killed them."*

*"Then why were you kneeling in front of the bodies with blood on your hands?"*

"They died of asphyxiation! The blood was my blood, I—I must have cut myself on the roses. It can't be their blood; they—"

"How do you know they died of asphyxiation if you weren't the killer?"

"I'm a medical examiner, it's my job to analyze cause of death."

"That must be convenient. How many times have you lied about the cause of death on an autopsy report?"

"Not once, I swear. Every time I do a report it is completely truthful—"

"LIAR!"

Stacy was sitting in an interrogation room. Henry was in the corner, watching her and smiling. There was one bright light shining in her face and Stacy couldn't make out who was asking her any of these questions.

"That's good, Stacy, say exactly what they want to hear," Henry whispered. "Just tell them what they want to hear, and I'll be free."

"What about me, Henry? What about my freedom?"

"It won't stick, you're innocent. I would never doubt your innocence. Soon we can go home, and this will all be a horrible nightmare."

"It has to be a nightmare, this can't be happening," Stacy said, shaking her head. "I want to wake up from this, I—someone please wake me up." She sobbed but that only made the lights turn brighter.

"We found this—" the voice said, dropping a bouquet of flowers on the table in front of her, "A dozen red roses with your DNA all over them. How do you explain that?"

"I was running... there were roses everywhere. The roses cut me, that's why I—"

"That's all the evidence we need. Book her for murder in the first degree. She and the fiancé, can go ahead and rot in jail for all I care."

"What!" Stacy screeched as invisible hands grabbed her under the arms and pulled her out of the seat. "This is crazy, there's zero evidence I killed those women. They aren't even dead! I saw them, their eyes were following me down the alleyway, it's all a hoax! It's a hoax, I swear, *none of them are dead. I don't know who is doing this to me, but — please, please stop, it's not me, I swear!"*

Stacy was thrown into a jail cell with Henry. He sat on the small metal bed meditating as Stacy paced the room.

"We have to do something about this."

"What is there to do? I told you to get away, but they got you too. These cops will stop at nothing."

"Henry, they can't really convict us, can they? We're innocent. I'm innocent, you..."

Henry opened one eye, "Me? What, you don't think I'm innocent?"

"Of course, I do. It's just—"

"What? They didn't bring you in until after I went to jail, is it? Do you think I sold you out? Don't worry, my love, I would never do that to you. They asked me where you were, and I told the truth. It was innocent enough."

"But that's what... wait, they asked you where I was? They asked me where you were."

"Well, I guess they were trying to trip us up in a lie. I told them the truth — I didn't know where you were, but that you loved walking in the rose bushes."

"The rose bushes, all that blood — they thought it was blood from them women but it was mine. It's all my DNA, but they ignored it!"

"They don't care about the truth. They only care about their case."

"That isn't true!" Matt's voice boomed in the darkness. "I care about you, Stacy, but my hands are tied. I can't do anything about it. If I had just known you were a serial killer, I could have stopped you. I would have stopped you before that night with Oliver."

"Stacy!" Maeve's voice joined the cacophony, forcing Stacy down to her knees. "Stacy, I heard you're a serial killer — does that mean you killed your mother? Oliver says you may have gotten rid of her because you were jealous and you felt guilty about being a horrible daughter, is that true?"

"Ms., you have to get away from the bars," an automated voice rang out as Stacy inched toward the voices.

*Henry was chanting 'om' behind her, there was too much going on at once. Matt appeared out of the darkness, sitting at his desk.*

*"My hands are tied," he said, showing that his wrists were handcuffed to a chair, "there's nothing I can do to help you. Stacy, I wish you had told me, I could have helped you, I could have gotten you some help. I can't believe you would turn on me like that, joining Henry on his rampage—"*

*"Hey! It wasn't a rampage; you have no proof!" Henry snapped, his meditative spell broken. "You're the one who put us in here, you're the one who has to get us out!"*

*"I didn't put you in there, you did this to yourselves. Why did you kill those people, what power could they possibly give you?"*

*Stacy's head was spinning. She had to be dreaming, she knew it, but there was no way out. She was starting to feel nauseous. Around her everyone was screaming — Matt and Henry were yelling at each other, while Maeve was crying about their dad. Stacy could do nothing but sit in front of the bars and hold her head. Eventually, the yelling died down, giving way to the sound of heavy footsteps coming down the hall. A guard stopped and opened the door.*

*"Follow me," he said.*

*Maeve and Matt stepped back, bowing their heads for Stacy and Henry as they passed. They walked for what felt like hours down dark hallways peppered with security cameras. It was a slow procession into a brightly lit courtroom covered in rose bushes.*

*"All rise, the honorable Judge Lewis presiding."*

*Stacy looked up to the judge's bench and watched her mother sit down. Heather Lewis looked once at her daughter before looking back down at the pages on her desk.*

*"Everything here looks pretty much in order. Do the defendants have anything to say for themselves?"*

*"Yes I—" Stacy started, but Henry pulled her down into her chair.*

*"Stacy? Do you have anything to say for yourself? Anything at all?" Heather asked.*

*Henry stood up and spoke with Stacy's voice, "Yes. I would like to say that I will go down swinging for the love of my life, Henry Goldberg."*

Stacy tried to protest, but no sound came out. She was powerless and Henry was controlling her fate.

"Stacy, do you understand what you're saying?"

"I do," Henry-as-Stacy said, "I understand completely."

"That settles it then. I sentence Henry Goldberg and Stacy Lewis to death for the murder of Gabrielle Unwin, Audrey Wells, Lacey Daniels, and all the other women with auburn hair and brown eyes who have been murdered in the past and who will be murdered in the future."

"Wait!" Stacy yelled, finally able to take back her own voice, "But that wasn't me before, it was Henry. Henry stood up; Henry was the one talking!"

"But you allowed him to speak for you, you are both defendants, and there is proof here that where Henry goes you will follow. You are powerless against the law, especially when it comes to guilt by association. I'm sorry, dear, I can't stand these kinds of shenanigans, you know that. I worked hard to make sure my life was free, I hoped you would do the same, but obviously I was wrong." Heather exited the courtroom.

Stacy was led away with Henry into another waiting chamber. The guards left them alone for the first time in ages.

"You tricked me," Stacy said. "You told me I had to run, but I ran into a trap."

"It was your choice to run. You chose to stand with me. It's just like Matt said, if one of us is a serial killer, it's likely the other was helping. You helped me with those women."

"How? How could I have helped you, I examined them fairly!"

"You looked for ways I could be exonerated. You might as well have handed me the knife. C'mon, Stacy, think about it, trust your own instincts for once. Deep down, did you really think I was innocent?"

"Yes, I did, Henry. I never thought you could do something like this. I never thought you would be capable of such an act of violence."

Henry shrugged. "What can I say, I guess you weren't really paying attention."

"Henry Goldberg," a voice called from another room, "you're next."

Henry turned and gave Stacy a peck on the cheek. "Wish me luck!" he said, winking as he was led away.

A bright light lit up in front of Stacy. As her eyes adjusted, she saw it was a two-way mirror into her autopsy exam room. Directly in front of where she sat was a metal gurney, and beside it was what looked like an oxygen canister. Henry was led into the room, and he lay down on the gurney. She couldn't hear what was being said, but Henry laughed at something the guard said. The guard clapped him on the shoulder and then gave a thumbs up to someone in the viewing gallery behind Stacy.

"Wait — Wait this is happening too fast. I want a retrial, or a mistrial, or another investigation. Wait—wait!"

But it was too late. The guard had fixed the oxygen mask onto Henry's nose and mouth. Henry twitched violently for a moment, and then he died. All the guards bowed their heads, and an attendant wheeled Henry out of the room. A crew came in to clean the room and change it over.

"Are you ready?" Matt asked, standing by the door.

"No, I'm not ready at all. This isn't right, this happened too fast. I didn't even get to defend myself; Henry spoke for me. I didn't have a chance at my own trial," Stacy said, backing away from Matt.

"Stacy, this hurts me just as much as it hurts you," Matt said, slowly walking toward her, "You have no idea how much this hurts me, but I have to do my job."

"You don't! These are fake charges, you know that, don't you? C'mon, Matt, for old times' sake, please will you let me go? Please, will you let me help you investigate? I'll help you find the real killer; I swear, I just need more time!'

"Stacy, we know who the real killer is. The killer is Henry."

"Then why am I here? Why do I have to die?"

"Because! He spoke for you! You're guilty by association! What was yours is also his, and that includes criminal prosecutions. I'm sorry, I didn't think you'd go through with it." Matt was barely able to speak *through his tears. He caught up with Stacy, her back against the wall. "You have to follow me now," he whispered, gently kissing her on the forehead.*

*"What if I had chosen you?" Stacy asked. "I could go back on my promise, I'll give back my ring."*

*"You're heart's not in it. Deep down you still believe in Henry's innocence, which means you are just as guilty as he is. I can't forgive your guilt if you keep Henry in your heart."*

*Matt took Stacy by the arm and dragged her into the exam room. The gurney was back, and there was a fresh new gas tank beside it. Stacy lay down listening to Matt's sobs. She watched as the attendant lowered the oxygen mask onto her face.*

---

"NO! NO NOT YET, I'M NOT READY!" Stacy screamed, sitting up in bed with a start. She clutched at her throat gasping for breath.

*It's okay, it was all a dream. It was just a dream.*

She took a deep breath trying to get her bearings — she was okay. She was sitting in her own bed, in her own house. She wasn't in prison, there wasn't any blood on her, Henry was still in jail, but no one suspected her of anything.

Stacy went to the kitchen for some water and a snack, her dream was still at the corners of her consciousness. She felt terrified and confused — it was a fucking weird dream. As it faded away all she could remember was Henry speaking for her. She couldn't decipher what it all meant, the dream was a melting pot of guilt, blood, murder, and suspicion. All she knew was that she needed to find a way to help Henry, or else he would get dragged over the coals because Stacy was too afraid to speak.

# CHAPTER
# TWENTY
STACY

She didn't go back to sleep that night; it was too scary. Every time she closed her eyes the memory of her dream floated past, and Stacy jolted awake. By the time it was morning, Stacy was tired and angry. She was angry at the sham trial in her dream, where Henry spoke for her and dragged her down with him. She was angry that they didn't even get a fair trial, there was no evidence against them; it was their word against the police! She knew this dream was a vision of her future. Not literally — she didn't predict she'd be running down an alleyway being chased by dogs anytime soon. No, it was a vision of what could happen if Stacy didn't stand up for herself.

If she allowed the police to continue their investigation, there's no telling what else they would find to pin on Henry. Any unclaimed strangulation from the past 30-something years could be spun as an "unknown" victim of his. No, Stacy wasn't going to let that happen. She had to come up with a plan to get Henry out of that prison, so they could talk and find a way out of this mess.

"Hi, can I talk to Dr. Carter?"

Dr. Callum Carter was her supervisor at the coroner's office. His position was mostly political and administrative, and he looked as though he'd been in the office since the Reagan administration, slowly becoming a corpse himself. He's the one who 'suggested' Stacy take a few days off, he's the one she had to talk to before coming back to work.

"Carter here."

"Hi, it's Stacy. Lewis. Ms. Lewis," she stammered — the exhaustion was peeking through her voice. Stacy blinked it away and continued, "Cal, I have to come back. I'm going crazy here, no one will tell me anything about Henry, not even his lawyers. My crazy sister keeps calling me, and there have been camera crews at my door day in and out since the arrest. I know you said I needed some days at home to rest, but I can't stand another day in my own head. Please, I have to come back to work, before I lose my mind."

Dr. Carter sighed on the other end of the line. He didn't ever do anything quickly; Stacy tapped her foot to control her impatience.

"Well, we don't want that. It's not a good look for the city to have the fiancée of a serial killer on its payroll, but you are the most efficient examiner on staff, we're getting behind and making silly mistakes without you. And it's only been a week, I can't imagine what will happen if you're gone for much longer." He sighed again, it was like listening to a turtle decide what to eat for breakfast. "Why don't I make a couple of calls and see what we can do. Maybe you can do the graveyard shift for a few nights, to reduce your visibility."

*Perfect.*

"That works just fine for me, Cal. I haven't been getting very much sleep anyways."

"Alright. Don't jump into your lab coat just yet, I'll get it approved and I'll let you know before the end of the day."

"Can I start tonight?" Stacy begged, eager to get out of the house and get her plan underway, "Y'know, assuming everything is approved."

"Might as well, the dead bodies aren't going to wait," Dr. Carter said, before hanging up the phone. It could work, he was on her side, he was willing to let her come back and do her job — which is exactly what she needed for her plan to work.

Stacy knew two things for sure when it came to the Alleyway Strangler. One was that he always targeted women who were taller than average, with auburn hair, and brown eyes. The second was that the only physical evidence available in the case was the DNA from the last victim, Lacey Daniels. She used her time not sleeping to do a little research online — according to all the trusted media sources, the police's case rested on this last fact — the DNA from Lacey Daniels. For all they knew, Henry killed Lacey Daniels as a copycat murder.

These two facts were easy to manipulate. Stacy thought about offering herself up as bait to the real killer, but that wouldn't result in reuniting with Henry, besides Stacy had a lot to live for. The other option was to find a Jane Doe, someone who fit the profile of the killer, and make her death a copycat. She looked over her notes for the three women again — the only marks on the bodies were caused by beating and strangulation. Both were pretty easy to manufacture, especially if the victim was already dead. She was going to be back in the coroner's office, and she was the official medical examiner on this case, so all she had to do was mark that the strangulation was the cause of death. Thankfully, a broken larynx looked the same whether it was broken pre-or posthumously. If Dr. Carter could get her on the night shift, that would make this whole plan even smoother — no one liked to work nights at the morgue, that meant there would be fewer people to accidentally walk in on her as she was beating up a dead body.

When this victim was found, the police would have no choice but to release Henry. The DNA evidence from Lacey Daniels was strong, but they were looking for a serial killer. They want the big fish, not some weak copycat. This had the added benefit of poking holes in whatever set-up might have been happening. If Matt was trying to frame Henry, his false evidence would fall apart when another anonymous body turned up. It wouldn't be consistent anymore, it would be a fluke, it could even be seen as the killer trying to shake off their scent.

*It's not exactly ethical, but at the moment I can't care about that.*

Stacy had spent days flipping her view on the situation. She was convinced of Henry's innocence, then started to doubt herself, then going back to the start. She was sick of listening to other people's opinions about the case, she wanted to find her own way, to finally speak for herself. Henry was her fiancé, she wanted to stand by him, but she also needed to talk to him, face to face. For some reason, the police and Henry's lawyers still hadn't found a way to allow visits between the couple. Something about the fact that Stacy was 'too close' to the case, and could leak sensitive information.

As much as she wanted to believe the police were just trying to figure out what the protocol was, she also couldn't help but notice how much easier it was for Matt to drive a wedge between her and Henry this way. Matt could finally be the knight in shining armor, who came over with flowers and ice cream and wanted Stacy to gently realize her fiancé was a murderer, and he had no one competing for his affections or opinions. Matt could be like Henry was in her dream — speaking through Stacy, for his own benefit.

It wouldn't take long to find a Jane Doe. If Stacy was lucky, the killer would strike again. He likely felt safe now that Henry was set to go down for his crime. He might be a little more careful, maybe hide the next body in a more secluded locale, but that drive to murder someone was probably itching at his psyche. He couldn't resist it for much longer, Henry had given him a free pass, the heat would be off for a little while as the police and politicians patted themselves on the back. There was a possibility

Stacy wouldn't have to do anything at all, but just in case she had to prepare.

---

MATT WAS RIGHT, the camera crews had grown bored of waiting for Stacy to finally leave their house, and they drove off in search of their next exclusive, leaving nothing but empty coffee cups behind.

*Rude, they could at least clean up after themselves,* Stacy thought. No matter, she'd clean it all up later, it would give her something to do while she waited to hear back from Dr. Carter. Despite the fact that the news had moved on, Stacy still left the house in sunglasses and a baseball hat. She didn't want anyone to see her while she went about her errands, at least not this first errand. Stacy drove to the farthest beauty supply store she could find, and roamed the aisles for the better part of an hour finding *exactly* what she needed.

"Can I help you with anything, honey?" two salespeople asked Stacy as she paced up and down the aisles searching for the product she needed.

"No thanks, doll," Stacy said in her fakest southern drawl, "just trying to find that perfect shade is all."

The salesperson nodded and proceeded to subtly follow Stacy around the store. Stacy didn't care, she let the woman think the worst of her, shoplifting was nothing compared to the crime Stacy was going to commit. It would have taken less time had she just asked, but Stacy was too paranoid that she would be identified. You never knew who'd been watching the news lately, and who might remember you at the worst possible time. Eventually she found it — the perfect shade of auburn that matched her hair color exactly. She bought four bottles with cash and scurried out of the store back to her car. Her whole body was shaking with the feeling that she'd passed the point of no return. Now

Stacy felt she had no choice but to go through with it — find a body, doctor a murder, get Henry out of jail.

She spent the rest of the day as visible as possible, getting coffee at a busy cafe, buying her groceries at the biggest market in town, slowly strolling through the streets of Seattle. It was overkill, but Stacy didn't care. She hadn't been out of the house in a week, it was nice to feel the breeze on her face and share small talk with the baristas and grocery clerks. These were simple pleasures she'd completely forgotten about while drowning in her personal problems. Stacy was sitting on a bar's patio enjoying happy hour when she got a call from Dr. Carter.

"You're all set. They don't want you to start tonight, let's reset your body's clock a little bit. We're putting you on the night shift, 4 p.m. to midnight. It'll be a little easier for you, you can still rest a bit during the day, but it won't be completely messing with your circadian rhythm, how does that sound?"

"It sounds perfect," Stacy said, "I'll see you tomorrow."

She put down her phone and watched the people walking along the street in front of her. Families, couples, women coming home from work, all completely oblivious, each one of them preoccupied with their own silly little lives. Probably contemplating what to make for dinner, or worrying about the price of eggs at the grocery store. Little problems for their little lives — Stacy envied them. She wondered what it would be like to deal with these mundane problems day in and day out. Her whole life was one long traumatic event, jumping from one unstable situation to the next. Stacy longed for the day when she would be truly bored.

"Can I get you another one?" the server asked, smiling down at Stacy, "you only have two minutes until the happy hour special is over, gotta do it now, can't wait another second."

Stacy laughed, she was charming and sweet. Blonde hair, brown eyed, bubbly personality who counted her tips at the end of the night and gossiped with her roommates until dawn. She certainly never had to worry about whether or not her boyfriend was a serial killer — how nice that must be.

"Sure, I'll do it, but please get it in quick." Stacy absorbed the server's bubbly energy, playing along with her silly joke.

"Okay, I'll do it, I'm gonna run." The server bounced away, making a meal out of reaching the computer in time to put in Stacy's order.

The two of them laughed from afar and she gave Stacy a thumbs up. Was it stupid for Stacy to think that in this moment, life was kind of perfect? She hadn't thought about Henry for at least a half an hour, and Matt hadn't crossed her mind all afternoon. She wished every day could be like this, sitting at a bar during happy hour, making dumb jokes with the server.

*Maybe it could be,* she thought, *if everything goes right.*

# CHAPTER
# TWENTY-ONE
STACY

Three days later, Stacy was beginning to lose hope.
She thought working the night shift would mean many Jane Does to choose from, turned out it was mostly the elderly who croaked after having a heart attack at dinner. It should have made her feel safe — Seattle was a place a woman could walk home alone at night and not get jumped or killed — instead, it made her even angrier. She was angry that she couldn't get a good body — one that didn't land on her table already in rigour, a woman of the right height and age, a Jane Doe so no one would really care if they couldn't find her body the next morning. The longer she waited, the longer Henry had to wait, Stacy was starting to get antsy, she worried that she might have to give up her plan.

On the bright side, Henry's lawyers notified her that she was finally able to visit Henry.

"He's in a medium-security facility while he awaits trial," Kitagawa said, "so his appearance will be... not quite what you're used to." He was preparing Stacy for her first visit, breaking down what she needed to know and the security measures that would be in place. "Your conversation will be monitored and recorded, typical phone-through-a-glass stuff, but you'll also have a guard in the room with you. The state would like to make sure nothing escapes their sweaty grasp. They're really pulling at straws when it comes to this investigation, Stacy, I think we have a good chance at a dismissal."

"That's great to hear," Stacy told him. *But we won't even go to trial, I will make sure of that.*

"Now you'll have to check all personal items, and unfortunately you are unable to give Henry any gifts, so you can pass those freshly baked cookies on to someone else." Kitagawa laughed, he was doing his best to lighten the mood, impossible as that was.

"Have you seen him lately? Is he okay?" Stacy asked. "I need to know how he is. I know he'll be a little disheveled and stuff, I mean he doesn't exactly have access to his grooming case, but I haven't heard anything, not from you or the police. It's like they want me to forget that he's in there or something."

Kitagawa paused, carefully considering what to say next. "They probably would prefer it if you forgot about Henry; that would make their case easier, to remove anything that can make a jury sympathize with him. They want to paint him as a psychopath, and I think his time in jail reflects that. He's been put in solitary confinement at least once, for insubordination. You know Henry, he's a very stubborn man, doesn't take to authority very easily."

"I was worried about that."

"It'll be good for him to see you. I think it'll raise his spirits to know you're coming."

"Does he know that I've tried? I've asked you; you've told him that right?"

"Of course, I have, I've communicated that the police and the district attorney have made it impossible for him to receive visitors, but I think he's feeling a little despondent at times. It's hard for him to recognize that some things may be out of your — our — control." Kitagawa's voice lowered as he said it.

Stacy could see it now, Henry's sullen face across a table, Kitagawa trying his best to explain the situation. Henry likely wouldn't have taken it very well.

"Do you have any other questions for me?" Kitagawa asked.

"No, I think that's it. I'll see you tomorrow?"

"Yes, bright and early. I'll have a car come pick you up at nine-thirty a.m. I'll meet you outside the prison, and we'll go in together."

"Sounds good. I'm looking forward to it." She tried to be bright and bubbly, but it was difficult to muster the enthusiasm. She worried about the state Henry would be in, and she wanted desperately to tell him of her plan. If their conversation was being recorded, she couldn't outright say what she planned to do, but maybe there was some kind of code she could use, or a note she could slip to him...

*Stacy, don't go crazy. Just visit your fiancé, and let that be it.*

---

KITAGAWA'S CAR arrived at exactly nine thirty. Stacy was sitting on her steps waiting with a mug of coffee. She took a deep breath and went down to meet it, feeling more like a widow on her way to a funeral than a woman going to see her fiancé. The driver was kind and tried to make conversation with her, but Stacy didn't feel like engaging in small talk about the Mariners or the weather they were having. She stared out the window in silence for most of the journey, slowly sipping her coffee and wishing she was somewhere else.

Their fight over a prenup felt like it had happened years ago. Stacy wondered if the winery kept their reservation, or if they decided it would be best not to host an alleged serial killer's wedding. She was sure they could get it back, once she was able to clear Henry's name, then the pair could go back to regular arguments about what to watch on tv and whether The American Journal of Forensic Medicine and Pathology was appropriate to keep on the living room coffee table. It had to happen soon, she looked online and found out his trial date was pushed back due to lack of evidence. The city was in an uproar about it, thirsty for the blood of the weak man who was strangling women in alleyways. Stacy felt bad, people didn't really care about the truth, they just wanted someone to blame so they could go back to feeling safe.

Mr. Kitagawa kindly opened the door for Stacy when she arrived. The driver left, never acknowledging where he was dropping her off. The benefit of having any money was that people didn't ask questions.

"How was the drive?"

"Fine, boring. Nothing to write home about."

"It's pretty around here. I think the air is cleaner when you get out of the city." He smiled.

She felt okay, she felt confident in her plan. This was one step in the direction of getting Henry released, she only wished she could tell him.

It took almost an hour to get through security. Stacy was patted down twice, her belongings had to go through a metal detector before being confiscated, and she had her ID checked at least five times.

"Is all this really necessary? Why did they have me go through a metal detector if they were just going to confiscate my bag?"

"It's a precaution. They want to make sure you aren't smuggling anything into your lover." Kitagawa winked.

Clearly this was part of the deal he struck so that Stacy could visit. If the system wanted to break Henry down, it would be easier to do without Stacy around. All these hoops she had to jump through were there to discourage her from visiting. *It's fine, they can try to break him down all they want, I know Henry is stronger than all that and I know I'll be able to get him out of here soon.*

"When will I get to see him?"

"I don't know what's taking so long, I'm sorry. Shall I ask?"

"No, it's fine. I don't want them to think I'm desperate, it'll just make the process take longer."

Another hour went by, Stacy sat there reading a book, pretending she wasn't screaming inside. The next waiting room was empty except for her, the lawyer, and a bored security guard. There was no one she could commiserate with, even if she wanted to, and Kitagawa kept getting up to answer phone calls. It seemed like they were mostly from press outlets, trying to get a comment from him, but he always answered the same way.

"Please refer to the press statement put out by our team of lawyers, as well as the board at St. Vincent's Medical Center. The charges against Dr. Goldberg are nothing but slander and we intend to prove this in court, though we hope matters can be resolved before it comes to that. Thanks so much." He ended each call with a smile, then turned to Stacy and rolled his eyes.

"So many nosy questions. I swear, some of them are just civilians who saw him on the news and want to talk to the 'Alleyway Strangler.'"

Stacy smiled and pretended he hadn't said the exact same thing, over and over again, for the past hour.

"Stacy Lewis for Henry Goldberg." Finally, the security guard came to life. "Room three."

Stacy walked over to the heavy door, and watched as the red light turned green. Kitagawa gave her a thumbs up, like a kindly father taking his kid to a driving test. There was a loud mechanical buzz and the door chugged open.

Stacy saw Henry before he saw her. He looked terrible. His face was gaunt and unshaven, his curls, while clean were unruly, and there were deep lines on his forehead and brow. His skin was sallow, and he had the general air of a ghoul, the kind that was angry you were living in his house, who didn't know he had died a hundred years ago. A second loud mechanical buzz, and there he was, standing in front of Stacy. She didn't know what to do or say, she could hardly smile, but didn't want to cry either. Henry looked as though he'd seen a ghost. She wondered if anyone told him she'd be visiting today. He shuffled over and sat down in the small plastic chair across from Stacy. Another mechanical buzz told them the phones were ready.

"Hi." Stacy smiled, touching her hand to the glass.

"I didn't believe you'd come."

"Well, here I am. I came as soon as they'd let me."

"You should have fought harder. I've been going through hell in here, meanwhile you're living your life as normal as can be."

"I haven't been— Henry, please don't be angry. I wanted to come earlier; I've been calling your lawyers every day, but they said the state wasn't allowing you to have any visitors. Today was the first day I was even allowed to know where you were being held. They told me you were in solitary for a while; that must have been hellish."

Henry nodded. Stacy didn't know what to say, she looked down at her hands. She wanted to tell him everything, she wanted to tell him about her plan, that she'd been looking at his case again, but nothing seemed right and there were too many people watching.

"Has Matt been around?"

"Only to ask me for an alibi." It was better to lie than make Henry any more upset. "I told him I didn't remember where you were, but you were probably asleep next to me, except—" Stacy cut herself off, but it was too late.

"Except what?"

She closed her eyes, bracing herself for the wave of guilt. "Except the day Lacey Daniel's was killed. I told him we'd had a fight; that was all. But I said you came home a few hours later, either way it wasn't enough time for you to—"

Henry held up his hand and Stacy stopped. It was enough for Henry. They were quiet for a while, Stacy just stared at the top of his head.

"Lillian's photography exhibit is coming up. She's really excited about it, apparently the gallery owner has been listening to her suggestions about where to put things, which I guess is quite novel because they tend to have overinflated egos or something? I didn't really understand it, but she was really excited over the phone."

"You should send me a postcard, tell me how it went. Or maybe we can video chat."

"Do you think so? Maybe if you were in the visitors room—"

"Stacy, how naïve could you possibly be? They won't let me out just so I can see your stupid friend's freakshow pictures," Henry snapped.

Stacy felt her whole body brace, a residual reflex from living with her father. Henry was angry, angrier than she'd ever seen him. He seemed irrational and restless; it was no wonder the guards were having trouble with him.

*If he only knew what I was about to do, he wouldn't feel so antsy.*

"Henry, I know you can't tell from... over there, but we're all working hard to get you out of her. Even me, I'm doing everything I can. We all know you're innocent, it's only a matter of time before it's proven and you're out of here."

"Stacy, I don't think you understand what it's like in here. I'm not at the spa, I'm not at an institution like your father. I get up every morning and shower in front of four guards, they won't even let me shave because I can't be trusted with a razor. You're not doing all you can, you're the coroner for Pete's sake, if you were doing all you could do, I'd be out of here. Can't you find some evidence on those bodies, some other DNA they could pull, or are you too busy having little reunions with your *ex-boyfriend* to remember that your *fiancé* is still in prison. I bet that's why you don't care, you have everything you need — my house, my car, and now you have me out of the way."

"Hey! That is completely out of line!" Stacy yelled "I get that you're annoyed, but there's no reason to take it out on me. I haven't heard anything, not even from your *lawyers*. You could at least instruct them to pass along what's going on, I had to find out about your bail sentence on the nightly news."

"We both know why I'm in here, Stacy. I didn't know if you'd be whispering information to your crooked cop exboyfriend."

Stacy's stomach churned. She felt guilty and angry at the same time. Guilty as the scent of Matt's cologne floated past her nostrils, and the memory of her head lying on his chest went past her eyes. Angry that Henry would think she was so easily swayed.

"I'm not that easy you know. I made a choice, months ago, to be with you. I've stood by you even when your mother hurled insults in my direction, and I have tried my best to make you feel better since her death. I've postponed our wedding, gone ahead with everything you asked—"

"Not everything—"

"Everything that was reasonable, yes. Still, you think I can wave a magic wand and get you out of here? Henry, I love you, but the fact is they found your DNA at the scene, and that's grounds for them to arrest you. The DNA wasn't on the body, I didn't have access to it. I did everything I could, I've gone over my notes a million times. I *know* you're innocent, and I know we'll get you out of here somehow, but you have to trust me."

"How can I trust you, when it feels like you're working against me? You say you're looking over your notes, but how do I know you aren't looking for more incriminating evidence?"

Stacy froze, this was beginning to feel like a conversation with Oliver or Maeve, not the Henry she was familiar with.

"Prison's really changed you, Henry." She could feel herself slowly disassociating from the situation. She thought she was going crazy in her self-imposed isolation, but that was nothing compared to the paranoia Henry adopted. "I don't know what else to say, except to ask you to trust me. We love each other, please don't forget that, don't let them take that away from us."

Henry stared at Stacy through the glass, his eyes were empty and his face expressionless. He was a brick wall, and Stacy knew he wasn't going to listen to anything else she had to say. Henry had already decided what to do, he decided how to control the situation.

"Do you want me to send Kitagawa in here? I'm sure he has—"

"Yeah, might as well. The man always tries to cheer me up, I won't deny him his daily pleasure of dragging me out of the dumps."

Stacy nodded, and hung up the phone. She meekly waved at Henry, and then indicated to the guard that she was ready to leave. Another mechanical buzz, another automatic door, and one last look at the man she was supposed to marry, and as soon as the door slammed shut behind her Stacy broke down in tears.

The weird thing about sobbing in a prison was that everyone who worked there was so used to it, they treated it as if you'd sneezed. A Kleenex appeared out of nowhere, a guard patted Stacy on her back, and everyone went back to what they were doing as if there wasn't a hysterical woman in front of them. Stacy sobbed until Kitagawa was done, and she quietly sniffled as they were escorted from the building.

"There, there, I know it must be hard to see him like this."

"I feel so bad. I could have warned him, I could have done something to help him, he doesn't deserve to be there, he doesn't deserve what is happening. He was so angry and paranoid, he's so out of control. I just don't know what to do or say..."

"He is under a lot of stress right now; Henry is not showing his kindest side." Kitagawa would make a good politician; that must be why he was such a good lawyer. He knew exactly what to say so Stacy would know he agreed that Henry was being an asshole, even though the words he said didn't convey that at all. "Your car is here, I told him to take you straight home, and I'm having some of my favorite teriyaki and miso soup delivered to your house as we speak. It should arrive just as the car pulls up to your door." He opened the door and guided Stacy inside.

She was still shaking like a leaf. "Th-Thank you. That's really sweet. I really appreciate that."

"Prison never brings out the best in people. He is scared, you should know that if there was anything more you could do, we would have asked you already."

Stacy couldn't help but cry the whole way home. She knew Kitagawa was trying to make her feel better, but Henry reminded her of her father, and she couldn't shake how scared that made her feel. He was a different person behind bars, which some people might expect, but the reason Stacy wanted to be with Henry was his constancy. She never knew this version of his was lying in wait, and she was scared to find out what would trigger a reappearance. She cried thinking about the freedom she had felt these past few days being alone at home. She cried as she mourned the fact that she would likely never have a home of her own, a little place where she could decorate just as she wanted and could maintain the house to her own sloppy standards. No one to ask if they liked the squiggly art print that she wanted to put over the mantle, no one who she had to compromise with when it came to buying furniture or finding a place for herself alongside theirs.

*That's selfish, Stace. Most people would kill to have a home like yours, and a meticulous partner to help keep it clean.*

Besides, this wasn't about the home. It was all a proxy for her feelings. As the car drove farther and farther away from the jail, Stacy felt the balloon of stress in her chest deflating. Henry took up all the space in her mind with his constant need for attention and reassurance. His life always took priority, even—

*You can't exactly blame him. You work in crime, he is accused of a crime he didn't commit, he thinks you know more than you do. It's pretty reasonable. Besides, you did know more than you let on.*

Stacy knew she should have warned Henry that the police were coming for him. She felt she ought to have told him they found his hair at the scene. There were a million things Stacy felt she should've, could've, would've done but the moment had passed now. She could complain all she wanted but it wouldn't alleviate the guilt she felt.

In the days leading up to the arrest, she had contemplated leaving Henry for Matt, wondered if this was the right marriage for her, and done nothing but complain about her lackluster sex life. Since his arrest, Stacy had reveled in her isolation, given up on reinvestigating the murders, and cuddled up to Matt in their shared kitchen. Sure, maybe Henry was being a bit difficult, but so was she, in other ways.

"Miss? We're here."

"Huh? Oh, that was fast." Stacy sniffled.

The driver smiled and opened the door for her. "We're always the most philosophical on the way home, right? I see Mr. Kitagawa's order came right on time." He took the food from the delivery driver and presented it to Stacy, declining her tip.

"It's on me, It's never easy visiting a family member when they're in the can. This is the very least I could do."

Stacy wanted to break down and cry all over again. The driver ushered her up the stairs before the waterworks could start, giving her a comforting squeeze as he did. Stacy collapsed in her living room and ate, barely tasting any of what she was eating. She couldn't do this anymore; the guilt trips and fear were too much for her. When all this was over, she had to leave Henry, but before she could do that, she had to stay true to her word and get him out of jail.

# CHAPTER
# TWENTY-TWO
STACY

Stacy had to set aside her feelings for a night and focus on the other person in her life — Lillian. The day had finally come when Stacy would have to leave the comforting nest that she had made for herself and actually interact with the rest of the world. Lillian's latest photography exhibit, her biggest yet, was opening tonight and Stacy had to go to the reception.

"No buts, no excuses, you *have* to be there. I need you, Stacy. I know you're going through a lot right now and I'm probably being a very selfish friend, but I'm going to lean into that just this once and say — you have to come to my art opening, and if you don't, I'll be convinced that Henry brainwashed you and I don't know if I can be friends with a zombie."

Lillian made her feelings very clear, and Stacy knew she meant it. Lucky for Lillian, Stacy wasn't in the position to feel much loyalty toward Henry. His words kept ringing in her head, the feeling of guilt kept rising and falling in her stomach, as Stacy went over their visit in her mind. She was beginning to doubt that Henry was the stable partner she had thought. Maybe he was the same as every other man — the second his ego or pride was involved all sense went straight out the window.

Stacy longed for time alone to really think this over, but she knew she could never ask him for that, not after what Henry had sacrificed. Instead, Stacy decided to have a night where she didn't talk about it. If anyone asked her about Henry or about her job, she was going to change the subject to the nearest piece of artwork. She got ready slowly, taking breaks to sit listen to music or grab a little snack.

*How dressy is this going to be?* she texted Lillian, crossing her fingers for a reply.

*Dressy-ish? More like artsy casual. Leave the ballgown, take the oversized Japanese trousers,* Lillian responded almost immediately, *I'm so nervy. What if ppl hate it? What if I never get another one of these? What if I get laughed out of town????*

*Literally impossible. No one will hate it, and if they do, I'll laugh them out of town, lol.*

*<3 thank u. I'll see u later. Whatever you wear, you'll look incredible.*

Stacy smiled at the phone and stared at her closet. Nothing in there screamed, 'artsy casual'. She tried looking online for inspiration but was stuck on where to go. She and Henry didn't go for dinner very often, and the places they went weren't very artsy. The rest of the time Stacy was wearing scrubs and a lab coat — she wouldn't dare wear anything she actually *liked* in the morgue.

After hours of staring at her closet, Stacy finally settled on a long black skirt paired with one of Henry's button downs — he wouldn't miss it, and she could get it dry cleaned before he was released. She braided a silk scarf in her hair and added every ring she owned, in part to add to her eclectic costume, and also to engulf the noise of her engagement ring. No one would think to look for it if she was wearing costume gems on other fingers, or so she hoped. A quick swipe of lipstick and Stacy sailed out the door, imagining for a moment that this was a typical Friday night for her — headed to a gallery before having a quick drink at a local cocktail bar, the latest scientific journal queued up on her e-reader so she could be deliberately mysterious.

Her skin prickled at the thought. Stability came in many forms, and Stacy was beginning to feel she had been hiding behind Henry, and Matt before him, rather than create a solid life for herself. Her world collapsed when she realized Matt wasn't the man that she expected him to be, and then her world turned grey once Henry became the man that she predicted he would be. Matt at least was an attentive and encouraging partner — not to mention, sexy as hell. He sometimes rolled his eyes at Lillian's extreme enthusiasm, but he never got in the way of their friendship, even told Stacy once that he thought Lillian brought out her true self —

"The version of you that was never marred by trauma. She's like your soulmate in a way, she reaches the real Stacy."

Stacy wondered…

*No way, he's way too busy to come to this.*

Stacy was wrong.

She walked into the venue, picked up a glass of champagne, and started floating around the room along with everyone else. She'd seen a lot of the artwork. This show was as much about morbidity as it was about life, Lillian was experimenting with painting and collage overtop of her photographs. All the portraits included some floral growth element either done in oil paint or using live moss. At first Stacy didn't believe it, but there they were, thriving under little humidifiers and looking as if they were growing from the hearts of their subjects. She got closer and closer to the moss, so close she could almost see it breathing under the soft studio lighting.

"Miss? Once step closer and I'm gonna have to ask you to go."

Stacy jumped and almost spilled her champagne on the photograph. A large hand reached from behind her and swiftly collected the glass before the bubbly had a chance to spill over. She turned around and was face to face with Matt, cleanly shaven and dolled up in what must have been a new suit. She gaped at him with her mouth open, unsure if she should run away or fall into his arms.

"I didn't realize how close I was, I—"

"Don't worry," Matt said, chuckling lightly, "I'm not here in an official capacity. Lillian said she'd have my head if I didn't come. I had to buy a suit, but now I think I might be overdressed."

"Not nearly artsy enough, you need some mismatched socks or something."

Matt smiled and pulled up on his trousers — one neon pink, one cloudy blue sock, both with metallic threads running through them.

"Maybe I should cuff them, to show it off? Here, hold this." He handed Stacy back her wine glass and bent down to adjust his cuffs, popping back up with a grin on his face, "Done. Tiny adjustment, hopefully a big impact."

They laughed and turned back to the moss.

"It's cool how she's managed to keep the greenery alive in here. She's been in and out installing for days now, I wonder if this went in last or if someone had to be here monitoring the humidifier and adjusting the lights."

"Probably some underpaid intern who isn't sleeping at night anyway," Matt mumbled. "I suppose I could have been in here; I haven't had much sleep either."

"Yeah, me either, we could have come in shifts." Stacy smiled, and the two settled into a comfortable silence, moving slowly throughout the gallery.

Stacy did her best to ignore the stares, and focus on eavesdropping where she could. She wanted to report back to Lillian later, maybe even gossip a bit at the afterparty. Right now, Lillian was surrounded by the gallery's curator and sales manager, explaining her technique of using pigment sticks as a growing medium for the moss. She looked over at Stacy, who winked back at her.

"This is Lillian's real element. The way her mind works is incredible, I'm just so jealous of her sometimes," Stacy mumbled into her drink.

"Why is that?" Matt asked, waving back at the star of the show.

"She has this ability to balance her whole life on spinning plates, and make it seem completely effortless. I know it isn't — I've been there plenty of times when a sale falls through or a show doesn't go well, or she's in a creative block and doesn't know what to do. But Lillian knows herself so well that she always finds a way to pull herself out of it. At the same time, her work at the morgue is impeccable, she's always there when I need her. She doesn't even feel bad at having a 'day job', I've been there as she argued with other artists that it's essential to have a menial job so you don't travel so far up your artistic ass that you can't even relate to real life." Stacy blinked up at Matt, Matt who had been hanging on to every word. "I'm sorry, I'm rambling."

"No, I get what you're saying. Lillian is true to herself, she's a very independent person and is stubborn enough to stick to her guns when other people might judge her for it. It's really rare in a person. Then again, not many people would think to attach live moss to a photo to examine the delicate relationship between life and death," Matt replied, before going quiet again.

Stacy wanted to ask Matt how the case was going, but she was determined to keep this night Henry-free. So, they just walked around the gallery, moving through the rooms from the moss to the oil-painted flowers, and drifting back again. Eventually, Matt grabbed a couple extra canapés from a passing waiter and pulled Stacy down onto a nearby bench.

"Need to rest my legs, and you're the only person I know here so you *can't* leave me. Besides, if I'm on my own, I look like an overdressed twat, whereas if you're next to me, I look like an adorably befuddled boyfriend who is very supportive and doesn't know how to dress for one of these things," he said, stuffing a puffed pastry into his mouth.

Stacy waved a waiter down for a few glasses. "What do you mean? I'm just as out of place as you are."

"No, you're not, you look perfect. Effortless, French, however you want to call it — you look like you knew you were coming to an art gallery." He sighed. "You look incredible, that's all I'm trying to say."

Stacy blushed, she didn't want to admit it, but Matt looked incredible as well. The cut of his new suit flattered his body, showing off his burly stature without looking like he was a stuffed sausage. Someone must have helped him out with that, hopefully a kind salesperson and not a girlfriend.

*Not that that matters, since you have a fiancé, remember?*

She wanted to resist, but she wanted to give in. She wanted to put her head on his shoulder, and she wanted to slowly unbutton his shirt and run her fingers through his hair. She also wanted to grab him by the collar and shake him until he truly understood how much he had ruined her life. Her confidence was shot, she didn't understand what she wanted out of life, and every day she was re-evaluating the health of her relationship. He also made her realize exactly what she was missing from her life — sex.

Matt showing up, revealing himself in a meet-cute moment, hanging on her every word and *touching* her, it all reminded her of what she had given up when they split. Henry was about as sexy as unbuttered toast, despite his good looks. There was a time when their relationship had that spice, but it seemed that as soon as Henry knew he had conquered Stacy's heart, he stopped trying. Or maybe his mother changed his mind, Stacy never knew, but she had been feeling that hunger for sexual contact even more since Henry went to jail, and her visit with him made her feel physically repulsed by her fiancé. He was so deeply self-centered, that she didn't even have a moment to connect. She couldn't have told him about her plan if she wanted to, because Henry was too busy taking his anger and frustration out on her.

"Stace? Where'd you go?" Matt asked, gently nudging her.

"Off in my own head somewhere," she said, looking into Matt's deep, dark eyes.

It would be easy, so easy to go back to Matt. She knew he missed her, deep down she also missed him, Henry was miles away...

"You came! You both came!" Lillian screeched, causing a very serious group nearby to roll their eyes and walk away. Lillian barely noticed. "I knew threatening each of you would work, you're so easy."

"Lillian, this stuff is great. I don't get it, but it's cool. I like how stuff is growing."

"Thanks, Matt, that was a very... visceral reaction to the work." She smiled, turning to Stacy. "What did you think about the 'growing stuff'?"

"It can only be described as 'cool'. There is no other word that could possibly express my feelings when I—"

"Okay, I can only take this for so long. I'm gonna go find more champagne and I'll be back when it's safe."

The two women giggled as they watched Matt wander off. For a moment it felt like old times, back when it was easy to have her boyfriend and her best friend in the same room. Henry would have thought of the perfect thing to say to Lillian, commenting on the politics of the artwork or how it related to some other artist's work. Lillian would have been annoyed because she just wanted to hear how he *felt* about the work, and she would have prodded Henry until he got frustrated and walked away. Matt said what he thought, and Lillian appreciated the honesty more than the demonstration of understanding.

"How's the night going?" she asked, wiggling her eyebrows at Stacy.

"Fine, I didn't realize he'd be here, but it's been...okay. Matt's been nice, hasn't mentioned work or the investigation at all. He complimented me on my outfit."

"Do my ears deceive me? Are you suddenly seeing Matt's positive qualities again?"

"Lil, please, I feel guilty enough just being near him. What if someone sees and it leaks to the press — Henry will find out and he'll be even more upset at me than he already is—"

"Wait—what? Why is he upset with you, what am I missing?"

Stacy opened her mouth to say something. She felt the rant at the back of her throat, wanted to spill her guts about how Henry made her feel when she visited him, his demands that she work harder to set him free, that she should have done more to get him out of jail — but it wasn't the time. She didn't want to dull Lillian's shine, and besides, she was having a good time pretending her fiancé didn't exist.

"I just meant he's upset at his situation, anyone would be, prison isn't exactly a day spa. Talking with Matt has been wonderful, but I can't help but think this will just complicate the investigation even more. If this really is about his bias…"

"…Then this night, where Matt is enraptured by your beauty and you two are slowly bonding again, won't help his neutrality in the serial killer case, I get it. Try not to think about it Stacy, ultimately, the evidence will speak for itself. Just allow tonight to be about… me!" Lillian laughed. "The best way to forget about your jailed boyfriend and enforcer ex is to focus all your energy on secretly persuading people you want to buy everything and if they don't offer top dollar, you'll beat them to it, and they'll be kicking themselves for years to come."

"Sounds good to me, now shoo or people will think we're in league."

Lillian giggled and swished her way through the crowd, off to charm another patron with her brilliance. Stacy went off in search of Matt, finding him near an abandoned tray of pigs in blankets.

"These art people have no taste. They're all fawning over the scallop-something, meanwhile an American classic is being neglected!"

"Where did you manage to find a beer?"

Matt winked. "Lucky for me, my favorite cheap pilsner is 'ironic' again. They have some at the bar, no one was drinking it until they saw I had one." From across the room a man wearing a crisp raw-denim Canadian tuxedo cheered with Matt. "I'm popular now, everyone's gonna be calling these pieces 'cool' by the end of the night."

Stacy could have jumped him right then and there. Matt had no business being this charming and comfortable in a room full of creative intellectuals. His ease was magnetic, and Stacy wanted it for herself. She wanted Matt's confidence, the way he encouraged her, she wanted his protection, she wanted the feeling of his arms wrapped around her as she fell asleep that night. There was no way she could possibly do it; she couldn't live with herself if she cheated on Henry. His mother's ghost haunted her as much as it did him, eroding her mental health slowly, like a steady drop of water that created a riverbed over thousands of years.

"You must feel so slick right now."

"Honestly? I kinda do. It's the little boost of confidence I need right now."

"Life's just not going your way, is it?"

Matt looked Stacy dead in the eyes, her heart stopped.

"No, it certainly isn't."

*I have to get out of here before I do something I regret.*

"I-I have to find Lillian and—um...I have to go home. I've got an early day tomorrow and I... think I've had too much champagne and—"

"Do you need me to drive you home?"

"No! No, that's not necessary, I'll just take a cab."

Stacy didn't wait for a reply, she stumbled to the coat check and out of the venue, waving at Lillian as she did. She'd text her later, Lillian would understand. Stacy needed fresh air, she needed a walk, and hey if the Alleyway Strangler found her that would make life a whole lot easier. *By all means, strangle me with your hands, maybe I'll finally feel something.* She barely paid attention to where she was going, but that didn't really matter, she could call a cab and get herself home, the walk was more important. Breathing fresh air that didn't smell like Matt's cologne was the most important thing she could be doing right now. He was protective, he knew something she didn't — that's what she read in his eyes in that thunderclap moment. He could see right through her, to the ghost of Amanda Goldberg that hovered over her shoulders stifling Stacy's ability to make any decision for herself.

A month ago, Stacy welcomed the idea of a stable, if sterile, marriage. She preferred it to the volatility of Matt's emotions, and whenever she thought about drifting back to her ex, the image of him beating up her father was enough to steer her back to Henry. Three dead women later and suddenly the attack didn't seem so bad, and Stacy was considering throwing it all away for one night in Matt's arms. He didn't make her feel guilty, or expect her to put his needs ahead of her own.

*It's all stress. The sooner this investigation ends, the sooner I can go back to my regular life,* Stacy thought. This investigation had upended her life and her mind, Henry might have made her feel guilty, but he was right about one thing — Stacy needed to find a way to get him out of there.

# CHAPTER
# TWENTY-THREE
STACY

"Jane Doe, coming right up," Trevor said, wheeling in a woman lying under a white sheet.

Stacy barely looked up from her desk, she had started to give up hope in her plan. "Thanks, you can leave her there. Are you done for the day, Trev?"

"Done for the quarter, my placement's over after today."

*Finally.*

"That's too bad, I feel like we were just starting to get used to you."

"Yeah, I get what you mean, not to worry though I think I'm gonna try and get a summer job here, I have it on good authority that a position is about to open up."

Trevor jogged out of the room before Stacy could say anything, but what did it matter, everyone had learned how to work around Trevor's uselessness, no point in getting used to someone else's quirks. Stacy got up and got ready for the examination, grabbing the woman's file along the way. Basic — average height, average build, no identification found around her, the body had been found less than an hour ago she was rushed over to the morgue, blah, blah, blah. Stacy gloved up and pulled back the white sheet—

She gasped.

This girl was perfect.

A quick scan for any marks or scratches showed nothing, she showed signs of mild strangulation, but there was no rope burn or anything like that. She was about as tall as Stacy, maybe a couple of inches shorter but nothing significant. Her hair was the right length, and a quick check... her eyes were brown. The same light, speckled brown as Stacy's. Rigor had yet to set in, she could easily manipulate this body if she worked quickly. Without giving it another thought, Stacy started punching the sides of the dead woman, in a way that would look like she had been kicked. Stacy muttered to herself as she calculated the logistics —

*The perpetrator had her on the ground when he started kicking her. Would he stomp on her? No — that's inconsistent, he beat them up, but he didn't step on them it was all kicking and maybe punching.*

She made sure no one was in the hallway before she continued — this part was a little more delicate. Stacy locked the door behind her, climbed on top of the body, and strangled the dead Jane Doe. She jiggled her hands as she did, simulating the grip of a man twice her size who had wider fingers than hers. She pressed down on the larynx with her thumb, right where she knew it would be weak and she could easily crush it. No one would know that it happened after the woman had died — no one except her. When she was finished, the body looked exactly like the other victims. Stacy checked her notes, comparing this body to the photographs of the other. They weren't identical — but that was good. This time the killer was rushed, she could say, he knew he didn't have much time, that the city was on edge, still fearful of a killer like him. For good measure, she climbed back on the body and punched her in the chest, the dead body bucked, and Jane Doe's head hit the edge of the gurney.

*Perfect, that's where her head hit the ground after the killer strangled her.*

Now the body was perfect — consistent bruising on a victim that matched the profile, with the same strangulation marks, and a broken larynx indicating how she died. There wouldn't be enough time to do a proper toxicity screen, Stacy checked the Jane Doe's file to make sure it was clean.

"Shit!"

*Suspected overdose, body found near drug paraphernalia.*

That was not exactly in keeping with the other victims, each one with a clear tox-screen and no history of drug use.

*Well, killers can't be choosers, can they? He started with a prostitute, may as well end with a drug addict.*

There was only one thing left for her to do. Stacy pushed away the little voice in her head that was screaming at her about morals and professional integrity as she opened four boxes of hair dye; auburn dye that perfectly matched her own. She followed the instructions on the box, crossed her fingers, and hoped for the best. As she waited for the dye to process, she sent an email to her supervisor.

*Sorry, Trevor, you'll just have to work at a coffee shop this summer.*

*"Hello all, I realize this is likely a moot point since today was his last day, but it seems that Trevor wheeled in a body that had already been examined? I'm talking about case number 04-66791, Jane Doe. I examined her yesterday, file attached, and was curious to find her body wheeled back into my examination room this eve. It's possible I didn't update her file in the internal service? He said it was a new JD that had been submitted this evening, but I can't find a record of a Jane Doe coming through the morgue within the last hour or so. Not to throw Trevor under the bus, and I know we're all fond of his calm demeanour and quirky attitude, but I think this is unacceptable as it can cause confusion for the families of victims, not to mention any potential investigations related to their autopsies. Again, I'm sure this is a moot point,*

*but in my opinion, Trevor isn't suitable to continue working in the office of the Seattle coroner at this time, thank you.*

She took a deep breath and hit send. There was no need to delete the intake record, once they 'figured out' this Jane Doe was a mistake, they could merge the files. Besides, it was municipal administration — the more confusing files that led nowhere and meant nothing, the better. It was less suspicious than deleting the paper trail. Stacy waited a few more minutes before checking on her manufactured victim. The dye took very well, thanks to her light-colored hair, after Stacy rinsed out the dye, this Jane Doe looked just like the other women who came through her exam room. A reflection of her, as seen through a fun mirror. All that was left was to dispose of the body, but that would have to wait. It was still early, and Stacy had a lot more work to do.

Stacy had to wait to put her plan in motion. There wasn't anyone around at this time of night; one medical examiner was usually enough for the night shift. She rolled the Jane Doe down the hall to an old service elevator that was rarely used — Stacy knew there were no security cameras in that part of the building. It was too old, and the city didn't have the budget to update it, and so it provided perfect cover for Stacy's crime. Earlier that night, after dying the Jane Doe's hair, she'd rented a van off a car-sharing app, using her sister's name for cover, parking it in a nearby lot that also didn't have much security. That was the van she'd use to dispose of this Jane Doe, hoping that it was so frequently used and cleaned, the police wouldn't have a chance to check it.

*Hopefully, the police wouldn't even think of such a thing.*

It didn't take her much time to figure out an alleyway to dump the body. According to her file, this Jane Doe was found in Capitol Hill, she could find somewhere around there, pass it off as though this Jane Doe was so close to the overdose victim, that they might have been one and the same. When someone was looking for a serial killer, they tended to look for what matched, rather than what didn't.

Next came the hardest part. Stacy had photos of photos on her phone; all vulnerable and embarrassing positions that the Alleyway Strangler had arranged his victims into. Legs spread, arms wide, women bent over garbage bags, one with her head in the air like she was waiting to—

*Don't think about it, Stacy, just get it done and go.*

There wasn't much choice for her anyway. The Jane Doe was starting to settle into rigor mortis, soon Stacy wouldn't be able to move the body if she tried. She spread the young woman's legs and draped her arms wide over an old box, like she was receiving the greatest pleasure she'd ever had, then she got out of there. Stacy walked in the opposite direction from the rental car, marking it as 'in need of repair' on her app, and then doubled back to the parking lot where she'd abandoned the coroner's van. She took the old elevator back up to her desk and collected her laptop. The whole process only took about an hour, Stacy was home in a flash, and she was in bed soon after.

Staring at the ceiling, Stacy prayed that it would work.

# CHAPTER
# TWENTY-FOUR
STACY

Stacy woke up late the next day. She had nightmares of the Jane Doe waking up and following her home, appearing in the backseat of her car, and waking up in the bed next to her. She woke up at noon to her phone ringing off the hook.

"Hello?"

"Stacy." It was Matt, his voice was stony and serious. "We need you down here, where are you?"

"At home." Her voice was groggy, and she felt hungover. It took a long time for Stacy to understand why Matt was calling her.

"Why are you at— you know what, I don't care, get over here."

"Excuse you, who do you think you are, and why do you think you can talk to me like that?"

"Are you drunk?"

"No, I just woke up, *Detective Ensor*. I've been working the night shift, so my schedule is a little off, apologies for not letting you know, it's just that I figured it's *none of your concern.*"

Matt sighed. "Just get to work. You'll find out when you get there."

When he hung up, Stacy saw what he meant. Notifications filled her screen from work, from Henry's lawyers, her sister Maeve, even a few unknown numbers claiming to be members of the press. Her plan had worked, early this morning the body of a Jane Doe was found in an alleyway in Capitol Hill. Media speculated this was another attack of the Alleyway Strangler, but that had yet to be confirmed, police were waiting on an autopsy. Stacy wasn't sure if she should shudder or cheer, either way she had to go perform an autopsy.

---

"The body was found in an alleyway behind a coffee shop. They were set to receive a delivery of beans that morning, the driver thought it was an addict strung out on the garbage bins. When he noticed it was a naked woman, he called the police right away," Dr. Carter explained as they walked down the hall. "You've been the examiner throughout the investigation, they need you to confirm whether or not this is the same guy as before. As you know, a suspect has already been arrested in this case so…"

He didn't need to say anymore. For what would likely be the only time in her career, Stacy knew exactly what she was walking into, and what would happen when she finished her report.

Matt and his Lieutenant, Anita Schafer, were waiting for her outside the examination room.

"It doesn't make any sense. We got the guy, his DNA was on the body, hair matching his description was found—"

"Matt, I don't want to hear this again, we need to treat every single body seriously, even if it is a copycat—"

If they were trying to speak in hushed tones, they were not succeeding.

"It *is*. It has to be a copycat; I just don't believe that I was wrong this time. I feel it in my gut, I know we have the right guy. Henry Goldberg matches the profile; he had the opportunity—"

"But he had no motive, and the criminal psychologist cleared him, and there was no evidence connecting him to two of the three bodies. You've already had people comb through those areas, canvassing for weeks, and not a single soul saw Henry Goldberg or a man matching Henry Goldberg's description on the nights in question. I'm sorry, Matt, but unless this body has evidence — physical, not circumstantial — connecting that man to this crime, we're going to have to let him go."

Matt tightened a fist and banged it on the wall. "That's a mistake, I just need a little more—"

"Stacy, long time no see!"

Stacy and Dr. Carter were now too close to be ignored. Stacy looked at Matt, his eyes were dark, and he was clenching his jaw as a large vein throbbed in his forehead.

"Very long, too bad it's under these circumstances. Dr. Carter was updating me, but I think I already heard. There's a chance the Alleyway Strangler struck again?"

"It sure seems that way. I'm just here to observe, please don't let me get in the way. I felt it was important that I see your autopsy report as soon as possible, since the press and the mayor have been hounding me all day. Matt is also here to *observe*." She directed that last part to Matt, who was pacing like a tiger in a cage.

Stacy hoped he didn't see that she was shaking like a leaf.

"That's fine by me, I understand the circumstances, but you two might be a bit bored watching me examine the body, why don't you wait with Dr. Carter? I'll come get you when I'm done, I promise you'll still be able to see the body. I'll do my initial reporting, and come get you when I'm ready to present, how does that sound?"

Matt stopped pacing then. He turned around and looked right through her, but before he could say anything, Anita Schafer answered for him.

"I think that's a good idea. Why don't we leave you to your

work, we'll be back in thirty minutes, and you can tell us how it's going."

It obviously wasn't what Matt wanted to hear. He looked back at Stacy as he walked down the hall, a strange look on his face. She was relieved to have some time alone. Stacy hesitated for a moment, wondering if maybe this was all a dream or a long and complicated nightmare. She walked in and was faced with her crime from last night. She had done an excellent job, from afar the body looked exactly like the work of the Alleyway Strangler. Beaten up like a man who was taking his anger out on a woman, deep strangulation marks that looked like they had been done by large hands, a woman who fit the profile exactly. All she had to do was doctor an examination.

*Just do what you would normally do, Stacy, this is a normal exam, it will be followed by a normal autopsy. What was in your notes before? Death caused by manual strangulation, and a crushed larynx. Deep bruising likely made by kicks rather than punches, indicating that the killer got her down on the ground and beat her after he killed her. No signs of sexual trauma.*

Shit.

She hadn't checked to make sure—

It was fine. Lucky for her, the overdose victim hadn't had any sexual encounters the day she died. Stacy stared into the face of the latest victim. Maybe her death would be celebrated a little more, maybe her family would welcome her back if they knew she had been strangled rather than died of her own hand. This could be a positive for everyone.

Or so Stacy kept telling herself.

---

"It's the same guy."

She was standing at the head of the Jane Doe, talking to Lieutenant Schafer and Dr. Carter. It was easier looking at them, they were ready to hear her lie.

"Once again, death by strangulation — a broken larynx, similar bruising around the throat, except this time I think he might have attacked her from behind."

"Why do you think that is?"

"Well," Stacy cleared her throat, "I noticed the patterning was a little different, so I examined more closely. It looks like there was deeper bruising around her neck, a little higher and tighter than it was on the other bodies, and the bruising was more progressed in this area. I'm guessing he pulled her in from behind with something, before turning her around and strangling her with his hands."

"I see what you mean," Dr. Carter said, "perhaps to incapacitate her before going in for the jugular. He learned from last time, doesn't want the victim to fight back."

"That was my thought as well." Stacy smiled — she had noticed that the markings Jane Doe came in with were still visible and needed another excuse. Incapacitated, a victim would be easier to handle. *Thank you, Lacey Daniels, for putting up a fight.*

"That isn't his usual mo. He's a big guy, why would he need to incapacitate a woman like this? She's weak, she looks like she hasn't eaten in days," Matt grumbled from the corner,

"As Dr. Carter said," Lieutenant Schafer countered, "he likely learned from his last mistake."

"It seems as though he did, I think he was in a hurry this time. The bruising is just as deep as on the other victims, but this time it's concentrated on the anterior side of the body. There's some light bruising on her chest and face, but it's mostly on her back and sides. I'm guessing this wasn't planned," Stacy continued, her voice starting to waver. She hoped she could pass it off as anticipation, rather than a reaction to the total bullshit coming out of her mouth at that moment.

"Well, if he's in the Seattle-Tacoma area, he's likely aware that we have arrested someone for his crimes. This might be a killer who got impatient and just couldn't wait for another kill, or he's frustrated that Henry Goldberg is getting all the credit," Lieutenant Schafer said. "Either way, we can't hold Goldberg any longer. I've already had calls from his lawyer and three members of the board of St. Vincent's, you'll be happy to know he'll be out later today, I'll have the prison start processing his release paperwork—"

"What? You can't! This doesn't prove anything, he—"

"Ensor, out in the hall, now."

Matt and Schafer left the room, but it didn't do much to hide their conversation.

"Lieutenant, you can't. I'm telling you — this is the work of a copycat or an accomplice, not the real killer. We have the real killer, and if we catch the person he's working with then—"

"Ensor, stop. You're too close to this case, I've said it before, and you promised me it wouldn't be a problem. I'm telling you now, it's becoming a problem. You arrested the wrong man; you were too eager. I get it, you were facing an impossible case with zero physical evidence and—"

"We need a second opinion. I want someone else to check over that body."

"You're kidding, right? You're the one who twisted my arm to get Lewis on this, and now you're trying to untwist it? Don't be ridiculous, Ensor. I have the mayor, a team of lawyers, and countless other 'concerned citizens' breathing down my collar, I do not have *time* to dedicate to your whims and the will-they-won't-they drama between you and your ex-girlfriend. She did good work, we'll have a tox screen and a rape-kit work up done soon. If you have concerns, feel free to *investigate* them and bring me hard evidence that supports your theory of the case. Otherwise, I am obligated to release the suspect from prison. Do you understand me?"

Stacy was very thankful that Anita Schafer was not her boss, she would not be able to handle it. Anita Schafer commanded a great deal of power, leaving many large men quaking in their boots. Stacy secretly crossed her fingers and hoped this was the end of the argument. She could go back to this sham autopsy, and hopefully get Henry out of jail by the end of the day. Matt must have nodded because a moment later Stacy heard footsteps going down the hall, and Anita popped her head back into the room.

"Feel free to continue with the autopsy. We'll let you know if we hear from family anytime soon, meanwhile I'm going to need a full workup — rape kit, tox screen, the works. I want it all on my desk by end of day. And Ms. Lewis — the sooner I have it, the sooner Mr. Goldberg can be released."

---

STACY DIDN'T EXHALE until she left for the day. After Schafer, Matt, and her boss left the exam room, she continued the autopsy and dug herself deeper into her crime. She knew the toxicity screen would come back and destroy the façade of a clean, easy murder victim, so she found someone with the same blood type and sent their blood off instead. Lucky for her, this victim didn't have any evidence of sexual violence, so the rape kit should come back clear. She got an email just after she sent the samples to the lab from Henry's lawyers telling her of the good news; she should be able to pick him up first thing tomorrow. There was some kind of delay with the paperwork, but there was no reason Henry should be held any longer. The suspicion against him held no water.

*No doubt Matt is dragging his feet around the precinct. No matter, the point is that Henry will be out, and everything can go back to normal.*

She didn't care about the Strangler anymore. She didn't care if she was in danger, or that she matched the profile or anything, all she cared about was seeing Henry's face when he found out she helped him get out of jail. Stacy could have floated on cloud 9 down the I-90, she stopped at her favorite takeout place for a special sushi dinner, grabbed a bottle of Henry's favorite wine to have when he got home, even bought herself a little sexy lingerie to celebrate the occasion with her fiancé. Nothing could bring her down, her plan had worked, there was no reason anyone would suspect her.

Except one.

Matt was waiting on the steps of her home as Stacy pulled in. There could be only one reason, and Stacy knew she couldn't break. If she did, Henry would be back where he started, she'd probably be criminally charged, and all that work would have been for nothing.

"Did they tell you?" he asked her.

"Yes, they said I had to wait for the prison to confirm, but I should be able to pick him up tomorrow."

Matt raised his eyebrows and whistled. "His lawyers must have put the screws to them. I was pushing for a couple of days."

"There's nothing you can do, Matt. Henry can't be the killer, it means you'll have to find some other ex's fiancé to pin this on."

"That's not fair! I told you I was going where the evidence led me, and unfortunately that led to Henry. From what I knew of him, he matched the criminal profile we were looking for. Obviously, I was wrong, okay? I came here to apologize, not to hear you beat me up about it."

The two were quiet. Stacy watched as a news van parked itself at the corner of her street, no doubt camping out ahead of Henry's return.

"Is that wine for him?"

"Yes, he really likes chardonnay."

Matt nodded. She didn't understand what he was doing here. If it wasn't to confront her, then why?

"You stand by everything you said today? That the killer was desperate, incapacitated the victim before strangling her and all that?"

"Of course. I take my job just as seriously as you take yours, if you're serious when you tell me that your bias had nothing to do with Henry being your prime suspect, then I'd hope you believe me when I say I was telling the truth today."

Stacy felt tears welling up behind her eyes. It hurt to lie to Matt, she knew doing so would break his trust and that he'd likely never see her the same way again if he found out the truth. *That's fine, Stacy. There's no reason he ever will, you won't tell a soul about what you did, not even Henry. He can go ahead and assume it was luck that got him out of jail.*

"Right. Sorry I even mentioned it." Matt stood up, staring into space for a moment before bending down and giving Stacy a kiss on her brow. "Good luck, Stace. I mean it, Henry doesn't deserve you, but he won out fair and square. You're right, he's way more consistent than I'll ever be."

Stacy was left standing on her stoop as she watched Matt walk away.

---

*"He's way more consistent than I'll ever be."* Those words echoed in Stacy's mind for the rest of her night. She barely tasted her sushi as she watched the news. Jane Doe still hadn't been identified, which was unusual for this case. The reporter made note of the fact that the killer reportedly used a new tactic, having learned to protect himself in case the victims fought back — another interesting development in the investigation. Stacy wondered if Matt's detective instincts were good enough to see through her façade.

*Impossible, Anita Schafer has been on the force longer than he has, she has more arrests and convictions under her belt than he does —*

*Matt's even said that Schafer is like a crime oracle, nothing gets past her. If she believed this victim was the work of a serial killer, there's no reason to think Matt doubts it.*

Still, whether it was nerves or anticipation, Stacy had a hard time sleeping that night.

# CHAPTER
# TWENTY-FIVE

*ey, I just wanted to say I'm sorry for yesterday. I was surprised, and worried for you. If this killer is still out there, you're still in danger, so please be careful.*

Stacy stared down at her phone, her eyes still blurry, barely registering the text message. At first, she thought it might have been Lillian, or her boss, it took a few minutes before she realized the text message was from Matt. His words chased her through her dreams, still terrified that Matt knew exactly what was going on. She took a cold shower to clear her head and wake herself up. It was an important day, and she didn't want to be thinking about Matt. She deleted the text message and decided, then and there, that it was best she blocked Matt's number. They could talk at the office if it was really important.

*Today, all that matters is Henry.*

She tried to have a slow morning. Stacy made breakfast and coffee for herself, sat at the table, and tried to read the morning paper. She turned on the tv, but the morning talk shows had barely begun. Her calls to Lillian went unanswered — far too early for the artist's schedule. Finally, she settled on getting dressed and tapping her foot as she waited by the phone. There was nothing she could do to get Henry's release off her mind. It had to happen soon, if Matt was so apologetic, he'd have stopped trying to block the release. There was no choice for him but to go back to the drawing board, and start surveying the crime scene, looking for evidence that didn't exist.

Finally, the phone rang.

"*This is an automated call from the Washington State Penitentiary system. Please hold the line, a member of our administrative staff will be with you shortly...*" Hold music took over the line, as Stacy's heart started racing. "This is a call for Ms. Lewis."

"This is she."

"This is a call to inform you that the inmate, Henry Goldberg, will be released at 10 o'clock this morning, thank you for your time."

The phone call didn't need to be any longer than that. Stacy checked the time and saw she had a little less than an hour to get to the prison, so she raced out the door and into her car. The car was packed with a fresh change of clothes, and Stacy made a stop at Henry's favorite coffee shop so she could greet him properly. Anticipating that Henry would want a woman's touch after his stay, Stacy wore the matching set she bought under her clothes. It was *not* comfortable for driving in, but what did that matter. All she wanted was for Henry to be home, for this matter to be behind her, and for her life to move on.

Stacy drove as quickly as she could without risking a speeding ticket. While she was driving, she kept getting calls from Henry's lawyers, but answering them would have done nothing but slow her down. She was determined to get there first, to be the first person that Henry saw when he was released back into freedom. There was no way she could ever tell him the truth — that she was the copycat, and the reason he had been released — but she could be the first thing he saw. She could be the light at the end of the tunnel for him.

At the end of her first and only visit, Stacy was in tears. She had never felt so guilty or powerless in her relationship, it reminded her of her mother. Heather was a strong woman, but Oliver managed to break her down every time. Stacy grew up around that guilt, watching powerlessly as her mother cried herself to sleep at night and bore the brunt of Oliver's verbal abuse. He often made her feel guilty, he was controlling, and he made it out to seem that Heather was stupid and helpless without him.

In many ways, Oliver was very similar to Henry. Sure, Henry didn't have the addiction problems or the erratic nature of her father, but he could be just as cruel. He replaced that inconsistency with dullness, but kept the need for control over everyone in his life. Even Henry's lawyers were afraid of him, that's the read Stacy got from Kitagawa that day. Henry had the ability to be charming and vapid at the same time; his eyes sparkled with their emptiness. Henry was stubborn to a fault, but always made it seem like it was Stacy's *choice* to change her mind, even when she was just doing it because he wore her down. Finally, his mother managed to engulf their whole relationship, both while she was alive and now that she was dead. Henry's suggestions about the wedding and the prenup, even Stacy pushing down her doubts about their marriage, all stemmed from his mother. Her death did nothing but strengthen the hold she had on her son.

Suddenly, Stacy was afraid of who she would meet outside the prison gates.

---

"I'M SORRY, ma'am, I don't know what else to tell you. He was released half an hour ago, and he left on his own accord. We don't hold prisoners back if they want to leave, they tend to dislike that kind of thing."

Stacy gripped the edges of the desk and tried not to scream.

She'd been waiting outside holding a coffee that was getting colder and colder by the minute. Ten in the morning came and went, but Henry didn't. Finally, Stacy crawled around the building and found an entrance, a reception desk, and the world's most bored receptionist.

"I don't understand; they said ten in the morning. Why would they let him go earlier than that? Why would he leave?"

"Listen, if you're asking me to tell you why administration does what they do, you have clearly never worked in a bureaucratic environment. All I have is the information in front of me, and that information says that an inmate by the name of Henry Goldberg was released at 9:30 this morning, on his own reconnaissance. Once they go out those doors, we stop keeping an eye on them — that's the whole point."

Stacy dragged herself back to the car. She tried to call Henry's lawyers, but no one had any idea what had happened to him.

"We assumed you'd be picking him up. My secretary tried calling to confirm, but when you didn't answer, she assumed you were on your way to pick him up."

"I was. I was driving, you're sure he hasn't called and maybe left a message with someone else? The prison, maybe, I got a call from them saying he was going to be released at ten, did they call and change anything?"

"I'm sorry, we received the same information you did. If there's anything else that we can do…"

"No, no that's fine, you've done enough, just let me know if he checks in, please." Stacy's voice was so small, it was as if she'd regressed into her childhood self. The feeling of not knowing where your loved ones were, of being abandoned in a strange place, was all too familiar for her. All she could think about was how disappointed Henry must be.

Stacy drove home slowly, her anxiety building with each mile. She wasn't even sure that Henry had his house keys with him, or enough money to get himself back there. She absentmindedly drank his coffee, and at one point she pulled over to take off the uncomfortable bra she'd put on for him.

*So much for a quick tryst in the car.*

There was no way for her to know when Henry made the decision to leave without telling anyone. He could have seen that there were no cars in the lot, and decided there was no point in waiting, or he could have decided days ago that he'd rather not see Stacy upon his release.

*This could be a positive thing,* she thought, *maybe he wanted to shower and get himself shaved before we saw each other.* Stacy couldn't think of anything else, except for increasingly complicated scenarios of Henry's departure from prison.

In one, he stepped out of the prison gates and Matt came out of the bushes, tackling him to the ground.

In another, the real killer slipped behind him and strangled him, throwing Henry's dead body into the surrounding woods.

In another, Henry secretly crept into the trunk of Stacy's car, and somehow found a way to strangle her from the backseat.

Each time she thought, *you're being ridiculous*, and each time she came up with something less realistic to take its place.

Lillian still wasn't answering the phone, and she didn't want to call Maeve who would do nothing but gloat that she had been right all along. Stacy turned on the radio, but the news kept playing bulletins about the latest Jane Doe and Henry's release. They read out the same statement from Henry's lawyers over and over again, always saying at the end that they were waiting on a comment from the man himself.

He had to be waiting at home for her, nothing else made sense.

But Stacy was wrong. She arrived home to news cameras and journalists camped out in her driveway, and a completely empty home.

"Hello?" she called out, "Henry, are you home?" The house felt eerily quiet compared to the roar outside her door. She tiptoed into the kitchen, but there was no one in there. "Henry? Come out, come out, wherever you are! I have a little surprise for you," she sang, but there was no one to listen.

She could feel how empty the house was, like it was missing more than just her fiancé. As she continued creeping through her own house, she started to take note to see if anything was missing. In the small dining room that separated the kitchen and living room, Stacy noticed one of the wall hangings was askew. There was a safe behind it, something Henry had insisted on when they first bought the house. She'd never known the combination to the safe because, apparently, she couldn't be trusted, and it contained some of his mother's jewelry. Eventually Stacy forgot it was even there; but now the wall hanging covering it was almost falling off the wall. She pulled it out and found the door to the safe was unlatched, but there was nothing in there. A chill ran down her spine as she dropped the picture and ran up the stairs to her bedroom.

He was gone. A watch that he kept on his side of the bed, half the clothes in his side of the closet, and a few pairs of shoes were missing, along with a suitcase to pack all that into. In their shared office, all evidence of Henry's existence had been cleared out; the drawers at his desk were half open and hastily cleared, his laptop and tablet were gone, as were the cameras and technical gadgets Henry liked to collect. All that was left was a post-it note stuck to Stacy's computer monitor.

*"Don't look for me."*

For a moment, Stacy thought she might collapse. Henry left, because he didn't want to wait for her. Henry hadn't contacted his lawyers, because he didn't want to be found. Didn't he understand that he was released because they couldn't keep him? The crime had been solved, he was framed, he could come back to his normal life — did no one tell him that? There must have been some confusion or miscommunication at the prison—

"Mr. Kitagawa's office, how may I direct your call?"

"I'm calling—I'm—It's Stacy. Lewis, Stacy Lewis I need to—"
"One moment please."

The hold music started, Stacy stared at the note, the room spinning around her.

"Ms. Lewis, have you heard from him yet?"

"No, I—I hope you had. I just got home I found a—"

She wasn't sure that was smart. There might have been conditions of his release, and Stacy didn't want to be the reason Henry got into any more trouble.

"Ms. Lewis?"

"I thought someone might have tried to break in, do you know if Henry had his house keys with him?" She sniffled, trying desperately to hold back her tears.

"Yes, I believe he did. I have a list of his personal effects right… here. Yes, his house keys were with him, shall I send someone down there? Are you two safe?"

*No, neither of us is safe, but there's no one you can send.*

"I don't think that's necessary. It's probably just some nosy member of the press trying to lure us out."

"Ahh yes, that should be all over shortly. We've put out an updated statement with the comments Henry emailed to our office, you can thank him for us. They'll be gone once they have a statement, I'm sure."

"Mmm-hmm, I'm sure you're right. Thanks, Kitagawa, you've been a big help, I'll be sure Henry knows it." Stacy hung up the phone before the lawyer could hear her cry out. So, Henry had the foresight to email his lawyers, but all she got was a note?

*Don't look for me.*

Why couldn't she look for him? What was going on? With shaking hands, she dialed Matt's number,

"Ensor speaking."

"M-Matt, it's m-me." Her voice shuddered as she spoke. "I need you to be honest with me — do you know where Henry is?"

"What? No, I have no idea. He was released this morning, wasn't he?"

"He was, but they let him out early and he didn't wait. I was there, I had a coffee, but he wasn't there. He wasn't anywhere, and now I'm home and his stuff is gone, I don't know what to do." She wiped away tears and snot with the back of her hand. "He knows he's free, right? He knows he's not a suspect anymore, that he doesn't have to run away, doesn't he?" Stacy couldn't help but let out her loud, desperate sobs.

"Stacy, please, take a breath, you aren't breathing," Matt said, "I promise you; no one is hunting for your fiancé. I don't know what the prison said to him, but he's wrong if that's what he thinks. Did he leave a note, anything that indicated where he might be?"

"It just says, 'don't look for me'. Matt, I'm worried—"

"I get it—"

"Do you? Do you even care? This is perfect for you, isn't it? My fiancé is out of the picture, he probably thinks the whole police force is after him, and he doesn't want me anywhere near him. You can swoop in and become my knight in shining armor and get me back, just as you wanted. You said as much when this whole investigation started, you told me you missed me and that you'd do anything to protect me, didn't you? So, what, was this all part of your plan?"

"No! Of course not, I would never— Stacy you have to listen to me. I can't say I would never stoop so low because believe me, I've thought about it. But I understand now what you need, and I have accepted that Henry is the man you chose to attend to those needs."

"You sound like a self-help book."

"That's probably because I got that from a self-help book. Take another deep breath." Matt waited until he heard Stacy exhale. "Do you know if he has his phone location turned on, or maybe on any of his other devices? Can you find him that way?"

"No, he only has location turned on for me, for safety and stuff."

"Is there anywhere he could go? Does he own a cabin, or does he have any family that he would turn to in a time of crisis?"

"No, it was always just Henry and his mother."

"Is there anywhere else he could have gone? Anyone who might have picked him up?"

"I called his lawyer already. He didn't seem to know anything about it, even told me to thank Henry for sending some statement to them? I don't know, I guess the press has been hounding them for comments and Henry emailed something in, but I don't know when or from where."

Matt went quiet again. Stacy sank to the floor, unsure of what to do.

"I'm worried," she said, her voice barely above a whisper. "When I went to visit him… Henry wasn't himself. He was so angry, so convinced that everyone had forgotten him in there. You know they put him in solitary confinement? He was never very good with other people's authority… I'm worried about him. Half the city is after him, you know, the press want a statement, they want to know if he's going to sue, what if they chase him down and he—"

"Don't start going down that road, it'll just make you feel worse. Listen, I'm going to write up a missing person's report for him, okay? It's a little unusual, we don't usually do this so early on, but it might be better than having a cop go after Henry right now. I need you to sit tight, can you do that?"

"Mmm-hmm."

"Is Lillian around, can she come over?"

"I haven't tried calling her in an hour, she didn't answer earlier."

"Okay, try again and see if she can come over. In the meantime, just sit tight and keep taking deep breaths, okay? If 'you're really worried about… never mind. I'll open up a report, hopefully he's just upset, and he'll come home soon. If you hear from him, or if he comes home, please let me know. Or better yet, call Cardoso, he'll help you out."

"Okay."

"You have his number, right?"

"Yes."

"Good, we'll do our best to find him, Stace." Matt hung up.

Stacy hugged her knees and cried, her whole body shaking with fear and disappointment. She thought she was helping Henry, but now she wasn't so sure.

# CHAPTER
# TWENTY-SIX
STACY

This time, it was raining in her dream. As Stacy ran through the floral maze, the thorns scratched at her face, arms, and legs, each stinging for just a moment until her whole body was throbbing from pain. She stopped for a moment to catch her breath, and watched as her blood fell onto the pavement. A body was lying beside her, legs spread wide her back bent over a pile of garbage bags. The body was familiar, Stacy crept toward it, and she saw her own face, all life drained away, but her hair was growing, and growing, and growing. It turned from auburn to blonde and back to auburn as it wound around Stacy's body trapping her in the alleyway. In the distance she could hear a police siren coming closer and closer and closer —

Stacy woke up with a start. It took a moment for her to realize she was in her bed, safe from the dead bodies and rose thorns; and that wasn't a police siren she was hearing, it was her phone ringing, a number she didn't recognize —

"Hello?" Stacy croaked.

"It's me."

Henry. It was Henry's voice on the other end of the line. Stacy pinched herself to make sure she wasn't dreaming, she looked again at the caller ID.

"Henry, is that you?"

"Yes."

"What is this—where are you? Where are you calling from, this isn't your phone number — are you okay? Where were you this morning, I waited and then I asked, and they said you had been released and—"

"I had to go, Stacy. It isn't safe for me."

"What do you mean? You'll be safe when you come home, I promise."

Henry scoffed. "That isn't true, I won't be safe anywhere in Seattle. You think the hospital will let me come back after I've been accused of being a serial killer?"

"They advocated for you; the board fought for your release!"

"That's all the media, they want you to think that because they don't want to be seen as heartless. Believe me, the second I step foot in that hospital my career is over. No patient will want to be seen by me, the board will probably give me some performative title that isn't a real job, and then they'll slowly wear me away until finally they 'suggest' that I resign."

He was drunk, he must be.

"Henry, you don't know that."

"I do. It doesn't matter, I can't trust anyone right now."

"You can trust me."

"No, I can't! I can't even trust that this line isn't bugged. I have to stay on the move, I just called to tell you that I'm alive, and you don't have to worry about me."

"Henry, please come home," Stacy begged, she was tired and on the verge of tears for the millionth time that day, "you don't have to stay on the move, you're safe *here*. Please, just come home."

"I can't do that, Stacy. You think this is over? You really think Ensor isn't going to try and pin this body on me, somehow? I bet he has wads of my hair stashed away for a moment like this, or a bribe ready to go to some junkie witness who will claim I put them up to this murder."

"Matt doesn't care about that, he's not—"

"Don't you dare say he's not that kind of guy. He's corrupt, they all are. Either they're corrupt or incompetent, there's no in between. Anyone who falls outside of that is too much of a coward to go against the status quo, you know that just as well as anyone. If Matt has a grudge against me, you can bet all of his little friends do too, and they'll make it next to impossible for me to—"

"Henry, you're starting to sound paranoid."

"I AM PARANOID!" he screamed, his voice guttural and raw. "I am paranoid. I'm terrified to show my face in Seattle, I'm scared anyone I run into is going to throw me back in that *prison*. Stacy, you would be paranoid too if you were in my position, you'd never be able to handle it, you're a *coward*."

"I did everything in my power to help you, Henry." Stacy's whole body was shaking, she wasn't totally convinced that she was awake. "You don't know the half of it. I—"

"Stacy, I don't want to hear it. Besides, this line is probably bugged, it's not safe for us to keep talking."

"Please, just tell me where you are."

"I can't. Even if I could, I won't. I can't trust you, Stacy, you're in bed with the enemy, you two are too close. I don't mean you were unfaithful; I just think you are too easily influenced. One word from Matt and you'll spill everything you know."

"Henry, please, you're worrying me. I'll do whatever you want, I'll cut Matt out of my life if I have to, just come home so we can deal with this properly. You have a team of lawyers that can help you, I'll be here too, but you have to just—"

But Henry had already hung up. Stacy sat in bed with her phone in her hand. She tried calling back the number, but it was already out of service. Henry must have thrown the phone away as soon as he hung up, that was the only explanation. She was about to call Matt but stopped herself — what if what Henry said was true? *Could the police even bug my phone if I'm not using a landline?* That must be impossible. At the very least, she had to call Matt to tell him Henry contacted her. She still didn't know where he was, but at least he knows how to contact her.

"Ungh," Matt droned into the phone, still half asleep, "Manhg huur."

"Matt? Matt, wake up, it's Stacy." Stacy spoke a little louder than usual to wake him up, Matt could be a heavy sleeper when he had the chance.

"Stace? Am I dreaming?"

"No, wake up! Please, I need you."

Stacy heard a snort, a grunt, and some commotion as Matt dropped his phone and picked it up again. The man did not appreciate being woken up in the middle of the night.

"Sorry, it's late. What time is it?"

"It doesn't matter, it's late. Henry called me, Matt, he called me just now from a phone number I didn't recognize. I tried to call back, but I don't know if he destroyed the phone or what, I got a message saying the phone number was out of service."

"Was it an automated message, like you hear from the phone company?"

"What kind of a question is that — yes, of course it was."

"There are a lot of companies that will dummy phone numbers these days, you pay a service so that any calls that come to your number get redirected, and it makes a fake number for you too. Henry might still be using his phone. Did you hear anything in the background?"

"Like what?"

"Sirens, nature sounds, a car driving past, anything really. You'd be surprised how much background noise can help pinpoint someone's location."

"No, I was tired, and I was busy begging my fiancé to come

home." Stacy sighed and fell back on her pillow. "The whole thing feels like a strange dream. I woke up from a nightmare into a weird dream, what do you think that means?"

"I think it means you're going through a hard time, and it's really late. What did Henry sound like?"

"Paranoid. He kept going on about the police force and how they're all corrupt and incompetent."

"Stace, you know he's not right. Yes, there are a few unscrupulous cops out there, but I promise I'm not one of them. We just want to find the killer and not have anyone start idolizing the guy. You know there are already forums on the internet dedicated to the Alleyway Strangler? He has fans. Some of them are women who want him to beat them up."

Stacy winced, she didn't want to hear about that right now, not while she could still feel hair around her neck strangling her.

"Tell me more about the call," Matt continued, "he sounded paranoid, and what else?"

"He kept saying he thought the line was bugged, that someone was listening. He called me a coward, and said that he couldn't trust anyone. He said I was in bed with the enemy."

"He sounds very paranoid. You said he spent time in solitary confinement? That can often have a deeply traumatizing effect on people. Weird, he was cleared by the court psychologist, and that was after he'd spent a day in there. You think this happened after he left?"

"I don't know, I don't know what state he was in when they released him. He left early and I didn't see him, remember?"

"Right."

They were quiet for a while, just listening to each other breathe on either end of the phone. Stacy stared at the ceiling, allowing herself to calm down and regulate her breathing with Matt.

"Stacy?" he asked, "Are you asleep?"

"No, I'm just thinking about Henry, and the killer, and how quickly my life has turned completely upside down."

"Oh?"

"Yeah, a few weeks ago it was boring. I knew exactly what to expect when I woke up and when I went to sleep. Henry and I weren't really intimate anymore, but I figured that was partly because of his mother's death. I felt so bad, I felt guilty because it kind of *was* my fault—"

"It's not your fault his mom was crazy."

"Whatever, I still felt guilty. You also can't always control how someone else's actions will make you feel. I never thought you getting involved in this investigation would make me feel…"

Stacy trailed off, unsure of how to continue. How did she explain to her ex-boyfriend that this investigation was making her think she'd made a mistake when she left him for Henry?

"Stacy, are you alright?"

"Huh? Yeah, I think so."

"You sound like you're miles and miles away…" He paused for a moment before he continued, "Are you okay at home?"

"Yeah. Yes. Obviously. Of course."

"I'm not convinced. You sound really lonely, and a little afraid."

"I'm fine, Matt, I don't need you to ride up on your white horse and save me." Stacy wavered a little as she said it. It was a complete and total lie. She felt terrified to be home alone. Before going to bed she locked all her doors and windows, and then checked them twice before she felt comfortable enough to go to bed. She wasn't safe when she *was* in bed either, her dreams were increasingly terrifying, they were all about another alleyway or dead body. Another dead woman, watching her, accusing her of something that Stacy couldn't quite put her finger on.

"I'm just saying," he said, "if you don't feel safe, that is very understandable in this situation. I can have someone watch your door. Whether it's press or Henry or anyone else, there are ways we can keep you safe."

*There are ways* you *can keep me safe,* Stacy thought.

She considered inviting him over, having Matt sleep on her couch and Stacy could be upstairs in her bed. Henry would be furious, but what did it matter now? Henry didn't trust her and was nowhere to be found. Stacy could explore what that tiny voice at the back of her mind had been saying since the day that first body was wheeled into her exam room — *maybe this wasn't the right relationship. Maybe there is someone else out there. Maybe Matt really has changed.*

"Who are you going to send? It's late. Just let the poor uniforms sleep, I can handle myself until the morning."

Now, Stacy decided, was not the time to explore those emotions. She had to get back to sleep, she could worry about Henry and her future when the sun was up, and her mind was clear.

"If you're sure."

The two of them went quiet again. Matt's breathing started to slow down, eventually his deep breaths turned into gentle snoring. Stacy slowly drifted off, regulating her rhythm to the soothing sound of Matt sleeping next to her.

# CHAPTER
# TWENTY-SEVEN
STACY

Stacy woke up in her lab, unsure of how she got there. "This must be a dream," she said, but everything felt so normal. She might have been taking a nap, it had been an extremely stressful few days, anyone would get a little narcoleptic. Stacy hopped in place a few times to get her blood flowing, before picking up the chart that was in front of her. There was nothing in there, the folder was filled with blank pages.

"Trevor!" she called out. "Did you check these files before you put them in my lab?" She waited but didn't receive an answer.

"Trevor!" she called out again. "Can you hear me, or are you ignoring me?" Stacy muttered under her breath as she walked down the hall. Trevor wasn't at his desk, instead it was a young woman with long brunette hair.

"Oh, sorry about that, for a second there I forgot that Trevor left. I'm sorry, I don't think we've been introduced —" Stacy stuck out her hand and the girl turned around.

"I'm Jane, it's nice to meet you. Is there a problem, I heard you yelling down the hall?"

Stacy's blood ran cold. Sitting in front of her was the Jane Doe she used to get Henry out of jail. She was alive again, but still had the markings at her death — the red ring of strangulation and the purple and yellow bruises Stacy made on top of it.

"N-no, it's fine. I'm sure everything is fine, I just, um..." Stacy gulped, she felt paralyzed with fear. This had to be a dream, or some kind of stress-induced hallucination. "The file is empty. The file that was in my lab."

"Oh! Oh my gosh I am so sorry about tha;, I'm still getting used to everything. I could have sworn — can I have the file?"

The interaction was far too normal. Stacy stuck her arm ou;, it wouldn't move the way she wanted. It was as though her body was going through rigor mortis, her muscles and joints felt too stiff to move. Jane, the receptionist, took the file and looked through it, shaking her head.

"I'm so sorry, there must have been something wrong with the printer...yes, you know what? The ink was low, and I didn't think to change it before. I'm so sorry, it'll just be a minute."

Stacy watched in horror as the woman stood up. She was completely naked, and Stacy could see where she punched the girl's body to create bruising that matched the killer's mo. Jane acted normal, puttering about at her desk looking for the inkjet cartridge like she wasn't a murder victim come alive again. Eventually, Jane figured out what was wrong, and reprinted the papers Stacy needed for her autopsy.

"So sorry about that," Jane said with a smile. "It won't happen again, believe me I've heard the Trevor horror stories."

Her teeth were starting to rot, and Stacy noticed that her blonde roots were starting to come through again. She took the file in her shaking hand and made a little noise in thanks. Her heart was racing as she walked down the hall, trying to figure out if she was dreaming or hallucinating. This must be some kind of stress-induced panic attack, triggered by her worry that Henry was in some kind of danger and the disappointment she felt that he still didn't trust her despite the lengths Stacy had gone to get him out.

Yes, that was the only explanation for what was going on. She'd drink some water and maybe get a chamomile tea from the staff kitchen *before she started her exam. No use going in there with shaking hands. She took her time sipping on her tea and reading through the file, it was pretty straightforward. A woman was found in her bed with a bottle of pills on her nightstand, an apparent suicide. The family wanted an autopsy to make sure there wasn't some kind of foul play involved. The name was only listed by the initials — A.G. It wasn't common, but on occasion when it was for private purposes a family might request that the name be redacted.*

*The whole autopsy wouldn't take too long, Stacy figured she could probably go home afterward and take a long bath. The office would live, they'd continue on without her. There had been no other Alleyway Strangler bodies since she doctored the Jane Doe, nothing she needed to supervise that couldn't be handled by another medical examiner. Once she was done, she could go home and rest.*

*By the time she got back to her exam room, two more bodies had appeared, their charts lying at the foot of each metal bed. She opened her mouth to call out to Jane, but no sound came out. Stacy shook her head and tried again, but she couldn't manage anything above a croak. Something weird was going on, she didn't know what. Was someone playing a prank on her? Stacy tiptoed over to the table, expecting a co-worker to jump off of it, but when she peeled back the white sheet, she saw a tag with "Gabrielle Unwin, #1" written on it. That wasn't the body that was in here before she left — was this the right room? Stacy looked and yes, she hadn't somehow wandered into someone else's autopsy. She whipped back the sheet and screamed — Gabrielle Unwin was lying, naked, on the metal bed, her eyes open and staring back at Stacy. She was supposed to have been buried already, what was she doing here? Her body was cold and grey, but the bruises that covered her torso and neck were bright blue. Her eyes followed Stacy as she moved to the next body.*

*Stacy pulled back the white sheet and was met with Audrey Wells' gaze. The girl's hair was matted, like it had been dug up, and her nose was still red where it was broken. Her body was cold to the touch, she was still dead, but her eyes followed Stacy around the room. The women* made no noise, they didn't groan like zombies in the movies did. They silently watched as Stacy uncovered the third and final victim of the Alleyway Strangler. Lacey Daniels' face was scratched up, her fingernails were bruised and bloodied, and her body was the warmest of the three. Her eyes were angry as they bore into Stacy, she didn't need words for Stacy to know how angry she was.

"What... who did this?"

"You did," Gabrielle Unwin said, slowly sitting u., "You did this."

"How? I cleared you all, you should be buried and resting at peace in some grave somewhere."

"How can we possibly be at peace?" This was Lacey Daniels — her mouth didn't move, but Stacy could hear her voice roaring in her mind. "You are letting the killer go free."

"What do you mean, we still haven't found the killer he—"

"Don't be ridiculous, Stacy," Lacey said, "you are allowing him to kill us."

Her voice was getting louder, her body was starting to shake. She was fighting the rigor mortis to make a fist with her hand. So far, Gabrielle Unwin was the only one who could stand up.

"Are you blind?" Audrey Wells asked, "Do you need me to lend you my glasses?" She stood up, struggling to get off the bed. It wasn't the kind of moaning and groaning Stacy knew from movies, Audrey moved like someone with arthritis, each gesture was deliberate and took effort to complete. Still, she moved quickly, soon she was standing face to face with Stacy. "Do you see me standing in front of you?"

Stacy screeched and ran to her desk, grabbing a scalpel along the way. Gabrielle Unwin had gotten up and was coming toward her.

"You haven't helped us at all. You've been judging us for getting caught, dismissed everything people have told you."

"She's been wishy-washy," Lacy Daniels piped in, "this woman doesn't have a backbone, she just waits for someone else's opinion to—"

"Don't say that, Lacey, she's scared. You can see it in her eyes, she's just terrified." Audrey was the most sympathetic of the three.

Stacy wanted to reach out to her and allow the ghoul to wrap her in a hug. It would feel so nice, she was so tired, if she could just give in — but Stacy recoiled the second Audrey Wells' cold hands touched her skin.

"What do you want from me!" she screamed. "I did everything I could for you but, but you don't understand—"

"We want you to open your eyes, Stacy! Stop listening to your sister, stop living in the past — take a look at what is right in front of you!" Lacey Daniels screamed again, as Stacy backed herself into a corner.

She squeezed her eyes shut and tried to wake herself up,

"You can't get away from us like that," Gabrielle Unwin hissed in her ear, "we'll be here tomorrow and the night after that and the night after that. We're dead, we have nothing better to do."

"You can stop this, Stacy," Audrey Wells' dulcet voice piped in, "you are a brave and intelligent woman, you can put an end to this."

"How!" Stacy cried, "How can I—"

"By opening your fucking eyes!" Lacey Daniels roared. "You can open your fucking eyes and stop hiding behind your guilt that's how! How many woman are going to have to die before you stop acting like everything is your fault?"

"Wh-wha—"

"Oh, don't you play dumb. Don't act as though your guilt doesn't drive all the decisions you make — you felt guilty over your father, so you broke up with Matt — even though your father had been stalking you for months and was about to attack you with a knife! You feel guilty about Henry's mother, so you've stayed with him even though you are unhappy under his control. You even feel guilty that your father paid more attention to you and was more obsessed with you than with your sister, so you entertain her absolutely idiotic ideas! Don't you see that, Stacy!"

It was true. It was all true, Stacy's guilt had driven her life for years, ever since her mother died, maybe even before then. Her guilt was the driving force behind most of her life, even the reason she left the hospital and came to work at the morgue. She felt guilty over what it could do for Henry's career, so when the position opened up, she left her job and came to work for the city. Sure, it was a better job, more prestigious title, but the reason she did it wasn't for her own gain, it was for Henry's.

"Look, I think she's starting to see it."

Stacy opened her eyes. The three woman were gone.

Standing in their place, were three duplicates of Stacy Lewis. She screamed as loud as she could trying desperately to wake herself up.

"It's not going to work, Stacy." Lacey Daniels still had her voice, but it was coming from one of the bodies that looked like her. "You can't wake up from this, not until you really and truly open your eyes."

Stacy was done with this. She pushed them away and ran past them into the exam room next door. She cowered under the small window and waited to see their shadows pass her. It was nothing but a dream, they couldn't hurt her, not physically at least. She just had to wait it out until she woke up, or somehow make herself wake up from this bizarre nightmare. Suddenly the lights turned on in the room, probably one of the victims hitting the switch from outside. There was no metal table in this room, it was empty except for a young woman close in age and height to Stacy who was lying face down on the floor with her legs spread wide. Her knees were bent at an awkward angle, and the woman's right hand was underneath her body.

"WAKE UP, STACY" Lacey Daniels roared from somewhere behind her. Stacy screamed and scrambled out the door, but her body doubles followed her. Stacy turned a corner and realized she was in the corridor with the service elevator. She could take that down to the parking lot and run out the building that way. If she got to the elevator fast enough, they might not be able to follow her. Stacy booked it, jamming her finger on the button.

"Please, please, please hurry, for once in my life please!" she screamed, tears streaming down her face. Finally, the ancient elevator doors slid open, but what she saw made Stacy fall back and scurry away on her hands and knees.

It was another woman, lying naked and bent over a garbage bin, her head lifted in the air and her mouth was open in a display of either agony or ecstasy, but Stacy couldn't tell which.

"WHICH DO YOU THINK IT IS?" Gabrielle Unwin screamed, as though she could read Stacy's thoughts.

Stacy didn't want to think about what it was, she wanted to get away from the women. She stumbled back into the kitchen thinking maybe she needed another tea, or a moment to sit down and collect her thoughts, anything —

But sitting across from her was another naked woman. Her mouth agape and her hands tied behind her back, legs spread wide again. This time Stacy couldn't move a muscle, she didn't even try. She sat there and cried. She cried for all three of these woman, and for herself. She cried for her mother, and even her sister Maeve. Stacy cried because she just didn't know how to help them, she didn't even know how to help Amanda, whose love for her son drove her over the edge.

"You don't have to have sympathy for everyone, you know." Audrey Wells appeared beside Stacy and gently closed the naked woman's mouth. "Sometimes you just have to have sympathy for yourself. That's where it starts, you set certain boundaries and then you are able to see things from a distance, without so much emotion tied up in it."

Stacy could do nothing but sob. She didn't understand. This was a dream, which mean her subconscious was trying to tell her something, but Stacy couldn't figure out what it was.

"What am I supposed to be seeing?" she cried, as Audrey Wells stroked her arm. "I know you're telling me to open my eyes, and I want to I really do, but I just don't know what I'm looking at."

"Why don't you take a walk? A walk always helps us work these things through." Audrey Wells helped Stacy to her feet, shooing away the other women. Stacy saw Lacey Daniels get scolded by Audrey and set off down the hall.

"She needs to work on some anger issues. She's very angry with what you did." Audrey smiled and guided Stacy down the hall, but she could only go to the exam room. Stacy had to keep going on her own.

"Hey," Stacy stopped as she reached the front desk, turning to Jane Doe, "are you angry at me?"

"No, I think it spared my family a little bit, probably got me recognized sooner than if I had died anonymously on the street," she explained. "That being said, I don't know if it was a very good idea."

Stacy just nodded. She was tired, she was going to walk home and collapse in her bed where maybe she could go to sleep. A proper, nightmare-less sleep where she woke up feeling rested. Stacy walked out of the building and down the street, but soon her surroundings became unfamiliar to her. Grass started growing beneath her feet and a canopy of roses appeared above her head. It was the same dream as before; she knew exactly where it led and had no choice but to follow the familiar path. Stacy walked slowly this time, trying to take in as much detail as possible, hoping it would help her to, 'open her eyes', but she could see nothing that helped. Nothing that clarified why those women were so angry with her. Stacy proceeded down to the alleyway listening to the police sirens as they got louder and louder and seeing the victim's naked body as she came into focus. Stacy's double was standing over her as Stacy approached, when suddenly Stacy's double attacked her and screamed at her again.

"OPEN YOUR EYES, STACY, OPEN YOUR EYES!" Stacy screamed as she woke up. She patted down the pillows, her arms, her head, all to confirm it was really her and she was really awake. She splashed cold water on her face and stared at herself in the bathroom mirror — it was her; she was the one pulling faces in the mirror. This time she really was awake. It was the dead of night; she'd fallen asleep with Matt on the other end of the line. He didn't seem to hear her screaming; his snores were still coming down the line. Stacy quietly hung up and went downstairs to her kitchen.

Her dream was still vivid in her mind. The three corpses that turned into her bruised body doubles, how angry Lacey Daniels was, how she kept telling Stacy to open her eyes and face the truth, but no matter how hard she tried Stacy couldn't figure out what the truth was. It was on the tip of her tongue, if she just *thought about it* hard enough then maybe...

The answer was probably staring her in the face, but she was never going to figure it out. Maybe she should follow her subconscious advice and stop feeling so guilty about everything. The feelings of others were not her responsibility. She was so used to putting her mother's feelings ahead of her own, so used to watching over her shoulder before she succumbed to emotion that Stacy didn't realize how much she was ignoring her own feelings. Stacy suddenly felt like she was living in a stranger's body, unsure of what her own likes or dislikes were. Maybe this was a strange blessing in disguise. With Henry gone, Stacy had some time to focus on herself, work through the feelings of guilt that colored everything she did.

Life could be very different without guilt, maybe without Henry she could find out how to experience that.

# CHAPTER
# TWENTY-EIGHT
STACY

The dreams kept coming back, and they were always the same. Stacy was confronted with the three 'official' victims of the Strangler, and with her Jane Doe copycat. They kept telling her to open her eyes, to confront what was right in front of her, but Stacy couldn't figure out what it was.

"TRY HARDER."

She had to try harder to get past the last block, to figure out what she was *so close* to. It never happened. It always ended with Audrey Wells telling her to take a walk, and then Stacy would get stuck in the rose bush maze, end up in the alleyway, and wake up screaming. It was a good thing the walls were thick, or her neighbors would have sent her to an asylum by now. "So, it's the same dream every time?" Lillian asked.

She was still glowing in the aftermath of her exhibit. Some tech-millionaire wanted to populate his ultra-modern penthouse with her living art, and the two were working on an app that would 'listen' to plants and calibrate their needs based on what they were 'saying'. Lillian sounded like she was falling in love, while Stacy was falling to pieces.

"The exact same dream. They all turn into me, and then I

leave, and I get stuck in this thorny maze that leads out to an alleyway, and then I wake up."

Stacy left out the part where she had a conversation with Jane Doe about her death, and how she was found. Her body was finally identified as Nicole Miller-Jones, originally from Bellingham, Washington, had moved to Seattle for school before her parents lost track of her. They had never expected to see their daughter again, and blamed the Strangler for getting in the way of their reunion. That little detail had reared its ugly head in last night's nightmare.

"What do you think it means?" Lillian asked. "'Open your eyes' — do you think it has to do with Matt?"

"No, because they always talk about my guilt."

"Are you feeling guilty because you've been getting closer to him? I didn't think he would actually come to the opening by the way, it wasn't a set up if that's what you're thinking, I know you love Henry and you're committed to marrying him."

"If I can ever find him," Stacy muttered.

She saw Lillian's smile. She knew it was a set up; Lillian had always preferred Matt to Henry, and she had stopped trying to hide it. Stacy, for her part, was trying to follow what her subconscious was telling her and not listen to Lillian too much. She didn't want to fall back into Matt's arms because she felt guilty over their closeness, but she also didn't want to push him away because she felt guilty for deserting Henry. It was a strange place to be in, taking advice from your nightmares, but Stacy figured it might help her "open her eyes" and finally get a good night's sleep.

"Stacy, maybe you should see a therapist. I don't know why you don't already have one —"

"I was seeing someone after my mom died, but she was more of a grief counselor. You're right though, I should be seeing someone, at the very least so I don't drive you away talking about my nightmares."

"You don't have to worry about that, you know how much I love zombie movies."

The pair settled back into a comfortable silence as Lillian took the photos she needed. Stacy was just hanging around her friend while she visited the coroner's office. Her day was light, since Dr. Carter was trying to give her room to 'grieve her loss'. Everyone around her was acting as though Henry had died, but Stacy knew he was still out there. He'd reappear when they least expected it, and probably act like nothing had ever happened.

"Maybe I should be single for a while," Stacy said. "Henry and I could have a trial separation, I could get a little apartment somewhere trendy like in Fremont or something."

Lillian didn't respond. She had learned it was best to let Stacy drift off into her own cloudy decision making, especially right now.

"Whatever you do, please don't ask me to help you move, unless you're planning on making me a Michelin-star worthy dinner after," Lillian said. "I have to go, I have a meeting with Mr. Millionaire. Call me tonight if you can't sleep, okay? We can stay up and watch some trashy tv over the phone or something."

Stacy nodded and walked down the hall with Lillian, hugging her friend goodbye. "Maybe I will, anything that doesn't involve zombies or eyes."

Stacy meandered back to her office, stopping in the kitchen for a moment, before doubling back. She'd never been this lazy or distracted at work before, and wasn't sure she could blame it all on lack of sleep. By the time she got back to her office, there was a pile of messages waiting for her.

*It happened again.* It was from Matt. Three short words that made her blood run cold.

Another woman had been found.

*"Moriah Bannon was found murdered in another attack by the Alleyway Strangler. She is the fifth victim of the serial killer who has been terrorizing Seattle's streets for months, and police have yet to make a successful arrest. Local figure, Dr. Henry Goldberg was initially arrested and held under suspicion, however when the body of Nicole Miller-Jones was found while he was imprisoned, police were forced to let him go. We're here with Lieutenant Anita Schafer for a comment from Seattle PD."*

Stacy didn't wait, she ran back to her exam room and donned her lab coat, ready for the body she was sure would come through. Her phone rang with a call from Matt as she was getting her gloves on.

"Stacy, we're—"

"I already saw the news. I'm ready for her."

Less than an hour later, Moriah Bannon was lying on a metal table in front of Stacy. She was the youngest of all five women, and looked almost identical to what Stacy looked like in college. She was found near her parent's home on Mercer Island. The police figured she'd been on her way home from class when she was taken and killed.

"The I-90 is closed, they're hoping he hasn't traveled too far," Matt said. "I have to go I have—"

Stacy waved him off. She didn't want Matt to see her cry, or worse — vomit on the floor beside the victim. They were of similar height and build, same hair color, same hair length. Stacy checked, and sure enough Moriah Bannon also had dark brown eyes. Stacy's vision started to blur, she kept seeing herself in Moriah Bannon, and she needed to sit down and collect herself before she could continue.

*"Open your eyes,"* a little voice said, but Stacy had to ignore it. She had a job to do, she couldn't get wrapped up in her own psychosis right now.

The markings were the same as the last time. A crushed larynx, made by large hands, likely male. This time there was a secondary ring around the girl's neck — either the killer had used something to incapacitate the girl, or he'd learned from Stacy's copycat and added the move to his bag of tricks. *Or maybe he's trying to send a message — I know you, and you might well be next.* The rest of the body was typical — bruising up and down the torso, as though he'd kicked Moriah Bannon when she was down, no sign of sexual violence, no DNA evidence on the body indicating that Moriah Bannon didn't fight back.

She was probably caught by surprise, all the other attacks had happened in Seattle's busier areas, no one thought a serial killer would go out to Mercer Island. She was probably living at home for that reason — why risk getting killed on your way back from class, when you could live with your parents and feel safe.

Stacy hadn't been to Mercer Island in a long time. The last time she was there was the first and only time she'd visited Henry's childhood home. His mother had still lived there, maintaining a shrine of her son's life. Stacy was a little weirded out by the fact that Amanda had kept her son's teenage bedroom exactly as he'd left it. She almost broke into tears when Stacy put something down in the wrong place.

*"Open your eyes!"*

No.

It wasn't possible.

There was no way— that was just something—

Stacy thought back to the murder of Gabrielle Unwin, how Henry refused to listen to the report or talk to Stacy about the body. He claimed it was 'morbid', but he'd never had such a visceral reaction to Stacy talking about her work before then.

The night Audrey Wells was killed was the day she and Henry had an argument over his mother. It was the 3-month mark since Amanda had killed herself, Henry came home late, and he was falling down drunk when he did. Stacy brought up counseling, but he didn't want to hear any of it. That was also when Matt started working more closely with Stacy, taking special interest in the case.

He was the one who first noticed the similarities between Stacy and all of the victims.

And then there was Lacey Daniels. The one who kept telling Stacy to 'open her eyes'. That was the day of their argument in Redmond, when Stacy was abandoned at the winery and woke up drunk. Henry came home with scratches all over his face and a rose in his hand.

He hadn't picked her a rose at all.

Stacy and Matt agreed that this was the work of someone who was extremely angry, who was taking his anger out on his victims. Stacy was always in awe of how Henry had a deep command of his own emotions, he never lashed out or yelled at her, that was part of his appeal. But maybe the reason he never lashed out at *Stacy* was—

"Oh my god," Stacy whispered, stroking Moriah Bannon's face, "I—I'm so sorry."

Matt had been right; it was Henry all along. Henry was the *"weak, evil man who hates women and probably had mommy issues."* It fit the description, at least in Matt's eyes. Henry's mother was overbearing and emotionally manipulative, he'd inherited those qualities from her. In the moments when Stacy wasn't conforming to his needs, he lashed out. He wanted his mother back, anyone would, but he blamed Stacy for her loss.

Not only that, Moriah Bannon was dead *because* of her. If Stacy had let things lie, Henry would still be behind bars, and Moriah Bannon would still be alive. Thanks to Stacy, Henry had been released, and he did what any fugitive would probably do — he tried to go home. She didn't know what could have triggered him this time; it might have been their phone call when she was begging him to come home. She pleaded with him, but he knew better, he knew he couldn't stay in Seattle because it was only a matter of time before all fingers pointed back to the only suspect in common — Henry. He must have known Stacy planted the last corpse, the ring around Moriah Bannon's neck was a message. It was meant to go directly to Stacy, it was Henry telling her that he was safe, and he was watching her.

The weeks Stacy spent in fear for her life, wondering when it would be her turn on the autopsy table, all that fear was for nothing. These women were being killed *instead* of her. Rather than beat her up, the way her father used to beat up her mother, Henry went out and looked for other victims. He killed them, and knew exactly how — Stacy should have known, all of the women were killed with medical precision. Henry used his experience as a doctor to suffocate them quickly and efficiently, and he did it the exact same way every time. What Stacy couldn't understand was the way he left these women. None of them were raped, but they were all naked in embarrassing positions — was Henry trying to work out some kind of sexual fantasy? Was this the reason they'd stopped having sex?

Stacy's head was spinning. She couldn't figure out what to do or who to call. She started hyperventilating and the room was spinning, she felt a wave of nausea hit her and she only barely made it to the bin. It all hit her at once, and suddenly the room was too small and too big at the same time. She could taste the salt from her tears, but didn't even realize she was crying. How could she not *see it*? How had she been so blind all this time — these women looked like her for a *reason*. Her hands shook as she reached for the phone. She wanted to call Lillian or Matt, but would either of them understand? They couldn't judge her for staying with—

Another wave of nausea hit her as she realized with horror that she had shared a bed with Henry on the nights he murdered those women. Not Moriah Bannon, but for all the others Henry had gone out, found a victim who looked exactly like Stacy, strangled her and beaten her and then driven home as if nothing were the matter. Maybe he was drunk, but his hands had been around a woman's neck, slowly draining the life from her body. Stacy felt her knees buckle under her, she heard a loud clang as her metal tray and tools fell to the floor, and then it all went dark.

---

"Is she going to be okay?"

"She should be fine, but we'd like to keep her here for observation for a night."

"Do you know what happened to her?"

"We're unsure, we were hoping one of you could tell us if anything unusual happened today, something that might cause her to go into a state of shock."

"She hasn't been sleeping well. She told me she's been having really weird nightmares and they've kept her awake. Maybe she was tired, and the formaldehyde did something? I don't know."

"Ms. Lewis is the lead medical examiner on the Alleyway Strangler case. We had another body come in today, and until recently her um... fiancé was the lead suspect in the case."

"Right, I thought I recognized her. Dr. Goldberg's fiancée; that could explain a psychiatric reasoning for her fainting. Well, we have her on an IV drip right now, that'll get her fluid levels and hydration up to normal. We'd like to do an MRI to make sure there's no concussion or anything. Once she's awake, we'll figure out arrangements to take her home."

"Can one of us be here? I know we're not family but um... she's not close with them."

"She's not in a state of emergency right now, so I'm sure that will be fine. I think we need to just let her sleep for a while. Why don't you come back in the morning. Once she's awake and one of our doctors speaks to her, we can figure out if she's going home, or if it would be better for her to stay here for a while."

Stacy could hear them talking, but they seemed really far away. She was so tired, her eyelids felt too heavy and swollen to open. She should sleep. Maybe this was all a dream, and when she woke up, everything would be normal again.

---

"IT'S NOT A DREAM, STACY." *Lacey Daniels was sitting on her bed, still naked and bruised. Audrey Wells, Gabrielle Unwin, and Moriah Bannon were standing behind her.*

*"I feel sick to my stomach. Please, can you just let me sleep? My eyes are open, okay? I get it. Henry was the killer, I let the murderer out of prison and now Moriah's dead because of me — please, just leave me alone!"*

*"I'm not dead because of you, Stacy. You aren't responsible for Henry's fucked up mental state. He was always going to try and get back to his mom's house."*

*"But if it wasn't for me—"*

*"Shhhh, stop it," Audrey Wells piped in, "stop blaming yourself. Just go to sleep, and in the morning you can start over."*

*The women slowly disappeared into the darkness. For the first time in what felt like years, Stacy fell into a deep, and truly dreamless sleep.*

## CHAPTER
# TWENTY-NINE
STACY

Stacy woke up the next morning to sunlight pouring in through the hospital window. A cheerful nurse greeted her with a tray of the hospital standard jello-and-orange juice breakfast. It may as well have been a spa retreat, she felt pampered and relaxed for the first time in ages.

"A doctor is going to come by and talk to you, okay? You had a nasty fall when you fainted, they want to do an MRI just to make sure you didn't bump anything too badly."

"Okay. That sounds good. Who brought me here?"

"Your boss called the ambulance; your friends beat them here. You have some good people around you." The nurse sauntered out into the hall.

Stacy vaguely remembered hearing Lillian and Matt's voices. She was surprised Matt came, he was even busier than ever trying to find some end to the case, after her fake corpse messed it all up.

Just as she was thinking of him, Matt came into her room carrying a coffee. He looked behind him and closed the door before sitting down on the bed.

"I pretended it was for me, just in case they stopped me. The nurse said you should probably avoid caffeine for a while, but I know if you don't have your morning coffee, you'll just be angry and probably get a headache."

"Thank you," Stacy groaned, "they gave me a breakfast fit for someone who had all their teeth pulled."

They both laughed.

Matt picked at her hospital-issue blanket. "They said you had a panic attack and you fell. But you probably know that already."

"I didn't, actually. They haven't said anything yet, just 'good morning, here's breakfast.' Well, they told me you and Lillian beat the ambulance to the hospital, but that was it."

"Wasn't exactly hard, I was in the area anyway."

Silence again as Stacy sipped her coffee. She wanted to tell him everything, that she finally realized Henry was the killer, and that she faked a copycat corpse so she could get him out of jail. She wanted to talk about the guilt that was taking her over and slowly ruining her life, but she couldn't quite find the words.

"My throat feels really dry, do you think you can—"

"I'll go find some water for you," Matt said, already halfway out the door.

Stacy let him; it was nice having a golden retriever around sometimes. She needed a moment to collect herself and try to decide what to say to him. Should she start with her revelation about Henry, or go with the fact that Nicole Miller-Jones was all her fault? What she really needed to do was get out of bed and re-examine Moriah Bannon's corpse. Henry wasn't perfect, she'd learned that from Lacey Daniels, she was sure if she went over that body with a fine-toothed comb, she'd be able to find something that connected her to Henry. Mercer Island wasn't a big place, there must be something at the crime scene and if she could provide evidence to back it up, she might be able to right her wrongs this time.

"Ms. Lewis! You're awake, I'm Dr. Young, we're gonna take you to get an MRI done, just to make sure there was no trauma to the brain when you took a bit of a tumble. I understand you may have hit your head on a metal gurney and then on a concrete floor, quite the journey on the way down."

The doctor interrupted her plans — she was going to have a hard time getting out of here.

"I didn't know, I blacked out. I'm feeling fine, I don't even have a headache. I think all I needed was a good night's sleep, which I got thanks to you guys. If you just discharge me, I can be on my way—"

"Not so fast, we don't want to see you back here anytime soon. It won't take as long as you think. We're just going to take some pictures of your brain... your boyfriend here can accompany you if you'd prefer."

Matt had just walked back into the room carrying a bottle of water, a cup of hot water, and a cup of ice chips. His mouth dropped open when the doctor suggested he was the boyfriend, and he almost spilled the waters all over the floor.

"He's not my boyfriend. Just a friend. And a colleague."

Dr. Young looked between them — whatever they were hiding, they weren't doing a good job of it.

"Sure. Well, your *friend* can accompany you down to get an MRI. Are you able to walk or should I get a wheelchair for you?"

Two hours later, Stacy's leg was bobbing up and down with impatience. Matt was outside her room on a call, one that looked about as frustrating as waiting for the MRI results. It was useless anyway; Stacy knew she wasn't concussed — she had also gone to medical school and knew the signs. She blacked out because of psychological reasons, and because she was exhausted, *and maybe a little dehydrated.* Rather than keep her locked in to this bed, the doctors could have sent her home to convalesce in comfort.

"Ms. Lewis?" A nurse popped her head in, just as Stacy started another internal argument with Dr. Young. "Just popping my head in to say you'll be able to go home soon. Do you have someone who is going to take you, or—"

"I'm taking her," Matt interrupted.

Before Stacy could object, he walked away with the nurse to finish Stacy's paperwork. It was probably a good thing; it would finally give Stacy a moment with Matt to talk to him about everything that had happened. She felt horrible about accusing him of framing Henry, and pushing him away when this whole time he was trying to protect her. Soon Matt was back with her file under his arm and a thumb up,

"They said you have to be wheeled out, hospital rules. Do you need help getting dressed?"

"No, it's fine. I think that's a little… that's not necessary. You've done enough. You're doing enough." Suddenly Stacy felt nervous. She'd been naked in front of Matt before, and this wasn't exactly a sexual situation, but still she felt like a teenager with her first boyfriend. She made Matt turn around and close his eyes before she got out of her hospital robe.

"It's not like I haven't seen it all before."

"Yeah, but that was different. We were dating, it's okay for you to see me like that when we're dating."

"Stacy, we are adults, you know. I've seen women in worse states than you."

She rolled her eyes and didn't answer. The last thing she wanted was Matt's charming humor right now, even if it did help diffuse the situation.

The two barely spoke as he drove her home. Stacy wondered if he was in trouble, or if there was some ulterior motive for Matt's care.

"Shouldn't you be on Mercer right now? Pounding the pavement and looking for evidence?"

"I took the day off."

Stacy gave Matt a questioning look.

"Okay, it was suggested to me that I take a day or two off the case and let Cardoso take over for a bit. That perhaps I was a little *too* close to some of the people involved, and that while I managed to keep it from affecting my judgement, it was making me a little more distracted than what this case required."

Matt's disdain for the command poured through his speech and Stacy had to bite her lip not to laugh. Anyone with half a brain could have told him that, but of course Matt was the last person to see it.

"You have to open your eyes, Matt."

Matt looked over at her. "Funny, you kept muttering that last night."

"What?"

"Last night. I stayed for a while, just in case you woke up or something. You kept muttering something about opening your eyes, or having opened your eyes? I couldn't quite get it. I thought you were waking up, but when I shook your arm, you jerked away from me."

Stacy's stomach did flip flops, she worried for a moment about how to tell him the truth.

"I've been having these recurring nightmares lately—"

"Lillian said as much. She told the nurse you hadn't been able to sleep because of them."

"Exactly, I hadn't. It was a weird... the bodies kept visiting me. I would be in the lab and then the bodies would sort of, wake up and they kept telling me to open my eyes. I couldn't figure out what it meant."

"Huh."

They both retreated back into their own little worlds. Stacy stared out the window trying to figure out what to say. She wanted to apologize and explain to Matt that she had seen the light, but didn't quite know how without also admitting to her crime. He wouldn't be able to forgive her for it, she was sure of that. It had set his investigation back to a point where it may never be solved. Even if they could find more evidence pointing to Henry as the killer, they would never be able to arrest him if they didn't know where he was. The state police had closed the interstate highway, but what if Henry was hiding out at his mother's house? Or if he had dyed his hair, grown a beard, changed his appearance in such a way that would—

"Home sweet home." Matt smiled as he turned into Stacy's driveway.

The stoop was empty, the camera crews had long since moved on, now that it seemed impossible that Henry was the killer. Matt held Stacy's arm as she got out of the car and climbed the stairs.

"I'm not an invalid, Matt, I can walk on my own."

"Okay, just making sure. You're in a delicate psychological state, remember?"

She let them in and immediately plopped herself down on the couch. Matt continued into the kitchen, coming back with water and the pint of ice cream he'd left there.

"Anything else, my lady?"

"You're not leaving, are you?"

Matt blinked. "I figured you'd want me out of here. It's kind of weird for us to be together... without him."

"It's fine. I don't think he's coming back anyhow; he made it very clear that I wasn't supposed to look for him, and he wasn't coming home," Stacy grumbled, now that she understood what was happening, her view of Henry's escape was different. He wasn't just trying to protect her; he was also taking the coward's way out. How long would he stay on the run? He couldn't practice medicine like that, and Stacy knew he could never survive a boring, dead-end job.

Matt sat down next to Stacy and patted her on the shoulder. "You don't know that yet," he whispered.

Stacy admired how hard he was trying to be supportive of her. Matt knew very well that Henry was the killer, he'd known it from the beginning, yet here he was patiently waiting for Stacy to come to the realization, accepting that she was still invested in her life with the man.

"You've changed a lot, you know that?"

"Have I?" Matt asked as he dug into the ice cream. "I don't know. I'm still very hot-headed, stubborn, all those things I used to be."

"But I don't think you would have been able to be friends with me. Or support me as my murderous partner disappeared out of nowhere, you would have wanted me to wake up and smell the blood on his hands. Instead, you—"

"Did you just say what I think you said?" Matt froze with the spoon halfway to his lips,

Stacy took a deep breath and continued, "Yes. That's what the — in my dream, the victims kept telling me to 'open my eyes', but I didn't understand why. I couldn't see what was right in front of me, until yesterday. When Moriah Bannon was laying there, I realized — she looks exactly like me. There's a picture on our fridge of me when I was in college. It's me and my mom the day she—"

"I remember that picture. You guys look really happy."

"Yeah — and I look *exactly* like Moriah Bannon in that picture. That's when it hit me, when I finally opened my eyes. It was always Henry. You asked me once if I could account for his whereabouts on the nights the women were killed, and all three of those nights we'd had a fight and he left the house to cool his head. One of the nights was the anniversary of his mom's death, the death that *I* caused. He sacrificed the most important woman in his life for me, so he couldn't hurt me, instead he went out and—"

Matt cut her off with a deep kiss. Stacy hesitated for a moment, but then she melted into Matt's arms and returned the kiss.

"Sorry, that was inappropriate. I should ask how you're feeling—"

This time it was Stacy's turn to cut him off. She pushed Matt back onto the couch and climbed on top of him, slowly unbuttoning his shirt.

"I don't want to think about how I'm feeling," she growled, "I just want you."

Matt dove his fingers into her hair gently tugging on the strands. She straddled his legs and slowly kissed his neck, burrowing herself in his shadowy beard, and then slowly kissed him down his chest. Matt moaned as Stacy slowly teased using her tongue, burying her fingers in his dark chest hair. With one hand on her back and one around her legs, Matt picked her up and carried her to the bed, and the pair made love.

Stacy was hungry for it, she had been fighting her attraction to Matt for too long. Matt was passionate, finally able to give in to his fantasy. Stacy moaned into his neck as Matt's hand traveled down between her legs. It was the release she needed; the release Henry could never give her.

They fell asleep after that. Stacy finally felt as though her body was recovering from her weeks of nightmares. A medical induced sleep, and a sex-induced one, were all she needed. Matt stumbled out of her bed and made them tea, they joked while they ordered some pizza, and had sex again. Stacy didn't bother asking if Matt had any where he needed to be — she was learning to put her needs first, after all. Lillian called a few times, but Stacy ignored it, until Lillian started calling Matt. Then Stacy had to answer her.

*I'm fine, I'm home and I've been half asleep all day.*

*Wouldn't hurt to answer the phone! But I'll let you sleep ;)*

Stacy ignored that last bit.

"What did Lillian want?" Matt asked, they were sitting on the couch again eating their lunch… it could have been their dinner, Stacy had lost track of time.

"She just wanted to be nosy." Stacy smiled, Matt turned on the tv and they ate in silence as they half-watched some cheesy soap opera.

"Matt, I need to tell you something." Stacy wanted to come

clean about the Jane Doe. They had just finished having sex, it seemed like a good time to tell him.

"Sure, go ahead."

She stared into his deep brown eyes, and she chickened out.

"I wanted to apologize for doubting you. Maeve got into my head, she said you framed Henry because of some grudge, that this was your form of revenge. I should have known you'd never do something like that, I don't think you'd put your job on the line just for revenge."

"I want what's best for you, Stace. I knew that might not be me, and I knew that even if I changed it might be too late. Ultimately, it's good I did change. Even if you weren't — aren't — willing to take me back, my head's a lot clearer these days. I have an outlet for all the shit that happens on the job."

"I really am sorry I doubted you," she said, trying to force herself to tell the truth. "Henry really did kill all those women. I mean… I guess he didn't kill that Nicole girl, but everyone else."

"It's hard to believe someone so close to you would do something so horrible," Matt muttered. They settled back into their comfortable silence.

"It's hard to believe, but not impossible. Henry was quietly manipulative, in a way that I didn't notice until it was too late. He put his mother on a pedestal, and I think he did blame me for her death, but it really wasn't my fault. I felt so guilty that *I* was the reason she died, that Henry effectively *chose* me over his mother, but I don't think he knew his mother would go through with it. She wanted to manipulate his relationship and break us up, no matter the cost, and ultimately that's not my fault. It's not his either, but I—"

"Stacy, no offense, but I don't think I'm qualified to have this conversation. I don't mean to shut you down, I really don't, but I think maybe you need to untangle yourself from Henry with the help of a professional."

Matt was right, Stacy knew it. She couldn't rant her way out of this problem, it required a lot more intensive help.

"Sorry, I didn't even realize I'd started to rant. I just wanted to say I'm really sorry for doubting you, and that it won't happen again."

Matt kissed her again. "It can happen again, it's healthy to have a little doubt. But I get what you're saying, and thanks."

They finished eating and went upstairs. Stacy had a few months of good sex to catch up on, and she didn't want to waste any more time.

# CHAPTER
# THIRTY
STACY

Stacy's fantasy only lasted one night. When she woke up the next morning, she knew she had to tell Matt the truth. If she didn't, he'd probably find out some other way and that would only make things worse. Stacy took a moment to breathe in the smell of his sweat — it was oddly intoxicating, and Stacy found that she missed it. She crawled out of bed and tiptoed down the stairs. Maybe if she told him over pancakes, it would lessen the blow.

She felt that pit of guilt at the bottom of her stomach. It was a familiar feeling, some delirious part of her thought she should give it a name. This time it wasn't about Matt being in her house, or effectively cheating on Henry, it was over how much of the truth she was telling. They talked about the case more as the night went on. Stacy told Matt about going over her notes for some evidence that would exonerate Henry, and how Maeve called and made her feel guilty for going against her fiancé and partnering with the 'brute who imprisoned their father'.

Matt laughed when Stacy talked about her mini-investigation, saying that it was because he was doing the same thing. He knew how much Stacy craved a sane and stable man in her life, and didn't want to be the one to break her bubble. All the while Stacy avoided talking about the fourth victim.

"The girl in Capitol Hill is the only outlier. It's obviously a copycat, but I don't know how to prove it anymore. He targeted Moriah Bannon in the same way—"

"Probably to send me a message—"

"Yes, but that also means there's nothing different enough about that fourth body to conclusively prove it was a copycat. I canvassed the area, asking some of the addicts around there if they'd seen her before, but they're all wary of talking to police, none of them would go near me the second I revealed I was a cop."

"You don't know she was an addict," Stacy said, trying to get him off the topic, "when I did some of my research, I found all these serial killer forums, they're so creepy. They have fan clubs and there are women whose fetish it is to sleep with serial killers. It could have been a fan, or a woman trying to show how dedicated she was."

"Maybe…" Matt trailed off and made a note on a scrap piece of paper.

Stacy's stomach flipped when he did, worried that she had doomed yet another person to jail without realizing it.

In the morning she decided she had no choice but to tell Matt the truth, no matter what the consequences. They had their night of passion, a night of reconciliation, if she lost him now Stacy could live with it. It might even be better; it would give her an opportunity to explore her life as a single woman.

---

"Wow, this is quite a spread." Matt smirked when he came into the kitchen.

"We have a lot of calories to make up for," Stacy replied nervously.

He kissed her on the forehead with the familiarity and affection she had missed. It would be hard to let it go, but she had to do it. She served him his breakfast and a coffee. Matt pulled a chair out for her and served her plate first. He made noises while he ate, complimenting the food and the chef. Stacy hardly touched her pancakes.

"What's wrong?"

"I ate while I made them," she said, quickly dismissing the topic.

She wasn't sure when to do it, when to set off the bomb that would explode the little shelter she had made. She wasn't even sure how this would affect Matt, or the repercussions it could have at her job. Stacy's heart started beating all over again, she had to chug an orange juice to keep from throwing up.

"Whoa, whoa, slow down there— is everything okay? Are you feeling alright?"

"No," she said, gasping for air. "I need to tell you something, and I don't know how, because I think it'll make you hate me."

Matt smiled and reached for Stacy's hand, but she flinched and pulled it away.

"Matt, the fourth body — the one you think was a copycat — it wasn't a murder at all."

"What do you mean?"

"It was me."

Matt was silent, his eyes narrowed as he tried to understand what Stacy was saying. "Did Henry force you to—"

"No. I was so confused, and desperate. Maeve had me convinced you framed Henry, and that I was being a bad fiancée because I didn't entirely believe that he was innocent. Then I went to visit him in jail and Henry was angry that I hadn't been doing enough to get him out — but I couldn't see him any earlier, no one would let me, I didn't even know where he was, and—"

"Stacy, you're getting off track. What does this have to do with the fourth victim?"

She wiped away her tears and continued, "When I got back to work, I decided I needed to lure the real killer out from hiding. For a while I thought I'd offer myself up as bait, but I figured that would be silly. Henry wouldn't know what I did for him if I was dead. So instead, I decided I would fake a body. I waited until a girl came in who looked the part. She was the right age, the right height, and she hadn't been dead for very long so I could manipulate her body a little bit. I dyed her hair, and I doctored her up so it looked like the work of the Alleyway Strangler. I used photos from the other murders to make sure they matched."

"But I don't understand, the strangulation marks were made by a man with big hands — I saw them myself; you couldn't have done it."

"Matt, I've worked on corpses for a long time. I jiggled my hands a bit, so they looked bigger than they were. Then I dyed her hair — she was a natural blonde. The girl was a drug addict who overdosed', she was a Jane Doe who needed to be identified. I knew she would be coming back to me, so it was easy to pretend she had a clear tox screen. I figured out her blood type and sent blood from another body to the lab, blood I knew would be clean from drugs. Just in case, the killer had never gone for someone who had a drug or alcohol problem before, and I couldn't stray too much from the profile."

Matt's face was hardening as Stacy told her story. She could see his fist clenching around his fork.

"Later that night I found an alleyway to put her in. I used one of those car share services to transport the body, then I marked it as in need of repair, so they'd pick it up and clean it. I did it so Henry would get out of jail. I did it because I needed to get Henry out so we could talk, so he could come home and see that I was committed to him. That I believed him. I didn't have my eyes open; I didn't realize what was going on. I didn't know he'd run away or that he'd kill again. Matt?"

Stacy looked up, but Matt couldn't meet her in the eyes. Tears stung her eyes as she watched Matt clench and unclench his jaw. Stacy reflexively tensed her muscles and prepared for the worst.

"I don't understand," he said, "I just don't understand why you did that."

"Because at the time I didn't understand the Henry was the killer. At the time I thought that there was some kind of a mistake, that Henry wasn't the type of man who would turn into a serial killer, I just thought he was upset with me for not helping him get out of jail."

"So, you doctored a dead body and compromised an investigation?" His voice was getting louder. Matt was angry and he was about to blow.

"Yes. I'm sorry, I know this made things harder for you—"

"It made things *impossible*, Stacy! Do you understand that there's a body out there where we couldn't *possibly* find any evidence? Now there's just this weird outlier, this one point where later on his lawyers could claim there is a shred of doubt that he's the killer. All they need is a little *reasonable doubt* and your abusive, serial killer boyfriend is out on the street!"

"I know!" Stacy cried. "I know, and I'm so sorry, I don't know what was going through my head. I'd been in this hellish bottomless pit for days and—"

"So, you decided to *fake a corpse* to make yourself feel better? You are the only person who benefits from this, you realize that? Sure, Henry gets out of prison for a moment, but then he's back to killing women. Not only that, but maybe if we'd caught him, he could get a little forced help, but you're here thinking you know better—"

"I don't know better! I just—"

"Meanwhile your sister who is the very *definition* of Stockholm Syndrome; your sister who you don't even like, *she* managed to persuade you that this was a good idea?"

"She didn't know, no one knows. I promise, you are the only person I've told."

That made him go quiet. He toyed with his fork, moving the last pancake back and forth on his plate.

"So, you chose to tell me, the lead investigator on the case, that the primary suspect's fiancée, a person I said could be unbiased, *doctored a dead body* to pass off as the killer, so that her fiancé could get released from prison?"

As his voice got lower, Stacy started to shake. She could only nod. Anything she said at this point would likely fall on deaf ears.

"Do you know how incredibly irresponsible that is? Not to mention selfish and *stupid*? What if someone saw you or caught you? What if your DNA or fingerprints were found on the body? It's like you weren't thinking, Stacy! You are a much smarter woman than this, I can't believe — no, I refuse to believe that you could do something so idiotic! Henry isn't some cult leader, he hasn't brainwashed you, and yet here you are telling me you *faked* a dead body — abusing your privilege and responsibility, might I add — because you felt *guilty*? What did you feel guilty for, doing nothing when your boyfriend secretly killed a bunch of women who looked like you?" He pushed his chair back and stormed out of the kitchen.

Stacy could only sit and cry. She listened as Matt stomped up the stairs and into her bedroom, stormed back down the stairs and burst into the kitchen.

"I truly don't know what to say to you right now. Stacy, I— I need some space," Matt said, and he left.

The whole house echoed with the sound of the door slamming shut behind him. Stacy had known he would react like that, she expected those kinds of outbursts from Matt, but still, she could do nothing but cry. She cleaned up after herself, and then went upstairs to her bed, where she buried herself in blankets for the rest of the day.

Eventually Stacy came down. She ordered food for herself and tried to call Matt. He blocked her call, or didn't answer.

Either way, he wasn't someone Stacy could rely on anymore, he clearly wanted nothing to do with her. She didn't feel like she could talk to Lillian either, how could she explain what had happened between her and Matt without revealing her crime? Instead, Stacy locked all the doors and windows, and resigned herself to being alone again. It felt strange to be here, the same place she was in when she decided to fake the fourth victim. Matt would be at the precinct by now, defying orders to lay off the case, probably telling anyone who would listen that the fourth victim was a fake. Soon they would haul her in for questioning, and then she didn't know what would happen.

*Pull yourself together, Stacy. It's the consequences of your actions and you know it.* She knew this was inevitable, but she still wanted to find some way to save herself. It had been a few hours since Matt had left, since no one had knocked down her door, Stacy could safely assume that his boss wasn't listening to this new theory of the case — that the Strangler had an accomplice, a woman he coerced into doing his dirty work for him. Stacy hoped Matt conveyed that she didn't *kill* that Jane Doe, only passed her off as a murder victim. There was big distinction between the two, especially when it came to sentencing. Even if Matt covered for her, she knew she wasn't safe in her home. If it wasn't the press coming after her again, it would be Henry tracking her down to finally take his anger out on her. Stacy needed a safe place, and she couldn't rely on Matt anymore.

The night prior he finally admitted that this whole time, he had persuaded a uniformed officer to be outside her door at all times, especially when she was alone. Matt didn't trust Henry, once the bodies started piling up, he trusted him even less. Even when Henry was in prison Matt kept someone on Stacy's door, just in case. If he was angry with her, that meant there was no one watching her anymore. There was no one to make sure she was safe in case Henry returned, which he inevitably would.

They hadn't spoken, except for a brief phone call, Henry

would want to talk to her, he wouldn't be able to resist. Stacy had to leave, she wasn't sure she could stay with Lillian, it was too familiar, and she didn't want to put her friend in danger. No, she'd stay at a hotel, somewhere she could check in under a false name, so Henry couldn't find her.

There was a chance he wouldn't come back. He'd been effectively exonerated, he could walk the streets of Seattle in broad daylight if he wanted to, but there was obviously some part of Henry that was driven to keep killing. If he stayed in Seattle, it was only a matter of time before he got caught. People were more careful, every woman was on alert, it was going to be harder for him to find victims; unless, of course, he finally went for Stacy. She didn't let herself wonder if Henry would really do that. Somewhere between her revelation and her night with Matt, Stacy realized she didn't know Henry at all. He was capable of anything, there was no point in worrying or wondering what he might do. Stacy knew that Henry was on a path of destruction that ended with her, all roads led to Stacy and her many betrayals. No, Stacy had to get out of this house and not come back until Henry had been caught. She needed an alias and a new phone — Matt had advised her to turn off her location, but she wasn't sure that was enough. Henry was too smart.

Stacy hurriedly packed a bag, making sure to bring everything related to her work. Clothes could be replaced, but she couldn't let Henry have access to her files, it might give him more ammunition. She took very little, figuring she could replace it all or find someone to bring it to her. Lillian would help, and she could defend herself against Henry. Besides, Matt wasn't mad at her, maybe he'd help. Stacy resisted the urge to collapse in tears and instead focused on what she needed to do. She considered taking her car, but couldn't be sure there wasn't a tracking device in it. No, the car would have to stay. She could use a car-sharing service or maybe a rental for the time being. The first step was getting to the hotel, the next was possibly getting out of the city for a while, until Henry was caught, or the danger was over. Stacy was a fugitive now, not much better than Henry, her actions were criminal, and her life would be too, until a time when it was safe to come back. Maybe Matt's anger would subside a little, and he would see her side of things.

She was so busy rushing around and packing her bag, she didn't hear the door open and close downstairs. She didn't hear the heavy footsteps making their way up the stairs, she didn't realize until it was too late that Henry had finally come home.

"Henry—"

That's when everything went black.

# CHAPTER
# THIRTY-ONE
STACY

Stacy's head was throbbing, and she felt like throwing up. She felt disoriented and couldn't tell if she was standing up or sitting.

*I think I'm sitting, my legs are—*

She tried to move her legs, but they were tied to something. She tried to move her arms, but they were handcuffed behind her. She tried to remember the last thing she saw but she was drawing a blank. Slowly, as her eyes adjusted to the darkness, the room around her came into view. In front of her, there was a light, her vision was still blurry from whatever knocked her out. The last thing she remembered was packing a bag, and then—

"Yes, yes, Matt, right there…"

That was her voice. That was her voice moaning, telling Matt what she liked, groaning with pleasure and climaxing as he moved between her legs. The sound stopped and started again from the beginning. The sound of her giggling and Matt making some cheesy joke. The sounds of the two of them kissing, the sound of his caress, of Matt talking dirty to her as she moaned with pleasure in his ear, until once again she climaxed with Matt between her legs. The light was coming from a tv, as her vision came into focus, she saw the grainy images of her having sex with Matt. Matt cradling her in his arms, Matt kissing her body, caressing her, talking dirty to her.

*What is this, where am I?*

Stacy tried to turn away, but she couldn't move her head. She was strapped to a chair that had some kind of a vice, she could only sit and watch the grainy footage of her and Matt having sex over and over and over again.

"Hello?" she called out. "What's going on?"

"You betrayed me," came Henry's measured tone from somewhere in the darkness, "and now you're going to watch until it tortures you like it tortured me."

Suddenly, Stacy remembered; she was throwing clothes and shoes into a bag, desperate to get out of her house when suddenly she felt a large presence behind her. She turned around and saw Henry's fist coming toward her, and then everything went dark. Her mouth tasted bitter and dry — he must have knocked her out with something chemical. She tried to look around her, but it was too dark, her eyes could only focus on the screen in front of her.

"How did you, what did you do? Why do you have this?"

"I couldn't trust you, not after your little *boyfriend* had me arrested. I waited until you were gone and came in to install one of those nanny cams. It's very subtle, you didn't even notice it was there. I watched as you slept fitfully for a few nights, then of course I watched as you betrayed me — multiple times, I might add. Obviously, I was not enough for you, you're just like my mother said — you're a slut who's after my money and my prestige. You cheated on me the first opportunity you had — and that was after I was released from prison. Who knows how many men were in *our* bed while I was locked away."

"Henry, you have it all wrong."

"Do I? Should I start this video from the beginning?"

He replayed the video, turning the volume as loud as it

would go. Stacy was in tears as the sound of her pleasure roared in her ears.

"Do you know how *hard* I worked to make sure I didn't kill you?" Henry screamed. "Every time I looked at you, I saw the whore I traded for my mother. My pure, wonderful, angelic mother who raised me and protected me my whole life. I was stubborn, I thought I had finally found the woman who could be the mother to my children, I thought you would stand by me, but my mother saw right through you, and she was right all along! I lost her for *nothing*!" Henry was crying now.

Stacy still couldn't see him, but she could hear his voice waver. Henry sniffled and there was a thud as he sat down in a chair.

"I did so much for you, did you know that? I wanted to kill you after Mother died. I wanted so badly to hurt you, so you could feel how hurt I was, but I resisted. I resisted and *this* is how you repay me?"

"I'm sorry, Henry, I really am. I didn't think you — you abandoned me. And you killed all those innocent women, how could you do that?"

"Would you have preferred that I do it to you? Why, so you could run along to your little friend Lillian or back to your *cop* for protection? No, no I knew I could still mold you into the wife I needed, but I couldn't do that if you ran away from me. I had to keep you close to me, but you never listen, do you? The prenuptial agreement, even the venue for the wedding, you refused to listen to my reasoning. You are so self-centered, always putting yourself ahead of our relationship, how was I supposed to feel? How was I supposed to trust you, if you always put me on the back burner?"

Stacy's mouth gaped open, unsure of what to say. She could only stare at the screen as tears streamed down her face. The guilt she felt over Amanda's death bubbled to the surface, mixing with her pangs of self-condemnation and inadequacy. Henry must have been right, she often thought about how sexually unsatisfying their relationship was and that was the point she leaned on when she wanted to leave Henry. She put her own needs before his as protection, and that probably made her a horrible partner—

"No, Henry you're wrong. I don't need to be molded into your vision for a wife, I am my own person. I deserve to be my own person, to have my own thoughts and autonomy. You wanted to control me, your mother knew that I wasn't going to let you and that's why she tried to turn you against me. You were convinced I would change, that you could manipulate me into changing, but you didn't count on the fact that I was just a little too stubborn for you. That doesn't make me a shitty partner, it doesn't make me self-centered, and you could still trust me. You could still trust me, Henry, if you just let go—"

"Shut up. I don't need to listen to the measly excuses for your infidelity. This isn't about *me*; this is about *you* and the fact that you drove me to murder those women and you don't even care. You don't care about a single one of them, if you really did you wouldn't have let me go—"

"You were the one who berated me for not doing enough to get you out! I left the prison in tears wondering what I had done wrong, thinking they were telling you lies about me!"

Henry kicked the chair, tipping it over. Stacy screamed and he grabbed it just before the chair hit the ground. Stacy's heart was racing, and she was crying uncontrollably. She didn't know what to believe anymore — it was her fault that Henry was in jail, her fault that he was released. She felt incurably guilty because those women were dead because of her, but she also didn't believe that it was her fault her fiancé was a sociopath. Her life felt completely out of her hands, she didn't know what to say to calm Henry down and make him face reality.

"It was you, wasn't it, who faked that body for me? I thought then I might be able to trust you, but I wasn't sure. You were supposed to try and find me, and instead, you cut me loose. I was so angry, you know that? When I was in prison, I made myself promise I wouldn't hurt another woman. It wasn't fair, I thought, that these beautiful innocent women were paying for your faults. But when you didn't even try to find me, when you went back to work like I meant nothing to you, I felt so angry. I thought that finally I could trust you, that finally you would come when you called, but you did the opposite. You were waiting until I was out of the picture — you probably worked together, you did, didn't you?"

Henry whipped her around so that she was facing him. His face was terrifying in the glow of the tv, illuminated by the grey light he looked like a gargoyle. Henry searched for the truth in Stacy's eyes, but he obviously didn't like what he found there. He spat in her face and walked off into the darkness.

Stacy tried to move her head, but she couldn't. She couldn't do anything but wait as the spit dripped from her face onto her lap, its path lubricated by her tears. She was exhausted and unsure of what to do or say. She knew this was over, this was the end for her.

"You know how hard I worked to keep you safe?" Henry asked, he approached with a box of tissues and started cleaning Stacy's face, gently dabbing at her tears. "The day my mother died I was so full of rage. I knew it was your fault that she killed herself. To you it was a threat, but I understood — she couldn't bear to see what you would do to me. I was stubborn, I told her you could change, but she saw right through my blindness. She couldn't handle seeing me sad, that was why she killed herself. That day all I wanted was to hurt you, because I wanted you to understand how I felt, I wanted you to understand the sacrifice she had made. You always compared Mother to Oliver, saying she was obsessive and controlling, but that's not true. Your father was a junkie and a drunk, my mother cared about me. You couldn't ever understand that kind of love. I wanted to make you understand, I wanted to hurt you, so you knew how horrible I felt. My whole body felt battered and bruised, and that's what I wanted to do to you, but I couldn't. If I did that to you, you would leave me. So, I had to find another outlet. I tried boxing. There's an abandoned punching bag down here somewhere...but you see that wasn't enough. I'd come upstairs and see you and your perfect skin, unbothered by life and I'd get angry all over again. Every day that passed my rage grew, until I knew I had to kill you."

Stacy sputtered, she wanted to cry, and she needed water. Henry stroked her hair and gave her a bottle with a straw to drink from. He turned the volume down on the sex tape. Stacy didn't think he did it for her benefit, but only so she would better pay attention to him.

"I couldn't kill you. I do love you, Stacy. I know it doesn't seem like that right now, but I am doing this out of love. I love you so much it makes me crazy, seeing you and Matt like that broke my heart. I've done so much for you, especially these past few months, and that's how you repay me. You understand why I'm upset, don't you?"

Stacy nodded; she was terrified for her life.

"Good. I wanted to kill you, but I couldn't. Then one day, while I was taking a walk, I saw this woman. At first, I was convinced it was you, and that you were hooking on the side. I went up to her in a rage thinking she was you; I didn't realize it wasn't you until it was too late — isn't that funny? I dragged her into an alleyway. She screamed, but no one really cares about hookers screaming anyway. I grabbed her by the neck to quiet her, and found it was just so easy to break her neck and suffocate her. I just held on until she finally died, then I realized she weighed just as much as a punching bag. And if I allowed myself...well she looked just like you anyway."

Henry turned back to Stacy and looked her in the eyes, he was so calm it made the hairs on the back of her neck stand up.

"You know the rest. Most of the time when I was angry with you, I could come down and use the punching bag. I conjured the image of that hooker in my mind, and I would just wail on this bag, and that would be fine. Sometimes... Stacy, you can really be infuriating sometimes. When I couldn't handle it, I would go for a walk or a drive and find a woman — it was easy to find them, easy to make them trust me, easy to get them close enough and kill them. Easy to clean them after as well."

"What about the bodies?"

Henry turned to look at Stacy, a quizzical look on his face. "What about them?"

"Why did you leave them the way you did? They were naked, strewn about like they were servicing a man or getting fucked. Why would you do that?"

"To embarrass you. I wanted to embarrass you the way you embarrassed me at every turn. You were always begging me for sex, because you're a whore, it was disgusting. Stacy, I don't think you understand — these women were a proxy for you. I wanted you to feel the humiliation and pain that I felt when you forced my mother into her grave, and the disgust I felt for you afterwards. I took their clothing because without it these women looked more like you, besides it was probably a bad idea for me to leave fibers at a crime scene, you saw how bad that could be for me."

"The scratches on your face—"

Henry broke out in peals of laughter. "I couldn't believe you bought that! Thorns from roses, it was so easy. You are so stupid, so willing to believe me. It's too bad, that was the quality I most liked in you, that you were so willing to just *believe me.*"

"I wanted to believe you because I loved you. I never thought you'd be capable of something like this, of hating me this much."

"Stacy, I don't hate you. I love you, that's why I killed those women. I killed them because I love you, and I trusted you, and if I didn't hurt them, I would hurt you and I didn't want that.

Now that I know you really are nothing but a whore, I don't know if I care anymore," Henry said as he walked away from her into the darkness.

Stacy struggled to adjust her vision to the dark, the light from the tv screen wasn't enough to illuminate the room they were in. They must be in the basement, a tiny room used mostly by Henry to store his mother's things after her death. Stacy never needed to come down here, so she didn't, it creeped her out anyway to be down in Henry's shrine to his mother. She wanted to scream, but her voice felt hoarse. She wanted to fight back, but her muscles hurt.

Henry walked back toward her holding a broom handle. He swung it in his hands, playing with the broom as Stacy cried.

"Now I know I can't trust you. Now I know for sure that my mother was right — you aren't the girl for me, you're not made from the right stuff. You will betray me at any chance you get, because for some reason I am just not enough for you. You are so wrapped up in your own... I don't know. I'm not a psychologist after all, but you are far too wrapped up in your own mind. And now you know my secret, you know without a doubt that I am the man who killed all those women — most of them, you helped with one of them. Don't get me wrong, I am very grateful, but I'm also sad. It gave me false hope that maybe you could finally come around. Imagine my disappointment when I saw *that*." He used the broom to gesture to the video, swinging it as he approached.

"This time, I'm going to beat you before I kill you. This time, I want you to feel every pang of betrayal, just as I did when I was watching you have sex with Matt Ensor over and over and over again."

Stacy braced herself for what was coming. The thwack of the broomstick hit her in the arm at first, and it wasn't so bad. She was in a chair, her head was protected in some kind of a vice, Henry didn't have much to work with. It was enough for him, he swung the broom down and it hit Stacy in the stomach, the broom whistled through the air as it came down on her legs. Henry loosened the ties on her arms and legs so he could get better leverage, he swung the broom up over his head—

But something stopped it from coming down again.

A hand, reaching out of the darkness, grabbed the other end of the broom handle, and shoved it back into Henry's chest.

## MATT

Matt left Stacy that morning in a rage. He couldn't believe she would do something so fucking *stupid*. Henry had a team of well-paid lawyers, the police department were having a hard time pinning him for the other murders, he would be released from prison in his own time, why the hell did she think it was her responsibility to get him out?

*Because Henry made it her responsibility.*

That stopped him in his tracks. Henry was notoriously manipulative; Matt had interviewed his exes for the investigation, and each said the same thing. Henry wanted to control and mold his wife. What was it that Katrina Foy had said?

"If it was possible for Henry and Amanda to mold a woman out of clay and animate her as a wife, they would have."

Henry used Stacy's vulnerable nature against her. He knew she was always going to blame herself first, he knew he could easily make her feel guilty — so he did. To test her, probably, to see just how far Stacy would go for him. The psychologist said abusive partners could do this sort of thing, test their partners to see how far they would go, or how much the abuser could 'trust' them.

Ultimately, Stacy's actions weren't really her fault, she was a puppet on a string and Henry was the puppeteer. He walked the whole way home debating whether or not Stacy was in the wrong. He didn't know, he would never know what it was like to have a partner like that.

He should call his mom more, make sure she knew he was grateful that she was just a boring but strict woman.

Matt was overcome with guilt by the time he got home. It was fair that he was angry, Stacy had compromised his investigation, made it even harder to solve this string of murders, but that didn't change the fact that she was in danger. He thought for a long time about what he should do, before he set out to make things right.

## CHAPTER
# THIRTY-TWO
STACY

Matt appeared out of the darkness and disarmed Henry. Stacy thought for a second that she was hallucinating, she kept waiting for the next blow, but it didn't come. She was strapped to the chair and could only watch as Henry and Matt scrambled in the darkness. She knew if she didn't get herself free that she would be the one who ended up hurt or killed. Henry had started to loosen the straps at her wrists and ankles, so he could get better leverage while hitting her, she worked to get her ankles free first. If she could get her legs free, maybe she could scramble up the stairs, or hit the chair against the wall and break it; that worked in action movies, didn't it?

Henry and Matt were fighting each other in the darkness. Henry was doubled over holding his chest where Matt shoved the end of the broom. Matt moved toward Henry, and Henry kicked him to the ground, but he was still clutching the broom handle. Henry stepped on his hand and tried to wrangle it out of his grip, but Matt was too quick. He struck Henry in the back of the knees, buckling his legs and giving Matt just enough time to roll away. Their scramble was quick, like a strange, choreographed dance. Finally, Matt was able to get away from Henry, but there wasn't far to go in the suffocating darkness.

"Stacy, can you find a light?"

"I can hardly move! I'm trying, just get close to the tv."

Matt stared at the tv for a moment. A confused look on his face.

"This is from last night," he said. "You filmed us having sex and didn't tell me?"

"No, asshole," Henry growled from behind, "I needed to make sure my fiancée was faithful. Obviously, I was wrong, she isn't the woman I thought she was." From the darkness there was a click, as Henry flicked the safety on a gun. "I didn't want to use this."

"Henry, please," Stacy begged, "don't do this to yourself."

Henry just laughed. "I meant on you. I have the gun for protection, but it leaves far too much evidence for my taste. It's quite disgusting and undignified. Even my mother had the sense not to use a gun. That's what I was going to do once I was finished with you, Stacy. I could join mother in a dignified way, just as she did, just go to sleep and never wake up again."

## MATT

"You're a fucking coward," Matt barked, "you won't even face the consequences of your actions. Those women had families, loved ones who miss them, who want to see someone brought to justice. You're taking the coward's way out."

"Don't you dare call me a coward!" Henry cried, shooting the wall behind them.

Stacy screamed and tried to duck, but her head was still

buckled to the chair. She struggled with the straps at her ankles, and Henry rounded back on her, but before he could reach Stacy, Matt bounded over and kicked him away. Matt drew his own gun, but Henry was too erratic and fast for him. Henry started shooting at everything he could, trying to corral Matt into a corner through fear.

"Henry, you have to stop this. We're in a basement, the bullets could ricochet and end up hurting you."

"I doubt that, you just want to lock me up again, like an animal. Have you ever been in prison, Matt, do you know what your little prison guard friends are like? They drove me crazy, those classless, brutish idiots, they wouldn't know real authority if it slapped them in the face — which I did, by the way." Henry seemed to take pride in that, smirking at Matt as he rounded on him.

Henry had the advantage, he knew the basement like the back of his hand, Matt had to step carefully in the darkness while Henry slid around the furniture like a cat.

"I want to get you help, Henry. I think you are a smart man, you could be brilliant, but not like this. You can't take your anger out on women like that; it's... it's not... normal." Matt was not well trained in de-escalation, he made a mental note to talk with a therapist a little, in case he was ever in this situation again.

"Not normal? That's what you landed on?" Henry asked, shooting at a table just beyond Stacy.

Stacy screamed again, but it looked like she was working harder to free herself. She seemed to have gotten some leverage with her toes on the ground.

"Listen, we're in a high-stress situation, I'm not thinking about my vocabulary." Matt had started to get his bearings. He figured the room must be around ten feet across, the ceilings were higher than he thought they were. Stacy was dead center, and the glow from the tv illuminated an area in front of her. That meant Henry was somewhere behind the tv. He tried to creep behind, but something tripped him up and he tumbled to the ground. His gun fell out of his hands and slid on the floor. He tried not to react. Henry was somewhere behind him, there was a chance he didn't see it.

"I heard that."

"I picked it up, Henry. I have a little more training than you."

"We're in a pretty small space. I'm not exactly worried about my aim," Henry said, shooting a target just to the right of Matt, as if to prove his point.

Matt managed to duck to the ground, hiding behind the tv. He found his gun, picked it up and unlocked the safety, using the tv as cover.

"Henry, please be reasonable. I can call someone right now and get the police here, if I go missing, they're going to look for me. This is probably the first place they'll search, and they'll find two dead bodies and your DNA, your gun, evidence of your existence everywhere. All you're doing is incriminating yourself even more, why don't we stop this little game and start acting like adults."

"If you want to act like an adult, why don't you stop playing hide and seek and putting your little slut between us."

"Henry, stop this!" Stacy cried as she continued to struggle to get free.

Matt was sure that Henry was ignoring her. "Let's call a truce then Henry, let's each put our hands up and come out from where we're hiding," Matt said. He knew if he could get Henry in front of him, he could disarm him, but he needed to see him. Henry was hiding in the darkness, for all Matt knew, Henry was standing just to the left of him. He needed to get Henry in the open, then he could negotiate for Stacy getting out of there. "This is between us. Leave Stacy out of it, okay? Let's talk, man to man."

"This isn't between us at all, Matt. This is between Stacy and me, and then you butted in, why don't you go back to the precinct and harass another inmate while you're at it?"

That was enough, Matt could hear that Henry was on the other side of the tv, near the door. If he stuck to the sides of the room, he could tiptoe toward him and disarm him that way, he just needed to keep Henry talking.

"Are you afraid of going back, is that it? You can't handle being on the run the rest of your life."

"Why not?" Henry laughed. "You think I'm not smart enough? Please, I know all I have to do is get far enough away. I have the money, I'll set myself up quite nicely somewhere else. Stacy, you would never know since you refuse to share your life with me, financially."

That was enough. Henry could keep ranting, Matt was halfway there, in the dim he could see Henry's tall figure with his gun pointed at Stacy. Henry took one step toward her, coming into the light.

"You refused to become my wife, really. Now I understand why, you were just stringing me along. This whole time I thought maybe I could turn you against him, Maeve was very helpful. I convinced her that Matt was doing this out of revenge, she told me you had finally changed your mind, and I thought my plan worked. My mother always said you were using me, and she was right. She's always right, and I can't believe it. Honestly, I ought to have gone with Maeve. She isn't exactly the woman I pictured for myself, she's a little stupid and fat and squat, but she is far easier to control than you—"

Henry's rant was interrupted by Matt leaping into the light, reaching for Henry's gun. Unfortunately, he slipped on the broom handle and fell backwards to the floor. The wood clattered on the ground as it rolled away, and Henry stepped on Matt's chest stopping him from going anywhere, aiming the gun squarely at his head.

"That was stupid, Matt. You know, it's really too bad your

name is Matt. It's such an anticlimactic name. I would much rather say, 'that was stupid, Matthew,' but of course you dumbed it down. I wonder, when they write your obituary, if it will say, 'Matt' or 'Matthew'. Well, there's only one way to find out."

Henry had Matt dead to rights. His foot was slowly breaking his ribs, spraining his wrist, as Matt struggled against him. Henry didn't even have to aim from this distance, there was nowhere else for him to go. Matt closed his eyes, and waited for the bullet.

He heard the gun go off.

He heard a scream, Stacy's agony cutting through the darkness as her chair clattered to the floor.

Henry screamed, "You fucking whore!"

Matt was alive, he didn't have any time. His gun was beside him, he picked it up and shot at Henry. Henry looked surprised as he fell backward, with a bullet in his forehead. Matt collapsed backward onto the ground, catching his breath. He listened as Henry's life drained out of his body. He felt dizzy; he was probably concussed, he struggled to push himself onto his feet. It was darker all of a sudden, he couldn't see Stacy or Henry anymore.

"Stace? Stacy, are you okay?"

He heard Stacy groan in the darkness. Behind him the television sputtered and crackled. Matt stumbled to the wall, scrambling to find a light switch, a cord, a flashlight — anything that would help him in the dark. There was a clatter as he dropped a flashlight to the floor.

*For fuck's sake, I don't even know if he's dead or if I imagined that.*

His head spinning, he slowly descended to the ground and picked up the light. With his shaking hands he surveyed the scene — Henry was dead, blood was leaking on the floor from his wound. Stacy was lying beside him, still strapped to the chair, her shoulder out of place. The bullet meant for Matt went into the television set, the one that hit Henry killed him instantly.

## STACY

Stacy's head hurt.

Her ears were still ringing, her head hurt, and her arm was sore. She could hear people all around her, there was beeping coming from somewhere, but she didn't know where. The room felt like it was spinning, and she didn't understand where she was. It was bright, so she must have been out of the basement, but she wasn't at home.

*"Is she awake?"*

Stacy wanted to say yes, but her throat hurt. She tried to move her arm, but a shooting pain in her shoulder stopped her. She wasn't in the chair, she was in a bed, there was a pillow behind her head.

"What happened?" she croaked.

"Stacy? Just rest, okay. Don't worry about it, just focus on getting better," Matt suggested.

But that was impossible, Henry killed Matt, she saw it happen. Matt slipped on the broom handle that he didn't realize was on the ground. She saw him slip and fall on his back, and Henry trapped him. He stepped on Matt's chest, pushed his foot into Matt's ribs, and pressed his other foot onto Matt's wrist forcing him to release his gun.

"There's only one way to find out," Henry said, pointing the gun at Matt's chest.

Stacy knew she had to do something, she hadn't got her ankles out of their restraints, but Henry was close enough, she could maybe reach him.

"Henry — where's Henry?" she said in a panic, trying to get up from the bed, but someone gently pushed her back down. "Matt, Matt's in danger—"

"She's delirious," someone said, "maybe increase the dosage of her…"

Stacy didn't hear the rest, she drifted off into the darkness of sleep again.

# CHAPTER
# THIRTY-THREE
STACY

Stacy had a dislocated shoulder, a mild concussion, and bruises where Henry hit her with the broom. Other than that, she was okay.

"It could be worse; I could be dead."

The nurses didn't find that very funny.

The investigation was wrapping up, with Stacy's house cordoned off as a major crime scene. According to Lillian, who went by to get some of Stacy's clothes, it was an absolute circus. There were news vans parked up and down the street day in and day out, to the point where Stacy's neighbors had started arguing with the camera crews over parking spaces. Stacy felt lucky she didn't have to deal with it, she'd finally had enough excitement for a lifetime.

Andy Cardoso led the investigation from then on, with Dr. Carter replacing Stacy during her recovery. All she had to do was give the same statement about a million times; first to Detective Cardoso, as he wrapped up the file on the Alleyway Strangler, then for Seattle PD's Internal Affairs unit, and finally to the city's HR and legal department, just in case they could somehow be implicated in Stacy's ordeal. By the time it was over, she never wanted to say the name 'Henry Goldberg' again. She wanted to forget him, to forget their time together and all the complications that came with it.

Matt was with her every day. He was suspended from duty for a few weeks, while they investigated what happened. Fortunately for them, Henry had hidden security cameras installed everywhere in the house, which recorded everything that happened — mysteriously, the tape that showed Matt and Stacy having sex had been irreparably destroyed. Somehow, in the confusion, a bullet had been shot into the ancient dvd player, destroying the tape he'd tortured Stacy with.

"Pretty convenient," Stacy said to Matt, a few days into their hospital stay when the two were finally alone, "the tape that Henry made of us was just destroyed. It's lucky he had such bad aim."

"Yeah, well it was pretty dark in there, at one point he was shooting the place at random, he happened to clip the dvd player. You can't trust old technology like that, you know."

"Strange that it wasn't on the cameras."

"It's there, you can't see it hit the DVD because of the angle, it looks like he's shooting *past* the tv, where I was hiding." Matt shrugged. "The world works in mysterious ways, and sometimes they really work out for us. The media isn't going to have a tape of you and me in the throes of passion hanging around."

Stacy had never felt so relieved. It wasn't just that Henry was dead, or that she'd found out his true nature before they were married, Stacy also felt she was finally surrounded by people who truly supported her. Lillian, and her new tech-millionaire beau, came by every day with specially catered meals for Stacy that blew the hospital food out of the water, and she brought Stacy her clothes and kept Henry's 'fans' from ransacking her home. Mr. Kitagawa, Henry's lawyer, came by to say hello and offer his services if she needed anything done with his property. Henry didn't have an updated will, he left everything to his mother, but Kitagawa said he'd help her sort out her part of all their assets.

"I think, after all you have been through, and since Henry demonstrated he was very intent on having you as his spouse, that there is something we can do with the estate." He smiled at Stacy and patted her on the head, leaving to go deal with the media storm Henry left in his wake.

Since she was stuck in bed, Stacy was glued to the news coverage about Henry.

There was reportedly a documentary series in the works, focusing on the strangely close relationship between Henry and his mother; there were podcasts going into detail about the five murdered women, their lives, and untimely deaths; and countless articles and profiles about Henry and other serial killers who seemed to hide in plain sight.

Stacy had been offered two different book deals to write about her experience, but she turned both of them down. Now was not the time to draw any more attention to herself, she wanted to heal both physically and mentally from the ordeal. No, instead she was happy to watch these stories as if it had happened to someone else — all this was just another piece of true crime, it would become fodder for a television series and then it would be as if it never happened, or maybe that it happened to someone else.

---

"Why do they keep saying five murders?" she asked Matt one day. The two of them were playing Scrabble in her hospital room, it was their first 'date' of sorts.

"What do you mean?" he asked, scrutinizing his tiles.

"In all the reports I've heard they talk about Henry's five victims. The four he was confirmed to have killed: Gabrielle Unwin, Lacey Daniels, Audrey Wells, and Moriah Bannon; *and* they mention the copycat, but it's implied that he was somehow involved in her death. It was a whole episode of that podcast, The Alley, they talk about Nicole Miller-Jones and how she was an outlier, all the ways her death was *exactly* the same as the other women, despite the fact that Henry was supposed to be imprisoned at the time. Some people think he managed to escape so he could commit a murder, because he was trying to hit all the neighborhoods in Seattle."

"Mm-hmm, I've heard it, there's lots of theories," Matt mumbled as he played a word, "Sweet, triple word score aaaand double letter score on a 'q' — I'm *crushing* you today."

He was avoiding answering her. She remembered telling him about Nicole, she remembered how angry he was, that he left the house in a hurry to avoid blowing up at her. Now, it was as if that conversation never happened.

"Matt, do you remember—"

"Of course, I do, Stacy," he said, levelling his gaze with hers, "I remember every minute of that day like it was yesterday. I remember what you told me, and then I conveniently forgot it. Besides, I haven't been back to the station since, they had me on a little *recommended* PTO stint, remember? When would I have had the chance to change my notes?"

Stacy opened her mouth to say something, but Matt put a finger over her lips.

"It's your turn, Stace."

Stacy stared at him for a moment before turning back to the board. Henry could take the fall for the Nicole girl, and there was no one alive to dispute it.

---

"Stacy, it looks to me like you are free to go," the nurse said, popping her head in the door, "we'll have a wheelchair up here for you shortly, is there anything else you'll need?"

"No thanks, Angie. You all have been the best, this is honestly the nicest hotel I've stayed at in years, I'm gonna make sure to break my collarbone and dislocate my shoulder every time there are repairs going on in my house."

Angie laughed and left to get Stacy her wheelchair. She had been in hospital for about a week, in part for observation and rehabilitation, and in part to give the police time for their investigation. Most of her time had been spent with either Matt or Lillian, or with the hospital's trauma psychologist, and she was nervous about being home alone. Her psychologist had recommended she ask someone she trusted to be there with her for the first few nights, in case she experiences some PTSD symptoms from her attack, but Stacy felt guilty asking Matt or Lillian to come over; they had already dedicated so much time to her recovery, it felt selfish to ask them for more.

"I thought I'd be late," Matt poked his head in, "Angie said she's going to get you a chair. How did you think you were getting home?"

"I was just going to take a cab."

"You can't even carry your bags, Stace, what were you thinking? I was going to drop you now that you're out of the hospital?" He picked up her bag from the floor and made room for the nurse to wheel in a chair.

"I didn't want to burden you or Lillian, you guys have already done so much."

"Stacy, we care about you, it's important to us to take care of you. You aren't a burden, and if you are, it's one that Lillian and I volunteered to shoulder. I know you would do the same for us." He silenced her protests with a gentle kiss on the lips. "Stop. Lillian's already at my house cooking something with Mr. Millionaire, you have no choice but to accept our kindness."

It was enough to make Stacy cry. She didn't want Matt to see, so she turned away and watched the city go by as he drove her home.

"I would like to propose a toast," Lillian said, holding up her flute of Veuve Cliquot, "to Stacy — a woman who is extremely strong and powerful, who is kind-hearted and loyal, and above all a woman who is alive to celebrate with us today."

"Cheers to that," Stacy said, laughing with her friends.

Matt held her hand under the table. They hadn't decided what was going to happen just yet, it was all a little too soon. Matt still hadn't heard back from the Internal Affairs, and Stacy wasn't sure jumping back into a relationship was a great idea. At the moment, they needed each other's company, and ultimately Stacy knew they would remain friends even if they weren't lovers. Lillian and her new boyfriend left, leaving Matt and Stacy alone.

"There's still news vans all over your neighborhood. I thought you might want to stay here for a few nights, or until you're ready to be back in that house."

Matt was sheepish, Stacy couldn't remember the last time he was like this. She felt like she was in high school, watching her awkward boyfriend ask her to prom.

"I have a second bedroom now. I know when we dated it was kind of a junk room, but I tidied it up a bit, over the past year. It's a proper guest room, with its own sheets and everyth—"

Stacy cut him off, planting her lips on his. "I don't want to stay in your guest bedroom."

Matt smiled and picked her up. "Good, I didn't want us ruining the sheets in there." He winked, and carried her to his bed.

That night they made slow, passionate love. Matt was gentle, maneuvering expertly around her broken collarbone. He kissed her gently all over her body, and Stacy moaned with pleasure as he did. She felt like she was in another world, as Matt cradled her in his arms and made love to her. She fell asleep with her head on his chest, stroking his hair with her good arm, listening to his gentle snoring. She couldn't believe how comfortable she was. Stacy looked up at Matt, bursting with love for all that he had done for her, and for the secrets he was willing to keep on her behalf. She wanted desperately to protect him, and knew that she would go to great lengths to make sure he was safe and happy. It was probably the endorphins or something.

*But it is true, people do crazy things for love.*

She knew it was love, not just Henry's manipulations that made her fake that dead body. She knew it was more than his emotional exploitation that led her down an immoral path, because in those moments she was completely convinced she was doing the right thing. Henry knew that, of course, her therapist was helping her to see it, he banked on the fact that Stacy loved and trusted his word above anything else. Love changed your brain's chemistry, especially romantic love. You took up hobbies that you hated just to put a smile on the other person's face. Stacy worried about leaning back to the side of immorality — of lying or cheating in the name of her partner. She didn't think Matt would ever ask her for that, but she couldn't be sure. After all, she would never have guessed that Henry was a psychopath.

# EPILOGUE
STACY

"Stacy, nice to see you again."

"Dr. Davis, nice to see you too."

It had only been two weeks, but Stacy was already feeling a lot better. She was living in the house she shared with Henry, but that was temporary. Mr. Kitagawa told her it was best to stay there while all the estate legalities were being worked out, so she could establish it as her home. Matt was finally back to work, after being cleared by Internal Affairs, and Lillian was preparing another showing of her living plant work. Stacy was left to herself most days. At first, she wanted to go back to work right away, but she had a panic attack once and Dr. Carter immediately sent her home and put her on a forced sickness leave.

"You do fantastic work, Stacy," he said, "and I need you well enough to continue that fantastic work."

He recommended she see an old colleague, Dr. Danisha Davis, who specialized in abuse trauma and criminal witnesses. She only worked with people whose lives had been turned upside down after witnessing a crime, or because a partner turned their whole world that way. Stacy never knew there could be a psychologist who specialized in Stacy Lewis. They started off by doing three days a week, which would be reduced to twice a week, and then once a week for the foreseeable future. Stacy felt an immense sense of relief that first week, which was spent crying in Dr. Davis' chair. It was the first time she felt she could really let herself go and not worry about the other person. Matt and Lillian were wonderful supports, but at the end of the day they couldn't give her the advice she needed.

"What do we want to talk about today?"

"I don't have a plan; can we just talk and see where it takes us?"

"Of course," Dr. Davis said, "as you know I like to let you lead these sessions."

They had already broken down Stacy's need to consume every piece of media she could about the murders. She was trying to understand it all, find a perspective that was not her own. The months she spent with Henry already felt like they happened in a hazy dream, Stacy wanted to remember it, so that she wouldn't get caught in that cycle again.

"Many abuse survivors have that fear. That they'll get stuck in that drain, but you can only work on yourself. There no way you can understand what was going on in Henry's head," Dr. Davis said.

"I know all that, intellectually at least, but I still feel like there's something I've been missing, you know. Like, there must have been clues to his psychopathic behavior, but what were they? I keep wracking my brain trying to figure it out, but I can't come up with anything."

"That's likely your nature as a medical examiner; you can get a lot of answers from a dead body, but Henry is the first dead body that can't answer the questions you have. You can't know if this… episode was triggered by his mother's death, or if this was something you did. You'll never know, either way it isn't your fault."

"I heard on a podcast that some men act like this because they don't get enough attention from their girlfriends or wives. They say that it's the woman's fault, for not attending to her boyfriends' needs."

"What podcast was that?"

"It was a podcast about men's rights."

Dr. Davis laughed out loud. "Why on earth were you listening to that?"

"Well, The Alley doesn't have any new episodes out yet, and all the major newspapers have done their Alleyway Strangler episodes already. It's the only opinion I haven't heard yet. It's the only analysis that is missing from my collection of psychiatric analysis of my dead fiancé." Stacy tried to make a joke out of it, but Dr. Davis just shook her head.

"Stacy, why do you need this psychiatric analysis? What is the answer you are searching for?" Dr. Davis had a voice that was as smooth as butter.

Stacy sometimes wondered if she and Dr. Carter… it wasn't important. The point was that Dr. Davis had a way of making her feel so comfortable that Stacy could answer any question put to her, and know she wasn't going to be judged.

"I guess I feel extremely guilty. I don't understand how I couldn't have seen it, and these podcasts and articles, they all tell me the signs I was supposed to see. I feel like I was blind, and I don't understand how I was blind for so long — I still believed it wasn't him after three woman, all of which looked *exactly* like me, turned up dead after nights where we had fought. It's so obvious to me now. There was a day where I went over all of my notes determined to find one iota of evidence that it wasn't Henry, I even accused Matt of doctoring evidence to pin the murder on Henry. I was so determined for it not to be him, and I just don't understand how I could be living in a state of denial like that for so long."

Stacy's therapist took a deep breath. "Well, to start, I don't think anyone wants to think they're living with a psychopath.

Anyone in your position would look to their partner last, or assume it was a nameless sociopath out there with a thirst for redheads. That's because no one ever wants to see the worst in their partner, it's part of the trust we have in our relationships. There's an unspoken rule between two people, especially two people who have decided to marry, that they're not going to assume the other person is a serial killer. That may sound facetious, but it's true, in any partnership no one wants to be sleeping next to a killer—"

"That's another thing that gets me. How calm he could be, after all of these nights he crawled into bed with me like nothing ever happened."

"That's not entirely true, you told me — and the police — that Henry was often drunk when he came back from these midnight walks. That indicates to me that he had trouble reconciling what he had done with his perception of himself."

"I guess that's true," Stacy said, chewing her bottom lip, "I still can't believe it though. I let him hold me just moments after he beat and killed a woman. Not only that, but he was holding me knowing that *I* was the reason for those attacks."

"Yes, by his logic the danger had passed. Since he took his anger out on his victims, he was able to safely come back to you without physically hurting you."

Stacy took a deep breath. She really wanted to go one session without crying, but that was starting to seem impossible. She knew there was no grade at the end of all this, and that Dr. Davis wouldn't judge her no matter how much she cried, but Stacy wanted to go one day where she didn't feel like a victim.

"Stacy, do you know what Survivor's Guilt is?" Dr. Davis asked.

Stacy just shook her head.

Dr. Davis silently pushed the tissues closer to her patient. "Survivor's guilt is when a person who survived a traumatic situation believes they've done something wrong by surviving it. Does that sound familiar at all to you?"

*Yes, of course it does. I feel guilty that I am still alive, that I helped Henry, I even feel guilty that my sister can't see our own father's true nature.*

She shrugged and let Dr. Davis continue.

"Survivor's guilt comes in many forms, it goes hand in hand with complex post-traumatic stress. It has a tendency to play with people's perceptions of the past, make them believe that they are responsible for things that they couldn't be responsible for. For example, you cannot be responsible for Henry's psychosis. You've said so yourself, that you encouraged him to go to a grief counselor after his mother's death, but he refused. If it hadn't been you, it would have been another partner, that is the nature of the ultimatum his mother gave him — it was always going to be a choice between her and someone else. Ultimately, it was Henry's responsibility to take care of himself, to get help, and especially to recognize murder was not the answer."

Stacy couldn't help but laugh at that. She knew the therapist was right, she'd studied this sort of thing, after all. It was her specialty, but there was this little voice at the back of her brain that still said she was selfish for not doing more.

When she told Dr. Davis as much, she asked, "What else could you have done?"

*Well, I could have not doctored a dead body, thereby releasing my psychotic boyfriend from prison. I also could have kept an eye on him, and believed the evidence in front of me rather than my sister. I could have been a little less blinded by love, I could have stopped him somehow.*

"I just hate believing that there was no way to stop him. When I listen to these podcasts and read about the murders, they all seem to point to signs of his mental illness. His ex-girlfriend, Dr. Katrina Foy, has been on these podcasts talking about her relationship and how much he and his mother tried to control her life. Ultimately she was able to leave him, and when I listen to her, it sounds like she feels I wasn't strong enough to do the same."

"That may be true, but Katrina Foy didn't grow up in an abusive household. She doesn't have that lived experience, she can't tell you — or anyone — what it's like to be gaslit or emotionally manipulated or physically hurt by the person who is supposed to be the protector in your life. Also, these pieces of media — they're all trying to tell a story, and they all have the benefit of hindsight. We look back and suddenly it's all clear, like a path through a dense forest. You can't see the journey until you're at the very end, sadly."

Her session went over time that day. Dr. Davis recommended some journals, a couple of self-help books, and a therapy model to help them going forward. All this was supposed to help Stacy with the way she saw the world. She took a long walk on her way home, trying to look at the world through neutral eyes. Without realizing it, she ended up at the botanical garden, near the alley where Lacey Daniels' body was found. Lacey had been the only victim to fight back, but of course no one knew why. The assumption was that Henry had been able to sneak up on the other women, but Lacey was a more paranoid woman, or she was stronger, or she was 'crazy' depending on which publication you were reading. Either way, she was the only one to have Henry's DNA near her. It was her body that led the police to her fiancé, and for some reason Stacy had been convinced that Matt somehow planted evidence to frame Henry. She brought that incident up to Dr. Davis, who just reiterated that what happened wasn't her fault.

"Stacy, at the end of the day you have to remember that Henry knew exactly what he was doing," she said, "he knew you were an abuse survivor, and he knew he would be able to manipulate you to his advantage. Look at the timing of your relationship — the two of you knew each other before you dated Matt Ensor, isn't that right? But didn't start dating until after the incident between Matt and your father. The violence you experienced was fresh in your mind when Henry courted you and asked you to marry him. Even if it wasn't, Henry *reminded* you of the incident, when he compared himself — a sensitive, stable, intellectual man — to your ex-partner — a brutish, impulsive, more physical man. He knew this difference was key in making you trust him, and in making you vulnerable to his manipulations. He even tried to separate you from your best friend — your voice of reason, as you've said. He learned from his ex-partners that he needed someone with more self-doubt who he could mold and gaslight as he needed, and unfortunately that was you. But that isn't your fault."

Stacy walked under the rose bushes in the botanical garden as she reflected on what her therapist said, and on what had happened over the past few months. There was a time, only a few weeks ago, when this canopy of rose bushes haunted her, and her dreams were telling her to 'open her eyes'. Now that they were open, she was going through the process of taking the rose-colored glasses and the cataracts off of them — she was undoing the work Henry did to manipulate her. Her therapist kept reminding her that ultimately, only Henry could be blamed for his actions. There was no one else controlling his mind, he still had free will. Dr. Davis loved to remind Stacy that she also had an overbearing parent, and she wasn't a serial killer.

*Not yet at least.*

Henry was dead, there was no one for her to apologize to. The families of the victims contacted her to ask if she wanted to be a part of their support group for those who were victims of Henry's violence. That was proof that they didn't see her as an accomplice to his crime. She didn't join them, unable to look Nicole Miller-Jones' parents in the eye, but she'd seen a profile on them in the Seattle Times. It seemed the group of them had become very good friends, and Janet Miller-Jones was happy to finally have community after her husband and daughter had both died. Some good came of her own crime, at least.

Stacy sat down on a bench and cried. She'd been crying a lot lately. There was a part of her that kind of missed Henry too, in a way. She had always wanted a stable home life, and for a few months that was exactly what Henry provided for her. Now she understood that he was just as emotionally manipulative in those times as he was in the final weeks of his life, but there was something comforting in the rose-tinted life she had. Stacy would come home to dinner on the table, she knew what to expect from her days. She didn't always know what mood Henry would be in, but she did know he would be there, waiting for her to be home.

Stacy had no idea if she would ever get that again, or if that was even possible for her. Henry shattered her illusions of what stability could be, now she associated it with abuse just as much as the erratic life she had before. Stacy cried as she mourned her naivety, the bliss she had felt when Henry asked her to be his wife. There was so much hope in her life just a few months ago, and now it was gone and replaced with guilt, confusion, and the lingering symptoms of a concussion.

She cried for a long time, people walking by avoided looking at her. She heard one of them whispering to their companion, *"That's her, I think. I'm pretty sure it is,"* as they walked by. Maybe she needed to move away from here, move somewhere that she wasn't quite so notorious. According to Dr. Davis, she couldn't run away from her guilt — but she could run away from being recognized on every street corner and having to dodge camera crews trying to interview her. Day by day she could feel a little more of her guilt melting away, it was a process getting there but it was happening. She understood now that it wasn't her fault, that Henry was his own man and could have made different decisions in his life.

There was only one part of her that she couldn't erase. No

matter how positive the outcome was, no matter how much her therapist or Matt told her, what she did was a trauma response, she still felt horrible for doctoring a corpse. The fourth victim could have been laid to rest quietly, there could have been some other way to exonerate Henry, in theory. The same way Henry made the decision to kill those women, Stacy made a conscious decision to help him get out of jail. If she hadn't, Moriah Bannon would still be alive, ready to go into her senior year of college. She knew she wouldn't have to deal with the consequences. There was no follow up when it came to the body, all the bloodwork matched since Stacy was so careful about it at the time. Even Trevor hadn't come back to the coroner's office, and true to city bureaucracy no one had thought to check the discrepancy in reporting Jane Does. The only person who knew what had happened was Matt, the only person she ever confessed to. He'd kept her secret so far, and would do so as long as they were still blissfully in love, but that could change any day. If Stacy decided she couldn't be with him, if they had a shitty breakup, he could still ruin her career, and cause her life to go into a tailspin.

*It's just like Dr. Davis said, you'll have problems with trust for a while. All you can do is focus on healing yourself, you just can't control the rest of the world.*

Her phone rang, jolting her out of her misery. It was Mr. Kitagawa — Marco Kitagawa, as she finally learned.

"I'm calling to see if you wanted to do a little interview. I've been refusing them for you as they come in, as I think it's been a little soon, but I have been overwhelmed with requests especially given the popularity of the podcast, The Alley."

"Just put it all in a pile with the book deals—"

"This one might be interesting. It's from Anad Studios — the production studio created by Dana Marks."

"Dana Marks? The interviewer? Oh my god, my mom and I used to watch her show every single day, my mom was devastated when she finished the show!"

"Well, she wants to interview you for her latest program. I specified it would have to be in at least a month, to give you some more time to heal, but she's such a famous woman I thought you would be—"

"Yes!" Stacy blurted out. "Yes, that would be incredible. If I only give one interview it should be to her, that's it. Thank you, Marco, this is incredible it's just—"

"Yes?"

"Marco, I can't afford you. You were Henry's lawyer, his family kept you on retainer for years, but there's no way I can afford your legal fees."

"You don't have to worry about that. I've worked it out from the estate, as the family's lawyer I'm able to become the executor and the firm believes that after everything, you deserve compensation and so do the other women Henry murdered. I'll consider this part of my duties as executor of Henry Goldberg's estate."

They sorted out the details and hung up the phone. Stacy couldn't help but feel excited, she knew Dana Marks was an advocate for women in abusive situations, she would be the most sympathetic interviewer — probably the only sympathetic interviewer. Stacy felt horrendously guilty, but she thought that maybe, just maybe, she could turn some of that guilt into advocacy. Rather than listen to Katrina Foy and her amazing ability to get out from under the Goldbergs with a healthy mind and self-confidence, people could listen to her experience and see how much work it took to undo years and years of trauma.

It was absolutely insane, and it might cause Stacy to go into hiding for a while after, but she felt she had to at least try.

---

IF YOU LIKED THIS BOOK, make sure to pick up newest book, Don't Open The Door!

. . .

DID you enjoy reading The Doctor's Secret? If so, I would love it if you would consider leaving a review on Amazon!

TO GET updates about new releases, please follow me on Amazon! You can also follow me on Bookbub! Or join my reader Facebook group!

ENJOY this short preview of my book Don't Open The Door…

# DON'T OPEN THE DOOR

**Be careful when you open the door to strangers...**

Successful, happily married former military contractor Samson Chase is spending his time alone while his wife Teresa is on a business trip enjoying beer, takeout, and terrible movies while he works on his latest psychological horror novel.

But things take an unexpected turn when a knock on the door brings two beautiful young women to his doorstep, claiming to be stranded after a double date gone wrong.

He lets them in to use his phone...not realizing that he's just made a terrible mistake.

. . .

Samson wakes up with no memory of the night before and into a nightmare. Not only have the women destroyed his house and stolen from him, but they blackmail him with a video of an inappropriate encounter he can't even remember.

Months later, abandoned by his furious wife, on the hook for the house repairs, and in trouble with his publisher, he is back on his feet and ready to seek his revenge. The two girls have made two mistakes: targeting a man of his talents, and stealing a phone with a tracker in it.

It's time for some payback…and nobody is more creative at revenge than a man who scares people for a living, and has absolutely nothing left to lose.

*Don't Open The Door* – **the gripping psychological thriller perfect for fans of Freida McFadden, Daniel Hurst, and K L Slater.**

Buy Don't Open The Door on Amazon today!
Or read the next page…

# CHAPTER ONE

Marc stood over the body of a monster he'd just killed, needing to make sure it was actually dead. He was panting like crazy, like he'd just run a marathon.

Aside from the sound his respiratory system was making, there was a distinct dripping noise. Small droplets of blood traveled down his bloodied hand, down his blood-drenched blade, and fell to the ground. The melodic sounds they made were almost soothing, almost beautiful.

Also, the sound was definitely in the dichotomy of the carnage that happened inside this abandoned house. Or was it?

Marc had no idea it took such a great effort to hack another man to death. He'd killed many times before; however, that was with a gun. The knife was a completely different story.

It felt more personal in a way, not to mention exhausting. His knife kept hitting bones, sticking into all the obstacles, and he had to use great strength to pull it out, to finish the job the way he wanted to.

Nevertheless, it was exhilarating to do it the old-fashioned way. Marc felt alive like never before. He was aware of his surroundings; all of the smells, sounds, and small flutterings in the air, like never before. With this small action, he felt transformed; reborn.

In other words, he liked it this way much better and couldn't wait to *get hold of a better knife for the next time. Because there would definitely be a next time. He needed to feel this again, this rush, and soon.*

"Samson?"

His wife's voice snapped him back to reality. He was so engrossed in writing about his protagonist that he'd completely spaced out and forgotten where he was.

Samson was sitting in his office, like always, writing on his computer, like always. He was not in a dark, stinky, rotting crackhouse following his favorite monster. And according to the New York Times bestsellers list, America's favorite monster as well.

It was important to be reminded of such stuff every once in a while. Of his whereabouts, not that Americans had a strange taste in literature. He almost chuckled at his bad joke.

Samson looked at the number of words he has just written. *Not bad.* Still, he was irked at the interruption. Marc was about to experience the surprise of his life when a true monster entered the game. It amused him to write about hunters becoming the hunted.

"Samson?" Teresa repeated impatiently.

With a sigh, he stood and followed the sound of her voice. She was in the bedroom, and he leaned against the door frame, taking in her frantic behavior. "Yeah?" He had to clear his throat. It had been a while since he'd uttered a word. It wasn't because they were in a fight or something – far from it – it was just because he had been writing all morning while she did this.

"Have you seen my blue sweatshirt?" she looked up long enough to ask before returning to her task. Their bed looked like she had dumped the entire content of their closet onto it.

There was a good chance she had actually done that. It certainly wouldn't be the first time. What was the question again? Sweatshirt. "No, I haven't."

"Could you check the laundry basket?"

It would not be prudent of him to point out how she was closer to the bathroom than he was, so he only said, "Sure."

Teresa looked stressed enough, like she always did as she packed for a trip. Being a real estate broker, she traveled for seminars a couple of times a year. That didn't mean it got easier over time.

She had the urge to pack the entire house just in case, never knowing what she might need while she was away.

He had tried explaining to her multiple times she didn't need any of those things, but it was in vain. She was simply stuck in her ways, feeling more comfortable like that, in peace, as though in control, and he had learned to let it be. Because he loved her, craziness and all.

"It's not in here," he reported dutifully. "Maybe it's in the laundry room."

He already knew she would send him there next and started walking on his own.

Usually, Samson would accompany her on these trips to act as a voice of reason, but this time, he had to stay home and write. His deadline was approaching, and that made him nervous since he was nowhere near finished. Like all writers, he had good and bad days. Lately, he felt like all of them were bad.

To make matters worse, Teresa wasn't traveling for business, she was going to visit her parents, and Samson was genuinely sorry he would miss that. He wasn't one of those people who hated their in-laws. Mike and Jenny were great people, and they treated him like a son, which he appreciated greatly, being an orphan and all.

At the same time, it would be nice to have the house to himself.

*Oh, the fun I'll have.* It would be true Netflix and chill in its literal meaning. He would watch all the movies he wanted and chill all by himself. He chuckled at his own joke.

"Is it there?" Teresa yelled from the bedroom.

For a moment, he'd forgotten what he was doing. He was sent on an important mission of finding one of his wife's sweatshirts that she liked to wear around the house. It was too old and mangy to serve any other purpose.

"It's not," he yelled back, returning upstairs. He could hear her curse.

Why would she need that old thing in the first place? He dared not ask. Eight years of marriage taught him it was better to stay ignorant regarding certain things. He returned to his previous position by the door, not daring to enter while she packed.

"Take one of mine," he offered.

"They're too big on me," she stressed in return, folding a third or fourth pair of almost identical-looking jeans and putting them in the suitcase.

She was on the petite side, and he was tall and lean, but he didn't see a problem. It wasn't like she was going on a business trip and needed to look her sharpest. She was visiting her mom and dad, and he was sure they didn't care what she looked like as long as she was healthy and happy.

At the same time, Samson knew Teresa cared what she looked like and needed to have appropriate outfits for all scenarios, which apparently included an old sweatshirt, and that was why he remained quiet and let her deal with this on her own.

She eventually found several substitutes, but he could see that she wasn't completely satisfied with any of them. So logically, she decided to pack them all.

Samson could only stare at his wife and shake his head when she wasn't looking.

Deciding to let her be until she needed him again, Samson returned to his office and started editing the section he'd written that morning. It didn't take him long to once again completely forget about everything else and practically become Marc on his killing spree anew.

A couple of hours later – or mere minutes, Samson couldn't tell for sure – his wife demanded his attention once again. She always interrupted him while he wrote, and that bothered him at times. It felt like she had no concept of the importance of what he was doing. To her, his writing was merely a hobby. The fact they were living quite well thanks to his hobby because millions of people bought his books never seemed to cross her mind.

"Samson, it's time for you to drive me to the airport," she yelled from someplace in the house. It was good they had such great acoustics.

Most of the time.

"Coming," he replied, making sure he saved his manuscript. It was tragic how many times he'd forgotten and learned to be more mindful the hard way.

This time, he wasn't annoyed by the interruption. He was fairly satisfied with the section he'd managed to write. Besides, he was the one who insisted on driving instead of her taking a taxi. It would be good to spend some extra time with her before his week-long solitude.

"Hurry up," she prompted. "I don't want to miss my flight."

It was rather ironic that she would blame him for her tardiness and not herself since she had an almost a chronic inability to pack like a normal person. Samson felt like he would sprain all his muscles while picking up the oversized suitcase she'd chosen for the trip. Of course, she had another, slightly smaller bag that she carried.

"Are you one hundred percent sure you packed everything?" he asked her as he dragged the huge, heavy, suitcase downstairs. The thing was heavy like a motherfucker, and he envisioned taking a week to nurse himself back to health.

*Cut the crap, you're not that old.*

Joking aside, if he didn't know his wife, he would suspect she was smuggling a hacked-up dead body in that thing. Stuffed with some rocks, was implied.

Seeing her worried expression, he realized too late what a mistake he'd made. *You stupid idiot.*

"I'm sure there are perfectly stocked stores in Pasadena, too, if you forgot something," he added in reassurance.

"You're right," she said offering a small smile as he sighed with relief.

*Dodged that bullet.* Teresa would most definitely miss her flight if she tried to open this monstrosity to make sure she had all the things with her that she would not need.

They were at the front door when Teresa dumped everything in her arms onto the floor and rushed back inside, running up the stairs.

"Where are you going?" he asked, although he already knew the answer. She'd forgotten something.

He tried so hard not to laugh every time he saw her running. Even he, who was supposed to be a writer, would have difficulty explaining what was happening with her legs in those moments. For some reason, from behind, it looked like she was making circles. It was strange that she didn't take flight at some point. Not to mention it was a miracle she wasn't constantly kicking herself in the ass. It was funny as hell yet endearing. She looked like a little girl in those moments and not a grown woman.

Teresa reappeared half a minute later, carrying her toothbrush.

"You could have just bought another one," he couldn't help teasing.

"Not like this one," she replied instantly, raising her nose ever so slightly. It was obvious that simply going to the store had never crossed her mind.

Teresa always had trouble admitting when she was wrong. Some would call that prideful, but Samson considered that one of his wife's many charms. Charms, by his definition, were all the quirks of a person, good or bad. Besides, her charms made teasing her that much more enjoyable.

"Ready?" he asked, preparing to lock the door. He really felt like he'd strained a muscle dragging the suitcase to the car. *I'm getting old.*

"Yes, and please hurry," she prompted. "I don't want to have to run across the airport to catch my flight."

He tried picturing that. There was no way she could run with the bags she had, but the image almost made him smile. Checking the time, he reassured her that something like that wouldn't happen. Even if they got stuck in traffic, she would still have plenty of time to spare at the airport, just the way she liked it.

Fifteen minutes later, he was cursing himself to hell and back for having that unfortunate thought because they were stuck in traffic.

*Damn it.*

"I really wish you'd taken a different way."

Samson gave his wife a look, because as far as he was concerned, the only direct route from their place to the airport was the airline, and the last time he checked, their car hadn't come with a pair of propellers to turn it into a helicopter. This was the only route.

He didn't feel like arguing, so he remained quiet. They sat in silence for the next couple of minutes. Teresa didn't care for listening to music, so he indulged her.

"Oh, come on. Move, you idiot," Samson burst out all of a sudden, startling his wife a little as he honked at the driver in front of him who was too busy texting to realize that the line had moved forward.

The line of cars in front of them looked like it went on forever. Although Teresa didn't say a word, he knew she blamed him as though she expected him to have some kind of a superpower to would help them avoid it. Her behavior irked him to no end.

It didn't take long for another moron to raise his blood pressure even further. "What the fuck are you doing?" Samson raged, using his horn profusely as another asshole tried to cut in front of him.

"Samson, calm down," Teresa snapped.

"Did you see what he did?" he yelled. "I could have hit him!" It would have been his fault for the crash and not that dipshit's, and he would be responsible for the damages.

"But you didn't," Teresa pointed out, as though that made all the difference in the world.

He couldn't believe that she was this calm about this whole situation. That was because she wasn't driving. If she were in the driver's seat and had almost hit that car, she'd be livid, too.

Samson wanted to get out of the car, drag the other man from his – preferably through a cracked window – and beat him to a pulp. Maybe that would instill some manners into him, and he would think twice next time before trying to cut in line.

"You're doing it again," Teresa's voice broke him from his reverie. "Calm down."

He was prepared to snap at her again and demand to know what she meant by that, but his jaw was clenched so tightly that he wasn't able to. He was also squeezing the wheel so hard his hands ached, so it was pretty self-explanatory what she meant.

It took everything in him to calm down enough to loosen his grip and relax his jaw. He was really losing it. The blind rage he experienced lately scared the shit out of him; not that he would ever admit it.

He was a man. It was perfectly normal to get angry. It was all the testosterone in him, causing havoc.

*Just keep telling yourself that, asshole.*

"Honestly, Samson, you really should get over yourself already," Teresa's words put an end to his inner monologue.

"Excuse me?" he inquired, turning to look at her. He knew Teresa became frustrated with his condition quite often, but she had never talked to him like this before. She certainly had never used that tone of voice before.

"Years and years have passed since you were in the war. You need to move on. It's not healthy."

Samson could only gape in return. He didn't know that PTSD had an expiration date and felt like thanking her for that piece of information.

*It* can *have an expiration date if treated properly,* he thought, then chastised himself immediately. He didn't need his conscience teaming up with his wife against him.

"I'm trying," he replied in a much calmer manner than he felt.

"I know, but it's all in your head. If you could just adjust your attitude, I know you can move past it," she encouraged. Teresa's tone was now much softer, so Samson nodded.

"I know."

Miraculously, the caravan of cars, trucks, and buses began to move forward again, sparing him from further discussion about his screwed-up head. After all that, he'd still managed to get his wife to the airport on time.

Teresa liked to be there a bit earlier, and she never expected him to linger with her, which he appreciated. If there was one thing he hated in this world, it was waiting for anything, anywhere.

The idea of having nothing to do but wait for his turn drove him insane, which said a lot about his personality when he thought about it. He was sure that his version of hell would be an endless line of people waiting for nothing, and never reaching their turn.

He banished that thought because it made his heart start to beat a little faster. That was some scary shit. He had to remember that for his next book.

Samson parked in front of the building. "Here you go, ma'am," he announced in a strange accent, trying to imitate a chauffeur from one of her favorite movies.

"Thank you kindly," she played along.

"That will be two passionate kisses and one big hug," he deadpanned.

She adjusted her glasses, somewhat lost in thought. "I don't know if I have that much with me."

"That's okay. I'm sure we can come to some kind of an arrangement." He waggled his eyebrows, and she chuckled before they kissed.

"Please do something about this hair of yours while I'm away," she said as they parted.

"Why? I thought you liked it shaggy."

It *had* gotten longer than usual, but he kind of liked it.

"It *does* make you look younger."

"Just what I've been going for."

"Behave, while I'm away, okay?" she warned in a teasing tone.

He laughed at the inside joke. To anyone else, it might sound like she was warning him not to cheat on her, and that was by design. In reality, she was warning him not to make a mess out of the house because he was known for making extreme messes when left to his own devices. Not even the military had managed to cure him of that.

"Yes, ma'am," he replied dutifully, earning himself another kiss.

Afterward, he helped her with her suitcases.

"Hug Mom for me, okay?"

"Of course."

"Love you."

"Love you, too."

Samson waved goodbye as she went inside. She was strong for such a petite woman, he had to give her that.

He hopped back into the car. Freedom awaited him, and he had no clue what to do with it. He loved his wife and their marriage.

Many of Samson's friends complained constantly about their

wives and children, but he could say with utmost honesty that these eight years with Teresa were the happiest times of his life. Their marriage wasn't a fairy tale; they had problems just like all other couples, but at the end of the day, this was it for him, what he aspired to achieve.

Before he'd met her, he had been in the war, patrolling deserts and fighting for his life. Killing insurgents was the only thing he knew how to do, and he was good at it. There was no room for love or happiness in those days. Samson had been constantly surrounded by death and destruction. He'd lost a lot of friends in that damn war.

So maybe he wasn't the most reliable to judge such things. Who cared, as long as he was living his dream and was happy? And he was, despite the horrors he still carried with him.

Thank God he had Teresa. She was the best thing that had ever happened to him, period. She evened him out.

He only wished she would be a little more understanding of his condition. He knew she loved him, and he knew she worried about him greatly, but at times she acted a bit callous.

She was impatient for him to get better. He was, too.

If he was being completely honest, he *had* gotten a lot better. He was a mess when he was discharged, but he'd learned to adapt to normal life over time and lost a lot of the triggers that plagued him.

An occasional nightmare or angry outburst could not be avoided, especially not while he was stuck in traffic with a bunch of idiots. All the same, it was getting pretty manageable, or so he believed. Teresa disagreed, of course.

He was triggered far less often than before. After the war, he was so trigger-happy that he got rid of his firearms, frightened he would end up harming someone, including himself.

Now when he got stuck in the traffic, he played his favorite music and sang loudly, and that helped a little.

"Move it, you asshole," he boomed, honking. The music

helped, but no one was perfect. Especially since there were idiots out there who understood nothing but a foot in their asses.

Samson drove home. Despite teasing his wife that he was going to throw a big party and invite the entire neighborhood, they both knew he would spend a quiet week at home, working and watching TV.

Maybe grab a beer with his best friend, Malcolm.

There was work to be done, and if anything helped with his PTSD, it was writing his novels. Through them, he managed to channel all the emotions, thoughts, and frustrations he wouldn't know how to deal with otherwise. The fact that his publishing house and readers loved them to the point that he could make a living out of writing was a big bonus and a true blessing.

*Come on Marc, let's play.*

# CHAPTER
# TWO

Samson went to work very dutifully, with discipline and full attention. He was slightly concerned that he wouldn't be able to meet the deadline his editor, Hunter, had set for him, so he didn't want to waste time. Although he was sad that he'd missed the chance to spend time with his in-laws, it was more important to stay home and write.

*Ah, the glamorous life of an author.* He spent time alone in a stuffy room, describing life and all the intricate circumstances, twists, and turns he wasn't getting to experience. *The irony.*

When he reached his word quota for the day, Samson decided it was time to eat. Standing up, he stretched, and that was followed by a lot of cracking noises. He loved what he did, but sitting down all the time was seriously fucking him up.

He'd been in constant movement, engaged, and mobile all his life, so all of this sitting-down crap was not for him. Alas, he was doomed to that until some genius invented a device that could convert his thoughts to paper without intermediaries.

In the kitchen, he opened the fridge and made a mental note that he would have to go shopping tomorrow. He couldn't live solely on pizza for a week, although he was tempted to give it a try.

Not feeling particularly hungry, he made himself a quick sandwich and ate standing at the counter. That was one of the things he learned while being a soldier: *Sleep wherever you can, for as long you can, and eat whatever you can, wherever you are.*

Those habits hadn't left him, although he struggled with the sleeping part. The nightmares had lessened, but they were still as brutal and soul-wrecking as the moment they first began. Usually, he dreamt about people he was forced to kill and people who were killed in return.

Samson had terrible nightmares about his time in Afghanistan. It was hard to watch his friends die in battle, blown to pieces by the makeshift bombs the terrorists liked to leave for them all over the abandoned cities.

He knew there were millions of ways to die on this earth but only a few were as torturous, monstrous, and sadistic as being blown to pieces.

The lucky ones would die instantly, but the rest... the rest could continue being for quite some time. And he intentionally chose that word – *being*, not living – because a pile of meat left behind wasn't capable of anything else.

Forcefully, he cleared those images from his head. For him, lingering on them felt like inviting the nightmares to be more frequent. Samson needed something to do because the worst thing for him was to sit around and think about the past. That never ended well.

He didn't feel like returning to work, figuring he'd earned some downtime. He knew his mind wasn't a well of words that could dry out, but he didn't want to take a chance. Especially not so close to his deadline.

Checking the time, he realized he had plenty of time before his workout session.

*What to do?*

Looking about as he finished the last bite of his sandwich, he knew exactly what he *should* be doing, and it wasn't Netflix and chill. He would leave that for tonight.

His tornado of a wife had left quite a mess in her wake, and since she'd warned him to keep a clean house, he decided to tidy it up a little.

He started with the dishes, both because he loved her and was just a tad bit scared of her, especially when she was pissed off. She was tiny but feisty. Samson smiled. He already missed her. This house felt especially empty without her.

He washed and dried the dishes by hand, not daring to use the dishwasher without supervision. There were a lot of things that could go wrong, hundreds of ways he could screw up, and he wasn't taking any chances.

Afterward, he folded all the discarded clothes neatly and returned them to the closet. He didn't bother to dust or vacuum, reserving that for the last day before his wife returned. Until then, he had no problem breathing his own skin cells. He'd inhaled a lot worse while serving.

With that settled, he was pleased to see it was time for him to go to the gym. Grabbing his gym bag, he hopped in the car. It was kind of ironic that he had to use a car to go exercise, but the gym he liked was a long way from home, and if he jogged there, that would be his exercise for the day, and he preferred something more rounding than a running session.

Samson had never cared much about working out, but one of the requirements when he was a soldier was to be fit, and he continued doing it because he wanted to stay healthy. He always felt much better afterward, although during the training, especially when dealing with large weights, there were times he felt like a sadistic bastard for punishing his body in the first place.

There was another reason he was so keen on exercising as much as possible: It was a great way to deal with his anger.

"Hey, Samson," a girl at the reception greeted him.

"Hey, Sam," he greeted back.

"Hey, Samson," another woman said in passing.

"Hey, Tina." She was one of the regulars that preferred to do her workouts in the afternoons just like he did.

"I read that book you recommended," Samantha said, offering him a locker key.

"What'd you think?" he asked, accepting it.

"It was amazing."

"Glad you liked it." He'd recognized early on that she was a fellow lover of the dark fantasy genre.

"Hey, Samson," greeted another girl whose name he couldn't recall.

"Hey."

After exchanging a few more pleasantries with the receptionist, he started walking toward the locker room to change. On his way there, his trainer, Pete, met him.

"Hey, Samson," he said in an overexcited way, in a high-pitched voice, mimicking the girls who'd greeted him. Pete was convinced that Samson could have any girl he wanted.

Happily married, he brushed it off easily, but it felt good on some level to hear it, anyway. He was pushing forty, and his deployments had left serious marks, physically and mentally.

So, it was good to know he still had it.

"Hey, Pete," he greeted in the same manner he had all the rest.

"Ready to party?"

"Sure."

Nodding, Pete went to prepare everything for them as Samson changed.

Although Samson would never act on anything, he had received a couple of invitations for drinks from regulars. He never told Teresa. He was faithful to his wife, but he was also no idiot. Some things did not need to be said.

He had turned all of them down, politely but firmly, making

sure they understood he would never cheat on his wife. Perhaps it was a bit ironic considering his former occupation, but Samson refused to cross certain lines.

*Kill a bunch of people is a-ok, but cheating is a big no-no.*

Changing, he went to find his favorite trainer. And it was no surprise to find Pete flirting with some woman. He was young and single, so it was allowed. He told Samson he had this job specifically because he could do two things he loved most: Train and hook up.

That didn't mean the kid was unprofessional. He abandoned his latest conquest the instant he spotted Samson, then grinned like a motherfucker. "Let's get down to business."

And he meant it.

Half an hour later, Samson had lost all the previous thoughts inside his head. There was only the here and now for him. The pushing, the pulling, the endless counting, and of course, the endless pain.

"Come on, old man, give me one more," Pete encouraged in his usual manner.

Samson gritted his teeth, mustering all his remaining strength, and pushed his limit ... or what he believed was his limit. It always surprised him when he did more than was expected or required. Pete always knew he could, and that made him a great trainer, even at his young age.

"Perfect." Pete accepted the weights from Samson as he tried to sit up straight. The last couple of pushes had almost killed him.

*But you did them anyway.*

His trainer threw a water bottle to him. Samson's hands shook so badly, he barely managed to catch it.

"This was brutal," he commented as he tried to catch his breath.

"You did great. I'm proud of you."

Samson greedily drank the entire bottle of water although his trainer cautioned him to pace himself. He couldn't.

"Ready for another set?" Pete asked him a minute later.

"You're a funny guy," Samson grumbled, which made the other man laugh out loud.

"You told me not to go easy on you," Pete pointed out between the cackles.

He had, and that was a clear sign he'd suffered brain damage in Afghanistan.

"I didn't think you would actually try to kill me," Samson deadpanned. That was saying a lot, coming from a retired soldier.

"Come on, it's time to do legs."

"Great." Samson followed behind him. Leg cramps would make him forget about the upper-body inferno he felt.

Another half an hour later, the torture known as exercise with a personal trainer finally ended. Pete was funny like that. He always insisted they stopped after an hour, saying how the body would simply get overtrained otherwise and how it wouldn't produce desired results. Samson's complaints that he only wanted to stay in good shape, not end up pumped like the Hulk fell on deaf ears. Pete had his own ideas, and that was that. Samson rolled with it.

A normal person would go straight to bed after that, but as was obvious, Samson wasn't a normal person. Besides, this was his first night of freedom, and he wanted to celebrate it in some way.

He honestly couldn't remember the last time he and Teresa had been apart. And he took that as a good sign that neither felt like running away from the other.

*Time to party,* he thought with slight amusement. His definition of a party had definitely changed over the years.

Returning home, he flopped onto the couch, deciding to relax for a bit. He had showered at the gym, and his hair still felt a little damp. *Maybe I do need a haircut.*

He fished his phone from his pocket and dialed Malcolm.

"Hey, Sam, what's up?"

He was the only one who called him that, and Samson never minded.

"Hey, Malcolm. Teresa went to see her parents, so I'm home alone."

"Home alone, you say? I hope you're behaving," the other man jibed.

"It's disturbing how much you sound like her," Samson lobbed in return. What it said about him – that his best friend and his wife shared so many similar traits – he wasn't prepared to analyze. Ever.

"Thank you for saying that, asshole."

"Want to grab a beer at the bar?" Samson offered.

Malcolm liked to visit a very specific bar since because it had flat screens on every wall on which all kinds of games were played nonstop. Malcolm was almost an addict when it came to sports. And it wasn't limited to football: If it was played with a ball, chances were that Malcolm knew everything about it and loved it, not to mention knew all the players and their stats. He was like a savant.

"I can't. We're having a family night and playing board games. Wanna join?"

"Nah, I'll pass."

Malcolm chuckled. "Can't say I blame you. We tend to get a bit competitive."

That was putting it mildly.

"Some other night, then."

"Sure," his best friend agreed before disconnecting.

Samson took a deep breath and exhaled loudly. The house felt empty. He missed Teresa milling about, telling him about her day. The daily things that happened to her simply because she dealt with people were insane. And people were crazy. He should know.

*Maybe I should write a book about her adventures,* he mused, but for that, she needed to be here, telling him all the stories.

Was it weird that he missed her so intensely?

Maybe he wasn't *missing* her per se, maybe he was just feeling the absence of noise. He fired up the TV. It was tuned to a golf channel, but he didn't bother to change the channel. The announcer droned on in an extremely monotone voice.

Teresa could talk for hours without getting tired, and he loved hearing her speak.

And the funny thing was he'd never had problems writing while she was doing that, mulling around, popping in to see how he was doing every once in a while, and having a quick chat. He liked those small breaks with her. Even when she was watching TV – and loudly – he could continue describing the world hiding inside his head without a problem.

He wondered if his ability to work despite the noise around him came from the fact that he had been in a war where he was compelled to do his thing in far worse circumstances, under pressure, and surrounded by danger.

What was TV noise compared to that?

As it turned out, the silence made him uneasy. He turned off the TV to prove himself wrong. He wasn't.

At times like this, when he was confronted with himself, warts and all, he was slightly saddened that he and Teresa had never had children. Teresa never wanted any, was enjoying her life too much as it was, and he was okay with that. Samson never felt like he was missing something in his life, at any rate. They shared a great life; why ruin it?

There was enough suffering, pain, poverty, destruction, and disease in this world. Why condemn an innocent child to all that? Was that too cynical? Hypocritical? Samson couldn't be sure. And where did that attitude come from, anyway? His childhood wasn't bad. He'd had a great mother who loved him and would have done anything for him. And she had. She was a single mom and had struggled greatly to raise him. They had been poor but happy.

Samson had nothing but respect for his deceased mother; however, there were times he felt like he was the reason she had struggled so greatly. Who knew what her life would have looked like without him in the picture? Better? He was sure of that.

They had barely managed to make ends meet, even though she had worked two jobs, sometimes three. It was expensive being poor; he understood that now.

Samson had enlisted as soon as he was eligible, to help the weight on her shoulders. Sadly, not even that had saved her from an early grave. She died while he was overseas. He didn't even have a chance to go to the funeral and say his goodbyes. That was why he still visited her grave almost every week. *I love you, Mom;* he sent a prayer to the heavens. *I hope you're happy.*

Realizing he was throwing himself into all the dark parts of his soul, Samson decided to stop his train of thought. Stop with the thinking, period. Nothing good came of it, anyway.

*I just miss Teresa,* he tried to reassure himself.

This was a moment when his brothers-in-arms would call him a wuss, or a whipped man. Samson never gave a fuck. He loved his wife and was never ashamed to admit it.

He texted Teresa to call him the second she landed because otherwise, he would worry about her.

With that settled and his mind once again locked tight, Samson grabbed the remote.

"Let's get this party started," he said to the empty house.

He browsed through a list of horror/action movies, looking for something new to watch.

There was no surprise he liked that genre. It was the focus of his writing as well.

*I wonder if they'll ever make a movie out of one of my books,* he thought. He was excited by that prospect. Not that anyone was offering, but it would be special.

Teresa hated horror movies, and she had never read his books. She found them too scary and gruesome, so with her away, this was the perfect opportunity for him to sit around and indulge since he wasn't one of those people who would torment their partners on movie nights simply because it was his turn to choose the movie. He made sure they watched something they would both enjoy.

But now, the TV was all his. That got him excited, like a little kid.

When he found something he liked, he set everything up and ordered a pizza. While he waited, he went to the kitchen and made a shitload of popcorn. He even found some stashed Twizzlers and grinned because Teresa hadn't found them and eaten them.

Samson was going for the full experience. Once his pizza arrived, he placed everything on the coffee table in the living room. The final touch was the bottle of cold beer he grabbed from the fridge before he parked his ass on the couch and started the movie.

*This is the life,* he thought, taking a sip of his drink and a mouthful of popcorn. It was pretty salty, just the way he liked it. He settled for a gruesome action flick.

Samson was sure this spot would become the center of his universe for the week, and that was okay. The movie he chose, *The Dark Road*, did not disappoint despite the cheesy title. Maybe cheesy titles were part of the charm.

Samson remembered a time when he liked a different kind of action film: He used to love watching war movies. But after living through such things, he preferred to watch something else. Watching actors playing war did something unpleasant to him. In a way, it pissed him off to remember how it looked. No matter how realistic they tried to make those movies, the reality was much worse.

That was why he avoided them. Who wanted to have all those negative feelings while trying to relax? Certainly not him. It was imperative to avoid any kind of triggers on his journey to full recovery.

Malcolm told him how one of their buddies from the war, Trent, cracked under the pressure and started going to therapy. Samson believed he wasn't so far gone to need to seek help from a stranger. He was dealing with it on his own and making money while he did.

Besides, he liked dealing with things on his own. After doing it all his life, Samson didn't know any different way to live; to be. That didn't mean he judged people who sought help. He felt everyone should choose their paths.

Then the main character on the screen just lost his head – literally – and Samson grimaced, taking a sip of his beer.

"Wouldn't want to be you, buddy," he said while saluting with his bottle.

Was talking to himself a bad sign? He brushed it off. Everything was fine unless someone talked back to him.

Not that he cared much either way. As far as he was concerned, watching horror movies and enjoying extremely greasy pizza that he washed down with domestic beer was pure heaven, insane or not.

Buy Don't Open The Door on Amazon today!

# ABOUT COLE BAXTER

Cole Baxter loves writing psychological suspense thrillers. It's all about that last reveal that he loves shocking readers with.

He grew up in New York, where there was crime was all around. He decided to turn that into something positive with his fiction.

His stories will have you reading through the night—they are very addictive!

Sign up for Cole's VIP Reader Club and find out about his latest releases, giveaways, and more. Click here!

*For more information, be sure to check out the links below!*
colebaxterauthor@gmail.com

## ALSO BY COLE BAXTER

The Doctor's Secret

Don't Open The Door

The Hollow Husband

I Won't Let You Go

The Betrayal

The Perfect Surrogate

The Perfect Surrogate

The Perfect Suitor

What She Witnessed

Finding The Other Woman

Going Insane

Prime Suspect

Trust A Stranger

Did He Do It

Follow You

The Perfect Nanny

**What Happened Last Night**

**Perfect Obsession**

**She's Missing**

**What She Forgot**

**Before She's Gone**

**Stolen Son**

**Detective Carrie Blake Series**
Deadly Truth - Book 1
Deadly Justice - Book 2

**Box Sets:**
**Psychological Thriller Box Set Volume 1**

Printed in Great Britain
by Amazon